Oct. 2020

THE HOUSE BY THE SEA

LOUISE DOUGLAS

D1500888

B
Boldw**o**d

First published in Great Britain in 2020 by Boldwood Books Ltd.

Copyright © Louise Douglas, 2020

Cover Design by Becky Glibbery

Cover Imagery: Shutterstock and Alamy

A CIP catalogue record for this book is available from the British Library.

Paperback ISBN 978-1-83889-278-4

Ebook ISBN 978-1-83889-276-0

Kindle ISBN 978-1-83889-277-7

Audio CD ISBN 978-1-83889-279-1

MP3 CD ISBN 978-1-83889-697-3

Digital audio download ISBN 978-1-83889-275-3

Boldwood Books Ltd
23 Bowerdean Street
London SW6 3TN
www.boldwoodbooks.com

For Marianne Gunn O'Connor, with love

1

I was walking the dogs along the footpath beside the River Avon when my sister, Martha, called to tell me that Anna DeLuca had died.

It was April. The air was cool, the tide was out and I was alone. The dogs sniffed the grassy fringes of the path, while I held the phone to my ear and listened as Martha described how my former mother-in-law had passed away peacefully in a sunlit room in a hospice in south London. As she spoke, I watched a boy cycling towards me. He was fourteen or fifteen, dark haired, slightly built. He could have been Daniel. I stepped aside as he passed. He stood on the pedals to keep the bike steady, leaned over the handlebars and nodded his thanks. He was wearing school uniform: rolled up shirtsleeves, a jumper tied around his waist, black shoes with scuffed toes, mud on the knees of his trousers. His cheeks were flushed with exertion.

'It was a lovely room,' Martha said, 'and Cece said the staff were angels. She said it was a good death. All the family were there.'

I watched the back of the boy, cycling away from me. The jumper flapped behind him.

'Edie?' Martha asked. 'Did you hear me?'

I would have liked to tell her about the boy who looked like Daniel, but I knew if I did she would make the face she always made when I told her about something that reminded me of my son. Even though I couldn't see her, I'd know that was what she was doing.

A silence grew between us. Martha was expecting me to say that I was sorry about Anna's death or to ask her to pass on my condolences to Cece, but I couldn't. I simply couldn't bring myself to say it was all for the best, or that at least it was an end to Anna's suffering, or some other cliché. I'd spent ten years picking at my hatred for Anna and the wound was deep and bloody. I could hardly say something kind about her now.

I watched the boy on the bike riding through the tunnel made by the overhanging branches of trees. He went around a bend and disappeared.

'Was Joe there?' I asked.

'Sorry?'

'Was Joe with Anna when she died?'

'Yes, I just said, all the family were. He's spent a lot of time with his mother over the last few weeks.'

I expect she was asking him for forgiveness, craving his reassurances. I could imagine him holding her trembling hand, telling her that what happened to Daniel wasn't really her fault and she, oh, she'd be doing her best to believe him, but deep down she must have known Joe was only saying those words because he loved her. In her heart she must have known he didn't mean it, because it was her fault, she was responsible for us losing Daniel, and even if Joe said he forgave her, it wouldn't be true. Daniel was his son as much as mine. How can anyone forgive the unforgivable?

I looked back towards the city, hoping I might catch sight of the boy on the bike, but I couldn't see him.

'Edie, are you okay?' Martha asked tentatively.

Was that the boy? Was that him over there, cycling on the other side of the river?

'Edie?'

No, it wasn't him. Only some man on a road bike.

'Edie?'

'Yes, I'm fine.'

Another pause, and then, in a less tentative tone of voice, Martha said: 'Cece asked me to tell you that the funeral's next Thursday at the crematorium. We could go together. You will come, Edie, won't you?'

'I don't think it'd be a good idea.'

'At least think about it. It would be progress for you; closure. It might help you put everything behind you and... you know... move on.'

Move on? No! I didn't want to move on. How could I want to do anything that would mean leaving my son behind? Forgetting him?

Martha talked and I half listened, letting my mind wander, watching the two dogs, side by side, cautiously sniffing at a piece of timber brought up by the tide. Sanderlings and avocets were feeding on the great slopes of pewter coloured mud that reflected a low, grey sky; trailing scribbles of bird prints below the tideline of driftwood and plastic. High above, gulls spiralled beneath the underside of the Suspension Bridge.

I would not go to Anna DeLuca's funeral.

I didn't want to see Joe again. He wouldn't want to see me either. It was his mother's funeral, let him deal with it on his own, in his own way. I'd rather be anywhere else in the world, than with him, remembering her.

2

FOURTEEN WEEKS LATER

The aircraft tipped to begin its descent and through the porthole I watched the southern side of the island of Sicily emerge from the glare of the sun. Beyond the breaching wing lay a hazy, mountainous land surrounded by turquoise water. Wispy clouds bunched around the summit of Etna, the shadow of a forest creeping up her flank. I saw the sprawl of cities, the pencil lines of motorways, the meandering loops of a river and the brilliant blue rectangle of a reservoir. My journey was almost over and Joe was somewhere down there, waiting for me. The last time I'd had a meaningful conversation with my ex-husband was ten years previously, and on that occasion, I'd told him I wished he was dead, and I'd meant it and he knew that I meant it. I'd watched him implode, emotionally, in front of my eyes. I'd turned away. I didn't know how I was going to face him again. I didn't know how either of us were going to cope.

It wasn't as if we had anything in common any more, save memories too painful to revisit. I knew very little of Joe's life now and I didn't know how much, if anything, he knew of mine. He probably didn't know that home, for me, was my friend Fitz's two bedroom house in Southville and work, the Special Educational Needs department of St Sarah's school, South Bristol. In my spare time, I walked Fitz's dogs or went to the Watershed cinema to watch European films with subtitles. Sometimes I meandered around St Nicholas' Markets and treated myself to a Caribbean wrap and a ball or two of knitting wool; some second-hand books. Most of my energy was taken up with keeping Daniel's memory alive, that was my raison d'être; I would not let my son be forgotten – never. It might not look much of a life, but it was mine and I was happy with it. I felt safe and I didn't have to worry about the worst happening because the worst had already happened. I was doing fine and if Joe thought I wasn't, well, he'd be wrong.

All this anxiety was his mother's fault. Anna DeLuca was the reason why I was on this plane and why Joe was waiting for me at the airport in Sicily. She was behind this, she couldn't leave us alone, she had to be interfering in our lives, pulling our strings, moving us around like the pieces on a chessboard, even now, months after her death. Hadn't she ruined our lives enough already? Hadn't she caused enough heartache? Martha had said Anna's death would be a line drawn in the sand for me, but Martha had been wrong. I thought of Anna's small, heart shaped face, her black hair, her pretty brown eyes and little white teeth, the peppermints she used to freshen her breath, and the old fury began to rise in me.

I was distracted by the passenger beside me, who knocked my arm as he reached for his seat belt.

'Sorry,' he said, 'so sorry.' His jumper slid off his lap and landed on my feet. It was unpleasantly warm. Surreptitiously, I kicked it back towards him. 'I'm all fingers and thumbs,' he said. 'I don't like take-offs and landings. Always make me nervous.' He laughed uneasily.

I moved closer to the window, turning my body away from his. I didn't like flying either. Last time, I'd sworn 'never again' and yet here I was, on a journey I hadn't planned, going to a place I didn't want to visit, brittle with nerves, resenting the time and energy I was expending, dreading what was to come, and all because of her, Anna DeLuca, and her stupid, manipulative will.

The intercom pinged and the pilot informed us that we'd be landing in fifteen minutes. She said the weather in Sicily was a fine and sunny twenty-five degrees. Good, I thought. It would be nice to have some sunshine. The British weather had been dull in the weeks since Anna's death and I'd been out of sorts. Nothing had gone terribly wrong, but nothing had been right either. I'd felt as if I had a persistent hangover, or jet lag; some affliction that dulled my mind and slowed me down. It was knowing that this trip was coming; knowing I had to use my precious holiday allocation to come to Sicily to meet Anna's lawyer; knowing I'd have to burn energy dealing with whatever mess Anna had left for me and Joe to clear up.

My paperback was on my lap and I'd been using a photograph of Daniel as a bookmark. There he was, my beautiful boy, sitting astride the skateboard that Anna had bought him for his fifth birthday. He'd been asking for a skateboard for months, begging for one, and Joe and I kept saying 'No,' because we didn't think he was big enough and back then we lived in a tiny flat on the second storey of an old house in North London. There was no way I could manage the creaky stairs with a child, a shopping bag and a skateboard in tow. But Anna being Anna, that didn't stop her. She presented the gift to Daniel on his birthday; his eyes were wide with delight as he tore the paper from the present, its shape and weight giving away what was inside. It was a fabulous board, the exact one he'd wanted. He kept saying: 'This is the best day of my whole life!' Anna told him the skateboard had to stay at her house, close to the park. She also – pre-empting objections from us – gave him a protective helmet and pads and told him that using the board was conditional on him wearing the safety gear. I could still recall the sinking feeling as I watched Daniel hugging his present, the half-hearted smile I dredged up, Anna's eyes flicking from Daniel to me, delighted at his joy, desperate for my approval, and Joe saying: 'Wow, that's great, Anna!' (he never called her Mum) and then reaching across to take hold of my hand to let me know he knew how annoyed I was.

I lay Daniel's picture back in the book, closed it carefully and tucked it into my bag. The closer I came to seeing Joe again, the more anxious I felt. Funny how it was always the relationships that once were closest that caused the most trouble when they were over.

We were lower now, so low that details of the landscape were revealing themselves: a water park, a motorway junction, a shopping mall. I saw the shadow of our plane swoop beneath me, a ballet partner mirroring the arc of the real thing. I thought of Joe, waiting for me, and had a rush of nerves. Here I was – a jolt as the landing gear mechanism lowered the wheels – here we were – a groaning of the air brakes – the two of us about to be reunited because of the machinations of his mother, and it was too late to do anything about it now; too late to do anything but comply.

The man beside me was breathing heavily. 'Oh God,' he muttered, 'Oh God, oh God, oh God!'

The roofs of the apartment blocks rushed closer and closer, a forest of aerials and chimneys and water tanks. We skimmed the power lines and the tops of the trees, the airport terminal came into view to our right and there was the bump as the plane touched down, a brace against the forward thrust as it braked, a spasm of relief.

'Hurrah!' the man beside me muttered. He grabbed hold of my wrist. 'We did it!' he cried. 'We're safe!'

He was the lucky one. For him, the anxiety was over. For me, it was just beginning.

3

We disembarked and I experienced my first blast of Sicily: hot and dry, streaky with the smell of aircraft fuel. We were shepherded across the tarmac, buffeted by gusts of displaced air. I managed to position myself behind a family I'd noticed at the departure gate back in London. The boy was about ten, older than Daniel had been when he died, but younger than Daniel would have been if he had still been alive. He was holding his little sister's hand, pointing things out to her.

Halfway between the plane and the terminal, the girl dropped her toy rabbit and none of the family noticed. I picked it up and quickened my pace to catch up. I tapped the mother's arm and when she turned, I gave the rabbit to her. She smiled her thanks. I wanted to say something about her son's gentleness and thoughtfulness, about how he reminded me of Daniel, but it might have come across as a bit weird. Sometimes when I tried to praise the children of strangers, I went over the top and everyone got embarrassed and it didn't end well. I was glad for that mother that she had such lovely children and it wasn't that I wanted them for myself, only that I wished Daniel was with me.

I would have traded the rest of my life if I could have had him back for a single hour, a minute, a heartbeat. It was a hopeless wish though. All the time in the world wouldn't be enough to compensate for the time that had already been lost.

We reached the terminal building and walked through sliding doors into the quiet, sanitised chill of a hallway. We shuffled across a marble floor towards the immigration desks. I stood a little apart from everyone else, keeping myself to myself and switched on my phone. Amongst the welcomes from various Italian service providers that lined up over the screensaver of Daniel's face, was a text from Joe.

I'm at arrivals.

Okay. Fine. Don't say 'hello' or 'hope you had a good flight' or 'looking forward to seeing you again.' The coldness and brusqueness of the message put me on edge. But what had I expected?

Up until Anna's death, all I'd heard about my ex-husband were bits and pieces of information that Martha passed on from Cece. For a year or two after I left Joe, Martha kept trying to tell me about his mental health issues and so on, but I wouldn't listen. In fact, I used to get quite angry with her. 'Why are you even telling me these things?' I'd say. 'I don't care about Joe. Really, I don't!'

I knew he was running his own gardening business in North Wales and as far as Martha was aware he didn't have a new partner: like me, he'd never come anywhere close to marrying again. I assumed he was better now – he'd sounded quite coherent in the emails he'd sent in the past few weeks. Still, this whole situation was ridiculous. It was a stipulation of Anna's will that Joe and I meet the lawyer together, but we had flown in separately and we should have arranged to make our way separately to the lawyer's office in the city of Ragusa. It had been a stupid idea to meet at the airport. It had been a stupid plan to share a car. What on earth would we talk about? How could we bear to be together?

I typed a reply.

You go on ahead, I'll follow in a taxi.

My finger hovered over the 'send' button. I didn't actually know how much a taxi would cost or if Sicilian taxi drivers had the facility to accept card payments and I didn't speak Italian so I wouldn't be able to ask. I wouldn't know if I was being charged a fair price for the journey, I didn't even know where Ragusa was in relation to the airport. What if it was 200 miles away? Why hadn't I looked it up beforehand? Why hadn't I thought this through? Did they even have Ubers in Sicily?

I deleted the text without sending it. My heart was thumping. My breathing was ragged. I heard Fitz's voice in my head: *One foot in front of the other, dear heart. One step at a time.*

* * *

I was desperate for a delay to give me time to collect my thoughts but was through immigration in record time and my suitcase was one of the first off the carousel. I extended the handle and dragged it towards the Nothing to Declare lane. The bag was a bulky, difficult thing that kept twisting on its wheels. As I approached the exit gate, I lost my nerve and hovered behind the sliding doors. I looked each time they opened, but I couldn't see Joe in the arrivals hall. Perhaps he was in a different terminal or perhaps I'd got the wrong airport. Such mistakes happened. Fitz knew someone who had once inadvertently bought a ticket for Birmingham, Alabama, when she only meant to go to the West Midlands.

The doors slid open again. The family from the plane went through and a cheer went up from the relatives who had come to meet them. The doors closed. I tightened my fingers around the handle of the suitcase. The doors opened and closed; opened and closed. Each time I leaned forward and looked, each time Joe wasn't there. I couldn't stay here forever. Still I hesitated. The doors slid open and this time a man with tanned skin and short, silver hair standing on the far side of the barrier, caught my eye and raised his hand. He waved vigorously. I looked over my shoulder, assuming he was trying to catch the attention of someone behind me, but he wasn't. He was waving at me.

Was it Joe? No! Oh God, it was! I'd been looking for the young man I used to know, not an older, sensible looking man wearing a dusty blue golfing shirt tucked into a pair of jeans. The shock unfooted me. Had he been watching each time the doors opened? Had he seen my eyes scanning the crowd, slipping over him without any hint of recognition? Embarrassment heated my cheeks. What should I say? Should I apologise? No, no. I'd blame my eyes. I'd say I was tired. Shit.

'Come on,' I murmured to the suitcase, and I went forwards.

Joe wasn't smiling as we walked towards one another. His expression was one I recognised from my work, that of a parent called in to school because their child had misbehaved, a parent who didn't want to be there, who'd rather be at the dentist's or unblocking the drains or anything. I was almost sick with nerves myself.

At the last moment, my bag unbalanced me and I stumbled. Joe caught me and there was a moment's awkwardness. I assured him I was okay, but still I dusted the place where he had touched me and he wiped his hands together. We two, who used to spend whole weekends in bed, who had known every tiny part of each other's bodies and used to delight in giving one another pleasure, we had become reticent about touching at all. It was painfully awkward and so was the silence that stretched between us so far I could feel the draught as metaphorical tumbleweed rolled sorrowfully by.

It wasn't a great beginning. I wondered how on earth we would get through the coming days.

4

'I can't believe you're still struggling with that old suitcase,' were the first words Joe said to me on our reunion. He stared at the case, battered and grubby and covered with stickers. 'You said you were going to get rid of it after Seville.'

Oh, Seville; yes. At Seville airport, I had inadvertently pulled the case over the toes of an elderly man, causing him to drop the duty-free bag he was holding. The bottle of Laphroaig contained inside broke, spilling its contents firstly into the plastic bag and then, when the old man picked the bag up, over his beige slacks, his sandals, his white socks and the floor.

I was pretty sure now that Joe was remembering the smell of whisky, the redness of the man's face and his refusal to accept our help or our offer to replace the whisky.

I hadn't thought of that incident in at least a decade and wished Joe hadn't reminded me of it; a thinly veiled criticism that carried all kinds of subliminal messages about my clumsiness, my carelessness, my inertia. At a time when I was already wracked with insecurities, it wasn't a kind thing to do. On the plus side, it was gratifying to find a valid reason to be angry with Joe all over again.

Now my ex-husband was staring at my face. If he said anything about me looking worn out or stressed, I would turn around and walk away. Really, I would.

Instead he asked in a grudging voice: 'Do you want some?' and offered me the bottle of water he was holding. He'd obviously been drinking from it while he waited for me because it was half empty.

'No, thank you,' I said primly and even before the words had been spoken, I regretted them because I was desperately thirsty.

'We'll get going then.'

'Right.'

Joe tried to take the handle of my bag, but I insisted I could manage and then had to pretend I wasn't struggling as I followed him through the arrivals hall.

If I hadn't known it was Joe in front of me, I wouldn't have recognised him. His whole shape and demeanour were different. It wasn't just the hair, although his ears were very brown against the silver; his shoulders were broader and his walk was no longer a relaxed lope, but more of a marching gait. He no longer hunched his shoulders. He no longer dragged his feet. I was probably different too. I wondered how other people saw us: a couple clearly not in harmony, the man walking ahead, the woman behind with her recalcitrant suitcase. They probably thought we were the kind of miserable, long married pair who had hen-pecked one another so comprehensively over the years that we'd lost the capacity for humour, or kindness.

What did it matter? Who cared what anyone thought?

I followed my ex-husband out into the brightness of the outdoors and the oven-like warmth. I breathed in the new, foreign landscape: herbs and exhaust fumes, a dry wind. The suitcase tipped again and Joe turned.

'Let me...' he said.

'No,' I said, tetchily. 'I can manage. I'm fine.'

We carried on, he striding ahead, the case bumping in my

wake. I followed him past taxi ranks and car parks to the bay where the hire car was parked, small and dusty, one of a number of Fiats in a line beneath the twiggy shade of a row of lime trees. The windows had been wound down a couple of inches.

The doors to the car beside ours were wide open and a young girl was sitting in the passenger seat, her bare feet up on the dashboard, staring at the phone she held in one hand while picking at her teeth with the thumbnail of the other. She looked at us over the top of round, pink plastic sunglasses, then turned back to the screen.

'It's not much of a car,' Joe said with a hint of apology in his voice – or perhaps it wasn't apology, perhaps he wanted to convey that he was used to driving bigger, better vehicles.

'It's fine,' I said.

'It was all they had.'

'It's fine.'

Joe put my suitcase into the boot and I climbed into the passenger seat and closed the door, pulling it shut with a thunk, just loud enough for Joe to intimate that I was annoyed. Then I wished I hadn't, because he would definitely have picked up on the fact that the almost-slam of the door had been deliberate. Or perhaps not. We had been apart for ten years; he would have forgotten how to read subtleties in my behaviour by now, wouldn't he?

My heart gave a flutter of panic. *Does he still know me? No! No! Of course he doesn't! But what if he...? Stop it, Edie. Stop, for God's sake!*

Joe climbed into the car and started the engine.

'Do you mind if I open the window?' I asked.

'No.'

'You wouldn't rather have the air conditioning on?'

'The window's fine.'

Was this how it was going to be between us? Stilted conversation and surly, monosyllabic answers?

I pressed the button and lowered the window. Warm air rushed in. I glanced at Joe. His face was as rigid as a mannequin's. Fine. Good. Be like that.

We jolted over a speed bump and queued for the exit barrier. Joe was staring pointedly ahead, I rested my elbow on the door frame and my chin on my knuckles and looked through the side window. Crows were pecking amongst the dusty grass at the verges. We moved forwards painfully slowly.

'Is this your first time in Sicily?' Joe asked. He put on his sunglasses and pushed them up his nose. As I looked at him, I was struck once again by the whiteness of his hair. Last time I saw Joe, his hair had been black and wavy. Before we had Daniel, I used to wash it for him sometimes. He liked me to massage his head, my fingers slippery with conditioner, and afterwards, if the hair washing hadn't led to sex, which it some-times did, I'd rinse his hair with the shower head and then blow dry it for him. I'd known Joe's head intimately, every lump and bump of it. I knew his hair; its texture and its whorls. In all the time we were together, I'd never found a single white hair on Joe's head.

'Edie?' Joe asked again, definite irritation in his voice now. 'I asked if you'd been to Sicily before?'

'Yes,' I said, 'I mean, no. No, I haven't.'

We'd been planning to come to the island the year Daniel died; he was supposed to celebrate his sixth birthday here, in the villa where Joe used to spend his childhood holidays. Anna and Anna's mother were going to be there and other relatives from the Italian side of the family who I'd never met. It was going to be a big celebration of a holiday. All kinds of treats and outings and parties had been planned: picnics and days on the beach and a visit to a nearby hilltop city to watch a festival. We never made it to Sicily that year, of course, and Joe's grandmother had died soon after, and Joe and I divorced and all our plans had come to nothing.

'What about Italy?' Joe asked. 'Have you ever been to Italy?'

'Florence, once, with the school I work at.'

'Right.'

'It was an art trip, Fitz – Miss Fitzpatrick – the friend I live with, she arranged it. We travelled by coach.'

He didn't respond.

'We saw lots of statues.'

Nothing.

'And churches.'

I'd been particularly taken by the tiny, hidden church of Santa Margherita de' Cerchi where Dante met Beatrice. I'd gone there with a fifteen year old with a range of disorders who couldn't cope with the organised tours the rest of the party were enjoying. I couldn't cope with them either, excursions were far more pleasant when it was just the two of us. We'd discovered a basket beside Beatrice's shrine filled with fascinating notes from people pleading for help with their love lives. Some were written in English: *Oh, Beatrice, help me! He is my world but he doesn't even notice me! ... I know she prefers this other guy but he's a dick, what shall I do? ...* We'd made up our own responses, matching broken heart to broken heart. Afterwards, we bought ice creams and sat on the wall beside the river. The girl, Keira, her name was, told me about how she wanted to do well in life to prove her mother wrong. 'Wrong about what?' I'd asked and she'd replied: 'Me being too stupid to make anything of myself.'

I considered telling the story to Joe but decided against it.

We left the airport and joined a dual carriageway. Cars and mopeds zipped past us.

'How far is it to the lawyer's office?' I asked.

'About two hours,' Joe replied.

Oh God! What are we going to talk about for two hours?

'We should use the time to discuss what we're going to do with the villa,' Joe said, so promptly that I wondered if I'd inadvertently voiced my thoughts out loud: how else could he have known to answer my question? It used to happen when we were married; one of us would pre-empt the other's unspoken question with a response, but surely that telepathy born of intimacy must have withered while we were apart? 'Do you have any thoughts,' Joe asked, 'about what you want to do with your share?'

'Of the villa?'

'Yes,' Joe said, and I heard the word 'obviously' even though he hadn't actually said it.

'If it was down to me,' I replied, 'a quick sale would be best. Do you want to sell it too?'

'I do, yes.'

'Okay. Good.'

Joe was still staring ahead and I couldn't see his eyes behind the sunglasses. I licked my lips; my mouth was dry as dust. 'I didn't think you'd want to sell,' I said, my casual tone disguising how intensely relieved I was at his response. I'd been expecting a battle; I thought he'd be determined to hold onto the villa, no matter what. It was the last strong connection with his mother's Sicilian family and family was important to the DeLucas.

'Yeah,' he shrugged. 'Well.'

'I know how much the villa meant to you, all those fabulous childhood holidays you had there...'

'I need the money.'

'Oh?'

'Yeah.'

I waited, but he said nothing more.

We drove on in silence. I resumed my original position: staring out of the window, my face turned from Joe, my shoulders aching with tension. We rattled along the slow lane of a dual carriageway, and were overtaken by a variety of ramshackle trucks, including a three wheeler towing a flatbed stacked with tractor tyres. The driver, a swarthy young man in overalls, grinned and saluted as he went past. Joe touched his forelock in response. I had a flashback to a holiday sixteen years previously, when Joe and I spent the summer driving around Ireland in a campervan; the windows open, my belly swelling with Daniel inside it, music playing on the radio and life feeling so good, so easy. I remembered the braids in my hair, the cotton pinafore I used to wear, the cheesecloth shirt, the sun in my eyes, Joe's hand reaching across the hot leatherette of the bench seat, to take hold of mine; how happy we were.

The happiness was long gone. Daniel was gone and our love hadn't been strong enough to survive the aftermath of his death. Now we were merely two people with nothing in common, save an inheritance that had been foisted on us in a clumsy attempt to make up for something that could not be compensated for; an inheritance I couldn't wait to offload.

5

Back in Bristol, when I was planning for this trip, I'd borrowed a linen trouser suit from my colleague, Meg, to wear to the meeting with the Sicilian lawyer. The suit was a mistake. It was of good quality, but it wasn't my style and it didn't fit. Beneath the jacket was a sleeveless, polyester shirt with a bow at the neck. I had to hold the ribbons of the bow to stop the wind blowing them into my eyes. Sweat was pooling in the ridge of my back. Meg always looked well-dressed, she looked right in her clothes. I'd thought that if I borrowed them, I'd look right in them too, but I didn't. I tucked the ribbons inside the shirt, sweated in the suit and watched the countryside pass by.

Soon, we left the flatlands behind and drove a winding road that led into lusher countryside. We passed a hobbled donkey and Joe's fingers clenched on the steering wheel. I remembered something I hadn't thought of in years. When we were eleven years old, Joe and I rescued a starling from a cat and put it in a box in the shed at the back of Joe's family's house in Muswell Hill. Joe looked after it, bringing it food and water, checking on it several times a day. The starling, which we named Stanley, was recovering and we had hopes of a successful return to nature, until Joe's father, the psychiatrist Patrick Cadogan, discovered it.

Joe and I found Stanley's body on the compost heap; we recognised him by the missing tail-feathers. Mr Cadogan told us he'd found the bird dead in the shed, but he was lying. Patrick Cadogan was a murderer; Joe knew it and so did I. When Anna saw the starling limp in Joe's hands, I looked into her eyes and saw that she knew it too. That was one of the reasons Joe changed his surname from Cadogan to DeLuca as soon as he was old enough to legally do so. Patrick Cadogan was a cold, cruel man and Joe wanted nothing more to do with him.

* * *

To reach Ragusa city, we had to drive through a tunnel hewn through the mountain. After that, we crossed a ravine on an elevated section of road. The drop on either side terrified me, but Joe was oblivious to my discomfort. He had no idea about the dark places to which my imagination had a propensity to turn, but I read the headlines, clear as anything: BRIDGE FAILURE – MULTIPLE DEATHS, ROGUE CONCRETE BLAMED.

We crossed the ravine without anything terrible happening, travelled a winding road for a while and then at last the old city of Ragusa came into view, clinging to the side of a mountain, materialising like a dream. It was built so high that its apex was wreathed in cloud. It was a fairy tale city; growing out of the landscape like something organic and ancient, one of its faces lit by the sun, the opposite side in shadow. I stared at it, awestruck, trying to imprint the memory in my mind because I'd never seen a city like it.

'Did you know it was like this?' I asked Joe. 'Did you know it was this beautiful?'

'I've been here hundreds of times,' he replied coldly.

Of course he had. No doubt this view was commonplace to him. I wished I'd kept my enthusiasm to myself.

We found a shady layby at the foot of the city where we could leave the car, before getting out, stretching and staring upwards. Anna would have known I would love this view, she would have known the effect it would have on me, but, even in death, I didn't want to give her the satisfaction. If she had imagined that bringing Joe and me here together would be the prompt we needed to start dismantling the wall we'd built between us, then she'd been wrong. Joe clearly had no interest in making friends with me and the feeling was entirely, one hundred per cent mutual.

Joe pulled a jacket from the back seat, shook it ineffectually to smooth out the creases and put it on. He leaned down to comb his hair with his fingers using the wing mirror as a reflector. To one side of us, the seductive city climbed the mountain. To the other, the land dropped away steeply into a shrubby ravine. Goats were grazing in sandy patches amongst the black shade of trees dripping with long, pale catkins.

Joe retucked the hem of his shirt into the waistband of his trousers. He had a small belly now that he'd never had before and I tried not to notice it.

'I should have brought a tie,' he said.

'I'm sure it won't matter.'

'You don't think it'll look disrespectful?' This was typical Joe, becoming anxious, craving reassurance, whenever he had any dealings with authority. It was a window back into the past, to the insecure young man who was never good enough for his father, who struggled to cope at the expensive and brutal boarding school Patrick had insisted on, who had, right up until Daniel's death, used humour to deflect criticism. Neither of us was laughing now.

'No,' I told him, 'you look fine.'

Joe said, 'Hmm,' unconvinced, and patted his pockets until

he found a folded letter with the address we needed on the heading. He tapped the street name into the map app on his phone and we followed the directions, climbing steeply uphill through narrow, stepped alleyways.

Close up, the city was as lovely as it had looked from the road, unexpected views announcing themselves as we turned tight corners: a wall overlooking a ravine with a church clinging to its side; falls of bougainvillea, swallows feeding above a grand fountain, splashing water poured from the urn of a statue into a great, green bowl; patches of dark shadow, patches of bright light, dappled ground around the trees. Birds sang from their perches on flag-poles jutting over secret squares; restaurants were tucked behind houses that were stacked tightly against one another; twisting alleyways barely wide enough for two people to walk side by side; steps leading upwards, or downwards to arched doorways and tiny, vaulted bridges; the smell of good coffee; the smell of cooked cheese. Carnations and pelargoniums planted in old olive-oil tins spilled red flowers like spots of blood; caged songbirds trilled from balconies; and washing dried on wire racks hooked to windows above our heads. If it hadn't been for the fact that it was Anna who had brought me to the place, if I could only have stopped myself from seeing the city through her eyes, imagining her imagining me and Joe here together, then I would have been utterly delighted by it. I had to clamp my mouth shut to stop myself from pointing out the wondrous views to Joe.

Eventually, hot and breathless, my skin burning and a blister forming beneath the ankle strap of one of my sandals, we found ourselves in the central piazza. In front of us the steps that led to the doors of the Duomo San Giorgio towered over the square. I would have loved to sit for a while outside the café and drink it all in, but Joe was focused on his phone. He shielded his eyes with his hand as he studied the names of the streets that led from the piazza.

'This way,' he said gruffly.

I followed him into a shady, cobbled alley lined with tiny, expensive shops. At the end of the street was a sign: Studio Legale Recupero.

'There,' said Joe. 'That's it.'

'It's very...' grand, I was thinking. It was nothing like the office of the solicitor who'd dealt with my side of the divorce. She'd been an acquaintance of Fitz's and every inch of available floor and table space in her scruffy little backstreet room had been piled with cardboard files. This was modern and elegant and impressive.

Our two shabby reflections looked back at us through the darkened glass. Above us, cameras fixed to the lintel blinked.

Joe reached up to straighten the collar of his shirt. 'Right,' he said. 'Let's get this over and done with.'

He raised his finger and pressed the buzzer. The door opened and in we went.

6

We found ourselves in an air-conditioned reception area, full of swathes of glossy wood and butter-soft leather furniture. Birds of paradise blooms stood proud above an enormous glass vase beside the desk. We introduced ourselves and the receptionist invited us to take a seat, which we did; sitting awkwardly side by side. I leaned down and tried to adjust the position of the sandal strap so it stopped rubbing on my blister, while Joe fidgeted with a loose button on the cuff of his jacket.

A few minutes later, the lawyer's assistant arrived and invited us to follow her into a tiny, darkly mirrored lift. I held my breath and pressed my hands against the wall behind me to prevent any part of my body touching any part of Joe's. The lift was slow and cranky and I was scared we'd be trapped. I had to stop myself reaching for Joe's hand. Ten years it had been. Ten years, and still my instinct was to lean to him for reassurance. Did the body never forget?

The lawyer, Avvocato Recupero, was waiting for us in a room on the first floor. He spoke no English, but he was courteous and his tone was kindly; he put me at ease. I could see how he would have appealed to Anna; she always liked nice things; attractive people. I imagined her imagining us meeting him for the first time. *Go away*, I said, *leave me alone*, but she was with us, almost as present in that office as if she had been there in person.

Joe and I were shown where to sit, side by side. There was a jug of water on the table and several upturned glasses. I filled one and drank the water so greedily I spilled some onto the faux silk blouse. The spots glared black. I filled the glass and drank again. This time I spotted the desktop with water. What was the matter with me? Why was I being so clumsy?

I wiped the desktop with the sleeve of my jacket. It left a smear on the wood. The assistant leaned over and passed me a paper towel and my cheeks burned hot with embarrassment.

Joe was fluent in Italian and talked for some time with the lawyer. I couldn't follow what they were saying although I heard Anna's name mentioned several times. I sipped my water and tried not to fidget. Eventually the tone changed and the formalities began and at this stage Joe took the time to explain what was happening. Every so often, a document was placed in front of me and I was shown where to sign.

'That's to confirm your inheritance of half of the villa,' Joe told me, 'that's the transfer of the deeds. That's to say you'll take fifty per cent responsibility for insurance.'

Every document I signed, he signed too, his name beneath mine, an uncomfortably intimate procedure that reminded me of signing the marriage register, and then, later, the papers that would finalise our divorce.

The business was completed quickly, more smoothly than I'd expected. When it was finished, the lawyer handed a leather folder to Joe, indicating with a small bow that the bundle belonged to me too. It contained papers, the deeds to the villa and a wallet of keys. Attached to each key with a short length of string was a brown paper label describing the door that it opened. The writing on the labels was sparse and neat; Anna's.

We all shook hands and the assistant disappeared and

returned a few moments later with a tray. On the tray were four small glasses filled with a pale coloured liqueur. We each took a glass.

'A saluti!' said the avvocato. He raised his glass to me and then to Joe. 'Congratulations and good luck to you both!'

I wondered if he'd ever had a couple drink a less enthusiastic toast to their future.

7

Back in the car, Joe passed the document wallet to me and I held it on my lap.

'I told the lawyer we wanted to sell the villa,' he said. 'He's going to put us in touch with an agent, but he's already had an enquiry from someone interested in buying it.'

'Do you know who?'

'Some friend of the family.'

Joe reached for his seat belt and pulled it across his body.

'So, it shouldn't take too long?' I asked.

'No.'

'And you'll get the money you need.'

'Yes.'

'What are you going to do with it?' I asked. He'd been evasive last time the subject was raised and I wondered if he was intending to spend the money impressing a new partner or something similar. His answer surprised me.

'I want to help young addicts.'

'Oh?'

'To give them the skills they need to set themselves up for

work. Practical skills, I mean: garden design, landscaping, that kind of thing.'

'Sounds great,' I said, and it did, and it was great that Joe was going to use his inheritance for the good, but of all the disadvantaged young people he could have helped, why had he chosen addicts? Well, I knew why obviously, but it irked me nonetheless. I couldn't help feeling badly about it.

'So, is that it?' I asked, to change the subject. 'Are we done now? Can I go home?' I'd bought an open ticket, not knowing how long I'd be in Sicily, but the prospect of returning so quickly was enticing.

'There's still stuff that needs doing.'

'What stuff?'

'The contents of the villa...' He glanced to me. 'We need to decide what to keep and what to sell.'

'You can do that,' I said. 'They're your family's possessions.'

Joe started the engine and lowered the windows.

'Some of it's quite valuable,' he said, 'and half of it belongs to you.'

I detected a note of bitterness in that observation and replied quickly: 'I don't want anything.' Certainly nothing that used to belong to Anna. 'You decide what to do with it. You'll know what to keep.'

Joe took off the handbrake and manoeuvred the car out of its spot. As we moved, a flock of sparrows fluttered out of the tree; tiny shadows flickered over my arms and face. Behind us, Ragusa's walls basked in the golden glow of the lowering sun.

'There's a particular painting,' Joe said. 'Anna meant to take it to the bank last time she was in Sicily, but she never got round to it. It haunted her.'

'The painting? Why?'

'She'd promised her mother she'd look after it.'

'Is it valuable?'

'I don't know,' Joe said. 'It's old.'

'I'm sure it'll be okay,' I said.

'Yeah,' replied Joe. 'Let's hope so.'

* * *

We drove on. The longer I sat beside Joe in the car, the less I wanted to be there. The prospect of spending days, weeks even maybe, going through his family's possessions – his grandmother's fusty old lady things, congealed pots of face cream and personal items belonging to her and to Anna, things I would not want to see or touch, filled me with dismay. I didn't know if I would be able to bear it.

After a while, a thought occurred to me.

'Rather than us having to do it, couldn't we pay someone to go in to the villa and sort out the contents?' I asked.

'Pay someone?' Joe sounded as if the suggestion had appalled him.

'There are people who'll do that kind of thing, look at what's valuable and what's not and…'

'A stranger? You want us to employ a stranger to go through my family's things?'

Oh for goodness sake, I thought, *you're happy enough to sell the villa, why make a song and dance about what's inside?* Although I was bristling, I continued in a perfectly reasonable tone of voice.

'Not some random stranger, but a professional. Someone without any emotional connection who could be more objective.'

Joe frowned. 'You sound as if you think an emotional connection is a bad thing.'

'I didn't say that, and you know that's not what I meant. I'm only trying to be practical. It would save you having to feel bad about throwing things away. It would be less hassle all round.'

'I promised Anna we'd deal with our inheritance together.'

Anna scheming again! She'd thought of every little way to manipulate the two of us.

'You might have promised her, but I didn't and it's not like it matters to her now. Why put yourself – and me, through all that?'

Joe's hands were gripping the steering wheel and I knew from his expression that I'd said too much. I should have stopped there, but I couldn't help myself.

'House clearance experts would sort it out in no time and we wouldn't have to go to the trouble of hiring a skip or whatever.'

Joe remained silent while we waited at a roundabout, but as we joined the road that would take us towards the coast, he said: 'You've changed, Edie. You used to be kind.'

That was hurtful but I didn't bite back at him. I didn't want our sniping to develop into a full blown fight.

'I'm being practical, that's all,' I said quietly.

'Whatever,' he said.

I twisted the ribbon of the shirt around my hand. Perhaps he was right, perhaps I had changed but if I had it was because of Anna and what she'd done to me. Grief had made me bitter and anger had made me harder, but that wasn't my fault, was it? I hadn't asked for Daniel to be taken from me. If I was no longer a kind person, then Anna was to blame. She had ruined everything.

We continued in silence. Joe was in a bad mood now, but he hadn't stopped to think how difficult this was for me. I was dreading seeing the villa for the first time, dreading it becoming real to me.

I stared out of the window, every atom aching with tension.

8

Some of Sicily was beautiful, but some of it wasn't. We passed scruffy smallholdings, little farms, glossy horses standing in the shade of trees in fields surrounded by drystone walls, their tails twitching away the flies. We went through ugly industrial and retail estates. We saw car parks and pylons and yellow McDonald's signs and overflowing, communal rubbish bins; a giant quarry. I made a mental note of the bad and refused to allow myself to be enchanted by the good. It made me uncomfortable thinking of Anna thinking of me; she imagining how I'd feel when I came here for the first time. I made up my mind not to appreciate any of it.

After we'd driven in silence for more than an hour, we crested the ridge of a wooded hill and the sea came into view below us, taking me by surprise; a sparkling, jewel green sea that faded into a turquoise haze at the horizon.

'Wow,' I breathed, forgetting to be surly.

'The light,' Joe said quietly. 'I'd forgotten the light.'

He slowed the car and pulled over to the side of the road. We both looked over the vista, taking the time to savour it.

'When was the last time you were here?' I asked Joe.

'Twenty years, maybe.'

'That's a long time.'

'Yeah.'

'The villa's down there,' he said, indicating a small headland to one side of the bay. On the other was a larger headland, with a road running along its spine and a little town at the end. I could just make out a harbour, masts bobbing distantly, and a light-house that looked as if it belonged on a postcard. 'We could drive down and have a quick look at what we've inherited before it gets dark.'

'Okay, but Joe, I haven't booked any accommodation for tonight. Have you?'

'Not yet.'

'Will we be able to find somewhere?'

'There's a hotel in Porta Sarina.' Joe nodded towards the town.

'They'll definitely have room, will they?'

'Yep,' he replied.

'Do you think we should call them now?'

'It'll be fine.'

He started the engine again and we carried on slowly, zigzag-ging down the side of the hill until we reached a sharp turn, the road looping around a ramshackle cottage surrounded by a higgledy-piggledy yard. Chickens were scratching amongst laundry hung from the branches of twiggy old trees that cast long shadows in the evening light.

'That's the mafia cottage,' Joe said in a quiet voice.

'Mafia?'

'Yep.'

'What, mafia mafia? Like *The Sopranos*?'

'Yep.'

We drove slowly past. An old woman in a headscarf sat on a step in the shade shelling peas into a colander. She peered forward as we passed, squinting to see better. Nearby, an old man sat on a stool in the shade of an olive tree. One hand was on the bowl of a walking stick dug into the ground beside him, the other was holding a length of plastic twine. The twine was attached to a head collar worn by a small, brown and white goat that was feeding from a bucket at the old man's feet. His shoulders were hunched, his ears stuck out like bats' wings, his head was shiny, sun-browned and age-spotted, with a wisp or two of hair. 'Is that him?' I whispered.

'Yep.'

'I don't think I've ever seen a Mafioso before. What did he do?'

'Killed a couple who were living in one of the beach houses.'

'Killed them? Oh God! Why?'

'To prove himself to the mafia bosses. The couple were gay and the mafia thought they lowered the tone.'

'That's awful! Did he go to prison?'

'He was never convicted. He was only a teenager, people believed he was too young to have actually done it. But he did. And he threatened a woman who was cheating on her husband and later she was found dead in the marshes.'

'He killed her too?'

'The story was that the woman got lost in the dark and fell in the marsh, but everyone knew she'd been murdered. Even her husband spoke of it openly.'

'Was he convicted that time?'

'No.'

'Why not?'

'Because the police, back then, were sympathetic to the husband.'

'Seriously?'

'Yep.'

I glanced back over my shoulder. The old woman was still watching.

'Didn't your grandparents mind having someone like him just up the road?'

'It was how it was. They used to have him in to do odd jobs sometimes, building work, that kind of thing.'

'*What*? They had a murderer in to fix their walls? Why would they do that?'

'Because he was a good worker, I expect. Convenient.'

'Oh my God!'

Joe gave a short laugh, but I was shocked. This was a part of his family history of which I'd been completely unaware.

We bumped around a hairpin bend and headed steeply downhill. The concrete track had disintegrated in places and was full of potholes. The car lurched as the wheels struggled with the uneven terrain. I braced myself against the dashboard, tried to stop my body bumping against Joe's. I could see the headline: Estranged couple drown after cliff plunge. Inheritance trip ends in horror. Was aged Mafioso to blame for British couple's death?

'We could leave the car here and walk down,' I suggested.

'We're nearly there.'

And then suddenly the view of a perfect concave bay opened out before us. In the far distance, the sea and sky merged in a shimmer. Closer in, the sunlight caught the tips of small, innocuous waves whose only purpose, it seemed, was to add some sparkle to the perfectly blue water that reflected the perfectly blue sky. Fishing boats were silhouetted on the waves, disappearing into the glimmer and then reappearing. I could see a swathe of beach and, beyond that, lines of villas built above the beach road and amongst the trees that covered the hill.

We carried on downwards, still bumping but at a shallower angle, the track eventually flattening out into an area lined with stumpy bollards.

Joe turned off the engine and pulled on the handbrake. 'This is it,' he said. 'We're here.'

9

We climbed out of the car and stood beside the ticking engine, looking up at an old stone wall eight feet high and topped with metal spikes. In its centre, two enormous wrought-iron gates were chained shut. My eye followed the line of the wall, high and solid, built to keep people out – or to keep them in. Plants tumbled over as if trying to escape the garden inside: bougainvillea competed with wild rose; thousands of flowers running wild. Drainage gargoyles had been built into the wall at intervals; plants crept between the lips of their gurning mouths and ivy clung to the stone. The scent was intoxicating; the buzzing of insects amongst the blooms deafening.

The shadows were lengthening. The sun was blazing towards the horizon, and the promise of evening hung around us. I breathed in air perfumed by jasmine, pine, resin and ozone.

'I didn't realise...' I began, but I tailed off, because I couldn't pretend I didn't know about the villa and what it was like. The year we lost Daniel, the year we were supposed to come here, I'd asked lots of questions about the villa and Anna had shown me photographs, even some old cine-film. In the wake of everything that happened after, I'd let those memories fade but being here now for the first time, I had a sense of having been here before. It was as if I knew the villa; as if it had been waiting for me to come.

Joe walked over to the gates and rested one hand on the metal, running his fingers over an ironwork vine.

'Every summer,' he said, 'when we came to Sicily, our grandfather used to meet us at the airport and drive us back here in his Alfa Romeo. I used to wear his sunglasses and leather jacket and sit in the front next to him; I felt like Steve McQueen.'

I'd heard that story many times. Joe loved telling it and Daniel loved hearing tales about his great-grandfather's car. He'd had a toy Alfa Romeo that he used to drive around the furniture in the London flat. Joe promised Daniel that one day they'd drive around Sicily together and visit all the football stadiums. He was probably thinking about that right now.

I wrapped my arms around myself and walked away from my ex-husband to the edge of the parking area. I looked down; glassy seawater lapped against the edges of a vertical wall of volcanic rock. I could see into the water, late sunlight glinting on the fish that darted amongst the weed. Beside me was a post, with a weather-worn wooden sign nailed to the top. Painted in slanted blue letters over a white background were the words: Villa della Madonna del Mare. The artist had decorated the letters with little blue waves, starfish and seashells.

I heard a clanking as the chain that held the gates together clattered to the ground. Joe took hold of one of the gates and heaved. It groaned monstrously and moved slowly. When the gap was wide enough, Joe squeezed through and disappeared into the gardens.

It felt strange to be alone.

It was so quiet; the only sounds were the insects and the gentle splashing of water against rock. After a moment or two, I too went through the gates, walking slowly, feeling as if I was trespassing. The heat contained inside the wall was stifling, and the smell of jasmine, sweet and musky, reminiscent of Anna's perfume.

I was standing on a driveway, gravel beneath the soles of my uncomfortable sandals; weeds and thistles and self-seeded grass and wildflowers growing through the small stones. On either side, shrubs and climbers tangled together. Flowers climbed through the trees, set free from their beds and their borders. Cicadas sang; birds fluttered between the branches. It was chaotic and creepy and magical, riotous; spots and splashes of colour and movement flickering on the periphery of my vision.

I took a few steps forward, turned a corner and saw Joe ahead of me, looking around with awe. Fading sunlight gilded the garden. Joe reached up into the leaves of a tree and picked a fruit. He raised it to his lips and bit into it, then he threw the fruit into the flowers.

I followed him through alternating patches of golden sunlight and deep shade as the drive meandered to the left, then to the right. At every step, something new revealed itself; a wild creeper scrambling over a statue; a patch of bright orange poppies, the veins of the petals picked out by the sun; sparrows dust bathing; a lizard posing on a giant sundial with a crack in its centre; a huge old olive tree, its trunk gnarled and solid as rock. Then, at last, behind a line of topiary gone feral, an old, low-growing tree masking one corner of the building, we found the villa.

It was classical in design, two storeys high with a red tiled roof, whitewash peeling from plastered stone walls. A stone balcony ran beneath the three central, first-floor Palladian windows and beneath was an open, colonnaded porch. Although weeds were growing from the gutters and there were holes in the roof where tiles had slipped, the villa hadn't lost any of its beauty. It was an ageing film star, a retired ocean liner –

beautiful, abandoned, fading, but not yet destroyed and sympathetically lit by the dying sunlight. Time kaleidoscoped. I swear I could feel Joe's ancestors moving around me, coming in and out of the villa. If I closed my eyes and concentrated, I would have heard the whisper of their voices.

A dove startled us, rising up from amongst the undergrowth, the sound of its wings like gunshot.

I came closer, until I was standing feet behind Joe; so close that I could smell the fabric of his shirt, his skin, his sweat.

The villa windows were covered by shutters reinforced on the ground floor by planks of wood nailed over them. They were strung with cobwebs, decorated with windblown petals, the paint peeling, the wood beneath bleached. The front door was barricaded too; two planks criss-crossing diagonally, bolted into the frame. The last people to come to the villa had made it secure before they abandoned it to the wildlife and ghosts.

In the next instant, I had the strongest feeling that somebody was watching from inside the building. I looked to the upper windows, my eyes scanning them one by one. If anyone was there, they were hidden behind the shutters and we'd never be able to see them from down here. Or perhaps they weren't in the villa, perhaps they were in the garden. I turned, half expecting to catch someone peeping from amongst the undergrowth, but the only movement was butterflies flirting amongst the flowers. Still, the visceral unease grew stronger; someone was watching. I was sure of it.

The colour of the light grew even more intense; scarlet and gold bled across the sky; one last hurrah before the sun died and the villa's façade glowed red. When the sun set, the garden would be plunged into darkness and then we wouldn't be able to see anything, we might not be able to find our way out, we would be at the mercy of whatever, or whoever, haunted the villa and its garden.

I shivered.

'Let's go now,' I said to Joe.

He didn't say a word, but turned and led the way back to the car.

10

While Joe locked the gates, I gazed at the sun sitting on the horizon and the darkness creeping over the bay. Mosquitoes murmured about my face. Across the water, lights were coming on in Porta Sarina, street lights and lamps in the windows of the houses clustered above the beach. A string of coloured bulbs was reflected beneath the harbour wall. Outside the Villa della Madonna del Mare, the water made soft, slapping noises against the rocks.

Joe moved from the gates, took out his phone and stared at it, his face illuminated by the screen. In that strange light, I caught a glimpse of Daniel. I hadn't seen Joe in such a long time that I'd forgotten how it was sometimes that I'd look at him in a certain way and see fragments of our son.

'There's no reception here,' Joe said. 'We'll have to drive over to Porta Sarina and hope the hotel has room for us.'

'You said they definitely would have room.'

'Yes, and I'm sure they will.'

'What if they don't?'

'You can have the car; I'll sleep on the beach.'

'Joe!'

'It'll be fine!' he said. That was obviously his favoured response to any potentially difficult question.

I wrapped my arms around myself, annoyed with Joe and also with myself for not sorting the accommodation earlier. Fitz had suggested I organise a room 'somewhere convenient' when I was booking the flight, but I didn't know the geography of the region so didn't know where 'convenient' would be and I couldn't bring myself to ask Joe. Deep down, I'd been hoping I'd be able to return to the UK the same day. Now that obviously wasn't the case, I desperately wanted the opportunity to be by myself, in a room of my own.

My emotions were knotted. I needed unravelling, stretching out. I needed a bath and a comfortable bed; soft pillows, space. I did not want to sleep in the car. Why couldn't Joe have sorted out accommodation before we arrived, if he knew we'd need it? Why didn't he ever think of these things? Why hadn't I behaved like an adult and addressed the issue with him before I left home?

We took our places in the Fiat. I scratched at a bite itching on my wrist. Joe started the engine and we chuntered uphill. The old woman from the mafia cottage was still out in her garden, pointing a torch down the track, looking out for us.

* * *

At Porta Sarina, I stayed in the car while Joe went into the hotel; he returned to say there was a room for each of us, which was a great relief to me. I attempted to give him some money, but he said we would settle up later.

I followed him into the hotel, the suitcase twisting and yanking at my arm. Inside was very bright, with mirrors every-where. I saw myself reflected behind the reception desk; saw how creased and crumpled I was, my hair a mess, dark circles beneath my eyes, the awful suit hanging from me, the ribbons of the blouse dangling, my pale, Northern European skin already reddened by the sun and shining from the earlier heat and exertion.

I scratched the lump on my wrist, found another a little further up my arm.

Joe caught my eye in the mirror. I looked away. He gave me the card key for my room. 'You're on the first floor,' he said.

'Okay.'

He hesitated, then asked: 'Are you hungry?'

'No,' I said. 'I just want to sleep.'

I was starving, but I'd be okay. Before I left Bristol, Fitz had come into my room and packed a bar of chocolate, some crackers and a couple of apples into my bag 'in case of emergencies.' Fitz was brilliant; she thought of everything.

* * *

The hotel room was small and clean: a bed, a television, a floor-to-ceiling window with a net curtain, an old air-conditioning unit leaning precariously over the top of the door.

I propped the picture of Daniel on the bedside table, took off the suit and blouse and folded them onto the seat of the chair. I bathed, wrapped myself in hotel towels and lay on the bed, sinking back against the pillows, holding the TV remote and flicking through Italian news channels, but most of the news seemed to be about football. I turned down the volume, called Fitz and was comforted by her dear, gruff voice. I didn't know where to start to relate all that had happened since she dropped me off at the airport that morning, so she made it easy for me by asking questions that I did my best to answer.

When it came to Joe, I told her that he'd been 'okay, considering'. I studied a bruise forming on the back of my calf where the bag had bumped into me. 'We won't be here for long,' I said, 'he wants to sell the villa, too.'

'Really? That's not what you were expecting.'

'No, and it's a massive relief! Honestly, Fitz, I can't even think about how awkward it would have been if he'd wanted to keep it. It could have taken months to sort out.' I sighed pointedly. 'As it is, we should have it all wrapped up in a week or two. He says there's a lot of stuff inside the villa that we need to deal with, but I bet it's mostly junk. Do they have charity shops in Sicily?'

'Don't be too quick to ditch it. You can sell anything online these days.'

'I just want to be rid of it. It's going to be mostly her stuff.'

'If it's mostly Anna's, then it'll be good quality.'

'I don't want anything to do with it.'

Fitz sighed.

'I told Joe we should get someone in to clear the villa, but he wouldn't listen,' I continued. 'If he thinks I'm going to sort through heaps of her disgusting old clothes...' I shuddered and tailed off.

Fitz was silent, which meant I'd said something of which she disapproved.

I wasn't sorry. I couldn't help myself. I couldn't help being bitter about Anna. It was as if there was a never-ending stream of bile inside me connected to her and whenever I opened my mouth some of it came out. Releasing the anger was the only way I could gain any relief, otherwise it built up inside me, a swirling mass of hatred.

'She's dead, Edie,' Fitz said gently.

'Yes,' I said. 'I know. But that doesn't make her any less guilty.'

11

The next morning, I dressed and went down to breakfast as soon as the hotel's tiny restaurant was open, drawn by the smell of coffee and the lure of sweet pastries, hoping I was early enough to avoid the awkwardness of having to share a table with Joe. No sooner had I sat down with a glass of orange juice and a plate of bread and cheese, than he walked into the dining room. His face fell when he saw me.

'Hi,' he said, with no enthusiasm whatsoever.

'Hi,' I replied in the same tone.

Joe looked around the room. One other table was occupied by a young man in a suit who was simultaneously eating and tapping messages into his mobile phone. Joe was faced with a difficult decision: to join me, or choose to sit as far away as possible. I could see the panic in his eyes and couldn't bear it.

I pushed back my chair. 'I'll go and eat in my room,' I said. I picked up my plate and my glass.

'You don't have to.'

'No, it's fine.' I scrabbled for an excuse, 'I'm waiting for a phone call.'

'Right,' said Joe, making no attempt to hide his relief. 'I'll text you when I'm ready to go.'

I took the food upstairs and ate alone, sitting at the table in my bedroom, with the window wide open and the curtain tied back, watching the hotel gardener water blood-red geraniums in their pots around the brilliant blue pool, watching the light catch on the plume of bright water that arced from the mouth of the hose. There had been times in my life when I'd have relished the opportunity to stay in a hotel like this one, to look out of this window and enjoy this view. Right now, it was the last place on earth I wanted to be.

* * *

There was a Eurospin store on the outskirts of Porta Sarina where we stopped on our way back to the villa. Inside, it was more like a warehouse than a supermarket, noisy, overcrowded and dark, smelling of cardboard and decaying vegetables. We filled the trolley with fresh and tinned food, bottles of water and beer, biscuits, boxes of matches, candles and cleaning supplies.

Joe paused by a display of sleeping bags.

'There might not be any bedding in the villa, and these are cheap,' he said.

'We're going to stay at the villa?'

'We don't want to be traipsing back round the bay every night, spending a fortune on hotel rooms.'

'But...'

'What?'

I was remembering the sensation of being watched; the conviction that someone, or something, was inside the villa already; the feeling of being a trespasser or usurper inside the walls of that lovely, lonely, abandoned place.

'It makes sense to stay there,' said Joe.

He was right, but apart from the unease I felt deep in my bones, I also disliked the prospect of staying in the Villa della Madonna del Mare, knowing that Anna had spent so much of her life there, knowing how much it was her villa. But Fitz was right. Anna DeLuca was dead and the sooner we cleared out the villa, the sooner I could leave it, and her, behind.

As we headed to the checkout, we heard a call and turned to see a small, slender-boned woman of about my age coming towards us. She was heavily pregnant, wearing patterned leggings beneath an over-washed cotton dress and dirty tennis shoes.

'Joey DeLuca!' she called. 'Is that really you?'

'Valentina?' Joe asked. 'Valentina Esposito!'

The woman put down her wire basket and half ran, half waddled towards Joe, and he held out his arms to greet her, a wide smile, like the smiles I remembered from long ago, brightening his face. They embraced, he leaning down to hug her with a warmth and enthusiasm that I hadn't seen since I arrived in Sicily.

I stepped back, closer to the shelves, to give them space.

'You look amazing, Valentina!' Joe said, straightening up. 'But what are you doing here? I thought you and Salvo moved to the States!'

Valentina shrugged. 'It didn't work out between us. Salvo stayed in New York, I came home. It wasn't all bad, we had a kid, Francesco, he's fourteen. I'm married to Vito Barsi now and this one, our first, is due in a few weeks! You remember Vito?'

Joe shook his head.

'No, you wouldn't. He was never part of our gang.'

'I'm glad it's all worked out for you,' said Joe.

'Yeah,' said Valentina. 'Thanks. What about you? Are you here on holiday? Is Anna with you?'

Joe shook his head and explained the reason for our visit.

Valentina paled when she heard Anna was dead. 'Oh my, I'm sorry!' she said, looking from me to Joe and back again. 'You've both had such a terrible time.' So she knew about Daniel. She gave me a sad smile. 'At least you have each other.'

Joe pursed his lips. I tried to make my expression neutral.

'Actually, we're not together any more,' Joe said.

'We're only here to sell the villa,' I added.

'We divorced after our son's death.'

'Ten years ago.'

Valentina said, 'Oh God. I'm so sorry! Me and my big, stupid mouth!'

'No, it's fine,' I said.

'Fine,' agreed Joe.

'It was a long time ago.'

'We're both fine.' *That's us. Everything is fine, fine, fine.*

There was a moment's awkward silence, then Valentina said, 'Vito and me, we run the pizzeria by the harbour. Why don't you come up one evening? For pizza?'

'Okay,' said Joe.

'Yes,' I said. 'Great.'

Valentina's phone pinged, an incoming text. She looked at the screen and her smile faded. 'I've got to go. Don't forget to come see us. Best pizza in town!' She blew us both a kiss then returned to her basket.

Joe put his hands on the handle of our trolley and pushed it towards the till.

'She seems nice,' I said, as we queued.

'She is.'

'She was pleased to see you.'

'We used to be good friends.' Joe scratched the bottom of his earlobe.

'What?' I asked. 'Why are you smiling like that?'

'Nothing.'

'Tell me.'

'Oh, it's nothing.'

'Joe!'

'Okay, okay. It's just... once, when we were teenagers, Valentina jumped off the floating dock into the sea and pretended she had cramp so I would dive in and save her.' His smile was wide now. 'She was a good actress! I believed she was drowning. I pulled her up, put my hand under her chin, like this,' he demonstrated with his hand on his own chin, 'and paddled her back to the beach, lay her on the sand and...' he tailed off.

'Gave her the kiss of life?' I asked.

'Something like that, yeah.' He grinned, delighted but embarrassed.

I knew there was someone in Sicily for Joe. I remembered how, when he came back to London at the beginning of September each year, tanned and taller after the summer holiday spent with his mother's family, he'd be different for a while, less friendly towards me. It always took a few weeks for our friendship to get back on course. Now I knew why.

'I only found out she'd been pretending ages after,' Joe continued. 'I boasted to everyone that I'd saved this girl's life, but then she told Anna she had a crush on me and couldn't think of another way to get me to kiss her.'

'Oh. Right.'

Joe looked at me. 'What?'

'If she liked you, why didn't she just tell you that she did? Why go to all that trouble?'

'I don't know. Maybe she was shy.'

'She doesn't seem shy.'

'Why are you making such a big deal of it?' Joe asked.

'I'm not. It's a sweet story.'

I didn't mean to be sarcastic, but that was the way it sounded. We both heard the scorn in my voice.

Joe turned from me, disappointed. I didn't bother trying to

apologise. I couldn't wait until all of this was over and we could go our separate ways and we'd never have to see one another again. Dear God, I hoped that moment would soon be here.

12

I needed some sun protection lotion and Joe said there was a pharmacy in town and that it would be quicker to leave the car and walk.

I followed him along the narrow pavements. He looked more like himself this morning. He was wearing a scruffy old T-shirt and a pair of shorts that had seen better days, together with a pair of working boots and mismatched socks. I'd put on an old cotton maxi-dress, trainers, a floppy straw hat and a pair of sunglasses.

Porta Sarina was not a picture postcard town. The buildings were shabby, pockmarked stone, cat shit in the gunnels and weeds growing from the guttering. Washing was strung between the upper windows of the houses across the alleyways: knock-off designer tracksuits, football shirts and shorts; lines of bright-pink baby vests. Recycling bins overflowed at street corners and there was a pervasive smell of fish.

As we approached the main piazza, we came to a wall covered in posters. They were mostly handmade, black and white. Printed on them were photographs, family snapshots or professional portraits, and beside the images were dates and lines of writing.

'What is this?' I asked Joe.

'It's the memorial wall.'

'These are dead people?'

'Yeah. People put up posters on birthdays and anniversaries.'

'Ugh.'

'"Ugh" what?'

'It's macabre.'

'Or you could look at it as being a loving tradition, a way of keeping people's memories alive.'

'I suppose,' I said, without conviction.

My eyes skimmed the posters. All the faces, dozens of them, united in death. Some of the faces were of young men who, according to their dates, had died in the war, decades earlier. There was a picture of a swaddled baby: Cancio, Egidia; nato morto, and next to it a small boy, about the same age as Daniel, Cancio, Matteo. Oh God, two children lost from the same family!

Beside me, Joe caught his breath. 'Look!'

To one side of the wall, amongst the many images, was a poster bearing the words: DeLuca, Anna, 66 years old. Beloved friend. Death will not keep us apart. Beneath was a photocopied picture of three young women standing in front of the Villa della Madonna del Mare, not as it was now, but as it once must have been, well kept, its gardens tended. The front door was ajar; the shutters on the downstairs windows opened wide. A young version of Anna was in the centre of the group; dark hair cut in a short bob. She was wearing pedal pushers and a gingham top with capped sleeves. To one side of her, a small girl with frizzy hair was grinning at the camera; to the other, a taller, more solidly built young woman stood slightly back. The face of the third girl had been erased; whoever had done it had scratched at the paper so viciously it was torn.

'Who could have put that up?' I asked Joe.

'I guess Anna still has friends here.'

'But the girl's face...'

'I know. It's weird.'

I picked at the edge of the paper, pulled at it. A small strip tore away in my hand.

'Leave it,' Joe said. 'Come on, let's go.'

* * *

I bought what I needed from the pharmacy and we returned to the car via the harbour. I felt uneasy, unsettled by the defaced picture on the memorial wall. Someone had cared about Joe's mother enough to put up a poster in her memory. And someone had cared enough to vandalise it. Someone loved and someone hated; someone wanted to remember and someone wanted to forget the past; to obliterate it.

As we walked through the town, my discomfort increased to the point where I was cold, despite the warmth of the day. It wasn't only the sinister violation of the face in the photograph, I had the exact same sensation I'd experienced at the villa the previous evening: that we were being watched.

I looked behind me, expecting to see someone dart into a doorway, but nobody was there. I looked up, to the windows of the houses that lined the narrow streets, but all I could see were the reflections of the houses opposite in the glass.

* * *

The waterfront, that had looked so appealing from the other side of the bay, was, close up, as scruffy and run down as the rest of the town. The street facing the harbour was lined with bars and the pizzeria, Vito's, was at the far end. A teenage boy was sweeping the terrace outside. He was dark haired and slender with heavy eyebrows; obviously Valentina's son. He concentrated on his work, pushing the head of the brush under the tables, making a pile of dust. His expression was serious, as if he was carrying the weight of the world on his shoulders.

'Ciao,' said Joe as we drew near.

The boy looked up. 'Ciao,' he replied.

His eyes were dark and sensitive, wary, his arms wiry and tanned. He still had the narrow shoulders of a young boy, yet he worked with the diligence of a man.

Joe walked on, but I stopped to watch the boy.

He was only a little younger than Daniel would have been if he had lived. How wonderful it must be to have a teenage son; Valentina was lucky. If only I'd had the chance to see Daniel grow up! If only Anna hadn't taken all that potential joy from me.

A wave of grief took me by surprise and in its aftermath I wondered if anyone had ever posted a picture of Daniel on the memorial wall: Anna or her mother? I couldn't bear the thought of that: Daniel's picture, out here, in this hot, distant little town, so far from home.

Valentina's son was beside me, concern in his eyes. 'Stai bene, signora?'

'I'm fine. I'm sorry. Ignore me.'

'American?'

'English.'

He looked at me, still worried.

'Really, I'm okay,' I said.

'I could fetch you some water.'

'No. I don't want anything.' I smiled reassurance. From some distance away, Joe looked back over his shoulder to see where I was. 'Joe over there used to be friends with your mother. We're going to come here for pizza one day,' I told the boy.

'It's the best pizza in town.'

'That's what we heard! I'll look forward to it. See you again...?'

'Francesco.'

'Francesco. See you soon.'

I grabbed the rim of my hat and trotted after Joe, catching him up at the harbour wall. The water was green tinged, glassy, a slick of fuel making rainbows on its surface. Boats rocked at the ends of their ropes. Tiny pink jellyfish were floating around the weedy chains that anchored the buoys. The sun was warm on my skin.

Joe pointed to the far headland, no more than a hundred yards away as the crow flies. I could see the wall that surrounded our villa, with trees behind it, thickly bunched together, the black tips of the cypresses. I couldn't see much of the building, only one edge of the roof, but the location from this viewpoint was like something from a film; the wall, the trees, the sea almost enclosing it.

'It looks mysterious,' I whispered.

'Mysterious?'

'Don't you think it does?'

'The locals think it's haunted,' said Joe.

'Really?'

'The waiter told me this morning. He said, if you stand here, at night, sometimes you can see lights inside the walls.'

I laughed uneasily.

'People always make up stories about abandoned buildings,' I said. It was an attempt to disguise my disquiet about what Joe had just said and at the same time convince myself that my sense of the villa being occupied was pure imagination.

'He said he and a group of friends were fishing close to the villa one night and they saw a woman drifting through the gardens.'

'Drifting?' I struggled to keep my voice steady.

'They were convinced it was a ghost. They said she almost looked human, but when she raised her head, she had no face.'

The woman standing beside Anna in the picture on the memorial wall didn't have a face either.

I looked at Joe from beneath the rim of my hat. He was staring at the villa. I thought he might have been teasing, but he wasn't smiling.

Before Daniel's death, neither Joe nor I believed in life after death or any other concept that Joe liked to term 'superstitious nonsense.' We weren't unsympathetic, but used to feel something akin to pity towards those who did. Back then, of course, neither of us had experienced the shock and the ensuing black hole of grief that came with losing the person you loved most, the one you were supposed to protect, the one who gave meaning to your own life. After Joe and I separated, although I felt guilty about it and sometimes faintly ridiculous, I'd found myself drawn towards tarot cards and mediums, standing stones and old churchyards, anything that might bring me closer to Daniel. He had to be *somewhere,* I reasoned, at least his spirit did. A soul so vital, so loving and bright and energetic couldn't just disappear. If I looked hard enough, for long enough, I would find him. I was convinced of it.

'Did your grandparents ever mention anything about the villa being haunted?' I asked.

'No. But...'

'What?'

'When they'd had a drink or two, they used to talk to their ancestors as if they were still there. They said the DeLucas never really left the villa, even the ones who moved away.'

'Even the ones who died?'

He nodded.

'There's nothing strange about it,' Joe said defensively, even though I hadn't said anything at all to suggest there was. 'It was a way of remembering, that's all. Keeping memories alive.'

'Sure,' I said. I wondered if, privately, Joe had been

harbouring hopes similar to mine, that some part of Daniel might still exist somewhere in the world.

And then I remembered something I hadn't thought about in years: a conversation I'd had with Anna when Daniel was only a few months old. She'd told me that before she was born, her mother had delivered three stillborn children; one after the other. Anna's three dead siblings hadn't been baptised and couldn't be buried in consecrated land, so her father had buried them in the villa's gardens. Her mother had kept the baptismal gowns she'd hand sewn for each baby and a photograph of each of them hung in an alcove in her bedroom, where she knelt to pray several times a day.

Anna had been drinking when she told me this story. When she wasn't drinking, she was quiet and private. After a bottle of wine, she became more willing to talk about herself and her feelings. That day, she'd been trying to explain her relationship with her parents and how heavily the burden of their expectations had weighed upon her shoulders.

I'd held my baby to my shoulder and rubbed his back as Anna had talked. Daniel's head had lolled against my neck, fitting the space exactly. Anna's breath was warm and musty and her face had softened as she recalled how, when she was alone as a child, playing in the villa's gardens, she used to go to the little graveyard and summon her dead sisters and brother to play with her; how they were her imaginary friends, older than her, and younger at the same time. She used to sneak into her mother's room to talk to the photographs of the babies; she brought little gifts to the graves to keep them happy. Usually they were kind: when she was lonely or frightened, they came to her and comforted her, but sometimes they were jealous of Anna, because she was alive and they were dead. Then they'd play tricks on her. They'd break glasses and plates and Anna was blamed, or they'd lock her out of her room or shut her in a cupboard.

'That must have been frightening for you,' I'd said. We were sitting together in the front room of her London house, sunlight streaming through the window.

Anna took another sip from her glass.

'I felt responsible for them,' she'd replied. 'I understood why they were angry. It didn't seem fair that I had everything and they had nothing.' Then she'd taken another sip and she'd laughed. Her teeth had been stained red. 'It wasn't real of course! It was all made up. I was just a lonely, introverted, stupid little child!'

Now I wondered if part of the reason for her bequest to us was to protect the graves of these lost children, these siblings who had never drawn breath but who had been such an important part of Anna's early years. And another thought came to me, one so crazy that I pushed it away and wouldn't acknowledge it.

Still, it was there.

If three stillborn DeLuca babies could come back to life, even in a small way, at the Villa della Madonna del Mare, was it possible, was there the faintest, smallest hope that I might be able to find Daniel there too?

13

Joe and I returned to the car and drove back along the spine of the headland, through flat, marshy land at the base of the cliff. The sun glinted from pylons and mechanical equipment at an electricity station in the distance. A giant billboard with a picture of a blonde woman modelling *Intimissimi* lingerie marked the junction with the coast road, which climbed steeply. I tried to relax but the cliff side fall to the left was perilous. There was no barrier and Joe drove quickly, one palm flat against the steering wheel, his fingers not even closed around it. I couldn't help imaging the Fiat bouncing down against the rocks, somersaulting, crashing into the backs of the holiday villas that were built along the beach. I was used to travelling at Fitz's ponderous pace, she gripping both sides of the steering wheel of her ancient VW camper, leaning forward, her foot hovering over the brake pedal, tensed and alert to any forth-coming potential hazard, real or imaginary. I could barely remember the last time I'd ridden in a vehicle driven by anyone other than Fitz. My life was mostly lived within a few square miles: Fitz's house, the school, the places I walked the dogs, the shops and the library, all of it travelled slowly, safely. My comfort zone.

This was different. Two thousand miles from home, the headland on which the villa stood was silhouetted against the dazzling sea, shimmering like a mirage, and Joe and I zipped along the coast road in the Fiat, he having no regard for the fact that a blown tyre or a patch of oil would send us hurtling to our deaths.

Soon enough, we reached the villa. Joe parked the car in the same spot as before. The sun was high in the sky, the colours dazzling. Light shone on the whitewashed façades of the beach houses, it glared from windows, roof tiles, parked cars. The beach was busy; littered with parasols and towels. Close to our end, a small white dog ran at the sea, chasing the rippling frill as the waves broke along the shore. A young woman in a red bikini clapped her hands and laughed at the dog's antics. 'Bravo, Toto!' she cried. 'Bravo!'

I helped Joe unload the bags of cleaning provisions and food and we carried them through the gates, up the drive and to the front door of the villa. The garden was lovelier in the bright daylight than it had been in the glow of dusk; its rampant, gleeful chaos, the jungle of greens and the jewelled colours of the flowers seeming more alive than ever: fronds and tendrils and opening blooms reaching up into the beautiful blue of the sky; lemons and oranges grew profusely on the trees, insects and birds were everywhere. I wondered where the graveyard was, where the three lost babies had been buried. The thought of them lying somewhere nearby sent a chill the length of my spine, but I dismissed it. It was a beautiful day and we were in a lovely place; the sun was shining and I'd be an idiot to be distracted by the darkness of my imagination.

Joe and I were outside the villa's front door, in the same spot where Anna and her two friends had posed for the picture reproduced on the poster on the memorial wall. I sat on a stone planter that contained nothing but dead foliage and waited while Joe prised away the planks that had been hammered over the front door with the claw end of a hammer. The wood splintered as he pulled. He tossed the planks down to one side, wiped the sweat from his forehead with his arm and turned to me. 'Where's the key?'

I gave it to him and he put it the lock, turned it. The door swung open with a sorrowful groan. We exchanged tentative glances and then Joe stepped into the gloom. I followed. Something crunched beneath the soles of my trainers.

'What's that?'

'Salt.'

'Salt?'

Joe kicked at a small ridge of grubby crystals spread the width of the front door. He picked up the plastic sack that had once contained the salt granules to show me.

'Why is it there?' I asked.

Joe mumbled something.

'What?'

'It's to protect the villa. It's a Sicilian thing.'

'Protect it from what? Slugs?'

'It's just what they do here,' said Joe, defensive again.

I heard something, like a sigh. I turned; nothing was there.

'What was that?' I asked Joe.

'I don't know.'

As he spoke, something fluttered from the darkness and darted towards us. I gasped and ducked, covering my head with my arms and Joe ducked too and then laughed.

'Oh Jesus, it's just a sparrow!' He stood straight. 'Poor little sod must have been trapped.'

I smiled, but inside my heart was pounding.

* * *

Because of the shutters, the interior of the villa was dark as a cave, but behind us sunbeams spread through the open door across the ornate tiles of the hallway floor. I stepped slowly over the ridge of salt into my own shadow. Despite the musty smell, the floor was clean, save a feather or two. A giant, crystal chandelier, draped with cobwebs, hung high above us, filling in the dome of the ceiling, glass droplets trapping the reflection of light from the floor tiles and sending them out again; twinkling the effect of an elaborate disco ball.

Joe tried the light switch, but nothing happened.

Slowly, my eyes adjusted to the gloom. Two large items of furniture stood in the hallway, both covered with dust sheets. To one side of the door was an arch shaped alcove with candle-holders on either side. The hallway opened into a long, dark room to its right and, to the left, stairs led upwards. Three other doors along its length were closed. A small brown object, like a fossilised croissant, lay at the foot of the stairs.

Joe picked the thing up and tossed it outside.

'What was it?' I asked.

'Nothing.'

'Joe?'

'It was a sheep's horn.'

'A sheep's horn?'

'It's to keep the villa safe. Don't worry about it.'

I gave a small laugh. 'A whole sack of salt and a sheep's horn. That's a lot of precautions.'

'When you live on an island that's been invaded so many times, you're bound to be worried about people breaking in to your property,' said Joe.

But that wasn't the reason for the salt and the horn and we both knew it. The villa had been made secure already; the planks over the doors and shutters would keep vandals and burglars out. These objects were to protect against a different kind of intruder.

Joe switched on the torch on his phone, directed the light into the alcove and moved the beam around, into every corner.

'It's not there,' he said.

'What isn't?'

'The painting, the *Madonna del Mare*.'

'The one your mother was worried about?'

He nodded and ran the flat of his hand along the ledge of the alcove. There was a brighter patch in the paintwork, where a picture had hung for many years.

'What does it look like?' I asked.

'The frame's about so big,' Joe described a rectangle approximately two feet square, the space of the brighter patch on the wall. 'The picture inside is quite small. The Madonna's praying but looking out of the image so she catches your eye. In the background are ships and the sea.'

He dusted his hands and wiped his palms on the sides of his shorts.

'We have to find it,' he said. 'I promised Anna.'

Anna, Anna, Anna. Always Anna.

We went upstairs, keeping close, me following Joe, our feet leaving faint prints in the dust. It was strange to think we were the first people to disturb this air, to breathe it, for years. If I narrowed my eyes, I could almost see other people, those who had been here before, passing us on the stairs, trotting down: adults with towels bundled under their arms, children in shorts and T-shirts running to play outside; Anna, trailed by her imaginary siblings; Daniel.

It made sense that Daniel should be here. He was a DeLuca. DeLuca blood ran through his veins. This villa should have been his destiny. It should have been where he came for his summer holidays, as his father had. He would have loved this place and it didn't seem such a large leap of faith to believe that he was here, now, somehow, with all the other lost DeLucas.

Joe looked over his shoulder. 'You okay, Edie?'

'Yes,' I said. 'I'm great.'

At the top of the stairs was a landing with the three arched windows we'd seen from the outside; seven feet tall at their highest point, rims of light at their edges. Joe opened the catch of the middle one and the two halves of the window swung open towards him. He pushed open the wooden shutters behind. They clattered back and light flooded onto the landing.

Joe stepped out onto the balcony and I followed. The ghosts retreated into the shadows. The sun sent its warmth and light into the Villa della Madonna del Mare, lighting the pale pink plaster on the walls, illuminating the fancy coving, the pictures and the fittings, the cobwebs, the floating motes of dust.

Joe and I rested our hands on the ornate balcony railings and looked through the trees out across the sea beyond and the perfect, blue sky. Gulls wheeled above the water.

When Anna wrote her will, she'd have had this exact scene in her mind. She must have known we'd climb the stairs to open the shutters and that we'd stand here, in the sunlight. She was probably imagining that Joe and I would fall into one another's arms and then be grateful to her for reuniting us. If that was the case, then she could hardly have been more wrong. But if, by bringing me here, she had inadvertently given me the means to bring Daniel closer to me, then I would make the most of every second I'd been given.

14

While Joe removed the planks from the downstairs windows, I opened the upstairs windows and shutters, letting light into rooms that had been dark for years. I gazed out across acres of gardens, which we hadn't yet explored, looking for the little graveyard, but the gardens were so overgrown it was a hopeless task.

From the rear bedrooms, I could see the old swimming pool, a derelict hole in the shape of two interlocking circles, one large, one small, surrounded by concrete tiles, and an abandoned pool house in the centre of what now looked like a wildflower meadow but probably used to be a fine lawn. I could imagine Joe and his friends playing in that pool: dive-bombing one another, seeing who could hold their breath the longest, sunning themselves around it. I could imagine Valentina there, a playful young girl, peering over the top of her sunglasses. I could picture Anna, standing where I was standing, watching the youngsters at a distance, enjoying their happiness. I wondered if, back then, she had any premonition of what might become of Joe; the terrible direction his life would take because of her. I wondered if, sensitive as she was to the past, she ever intuited my future presence, the former daughter-in-law who hated her.

When the upstairs windows were all open, Joe called me down and we went through the ground floor rooms together. The villa had been closed up with care, and carefully we set about reopening it. Years of darkness meant the colours on the soft furnishings hadn't faded. The rooms were tidy: good furniture shrouded in dust sheets; glasses and ornaments put away in cupboards to keep them clean.

I was awed by the stillness inside those rooms, the huge chandeliers, the beautiful old paper on the walls. I walked through the villa, hearing my footsteps, my heartbeat, not spooked exactly but unwilling to look too closely at the white sheets that covered the furniture – they looked as if they might undrape themselves at any moment and in the extremes of bright light and dark shadows it was difficult to guess what lay beneath.

When the shutters were open and the villa was airing, Joe and I went outside into the garden. We coughed the dust out of our lungs and picked cobwebs from our hair and clothes. Joe's face was grey with dirt and mine must have been the same.

'Is there anywhere we can wash?' I asked.

'There's the sea.'

I followed him through the garden, through a gap in the hedge, past the swimming pool, a tarpaulin that once covered it wrinkled in the bottom amongst dead leaves and dirt, and across the old lawn. At the farthest end, a path wound between overgrown oleander trees to steps that led down to a decked area a few feet above the sea. The rusting skeletons of two sunbeds had been pushed up against the steps. Someone had gone to the trouble of attaching a metal ladder to the far end of the decking in a narrow gap between the rocks so it was possible to climb over the sharp rock face down into the water without scraping one's knees and elbows. The sea slapped laconically against the scarred face of the rocks.

I held onto the side of the ladder and looked down. The water was crystal-clear, and very deep. Different kinds of fish swam in layers close to the rocks, sunlight glinted in the water, and deeper down, weed the colour of rubies waved its delicate fronds. The sun beat down on my back. The water was enticing.

Daniel would have loved this, I thought, and for the briefest instant I felt him with me, holding on to my hand, looking down into the water.

Joe had come to stand beside me. He looked over my shoulder, almost, but not quite, touching me. I could feel the warmth of his body.

'Fuck it,' he said. 'I'm going in.'

He stepped back, took off his boots and socks, pulled his T-shirt over his head and dropped it on the decking. He pulled down his shorts and stepped out of them. He was wearing dark blue boxer shorts beneath, with a black, elasticated belt. He ran past me, leapt over the steps and somersaulted into the water. He reappeared a way away from the decking, shaking his head, droplets flying from his hair and sparkling in the light. He did not call to me but swam out to sea.

I wanted to be in there too.

Beneath my clothes, I was wearing ordinary, mismatched, comfortable underwear. Fitz had insisted I bring my swimming costume, in case the opportunity to spend some time at the beach arose, but the costume was in my suitcase, which was still in the boot of the Fiat. It would be a long walk to retrieve it.

Fuck it, I thought. I was too old to be self-conscious about my body, too dirty to make a fuss, and even if Joe had been looking, which he wasn't, he wouldn't have cared what I looked like or what I was wearing.

I pulled my dress over my head and dropped it onto the decking. I went to the ladder, turned around and climbed down the steps, one by one, the water rising up my legs, deliciously cold, then my hips, and it had reached my waist before I ran out of steps and let myself fall back.

At first, the sea was shockingly cold, but in a few moments I was used to it and joy ran through me. I ducked my head beneath the surface, and when I came up again, gasping and refreshed, I swam, not towards Joe but parallel with him, enjoying the feeling, the water, the freedom, the sun on my face.

Almost six year old Daniel would have loved it here! He'd have been doggy paddling between us, his armbands keeping him afloat, his head held artificially high above the water, that wide grin on his face, those missing teeth; he'd have called to Joe and then me, asking us to play with him, to chase him, to pretend he was a shark, clinging onto our shoulders, wrapping his skinny legs around our waists. Teenage Daniel probably would be heading off alone, swimming out to the floating dock anchored off the beach – that must be the same dock that Valentina once jumped off, pretending to drown. And Joe and I, we'd watch him go and we wouldn't know whether to be happy that our son was so independent and confident, or sad that he was already growing away from us.

I thought of those two versions of Daniel, and all the other Daniels in between. Every one of those lost boys would have loved this place and I grieved the loss of every single one of them and every loss was because of Anna DeLuca. My endless grief was because of her.

* * *

After the swim, reunited on the decking, awkwardness returned to Joe and me. We dressed with our backs to one another, pulling dry clothes over wet underwear, not talking. We returned to the villa with embarrassing damp patches forming on our clothes and went into the cool of the villa's cavernous kitchen, where we'd left the food. I unwrapped the bread and was slicing it when we heard voices outside. Joe went to investigate and returned with two Italian men, one stocky and muscular, the other taller and thin with spectacles and receding hair, the three of them conversing in a friendly way, bumping into one another and patting one another on the shoulders.

'Ciao!' the men called when they saw me.

'Ciao!' I replied, conscious of my wet hair, the dark, wet patches showing exactly the shape of my underwear beneath my dress.

'Edie, these are my friends Liuni and Fredi,' Joe said.

The men each gave a small bow as he introduced them.

'Valentina told us you were here,' said the tall one. He spoke good English. 'We had to come and see our old pal, Joey DeLuca, again! We've missed him!'

'I'm pleased to meet you,' I said. 'Would you like a sandwich?'

The men declined, but Liuni had brought some beer in his backpack. He offered a bottle to me, but I shook my head. The men took a bottle each and went outside to drink, talking Italian to one another, laughing, catching up on decades of news.

I sliced a tomato and some cheese, put my lunch on a plate and went the other way, through the house and out of the front door. I wandered a little way into the garden and found an old metal bench where I could sit and eat in the dappled sunlight. I could hear the men's laughter, distantly: Joe and his friends.

Me, I was alone, but I was all right. I thought about Daniel and it seemed to me that he was somewhere close. I sat there, quietly, thinking of my son and it was peaceful. It was good.

15

The swim must have tired me because I fell asleep on the bench and when I woke, I was stiff, my hands prickled with pins and needles. The temperature had cooled and the airplane vapour trails that criss-crossed the sky were tinged gold.

I picked up my plate and went back into the villa. Half a dozen empty beer bottles were lined up alongside the wall at the back of the kitchen. I could no longer hear voices but followed the sound of chopping into the garden and found Joe hacking away at the oversized creepers with a long handled axe. I said, 'Hi.'

He put the head of the axe on the floor and leaned on the end of the handle.

'I found the axe in the log shed,' he said. 'It's not great, but it'll do for now. The guys are going to lend me some power tools.'

'That's great,' I said.

'Yeah.' Joe wiped the sweat from his forehead. 'I'm going for another swim.'

He headed off towards the decking without inviting me to join him, which was fine, I hadn't wanted to go anyway. I went in the other direction and fetched my suitcase from the car. I dragged it across the gardens and into the hallway, up the stairs.

From the landing window, I could see Joe crawling through the sea across the bay towards the floating dock. He was a long way away and it was unnerving to be in the villa with no other living being nearby. All around me, I sensed movement, whispers as if the shadows of the people who'd inhabited the villa were there with me; generations of DeLucas.

The child Anna used to play marbles here, on this landing. She'd told me she liked to come up here, out of sight of the adults downstairs who were always encouraging her to play the piano for them, or sit with them, which she found boring. She preferred to be alone. She'd sit on the landing, beside this very bookcase, and line up her collection of marbles according to her favourites, as if they had personalities. I'd played similar games with inanimate objects as a child. Had Anna imagined her dead brother and sisters here with her when she played?

As this exact question troubled me, I heard a gentle rumble, unmistakably the sound of a small glass ball rolling over the floorboards. I stepped back, against the wall, afraid that I'd inadvertently summoned the spirits of Anna's lost siblings. I didn't want to tread on a marble or step on the outstretched hand of an imaginary child.

Feeling light-headed, conscious that it was my overwrought state that was seeding these psychic fantasies, I hefted the awkward suitcase into the nearest bedroom and changed into a pair of shorts and a jumper. Then I ran back downstairs and out into the garden.

The sunset was lighting up one side of the villa, turning it red as if it was on fire. The kitchen was at the back of the villa and immediately beyond was a paved courtyard and behind that was the overgrown lawn and the derelict swimming pool. Wooden trellising supported an ancient vine with a trunk as thick as my thigh, a vine that had been trained to climb up and over the courtyard, giving it shade from the sun and some protection from the rain. Beneath the vine was a sturdy wooden table, covered with fallen leaves, desiccated grapes and bird droppings. Joe and his friends had moved three of the chairs earlier so they could drink their beers in the sunshine.

Joe and I could eat out here, this evening, I thought. We would have to eat together because the alternative, being in separate rooms inside the old villa was untenable to me. I couldn't be alone in this place, in the dark. The very thought made the hairs on my body prickle, brought the whispers of the villa's ghosts closer. I was so uneasy that I contemplated going back to the decking to find Joe, but I was afraid I might lose my way in the gloaming and accidentally wander into the graveyard of the still-born.

Instead, while I waited for him to return, I kept myself busy, moving the chairs back to the table and dusting the seats. If I prepared the table for our evening meal, then it would be difficult for Joe to walk away.

In the kitchen, I found glass jars containing candles, each jar covered by a dusty saucer that had kept the candle clean beneath. We'd bought matches, and although the candles had been left for so long, they lit easily. I set the jars on the table outside and some along the ledge of the window in the kitchen, where they flickered cheerfully.

Next, I swept the tabletop, and then the area around the table. In the candlelight, the courtyard took on a cosy atmosphere. The first stars began to twinkle in the night sky.

Joe returned, his T-shirt clinging to his damp shoulders. Beyond the black silhouettes of trees, silver moonlight was caught in the small waves rolling in from the bay and breaking against the rocks. The cicadas sang their song. Joe did not comment on the preparations I'd made. Perhaps he was thinking about the evening before, when I'd rushed off to my hotel room rather than eat with him.

I tried not to think about Anna's dead siblings watching from the shadows as I laid out the food, bottles of water. I unwrapped the wax paper from the cheese, opened a jar of olives, sliced tomatoes. Joe opened two bottles of beer and passed one to me. We sat at the table in the candlelight. I pulled the zip on my jumper up to my chin. Joe was thoughtful, staring into the mouth of his bottle. It was peaceful and I didn't want to spoil the atmosphere, so I tried to think of something to say that would be friendly, without compromising my anger; something that wouldn't summon the spirit of Anna to the table.

'Did you used to eat out here,' I asked Joe, 'when you came, before, on holiday?'

'All the time.' He looked around as if remembering the people who used to occupy the empty chairs. 'My grandmother used to love entertaining. There'd be lanterns hung in the trees, lights everywhere.' He trailed off and fell silent again. 'There was a housekeeper then, did I tell you? And a caretaker, a married couple. They lived together in a cottage behind the garage. They had a little dog. They were very good to me and Cece.'

'Was Cece upset that Anna left this place to you and me?'

'She got the London house. She thinks she came off best.'

Oh, Anna. More evidence of your scheming; you giving the uncomplicated London house to your uncomplicated daughter and the abandoned, difficult Sicilian villa to the abandoned son and his difficult ex-wife.

'Did your father ever come here?' I asked to change the subject.

'No,' Joe replied.

'Never?'

He raised the bottle to his lips, tipped back his head and drank. 'He didn't like the heat. And he thought Sicily was a shit-hole of an island.'

That sounded exactly the kind of thing Patrick Cadogan

would have said. He might have been a psychologist but he had the tact of a meteorite.

I pulled my left leg up onto the chair, wrapped my arm around it and rubbed the ankle. Moths were batting at the candle jars. Bats darted overhead, blacking out tiny parts of the sky.

We finished our beers and opened some more, becoming more relaxed. We told one another a little about our lives now. Joe talked about his gardening work, the van he drove, the long, solitary walks he took around the mountains and coastline of North Wales. I talked about the dogs and Fitz, how we joked we would grow old together, becoming more set in our ways until we turned into two eccentric old women surrounded by rescued pets.

We didn't talk about Daniel, but I could tell from the careful way Joe stepped around telling certain stories that Daniel was in his mind as much as he was in mine. Our son was as present at that table as if he'd been asleep on my knee, my arms around him. I could almost feel the weight of him. I could almost look down and see his lashes flickering, his lips apart, the thumb that had been in his mouth now hovering close to his chin. I could almost feel the heat of his body pressed against mine. If I closed my eyes and drank another beer, I could almost bring my darling boy back to me.

Almost.

16

Joe and I needed somewhere to sleep, but we hadn't had a chance to clean the bedrooms and the beds were still shrouded. There was no power inside the house, no light, no water. Neither of us wanted to settle in the big, downstairs rooms, so we decided to sleep under the stars. It wasn't cold and the courtyard was sheltered; we had a good stock of mosquito repellent.

Joe found a waxed table cover and lay it down as a ground-sheet. I watched from outside as the light of his phone torch moved about in the villa before he returned with cushions that he lay on the table cover to make makeshift mattresses and pillows.

We brushed our teeth using bottled water over the kitchen sink, big as a trough and then settled down in our sleeping bags, side by side, but with a wide space between us. The candles were still flickering in their jars on the table.

I turned towards the house so I wasn't looking out towards the old swimming pool. I wanted to be sure I wouldn't catch a glimpse of a faceless woman if I woke during the night. I had drunk enough beer to be sleepy and for my edges to be blurred.

Joe turned his back to me without saying goodnight. We did not talk any more.

I was tired in my bones and soon fell asleep. I must have slept well, because nothing disturbed me and my dreams were pleasant ones of children running in and out of the villa, crossing the courtyard to reach the swimming pool, which was full of clean blue water, the sunlight making shifting patterns on its base.

By the time the aching from the old wound in my hip woke me, a pale dawn was breaking, the night sky streaked with watery light. Although the sun was not yet risen, the dawn chorus had begun to chirp. I eased myself up onto an elbow and looked, sleepy eyed, at the garden, so different in this new-day light, its colours soft and hazy.

Joe had turned over in the night and was facing me now. His mouth was open and he was snoring gently. His jaw was stubbled. His eyes were surrounded by dozens of lines that were more defined because of his tan. I saw the pouches of flesh beneath his eyes, and the slackened skin at the jaw, the pores on the sides of his nostrils. Because he was sleeping, I had the chance to study his face and I had that surreal sense that often comes when you meet someone you haven't seen in years: simultaneously recognising every tiny thing about that person and at the same time seeing how much they have changed.

I manoeuvred my sore body into a sitting position, rubbing my elbows and massaging my wrists. Sparrows were pecking amongst the detritus of last night's meal. The candles were burned out, a small, withered piece of black wick submerged in a congealed pool of wax at the base of each jar.

I could hear the sea beyond the birdsong and now the sun was rising, the sky glowed incandescent. My throat was dry.

Quietly and carefully, I unzipped my sleeping bag and pushed myself up onto my bare feet, pulling down the jumper that had ridden up in the night, stretching out the pains in my back and hip.

The villa was behind me. In the early morning light, it seemed bigger and lovelier. I noticed details I hadn't noticed before: the chimney pots, window boxes and ornamental down-spouts; valerian growing from cracks in the walls. If the villa and its gardens were restored, if it were made to look as it had been intended to look, I could see that it would be the most heavenly place.

A stone beneath the roof coping had been carved with the year of its installation: 1806. So, the villa had been in Joe's family for more than two centuries. How many generations would that be? No wonder the DeLucas felt it was a place where they could connect with their history. And we were going to abandon it.

A tiny shiver of regret touched me like a whisper and in the same instant I heard a rustling in the gardens, as if someone – children – were moving swiftly through the undergrowth.

'Stop it!' I murmured to myself.

The kitchen door had been painted a dusty green; its orig-inal black metal hinges and architecture were still attached. I trod carefully towards it, avoiding sharp stones and the tight little yellow snails that had emerged on the flagstones during the night hours. There was an old water pump close to the back door and running along the back wall was a herb bed that had been taken over by a profusion of dill, sage and a leggy rosemary bush. Beyond that, still close to the kitchen, were fruit cages, though the fruit had grown through the netting, lifting the framework from the ground. The berries would provide feasts for the birds in late summer.

I pushed open the door and went into the kitchen. Jugs and plates lined the shelves, their colours muted by dust; pans hung from a rack on the wall. There was an enormous range for cooking and warming the water. A plastic clothes line was strung across the room, from one corner to the other, and fastened to it with coloured clothes pegs were faded postcards, photographs and pieces of paper. I hadn't paid attention the previous day, now I reached for the nearest scrap of paper, yellow, lined, torn from a notebook. Written on it was a recipe: 3 limone, 250g zuccero, 3 uova. Beside it was a photograph of a man and woman I didn't recognise, she wearing a headscarf, he with rolled up sleeves, a spaniel sitting at his side. The caretaker couple Joe had mentioned the night before, I guessed. Logs were stacked in the hearth and on the side was a plastic cutlery tray covered with a linen cloth; a folded magazine article tucked into the frame of a huge old mirror; a statue of the Virgin Mary. Everything in the kitchen spoke of a villa used, and loved, and lived in. It spoke of a thoughtful and attentive housekeeper. It was a place that had been cared for, where people were made comfortable, where stress was avoided.

The remnants of the shopping Joe and I had done the day before were on the drainer beside the sink. I took a bottle of water and hesitated – I thought I'd heard a noise from within the house.

'Hello!' I called softly.

I held my breath and listened, but heard nothing more.

A mouse, I thought. Or maybe it was house creaking as it warmed; wood expanding, the sunlight on the eaves. I wouldn't let my mind go towards an alternative.

I held the bottle under my elbow and struggled with the plastic lid. It wouldn't budge. I put it in my mouth, gripped with my teeth and tried to turn the bottle. At the exact moment the seal broke, I felt the air displace behind me and a voice barked a command I did not understand.

I dropped the bottle and it bounced on the floor, spraying my legs and ankles as it spun. I turned to see who it was who had spoken and my eyes focused on the closest thing to me: the barrel of a gun; a shotgun. My eyes made their way up the barrel. At the other end was an elderly woman, her eyebrows thick and bushy, her face set in a determined grimace. She was standing in the frame of the internal kitchen door, wearing men's trousers tied at the waist with a piece of rope and a checked shirt beneath a leather waistcoat. Bullets were strung on a loop around her shoulder.

The bottle stopped spinning. The water pooled. My heart was beating so hard I thought it might burst from my body. I could not think of a single word of Italian. I was so frightened, my mind had shut down.

The woman shouted something at me. Her voice was gruff, like a bear.

'I don't understand,' I replied shakily. I showed her my hands, turning the palms towards her so she would see they were empty. My fingers were trembling – she must see how they shook, she must see how scared I was. 'Take what you want,' I murmured, gesturing. 'Take it, but leave us alone.'

The woman said something else, the same bark, like an order.

'I don't understand. No parlo italiano!'

Two butterflies, oblivious to the danger, came in through the open door and span a dance in the pale air. My toes clenched. The floor was slippery and cold from the water. If the old woman shot me, I would fall into the puddle. I imagined my blood mixing with the water, turning pink, fragments of bone and flesh like meat. WOMAN SHOT IN COLD BLOOD. WOMAN FOUND MURDERED IN SEASIDE VILLA. Would I become one of the villa's ghosts if I was killed here? Would I be forever trapped amongst the DeLuca ancestors? And it was such a beautiful morning; I didn't want to die!

'Inglese?' the woman barked and I hung onto that word like a lifeline.

'Si, si! Inglese.'

The woman gestured with the gun towards the door, breathing heavily, licking her dry old lips, saliva bubbling in the corners of her mouth. She asked a question I did not understand and then shouted: 'C'è qualcun altro qui? Qualcun altro? Eh? Eh?' The gun barrel jabbed at me like a pointed finger and then jabbed towards the open door, signalling me to move.

I turned to the door, took a step, my foot slipped and my legs splayed. I almost fell. Through the gap in the door, I saw Joe sitting up in his sleeping bag, rubbing the lenses of his reading glasses on the hem of his T-shirt. He frowned when he saw me. I made a face at him, *Help!* I mouthed.

'What?'

'Help!' I indicated the old woman behind me with my eyes, and Joe spotted her.

He scrambled out of the sleeping bag and set off across the lawn, scampering on all fours like an animal. He was going to circle round behind us. I turned back to the woman who was right beside me now, looking over my shoulder. She hadn't seen Joe, but I could see his footsteps, dark where he'd crushed the long grass, and the two sleeping bags. I could smell her breath, stale, foul with garlic and old coffee, see the whiskers growing on her chin. She pushed me aside and at last the gun wasn't pointing at me. In one heartbeat, I was as scared as I'd ever been, in the next my fear flipped into fury. How dare she come in to our villa and threaten us with a shotgun? How dare she?

I lunged forward, throwing my weight at the woman and she, surprised, lost her balance and the two of us ended up on the ground. She was shockingly strong for her age and violent. We fought, she grabbing viciously at my flesh, me trying to push her head back and then Joe was there and he had hold of her, dragging her off me.

'Get the gun,' he cried, and I grabbed it and pointed it at the old woman while he pulled her to her feet, holding her arms behind her back so that she could not escape, although she twisted and raged, trying to bite him.

'Shut up!' I screamed. 'Shut up, you crazy bastard bitch!'

The woman screamed at me and I screamed right back at her. I stepped back, bumping the handle of the gun against the wall of the house and it went off, bang! The gun jumped in my hand and I heard a series of pings as the shot hit something and then more subdued pings as it bounced off something else.

'Jesus!' Joe cried. 'What did you do that for?'

'I didn't mean to... Did it hit anyone?'

The woman was looking all around her, trying to see where the shot had gone.

'It's okay,' Joe said, 'it's okay, we're all okay, let's calm down a bit.'

He let go of the woman's wrists and she, shocked by the gunshot, calmed down. She rubbed at her wrists, scowling ferociously. Her hair was wild, sticking up in all directions; there were scratches on her face and arms.

'Chi sei?' he asked. Who are you?

'It's her!' I cried; now I was marginally less panicked, my brain was functioning again. 'The woman from up the hill. The Mafioso's wife!'

At the word 'Mafioso', the old woman set to her screeching again, spitting as she spoke and directing most of her invective towards me. Joe let her finish, then spoke to her in Italian, and she replied to him; she was furious, his tone was conciliatory.

'Shall I call the police?' I asked, pacing warily, keeping my distance, feeling the weight of the gun in my hands. 'I'll call the police!' I said. 'Polizia!' I said to the woman. 'Prisone for you!' I didn't have a phone signal here, but I would damn well run up that hill and all the way back to Porta Sarina if I needed to.

'No,' Joe said. 'This was a misunderstanding.'

'A misunderstanding?' I cried. 'She breaks into our house, with a gun, she threatens us and you call it a misunderstanding?'

'She thought we were the intruders.'

'So why didn't she call the police instead of barging in here like Clint bloody Eastwood?'

'The old people round here don't trust the police. Signora Arnone's been keeping an eye on the villa for years. She looks out for trespassers, chases away teenagers...'

'Chases them away? Or shoots them and throws their bodies into the sea?'

Joe gave me a look that signified hysteria wasn't helping the situation.

The woman, who was a little calmer now, asked him a question.

He replied: 'Anna DeLuca era mia madre.'

'Ahh! Il figlio d'Anna! Il ragazzo! Bello! Multo bello!'

The old woman's expression changed instantly into one of grandmotherly affection and she and Joe fell again into conversation, the old woman looking as if she'd like to pinch his cheeks.

I paced beside them, working the stress out of my body. From time to time, Joe translated a snippet of information to me in English. The old woman had seen us go by in the Fiat the previous afternoon and, when the car didn't come back up the hill, had presumed we were up to no good and had come down at first light to chase us away from the villa, for which she felt some responsibility because the DeLuca family had always been so kind to her and her husband and because of the long-standing links between the two families.

This misunderstanding now cleared up; Joe was greatly relieved. The old woman put a hand in her pocket and withdrew a handful of bits and pieces: a manky handkerchief, some string, what looked like pony nuts, a metal screw. From this mishmash, she extracted a dirty business card, its edges frayed and curled, which she handed to Joe.

'Vito Barsi,' the old woman said.

'From Vito's pizzeria in Porta Sarina?' Joe asked.

'Si! Si! Vito! Si!' She patted Joe's hand.

'Vito's her nephew,' Joe explained. 'He used to come and help Signora Arnone's husband with odd jobs around the villa. He'll know how to get the electricity going.'

The old woman nodded, her wrinkled old lips pursed as if she'd decided everything was now resolved. She was even crazier than she looked if she thought I'd let any relative of hers anywhere near the villa.

'Dammi il fucile,' she said, holding out her hand to me.

'She wants her gun back,' Joe translated, unnecessarily.

'Well, she can't have it! She's crazy!'

'She didn't mean us any harm, she was only trying to protect the villa.'

'Joe! Stop being so reasonable!'

The woman interjected, addressing me directly, speaking very slowly. 'Mio marito, Gabriele, è solo in casa.' She pointed up the hill and made the gesture of an old man, hunching over a stick. 'Ha la demenza,' she said to me. 'De-men-za.' She twirled a finger to her temple.

'You should have thought of that before you came charging down here pointing your bloody gun at us!' I told her.

'Give her the gun,' Joe said. 'It'll be okay now.'

'Just because her husband's old and sick...'

'It's okay, Edie. Really. It's okay. Give her the gun.'

Reluctantly, I stepped forward and held the gun out to the old woman. She snatched it from me, slung it over her shoulder. She gave me one last, dismissive look, smiled fondly at Joe, then she turned and stomped away.

We followed her back through the villa, out of the front door and then all the way along the drive and out of the gates. I pushed the gates shut behind her, threaded the chain through either side and fastened the chain with the padlock.

'Don't let's ever forget to lock them again,' I said.

'We're safe enough with her at the top of the hill acting as lookout.'

'I bet she's the reason for the salt and the bloody sheep horn,' I muttered. 'I bet she's the bad luck they wanted to keep away.'

17

Joe and I walked back to the villa. I wrapped my arms around myself. My teeth were chattering.

'Here,' Joe said. He took off his jumper and offered it to me.

'No, it's okay.'

'Take it.'

'I don't want it.' I was still furious with him for giving the gun back to the old woman, a gun that had probably killed people, that might have killed us.

'Edie, you're shaking.'

I took the jumper crossly and pulled it on over my head. The smell and the feel of it, the warmth, were familiar. Immediately, despite myself, I felt better.

'Nobody's ever pointed a gun at me before,' I said.

'Me neither.'

'We could have died.'

'We were never in any danger.'

'What?'

'We weren't. She never intended to shoot us.'

'For God's sake, Joe, you told me that that woman's husband had killed loads of people!'

'Three people.'

'Oh, only three! That's nothing to worry about then.'

'Edie...'

'I mean, that's fine, isn't it, three murders, hardly worth mentioning...'

'Edie!'

'No, no, let's get this in perspective. Don-bloody-Corleone up there has killed three innocent people – three that we know about – for no good reason and then his mad, crazy wife comes down here brandishing a shotgun, probably the same shotgun that killed the others, and you act like it's fine, like it's completely normal, like it's no problem! You're still the same, aren't you? Still refusing to acknowledge what's under your nose!'

'What does that mean?' His tone was sharper, defensive.

'You know what it means! You always think people are going to do the right thing even when it's obvious that they aren't! Criminals don't pick up a gun for fun any more than alcoholics stop drinking because they've promised you they won't touch another drop!'

'Seriously, Edie? Seriously, you're bringing that up now?'

We glared at one another for a long moment then I clamped my mouth shut, huddled inside his oversized jumper and walked away from him, the grass spiky and cold beneath my bare feet. I hurried back towards the villa, ran upstairs, found a sunny corner on the landing and I curled myself up in a ball and cried. I cried until my stomach ached and my eyes were sore. I cried until I couldn't cry any more. I felt entirely alone, sensing no other presence. I hoped Daniel might come, but he didn't, and if the DeLuca ancestors were watching me, they decided to keep out of my way.

While I was upstairs, Joe made a little fire in the courtyard behind the kitchen. When I came down, I found him crouched beside it with his sleeping bag wrapped around his shoulders like a cloak, his eyes narrowed against the smoke. He didn't look at me, but poured a steaming liquid from the pan he had balanced over the fire into a cup and passed it to me. I took it, sniffed. Coffee.

Joe poked the fire with a stick.

We sipped our coffee. We didn't look at one another. We didn't say another word for ages.

* * *

Later that morning, Joe came to find me with the car keys in his hand. He said he was going to drive into Porta Sarina to pick up some tools from his friends.

I said: 'Okay.'

He hesitated, as if he was about to ask if I'd like to go with him.

'I'll stay here,' I said. 'I'll take a look in the bedrooms, see if I can find the painting.'

'Okay,' Joe replied. He hesitated again.

'Go on,' I said. 'I'll lock the gates after you.'

I watched the Fiat drive away, following its progress up the hill via a column of dust that rose through the scrubby trees and prickly pear cacti at the side of the track. I watched until I couldn't see it any more, then I locked the gates and wandered back towards the villa, through the dappled shade of the dipping trees.

I saw a little black and white cat crouching in the undergrowth, a skinny, sore eyed little thing. I crouched down and called to her, but she wouldn't come near me.

Upstairs in the villa, shafts of sunshine fell through the bedroom windows, making slanting oblongs of light on the dusty floors. I searched each room in turn, pulling aside dust sheets and looking in wardrobes and drawers. The master bedroom was by far the largest and grandest room, with a huge four poster bed, an elaborate rug on the floor, exquisite furniture, a marble fireplace and gilt-framed mirrors on the walls. In the far corner, a heavy curtain hung on a rail. Behind it, I suspected, was the alcove where Anna's mother used to pray for the souls of her lost children. I didn't want to touch the curtain, but I made myself reach out to draw it back. At the last instant, before my fingers touched the fabric, a spider scuttled from its folds and dropped onto the floor. It felt like a warning and I stepped away. It was possible the painting was in the alcove, but I wouldn't look, not now, while I was alone, knowing the photographs of the three dead children were hung in that corner.

The last room I searched was in the far corner of the villa, with windows on two walls. It seemed a bright and friendly room. I pulled the dust sheet from the bed, folding it over itself to trap as much dust as I could. Beneath was an ornate brass frame and a large mattress on a sprung base. Another dust sheet concealed a dressing table and stool, a third an armchair and the fourth a wardrobe. The room was nicely decorated: wild roses on the wallpaper, a big mirror, the chair and stool upholstered in green, yellow and pink. It was the kind of room that made me want to curl up in a chair by the window and read while the day settled around me. I knew I wouldn't feel afraid in this room.

In the wardrobe was a mishmash of clothes hangers with several objects beneath. I reached into the gloom and lifted out a painting. For a moment, my heart raced in anticipation, but when I held it to the light, I could see it was not some ancient picture of the Madonna but a portrait of Anna DeLuca as a young woman, seventeen or eighteen years old. She was wearing a blue dress, leaning on a stone balustrade overlooking a ravine. Her face was turned towards the artist, and she was smiling. The artist had captured the spirit of the girl, her liveliness, her sense of fun. It was a version of Anna I'd never known; to me she'd always been troubled, introverted, withdrawn.

I propped the picture against the wall and reached into the wardrobe again. This time I removed a bottle containing a few inches of clear liquid. I unscrewed the lid and sniffed. Vodka. I put the bottle back where I'd found it. There was also an old travel guide to Australia and a page-a-day diary, one of those that can be used during any given year. On the inside front cover was the name Anna DeLuca, and her age, fifteen. The diary was written in English. I flicked through until I found an entry.

> *School's finished at last, I'm so happy to be back in the villa! Signor Ganzaria has pumped up the tyres on my bike so I can cycle into Porta Sarina in the morning to see Gina and Matilde. I can't wait! This is going to be the absolute best summer ever!*

It was hard to marry the version of Anna in the portrait, and in that happy-go-lucky diary entry, with the version she'd become, the lonely woman married to the bullying husband; the woman who left the vodka bottle hidden at the back of her wardrobe – and there would be other bottles hidden about this room, I was sure of it: the woman who'd destroyed my life.

I didn't feel pity. Anna had chosen her own path. She chose to keep the extent of her addiction a secret. If she'd been honest, then she could have been helped and Daniel would still be alive today. All my pain, and Joe's, all of it was her fault. It was down to her and her pride.

I laid the diary down and wandered over to the window that overlooked the back garden. There was something about the villa that softened me; that brought down my barriers. Now I was alone, thinking of Daniel, I could indulge myself here, in a way that I could never do in England. If I narrowed my eyes, I could see my darling boy running across the patch of open lawn below, chasing after someone who was out of sight, running towards the pool. I leaned against the frame and listened to the sound of his laughter in my mind.

'Daniel,' I whispered, imagining him down there, safe and sound, having a wonderful time. I pictured myself going down to him, taking a towel to wrap him in, and he, wet and slippery from swimming, his goggles leaving a red line around his fore-head, holding onto me as I patted him dry, wriggling on my lap, asking what he could have to eat, what we were going to do next.

I might have stayed there for hours, lost in my beautiful daydream, but a movement on the track beyond the boundaries of the garden caught my eye. A large, black car was bumping down the hill. I watched its approach. Joe hadn't said anything about anyone coming, and given the morning's events I would be cautious about unlocking the gates to another visitor. I put the diary in one of the three dressing table drawers, and, anxiously, went outside.

18

I arrived at the gates as the car pulled up and watched from behind the shrubs, where I could not be seen. The vehicle was a big old Mercedes, so battered its body had the texture of a hammered-out metal drum. On its roof was a Taxi sign, the plastic yellowed and the letters worn away. The car shook like a dog coming out of water as the driver killed the engine, then the door opened and a tiny woman climbed out, jumping from the seat down onto the ground.

She was as small as a bird, with a mass of black hair streaked white at the front, a little pixie face with pointed features, and spectacles in winged frames. Her shoes were black, slip-ons. Her dress was a floral print and over it she wore a lacy blue knitted cardigan. She looked like a character from one of Daniel's favourite storybooks, Grandma Mouse. As she stood beside the car, I saw that she had put two cushions on the seat to raise herself to sufficient height to see over the steering wheel.

This elderly woman looked about her nervously, pushing her glasses up her nose. She was no threat to me.

I stepped out of the shadows and stood at the gate. I called: 'Ciao.'

The woman raised a small hand. 'Good afternoon! Hello! Edie, isn't it? How lovely to meet you!' She spoke Queen's English the old-fashioned way, pronouncing every letter. 'I've brought you a gift,' she said, 'to welcome you to the island.'

She reached into the car and produced a box from the passenger seat. I unlocked the padlock and pushed the gate open. We met at the threshold between the parking area and the garden.

'Here you are,' she said, handing the box to me. 'It's a traditional Sicilian keepsake. My father can't do much these days, he's stuck in the house but he made it for you.'

'Thank you, that's so kind.'

'You're most welcome. I hope you won't mind me dropping in like this, but we need to talk. My name is Matilde Romano and since childhood I was your mother-in-law, Anna DeLuca's one true friend.'

I recognised her then. She was the small girl from the photograph on the poster on the memorial wall in Porta Sarina, no doubt the 'Matilde' Anna mentioned in her diary.

'I expect Anna told you about me,' she said. 'We had so many happy times together!' The smile on her lips faded. 'She was such a lovely person! Such a dear friend and yet she suffered so many unnecessary tragedies. If only she'd been stronger! If only she hadn't let people take advantage of her! If only she'd listened to me!'

She plucked a handkerchief from the sleeve of her cardigan and held it to her eyes. I stood beside her, while she dabbed at her tears, waited while she blew her nose violently and then struggled to compose herself. When next she looked at me, her eyes had a bright, blurry look to them.

'I'm sorry,' she said, 'it's just that it's so sad about Anna. It's so very sad. I haven't come to terms with it yet.' She managed a small, quivering smile. 'Anyway, at least you're here, you and Joe. I'm glad to have the opportunity to meet you.'

'Thank you,' I said.

The woman hovered beside me and I realised she was expecting to be invited in. I didn't want to take her into the villa while Joe wasn't there. Legally, I might own half of it but it didn't feel as if it belonged to me at all.

'I won't ask you in because nothing is working,' I said, by way of an apology.

'That's all right,' the woman replied. 'I didn't come to be entertained. I came because I've heard Anna left the villa to you and Joe. Now, don't look so surprised. Nothing happens in Porta Sarina without everyone knowing. You two turning up is big news for the town gossips, especially with things being the way they are at the pizzeria.'

'Excuse me?'

'Valentina Barsi so unhappy in her marriage.'

She did not elaborate further but sighed and looked past me, to the villa. For an instant, the sadness left her eyes and was replaced by something else; something troublesome – fear, perhaps. Whatever it was, it disappeared as quickly as it came and she turned to me again.

'I have a second motive for visiting today,' she said. 'When I heard of Anna's death, I contacted the family lawyer to express an interest in purchasing the villa if it was to come up for sale. Now, I've received a letter from Avvocato Recupero informing me that you intend to sell.' She opened her handbag and took out an envelope with the lawyer's motif printed in one corner. She offered it to me, but I didn't need to see it. 'Is that right?' she asked.

'Yes.'

'In that case, I would like to buy the villa from you.' She tipped her head to one side. 'I've loved this place since I was a child. I've always dreamed of owning it, but I've never had the chance before. I think Anna would be pleased if it came to me, don't you?' She tilted her head the other way. 'I was her best friend. I as good as lived here when I was younger. I'm practically family.'

I wondered if Signora Romano, this sweet little old woman, had any idea of the villa's worth and if she could actually afford it.

'We haven't engaged an agent yet,' I said tentatively. 'We haven't had the villa valued.'

'Of course, you must get an independent valuation, but there are villas of a similar size in the vicinity, so I have an idea what to expect. I can pay cash, so, if you're agreeable, we should be able to progress quickly.'

'It seems almost too good to be true,' I said.

'Not at all. It's a practical proposal that will benefit us all.' She took a telephone from her pocket. 'What's your number.'

I gave it to her and she tapped it into her phone. 'I'll call you so you have a record of mine and as soon as you have the valuation, let me know.' She turned back towards the taxi. 'I'm glad we're in agreement about the villa, Edith. Don't waste money going through the estate agent, let's deal with one another directly. Regard me as a friend; a dear friend who wants to help you in any way she can.'

* * *

When Signora Romano was gone, I walked back to the old villa, warming itself like a decrepit, elderly relative in the sun behind me. It creaked in the heat.

'Well,' I said out loud. 'That was an unexpected development.'

The villa seemed to sigh and settle as if it had been holding its breath.

I put the box Signora Romano had given me on the kitchen table, picked off the tape that held the lid down and opened it. Inside was scrunched-up newspaper and inside the paper was a wooden doll, a puppet, about eighteen inches long. It was dressed as a medieval lady, with a painted wooden face, crudely made clothes.

I lifted the marionette out of the box and dangled her by the handles. She did an odd little dance, then swung on the end of her strings as if she'd been hanged. I could appreciate that some skill had gone into making the doll, but it was an ugly, unpleasant thing. I imagined myself showing it to Fitz, the two of us laughing over its macabre dancing, its bland face with two red circles for cheeks and spidery, drawn-on eyelashes, the tiny hooks screwed into the backs of its hands, feet and head to thread the strings that made it move. Its hair was brown, wiry and curly. I shuddered and put it back into the box, replaced the lid so I didn't have to look at it.

Instead, I turned my attention to the wallet the lawyer had given us which was still on the kitchen table and found a typed document labelled Inventario which could only mean 'inventory'.

In the glass-fronted bookcase in the living room, there was an Italian/English dictionary. I took it back to the kitchen and sat at the table. Helpfully, in the wallet was a plan of the villa, with the different rooms labelled, so I had no troubled identifying the hallway – corridoio, and from there I translated the items within it until I came to quaddro, which meant 'painting', together with the title – *La Madonna del Mare* – and the name of the artist – Guido Reni.

At the end of the inventory were three signatures, each witnessing the others: Claudia DeLuca, Joe's grandmother; Anna Cadogan-DeLuca; and Ignazia Ganzaria, domestica, the housekeeper. I tapped my fingers on the tabletop and stared at the inventory. So, the painting had been in the hall when the villa was closed up. Either it had been stolen, or it must still be here, somewhere.

There was the curtained alcove in the master bedroom.

No, I wouldn't look there on my own. Anyway, the inventory clearly stated that the picture had been left in the hallway.

I searched again, checking behind the large dresser that had previously been hidden beneath a dust sheet, and inside its cupboards and drawers. I patted my hands along the wall in case there was a hidden cabinet, or a door that might open into a secret room. I looked in the walk-in cupboard under the stairs that was full of junk, toys and games, suitcases, an old vacuum cleaner; an assortment of objects, but no picture. So it wasn't where it had been left when the villa was closed. Someone must have moved it since.

* * *

When Joe returned, he spent a while carrying tools from the car into the villa. I told him about our visitor, but he did not look at the puppet nor make any comment about Matilde Romano, his mother's one true friend.

'She looks exactly like Grandma Mouse,' I told him as he ran the pad of his thumb along the blade of a shear. 'You must remember her.'

'Grandma Mouse?'

'No! Signora Romano! She must have been here often if she was Anna's best friend. She's tiny, like a bird. Don't you remember a very small woman with frizzy hair?'

'I never paid much attention to the adults out here.'

No, I thought, *you were probably too busy having fun with Valentina.*

'Anyway, she wants to buy the villa,' I said. 'She used to love coming here and she has great memories of the place. She says she can pay cash. We don't have to do anything, just get it valued, and she'll take care of everything after that.'

He was silent.

'Aren't you pleased?' I asked.

He shrugged. 'It's just a bit odd, some random woman turning up like that.'

'She's not some random woman, she was your mother's best friend.'

Joe wasn't reacting as I'd expected. He didn't look as if I'd just told him about a stroke of good fortune that would save us both a great deal of time and trouble. Instead, his face clouded and he turned from me and walked away.

I thought I knew what was wrong. Despite what he'd said, he was going to find it painful to part with the villa, even knowing it was going to someone who knew it well, someone who was likely to look after it. He'd been expecting to have more time to get used to the idea of selling. It was all happening too quickly.

I could have gone after him and tried to reason with him, but I remembered how he used to be when we were married, when he was upset about something. The best thing to do was to leave him alone and wait until he'd sorted things out in his head.

All he needed was a little more time to process his grief and accept the inevitable.

19

While Joe made a start on clearing the old footpath from the gates to the front of the villa, I went back upstairs and made up the beds in two bedrooms, Anna's old room for Joe and the one beside it for me. I closed the door to the master bedroom so I didn't have to think about the curtained alcove, but as I passed, I heard a scuttering on the other side of the door. It would be a draught from the window disturbing the curtain, or, at worst, mice, I told myself. It was only my anxious mind trying to persuade me it sounded like children trying to keep quiet.

The villa's original linen was stored in a cupboard on the landing. It was fine quality, but damp, it smelled musty, and moths had been at it. When we had water, I'd wash it and save what I could. For now, I lay our sleeping bags on top of the old mattresses and folded our towels over the old pillows to mask the scents of the past: old heads, old dreams, old lovers. I propped the painting of Anna up against the dressing table mirror in her room, where Joe could see it. I thought it was a thoughtful gesture, and one that I hoped he'd appreciate.

* * *

That night, when we were satisfied the villa was secure, we used bottled water to wash and brush our teeth at the kitchen sink by candlelight and went upstairs together, our footsteps echoing in the stairwell. At the top of the stairs, shadows flickering on the walls, Joe asked if I'd searched all the bedrooms for the *Madonna del Mare*.

'Pretty much,' I said, 'except for the master bedroom. I didn't want to disturb the place where your grandmother used to pray.'

'That's where it'll be!' Joe said. 'She used to keep all kind of religious pictures there.'

He moved towards the door.

'No!' I cried, making us both jump. 'No, not now, Joe.' I didn't want him to open that door, not while it was so dark. 'There's a draught,' I said, 'it'll blow out the candles. And mice. There are mice. Don't go in there. Wait until it's light.'

He shrugged and went into his room. I went into mine.

My bed was so high that an average sized spaniel could have walked underneath without the top of its tail touching the underside, the mattress decadently soft.

I heard Joe moving about in the room next door, drawing the curtains. I left mine open, preferring to have the view out to the night sky, to the stars and the moon. My candle burned brightly in its jar at the side of the bed. I propped up my pillow and picked up the Agatha Christie novel I'd found downstairs. I tried to read by the light of my phone, but it strained my eyes to see the text, and I ached with tiredness, so I put the book down and lay on my side, looking out through the windows into the deep velvet darkness of the night.

As I drifted in that dreamy stage halfway between wakefulness and sleep, I found myself back in our London flat. It was the last night Joe and I slept together, the last time we shared a bed. The memories were distorted, and in some part of my mind, I recognised it wasn't real, but it felt real. The bedroom was exactly as it had been: small, untidy, the bed taking up almost all the floor space, we could only walk around it if the wardrobe doors weren't open. I knew that it was after Daniel's death because of the mess: clothes were heaped on the floor, empty cups, wine bottles. It was claustrophobic, dirty, awful. We hadn't cleaned the flat since we lost Daniel, neither of us had the heart to do it, we were afraid of destroying any last vestige of our son. The pyjamas he'd slept in the night before he disappeared were tucked beneath my pillow; I held them to my face a hundred times a day, inhaling whatever was left of Daniel, trapped in the fibres, wishing I could breathe him in and exhale him, fully formed again, flesh and blood, heartbeat, smile. I'd slept in Daniel's bed many times since his death, but that last night before I left Joe, I stayed in the double bed beside my husband, resentment hardening in every artery and capillary until I was more statue than human, until my heart barely beat, until I was barely capable of feeling pain. I listened to Joe's snores, and each time he inhaled, my anger calcified. I used to love him, but the soft, mushy love was gone; needle sharp hate had taken its place. It was cold, it eclipsed my grief; hate was the best anaesthetic.

I couldn't get comfortable that night, and I blamed Joe for that too, because I was the one who had reached the shaft first, I was the one who had fallen, I was the one who'd broken my hip and all the bones in my leg and my ankle. I'd rolled from one side to the other, shifting my weight, trying to find a position that didn't hurt. The bed was too small, the room too small, I was too hot; Joe, beside me, snored drunkenly. His sweat stank; he hadn't brushed his teeth for days; he was disgusting; he disgusted me. I welcomed the hate; I embraced it. That night, we lay together, in the dark, so close you could hardly fit a cigarette paper between our bodies, and yet we were a million miles apart, and even if I'd had any idea how to bridge the gap between us, I wouldn't have wanted to. I hated him because of what Anna had done. Because of Anna, Joe and I had lost Daniel, and everything else we had, everything that was meaningful or precious, everything we had nurtured and worked for, turned out not to mean anything or be worth anything after all. It was Anna's fault, but Joe could have stopped it happening. He could have.

I had risen early the next morning and left the flat. I didn't take anything. I didn't leave a note, I just went, and after that I only communicated with Joe through solicitors. In my half sleep, ten years later, I felt regret I hadn't felt before. I saw how easy it would have been for me to turn towards Joe, instead of away from him. How little effort it would have taken to try to make things better, how few gentle words. But I hadn't seen it then and neither had he. It was too late to try to change things now, point-less apologising for what we had and had not done or said a decade before.

20

Joe was already up when I woke the next morning. I heard his footsteps on the landing, muffled sounds from one of the bedrooms. I lay for a while, but soon curiosity compelled me to get up. The door to the master bedroom was open.

'Joe?'

He didn't respond.

I crept along the landing and looked through the open door. There was no sign of Joe, but the curtain that separated the alcove from the rest of the room had been drawn back.

I walked forward, slowly, floorboards creaking beneath my bare feet.

The alcove was narrow, little more than a cupboard. Its walls and ceiling were painted white. At the back was an altar, covered by a white cloth. Above it was a large, oval painting of the Madonna holding the baby Jesus, one hand raised and a dull gold halo around her head; clearly not the *Madonna del Mare*. In front of that was a brass crucifix with silver candlesticks on either side. The rest of the altar was covered with framed photographs, candle jars and miscellaneous objects: a cigarette box, a cup with an ancient lipstick imprint at the rim, a folded handkerchief embroidered: Ernesto DeLuca. Silk flowers, their colours faded, sat dustily in a silver vase; beside it was a worn gold ring and a child's bracelet.

I stepped inside the alcove. To the left, three framed photographs hung on the wall. Three babies lying in the same, small cot. Three babies, their skin and hair hand coloured in the photographs, dressed in bonnets and gowns, little white, beribboned booties, their eyes closed, their lips pressed together. Their heads rested on the same satin pillow, trimmed with lace. The babies could have been sleeping, except for the fact that their heads and hands and bodies had been so carefully arranged. Each was surrounded by flowers.

I read the names inscribed on the frames: Elena, Giosepa, Custanti. Custanti, the boy, must have been premature; his face was tiny and wizened; the two girl children looked, to my eyes, to be full-term. The images were heartbreaking. I could hardly imagine the pain Anna's mother must have felt as she prayed for the salvation of those three, unbaptised little souls.

I pictured the child Anna sneaking into the alcove and looking at these same faces sleeping amongst their buds and petals. I could see how she would feel a storm of conflicting emotions about these three angel children and how it would be hard for her, the only surviving child, to be strong enough to carry the weight of her parents' grief and expectation. Oh, dear God, was I feeling pity for her?

'Edie!' Joe's voice made me jump.

I pulled myself back to the present.

'Here!'

I stepped out of the alcove as Joe came into the bedroom, frustration etched on his face.

'I was looking for you... Did you find the *Madonna del Mare*?' I asked.

'No.'

'Did you look under the altar cloth?' I pointed into the alcove.

'All that's under there is a suitcase full of old baby clothes.'

This made me feel sad. 'Sorry,' I murmured. Joe didn't hear. The apology hadn't been meant for him anyway.

* * *

Later, downstairs, I showed Joe the puppet that Matilde Romano had given us.

'It's gross,' he said. 'The hair...'

'I know.'

'It's like a voodoo doll.'

I laughed uneasily. The same thought had occurred to me.

'It's such a weird present,' I said.

'Puppets are a Sicilian thing. There's a puppet theatre here somewhere. Don't you remember Anna telling Daniel about it? How she used to like to play with it, making up stories?'

I winced at hearing Daniel's name mentioned in the same breath as Anna's. I tried so hard to keep them separate in my mind. When love and bitterness met inside me, they curdled like vinegar and milk.

Joe said he was going to walk up the hill to find a phone signal so he could call the estate agent 'to get things moving'.

While he was gone, I wandered out into the garden. The morning was beautiful as ever; the sky as blue. The birds were singing and I glimpsed the little cat hunting in the undergrowth. I followed it, pushing aside swathes of overgrown foliage with my hand as it crept its secret trails. The cat disturbed butterflies and crickets and soon I lost sight of it amongst the scrubby feet of plants grown wild and strong. I pushed my way past some kind of creeper with papery, purple flowers, the petals folded around bright orange stamens that released a musky scent. Twines caught around my ankles. I didn't know in which direction I was moving. I could not hear the sea, only the singing of the insects and the sound of my own heartbeat. It was like being a child again, or a character in a fairy tale; I was lost.

I wandered for a while, knowing that sooner or later the vista would open up and I'd be able to work out where I was. Eventually, I stood on something hard and when I pushed away the dead leaves that covered it, I saw it was a grave marker, lying flat. The name on the stone was Elena DeLuca. I hadn't been consciously looking for the part of the garden where Anna's still-born brother and sisters had been laid to rest but had been drawn towards it anyway. I scraped away dirt and pebbles and I found the other two graves. One for Custanti, one for Giosepa. Beneath Giosepa's name was the inscription: E la morte non avrà più dominio. Although it was in Italian, the phrase was familiar enough for me to guess it meant: And death shall have no dominion. I had studied the Dylan Thomas poem of the same name at school.

The marker stones were at the foot of one of the largest trees in the garden, an oleaster with a muscular grey trunk. Not much would grow in its shade. This would have been a quiet, forlorn place, somewhere for Anna's mother to sit and mourn her dead babies; somewhere for Anna to come and play. Perhaps she asked her mother about the inscription. Perhaps her mother told her it meant that death was not eternal. Perhaps that was why Anna found it so easy to resurrect her siblings in her imagination.

I crouched beside the graves. If this was where the lost DeLuca children played, was there a chance that Daniel might be here too?

Daniel's body had been buried in a woodland graveyard in the Yorkshire countryside, close to a campsite we used to frequent as a family in the holidays. It was a part of England Joe, Daniel and I loved, where we used to go to escape the stress and busyness of London. It was somewhere that only held happy memories for us; somewhere Anna had never been and I'd been determined to keep my baby away from cold, grey, London churchyards and the dismal tolling of bells. But it had been a mistake laying our child to rest so far from home. It made visiting his grave difficult; not something that could be done on a whim so those times when I missed Daniel so much that I thought I would die could not be alleviated by the ritual of going to his grave. And when I was there, although the tree we'd planted above Daniel's body thrived, I never had any sense of my son being nearby.

But here; this was different. Here, in the grounds of the villa, it felt as if the boundaries between life and death were blurred. It felt as if the history of the DeLucas was so strong, that anything might be possible.

I stayed very still. I listened. The heat was so strong that morning that I felt it like a heartbeat; the air was treacly with it. I was as still as an insect preserved in amber, my senses alert. I closed my eyes. I tried to feel my boy, tried to bring him to me. I heard a subtle movement in the plants around me and adrenaline rushed through my veins. I caught my breath.

'Daniel?' I whispered. 'Are you there?'

There was a sound like a child's laughter, close; a soft sigh and a rush of cool air that touched my arm and the side of my face and disappeared. It was over in a second and the heat slid back and it brought with it the stillness of the day. I waited a few minutes more, but nothing more happened; nobody else came.

* * *

Back at the villa, I lit a small fire and boiled water for coffee. When Joe returned, I poured hot water into a cup and passed it to him. I was holding my precious secret inside me; turning it over in my mind. I had found a place where I might be able to reach Daniel; but I couldn't talk about it yet; especially not to

Joe. It was too fragile a thing to put into words, something that might dissolve if it was scrutinised, and I didn't want to lose it. It was best I kept it to myself.

'Did you speak to the agent?' I asked brightly.

'He's going to come out to give us a valuation. He says they can sell the villa as a job lot, with the furniture – if this woman wants the furniture.'

'Her name is Matilde Romano and I think she probably will.'

Joe sipped his coffee. His eyes were downcast.

'It'll probably take a while to sort everything out,' I said, to comfort him. 'These things usually do. There's no rush, is there?'

'No. But we need to find the Madonna. I don't care about anything else, but I promised Anna I'd find the picture.'

'We will find it,' I said. 'We will.'

* * *

Joe searched the upstairs rooms that I'd already searched in case I'd missed anything, whilst I tackled the downstairs methodically. I went from room to room, lifting the dust sheets from the furniture that hadn't yet been exposed. In the living room, I discovered a nest of mice living inside the grand piano, the babies hairless, blind, half formed, so I left them alone. I uncovered elegant sofas and one delightful and louche chaise longue upholstered in aqua velvet, the colour hardly faded at all. I found a pair of matching glass-fronted display cases tucked into alcoves in the snug and a table, its surface as glossy as oil, the patterns of the old wood as clear as if they'd been drawn onto the surface the day before. I wondered who had furnished this lovely room; who had chosen the wallpaper, a shimmering pattern of bamboo stalks and leaves in muted golds, reds and greens.

A photograph of a couple I recognised as Anna's mother and father was displayed inside one of the cabinets. From the style of the clothes, I guessed it must have been taken in the 1960s. They were dancing in this very room; she, with her black hair set in waves, was wearing a satin off-the-shoulder dress and heeled shoes, her feet precise, her neck taut, her chin pressed up to the air and a delightful, unselfconscious smile on her lips. She was a happier, more carefree version of the woman her daughter would become. He was handsome as a film star with his natty moustache and oiled hair, wearing a fine suit, a pressed shirt, one hand holding hers, the other resting on her waist, his eyes fixed on her face. Perhaps they danced and then he, Signor DeLuca, took his wife's hand and led her outside. Perhaps he lit a cigarette for her, passed it to her and then, while she smoked, he made cocktails for them both. I liked to think of him handing a Martini glass to his elegant wife. And where was Anna? Had she watched her mother and imagined herself following in her footsteps, dancing with her devoted husband in the Sicilian villa she knew she'd inherit one day? Had she imagined herself married to a man who would love her more than life itself? And if she had, then what had led her to Patrick Cadogan, to that cold, emotionless man, the man who humiliated her at every opportunity, who bullied his children, who made it clear he had no affection or regard for his family at all?

I put the photograph down and carried on searching. In the cupboards built in to the recesses behind the huge old chimney breasts in the downstairs rooms, I found boxed board games, candles, bowls, crayons, paper and more mice, but no paintings. In the smaller of the three reception rooms, I found a music cabinet that could play everything from vinyl records and cassette tapes to CDs. Boxes of eclectic music in its different formats were stored beneath. In another huge cupboard off the kitchen, I found an old vacuum cleaner, a disintegrating bag containing several pairs of trainers, tennis rackets, balls, a child's satchel, a tangled badminton net and some ancient fishing equipment. Everywhere I looked, I found the paraphernalia of family life, but no painting of the Madonna.

Joe came downstairs.

'Any luck?' he asked me.

'Nothing.'

'Me neither.'

Together we manhandled an old wooden ladder from the linen cupboard into the smallest bedroom, where an abandoned wasps' nest hung in one corner and a tiny door in the ceiling opened into the attic. Joe climbed up while I used my weight to steady the ladder. I watched him disappear through the hole. He called down to me that he was in a space that ran the length and breadth of the building. I heard his footsteps above, drawing away from me, and the occasional bump and thump from somewhere distant. When I heard nothing for a while, I became uncomfortable.

'Joe?' I called. 'Joe! Are you okay?'

He coughed in response. 'Fucking dusty.'

Eventually, he backed out and came down the ladder, bringing with him feathers, dust and cobwebs. There was nothing there, he reported, apart from old birds' nests, chewed insulating foam, bags of old clothes and the lanterns that used to light the gardens during his grandparents' parties.

'The Madonna's not there,' he said. 'Nobody in their right mind would put anything of value up there anyway.' He shook himself, dislodging the black, desiccated corpses of insects from his clothes.

'Why don't you go for a swim?' I suggested, but he held a finger to his lips. I listened and heard what he had: the sound of an engine; a vehicle coming down the track; another visitor on their way.

21

This time it was a battered old truck that drew up beside the hired Fiat, coughing thick smoke from its exhaust. The truck's bodywork was dirty, dented in unlikely places, the bumper held on with duct tape. Hand painted livery informed us that it belonged to Vito Barsi, Tuttofare – handyman. Next to a scrawled mobile phone number was a crudely drawn cartoon plumber, a rip-off Mario Brother with a full moustache and overalls, holding a plunger in his hand.

'Shit,' Joe hissed, 'what's he doing here?'

'Did you ask him to come?'

'No! I didn't say anything to Valentina either.'

'You saw Valentina?'

'I called in to the pizzeria yesterday while I was in Porta Sarina.'

'Oh,' I said. 'Well then, you must have said something to her.'

'I didn't.'

'You must have.'

'I might have said we didn't have any water.'

I pursed my lips. 'There you are then.'

The truck rocked on its wheels as the driver's door opened

and a short, heavily muscled man climbed out, a sweat stained baseball cap on his head. He was bullet shaped, with a domed head, broad shoulders and a thick neck; his features were large and uneven. He was good-looking in a bulldog-ish way and his jaw rotated as he chewed gum.

A young boy, slender as the man was thickset, slid from the seat on the passenger side: Francesco. He held himself in that way that boys do when they feel uncomfortable, his chin down low to his shoulders, his back hunched, flicking nervous glances from beneath the rim of his cap. He put his hands in his pockets and stood beside the truck, looking down at the ground.

'Ciao!' the man called, raising his hand as he strode towards us. The laces in his filthy boots were undone and his overalls were tied by the arms around his waist. He had a cowboy swagger. 'Vito Barsi at your service!' he said, touching the rim of his cap comically as he drew near. His accent was New York Italian.

'Tell him to go away,' I whispered to Joe.

'Hi,' Joe said.

'Hey,' Vito said, 'good to meet you guys. Word is, you need to get your power hooked up and your boiler working.'

'We appreciate you coming,' said Joe, 'but we've been recommended a business in Ragusa that...'

'Ahh,' Vito made a dismissive, swatting motion, 'you don't want to be bothering with no business in Ragusa. They charge over-the-top prices, bunch of crooks, the lot of them. I'm here now; I'm not even going to charge. I used to help my Uncle Gabriele with odd jobs here. I know this old place like the back of my hand and I'll have you fixed up in no time.' He nodded in the direction of the cottage at the top of the hill. 'My Auntie Irma said you guys got off to a bad start. She asked me to come and see you as a gesture of goodwill and I like to keep my favourite aunt happy, so here I am!' He grinned widely. The grey gum snapped between his yellowing teeth, a glisten of saliva. 'I brought my assistant,' Vito continued. 'C'mon, Ciccio.' He waited until the boy was level with him, then gave the boy a push forward. 'This is my stepson. He's not up to much right now, but I'm knocking him into shape. I'll make a plumber of him yet!' His hand gripped Francesco's shoulder, the fingers digging into the boy's flesh. Francesco did not smile.

'Ciao, Francesco,' Joe said.

'Ciao,' the boy said quietly. His hair had been cut very short beneath his baseball cap and the skin at the base of his neck was pale, apart from a smattering of tiny, dark moles.

I knew Joe didn't want Vito Barsi inside our villa any more than I did. I also knew that he didn't want to do anything that might cause trouble for Francesco. We hesitated, exchanging glances, and then Vito gave Francesco a prod to make him stand up straight and Joe said: 'Right, this way; follow me.'

We trooped through the gates and into the gardens.

Vito whistled between his teeth. 'Jesus,' he said, 'what a mess!'

I stiffened. When I looked at the gardens, I did not see a mess, I saw wild beauty. I saw a place where children could run and play, where babies had been buried, where generation after generation of the DeLuca family had grown vegetables, fruit and flowers. What right did this man have to come and criticise our villa? I felt a buzz about me, a swirl of anger. Vito Barsi was an intruder. The DeLuca ghosts didn't want him here any more than I did.

'These old palazzos are money pits,' Vito continued in the relaxed way that people talk when returning to a favourite theme. 'You spend money fixing one thing and before it's done, the next thing goes wrong. Plenty of folk have gone bust trying to live out their pipe dream in some place that was beyond saving. Most times, it's cheaper to knock them down and start again. Most times, the land's worth more than the buildings.'

I didn't like the thought of the villa being demolished to be replaced by a huddle of carbon-copy holiday lets. But it'd be all right. Matilde Romano had no intention of knocking it down. She loved the place.

We came round the corner and there was the villa in front of us. Each time I saw it, its size and its beauty took me by surprise. That afternoon, the sun was lighting the façade in a particularly lovely way. If I narrowed my eyes, I could blur the slipped roof tiles and the holes in the plaster; the weeds growing out of the cracks in the wall. If I didn't look too closely, I could make the villa perfect.

'Look at that,' Vito said. 'It's a miracle it's still standing. You want to offload this as soon as you can – that's if you can find anyone mad enough to take it. A developer's your best bet. Someone looking for land to build holiday homes. Have you been down the cellar yet?'

Joe and I looked at one another. 'We didn't know there was a cellar.'

'Where there's a palazzo, there's always a cellar. Rich folks always need somewhere to store their wine!'

'There's no cellar inside the house.'

'Nah, the entrance is round the side. Follow me.'

Vito led us round to the back of the house, past the terrace with the table and the vine. Beyond, separate from the villa, was a dilapidated archway, and beneath the arch were steeply descending steps.

'There!' said Vito. 'What did I tell you? Once I've been in a place, I never forget it.'

We followed him down the steps. The step-well was full of dead leaves, and broken pieces of roof tiles.

Vito tried the handle of the door at the bottom. 'Look at that! It's open!'

He took a torch from his pocket, and we followed him into a huge cellar. It was built partly into the foundations of the house and partly into the volcanic rock on which it stood. As the torch beam swung around the space, it flashed upon piles of boxes and old-fashioned trunks, bicycle parts, tractor parts, a pile of old plates and dozens of empty glass jars. Tipped on its side was the proscenium arch of an old-fashioned puppet theatre.

My heartbeat quickened. If the missing painting was going to be anywhere, surely it would be here. Joe looked around keenly, his eyes searching, as mine were. Francesco hesitated behind us, at the door.

'Lotta junk, huh?' Vito asked, kicking a box. He went beneath a bricked archway, further into the cellar. 'Mind your heads, folks.' We followed. Now we were in the service area of the cellar. It smelled of oil. There was a generator, a boiler, some kind of pumping mechanism. 'There's a reservoir under the villa that collects the rainwater that runs off the hill,' Vito explained. 'This pump here sends it up. You'll want to boil it before you drink it, but it'll be good water for bathing; make your hair shine.' He winked at me. 'My wife swears by the water that comes off the hills.' He directed the torch into various nooks and crannies in the complex system. 'Jesus H Christ, it's in a terrible state. I don't know if I'll be able to do anything with this.'

At the far end of the service area was a second archway. I walked towards it. 'Can we take a look through here?'

Vito said: 'Go ahead. Me and Francesco need to get the tools out the truck.'

He tossed the torch to Joe. It was a poor throw and Joe didn't catch it and the torch rolled towards the foot of the boiler, the beam spinning chaotically, lighting up wires hooked to the roof of the cellar, tools on the walls and, in one high corner, a line of tiny, hanging bats.

Joe picked up the torch and directed the beam towards the far arch. I followed him into the third part of the cellar, vaulted and fitted out from floor to ceiling with wine racks. Most of the racks were empty but, at the far end, were dusty bottles, stacked in rows.

'How come you didn't know about the cellar?' I asked Joe.

'This was the Ganzarias' territory. The housekeeper and the caretaker. The family would never have come down here.'

I looked over my shoulder. There was no sign of Vito or Francesco.

'What if he's something to do with the mafia too?' I whispered.

'Vito?'

'Yes! He's Gabriele Arnone's nephew. Mafia is a family thing, isn't it? Isn't that the whole point?'

'Shhh,' Joe replied.

'But what if—'

'Edie, don't. Don't go there. His aunt gave us a fright and she's sent him here to make things okay between us. That's what the people round here do. That's all there is to it.'

'I don't like him. Can't you make him go away?'

'Let's let him do what he's come to do and then he'll go. Irma Arnone's pride will be restored and we'll have water and power and he'll have no reason to come back.'

I didn't like it, but it made sense.

Joe flashed the beam of the torch around the cellar. To the left of the wine vault was a smaller archway, smaller than a door. 'You coming?' he asked.

I was hardly going to stay in the cellar on my own, in the dark.

We had to duck to get through the arch. Beyond were more steps, this time cut into the rock, leading sharply downhill. I followed Joe closely. There was nothing to hold onto and the rock was razor-sharp. Darkness settled behind us, cold and cloying. Ahead, I could hear a weird shifting sound, like some giant creature flopping about in a cave.

It wasn't far, only a few yards, although the steps were steep and sharp and the passage small and narrow and then Joe whispered: 'Wow!'

We were standing on a natural shelf, in a cavern. Half the

base of the cavern was rock, the other half was water; the sea. At the far end, some way away, the cavern opened to the elements; it had a small, shallow mouth, and beyond was the sky. A lovely turquoise light, pure and magical, spilled inside.

Joe passed the torch back to me and stepped down onto the cavern floor. The rock was jagged and he walked tentatively. His body hunched, arms outstretched, taking care to balance.

The further he moved away from me, shrinking from me, the larger I realised the cave was. I was transfixed by the dancing reflections of the water on the rocks.

When he reached the cave mouth, Joe turned and waved to me. 'There's a landing stage! You could get a boat in here! This must be how they brought supplies from Porta Sarina to the villa in the old days!'

Distantly, the sea slapped against the rock; the smell was of salt and seaweed and sea. Joe seemed a very long way away from me. Plastic was caught on the rocks, close by me. I reached down and picked it up. It was an old salt bag. The contents were long gone, but the bag remained there and beneath it was a brilliant white goat's skull with two brown horns. The salt bag had decayed over the years, the plastic so brittle it flaked in my fingers. It had an unpleasant texture; like something long dead. I let it fall and the torch beam picked up something else, an object on the cave floor a little distance away.

Treading carefully, I stepped over the sharp rock and shone the torch down on the object. It was a puppet, a similar size to the one Matilde Romano had given me, lying face down on the rock. Its handle was missing, but the strings were tangled around the puppet's torso as if it were caught in a net. It was wearing a tiny suit of armour, like a knight. I prodded it with the toe of my sandal, turned it over and gave a gasp of shock.

Beneath the raised visor of its helmet, the puppet had no face. Its features had been chiselled away.

22

'It's nothing,' Joe said when I showed him the puppet. 'Don't let it bother you.'

'Doesn't it bother you that someone put this disgusting thing here?'

'We don't know it was put there deliberately. It might have been washed up by the tide.'

'Oh, come on, Joe!'

'Whatever, it's been there for years. It's no concern of ours.'

'Is removing the faces from things a Sicilian tradition?'

'No, but there's probably some rational explanation.'

'It's like a kind of black magic.'

'Edie, that's ridiculous.'

'Is it? You were the one who brought up voodoo.'

'I was joking.'

We were talking in hushed whispers as we retraced our footsteps up the dark rock steps, through the cellars, up the stairwell and back into the daylight. As we blinked and shaded our eyes, Vito came around the side of the villa carrying a large metal toolbox. Francesco trailed in his wake, a canvas bag slung over his shoulder so heavy that it pulled his whole body down. Vito was telling Francesco to hurry, jabbing him with bullying words, but when he saw us, his expression changed and he grinned broadly. He took the gum out of his mouth and pressed it into a crack in the old wall. I saw him do it and Francesco's eyes followed his stepfather and then the boy looked at me. We exchanged a quiet glance and in that moment I felt a connection with Francesco. It was the beginning of something; a relationship, a friendship. I didn't know what exactly, but it was real.

'Vito, could you spare Francesco for a while,' I said. 'I need some help moving furniture.'

'Take him,' Vito said cheerfully. 'He's no use to me.'

Joe took Francesco's bag and hooked it over his own shoulder. 'Right then, Vito,' he said, 'I'll be your assistant. What first?'

* * *

I took Francesco into the villa, gave him some Coca-Cola and a snack, and then the two of us spent a pleasant hour clearing out the kitchen cupboards while Vito attended to the power, reconnecting us to the grid in a way that he told Joe was 'not technically illegal'. After that, he went back to the cellar to work on the pump while Francesco and I went around the villa testing switches and plugs. Power had been restored to some of the downstairs rooms, but the upstairs remained unconnected. Francesco said the upstairs must be on a different circuit. 'You probably need a qualified electrician,' he said quietly, being careful not to criticise his stepfather.

'We probably do,' I agreed.

To Vito's credit, he worked out what was the problem with the pump and soon enough we could turn on the taps in the kitchen and the bathroom. At first, filthy brown water spurted out, and the pipes rattled as if they were about to explode. After a while, the water became rusty red and eventually the red faded and the water ran clear.

The boiler proved the most problematic of the villa's hardware. Vito told Joe that the mechanism was 'screwed' and needed replacing, but that a replacement would cost thousands of euros. He'd managed to get it going for the time being, but it wouldn't last for long. 'The quicker you get rid of this place, the better,' he said. 'The whole thing's a liability.'

* * *

After Vito and Francesco left, Joe and I went back into the cellars. We searched every spidery, dark corner, we looked behind every wine rack and inside every old box. We found backdrops for the puppet theatre and scenery and puppets, tangled together in weird, orgiastic poses; I thought I detected the hand of Signora Romano's father in some of them. We found old shoes and hats, rusting paint tins that were almost empty and a machine for putting corks into bottles. We found plant pots and lampshades and an old crib and a crate full of jam jars.

We didn't find the *Madonna del Mare*.

Joe said the only places we hadn't looked now were the outbuildings. They were hidden somewhere in the overgrowth of the gardens and we'd have to cut our way through to them and search there.

* * *

Later, when we were eating, being lavish in our use of plates and glasses because we now had the facility to wash up, I told Joe what Francesco and I had talked about.

'He loves cars,' I said. 'After he's finished school, he wants to find an apprenticeship with a garage and learn how to fix engines. Eventually, he'd like to have his own business.'

Joe nodded. His eyes had become wistful. He was thinking about Daniel, who had been crazy for cars too. His first word was: 'Brum,' making the noise as he pushed a toy car along the carpet in the living room of our London flat. He loved to stand at the window, watching traffic passing on the road outside. When people asked him what he wanted to be when he grew up, he used to say 'a car man'. That was until he discovered heavy machinery and fell thrall to the wonders of bulldozers, cranes and piledrivers.

'Brum,' I murmured. I hadn't meant to say the word out loud, but it came, and Joe looked up so sharply, I knew that he knew exactly what was going through my mind.

He held my eyes for a moment and then he looked away.

It had been an opportunity for the two of us to connect and to talk about the son we had lost, but once again, we let it slip. We'd spent so long missing Daniel separately; it had become impossible for us to share our grief together.

23

A few days later, the estate agent came, together with his assistant, a cocksure young man in a tight-fitting grey suit. The younger man went about the villa's grounds taking photographs and measurements while Joe showed the agent around, the two of them talking Italian.

After they'd gone, Joe and I walked together through the gardens.

'Vito was right,' said Joe. 'The villa's not worth anything.'

'It can't be worth nothing! Look at it, it's beautiful,' I lowered my voice, as if to protect the feelings of the villa; to keep our plans secret from its ghosts.

Joe shrugged. 'The agent said people don't want draughty, old palazzos any more.'

'He called our villa a "draughty old palazzo"?'

'They want insulated new-build apartments with loads of bathrooms and smart air-conditioning systems and maybe a little balcony outside. He said whoever buys the place will buy it for the land and then apply for a redevelopment grant to build holiday homes. That's the only way to make money from it.'

'Signora Romano's not going to do that.'

'She says she's not.'

'No, honestly, Joe, she's not. She cares about the villa. She loves it. She wants to buy it to live in it, to keep all the memories alive.'

I glanced towards the building, basking in the sunlight, birds singing in the trees. I could see the top of the oleaster that spread its branches above the graves of the three babies. When she buried her children, Anna's mother must have believed they would be safe in the garden forever; their graves undisturbed. 'Even I would feel awful selling the villa to someone who was going to knock it down,' I said. 'She might be a bit odd, but at least by selling it to Signora Romano we know it's going to be safe.'

Joe was unconvinced. 'It's none of our business what happens to it after we've sold it. Signora Romano might have told you she wants to keep it, but really she might be planning to sell the villa on to some other party or obtain a redevelopment grant for herself.'

He was right, of course, but I still didn't think she would.

We walked on a little. Then I asked: 'If the estate agent was right about the value, does that mean the sale won't generate enough money for you to set up your scheme for young addicts.'

'Probably not.'

'Not at all?'

'Maybe on a very small scale.'

'That would still be something.'

'Yes,' said Joe, but he said it in a 'no' tone of voice.

He was gazing out towards the horizon and I could feel his disappointment.

I'd promised to let Matilde Romano know when the valuation had taken place, but Joe wasn't in the right frame of mind for me to broach the subject now. I decided to let it drop for a few days. Once Joe had time to come to terms with what the estate agent had told him, I'd raise the subject and ask if he was ready for us to progress the sale. Then, at last, I could think about going home.

* * *

I walked up the hill and texted Fitz.

Have you heard of an artist called Guido Reni?

She replied with a thumbs-up emoji.

Is he famous?

Yes. Why?

One of his paintings is here somewhere.

A surprised face emoji.

We don't know where it is, is the problem. We've looked everywhere.

Sad face emoji. Head scratching emoji. Chin in hand emoji.

You'd better look harder.

24

The next morning when I came down, Joe was already in the garden, clearing a path to the old outbuildings, a last-ditch attempt to locate the painting. This was the last section of the garden to be cleared, and also the most densely overgrown.

The villa was quiet and still around me, as if it was holding its breath, waiting to see what would happen next. The morning was oppressively hot. I thought of the little graveyard in the shade of the oleaster tree. The thought of abandoning the graves troubled me. I reassured myself that they'd be looked after. Matilde Romano must know about the graveyard if she and Anna had been so close. She could be entrusted with its care.

But then Joe's words haunted me. He was right; once the villa was sold, we would have no say in what happened to it. The prospect of the graves being bulldozed was unbearable.

I tried to put my worries from my mind. I dawdled around the villa, boxing up books and old toys and fighting off a headache. Mid-morning, I came to the kitchen for a drink of water and saw that Joe had left his shirt, crumpled and sweat-stained, on the table. Irritated by his untidiness, I pushed it to one side and something fell to the floor: his wallet. I picked it up and it opened in my hands like a book. I could not help but see the photograph, an old-fashioned colour print tucked inside one of the pockets. It was a picture of a young girl, fourteen or fifteen, a smiling young girl with a neat little body, skin tanned a deep brown, long, dark hair, tousled and wet, standing barefoot on the beach with the sea, and the floating dock behind her. The girl was wearing a bright red, halter-neck bikini with a frill around the waist and a matching bracelet of plastic flowers around her wrist. Her head was tipped back and she was laughing, her teeth straight and white. Beside her was a young man, Joe, about the same age as the girl but seemingly younger, his legs and hips skinny, hair beginning to grow on his navel. He was looking at her, grinning broadly; his hair was wet too. Their wet skin shone in the sunlight.

I took the picture out of the wallet and turned it over. Someone had written on the back, it was adult handwriting, hard to read and in Italian. I couldn't make it out, but I recognised the signature at the bottom, Valentina, and the crudely drawn heart.

She must have given it to Joe when he dropped by to see her, a reminder of their teenage romance, a keepsake that she'd held onto for all these years, through her moves to New York and then back to Sicily. Did a flame still burn in her heart for Joe? Did she wish she'd stayed with my husband instead of going off to marry her two Italians?

It took all of my willpower not to crumple the photograph in my hand.

I imagined myself telling Fitz about it and I knew she'd say: 'It doesn't mean anything. It's a gesture of friendship, that's all. It's what middle-aged people do, Edie, they remember their youth. Valentina probably kept the picture because it reminds her of how she used to look. It's probably nothing to do with Joe.'

Why did it bother me anyway? I had no right to care. I didn't care! Joe could do whatever he wanted, see whomever he wished to see, carry whatever photographs of whatever teenage girls he wanted to carry in his wallet. It was nothing to do with me, of no interest to me what-so-bloody-ever. No. It was just that my headache was making me feel tetchy. It was the weather. It was the graveyard. It was everything.

By now, the temperature had risen to the mid-thirties. I couldn't stay in the villa any longer. What was the point being a stone's throw from the beach and the sea if you couldn't enjoy it?

I collected my towel, swimsuit and book and went outside. Joe was hacking away at the overgrowth furiously, as if trying to make a point. He had stripped down to his shorts and boots and his skin glistened with sweat. He turned round when he saw me, and wiped his forehead with his arm. I was cross with him about the picture in the wallet. I knew my anger was unreasonable, but I couldn't help it and that put me in a worse temper.

'I'm going to the beach,' I said.

'Right.'

There was a moment's silence, in which I could have asked him to join me but didn't.

Do you still like Valentina? I wanted to ask. Do you wish you were with her? Did you keep a photo of the two of you together somewhere? When you were with me, married to me, did you wish you'd chosen Valentina instead? Do you wish that now? Do you?

Joe said: 'Liuni and his brother are going to stop by.'

'Oh, good!' I said. 'It's great you're still so close to your old friends. I guess those bonds you forge when you're young run deep.'

Joe looked confused.

'Roots, I mean,' I said. 'Roots run deep. Bonds hold strong.'

'I don't know what you're talking about, Edie.' He frowned and rubbed the blade of the shears against his boot.

I left the villa, trying to push away the black cloud of bad temper that followed me. I walked up the concrete track to the place where a little sandy path made a shortcut between the rocks down to the beach.

'Roots!' I muttered. 'Bonds! Bastards!'

The sun beat down on my head and shoulders and the track was stony; my shoes slipped on the pebbles as I descended. I picked up a stick and swiped it at the weeds that grew in the clefts in the rocks. The path was deserted except for tiny, basking green lizards. I was alone, the world was almost silent, the heat weighed heavy above me.

At its end, the path dropped down into the sand. This far corner of the beach was empty; all the families and sunseekers were congregated further up. I took off my trainers, hooked my fingers into the heels and walked on the hot sand. The sea was pale blue today, the light silvering the tips of the waves, a heat haze shimmering around the headland making the villa appear as if it was floating. A bird rose up from the trees. A red-sailed boat drifted close to the horizon. Teenagers were jumping off the floating dock – the dock from which Valentina had once jumped. I scuffed my toes in the sand. Was this where Joe brought her and lay her down? Was this where he leaned over his sweetheart to give her the kiss of life? Was she wearing that pretty red bikini with the frill around the waist? Did he look at her then in the same way he was looking at her in the photograph? What was he thinking when he kissed her?

I kicked over the sand and walked on until I reached the halfway point and then I stood and looked back at the villa on its hazy headland, I saw a movement on the far side of the water, a distant figure coming towards the sea. I watched, my hand shielding my eyes from the sun, as the figure came to the top of the steps at the edge of the decking; I watched the figure dive into the sea.

Joe. On his own, the same as me.

25

I found a spot by the rough dunes that backed up against the road where there was a little shade. I spread out my towel, covered my skin in sunscreen, lay down and slept. I would have slept for longer, but I was woken by the phone alert to an incoming text.

Matilde Romano here. You haven't sent me the valuation yet. I'm eager to proceed. Please send at once.

I drafted several texts in response but couldn't find the right words to explain why I hadn't been in touch, so in the end, I turned off the phone without replying to her.

I was hot and my left leg and hip were stiff, I tucked my bag under my towel, pushed myself up and walked to the water's edge. The sea was foamy where it met the sand; glassy and cool, little silver fish darted about my ankles. I walked out until the water reached my thighs, then I slid into the sea and swam out to the floating dock. The water was greenish, clear, like wine-bottle glass. A dark haired woman of about my age was drifting on a lilo. She smiled at me and I smiled back, but I swam on past her. What was the point in making friends when I'd be leaving soon?

I reached the dock and climbed up the ladder, onto the wooden planks where Joe and his friends used to gather when they were young. The dock rocked beneath me, the sea making sucking, splashing noises. Joe must have felt the same wood, warm beneath the soles of his feet and the palms of his hands, when he came here as a teenager. I could almost see Valentina sitting here wearing her red bikini, sun glistening on her wet skin, dangling her legs over the side, leaning back on her hands, long, dark hair tumbling down her back, and the boys gathered around, dive-bombing into the water, play-fighting, laughing. Twenty-five years ago, everything would have looked pretty much the same as it did now. The beach, and the billboard at the junction, just visible from here; the town on one side of the bay and the villa on the other.

Daniel would have loved it here. He'd have loved the dock and the sea and the beach. It was perfect for young people, the two headlands reaching out like protective arms, the bay a safe playground. If only he could have had some summers here! If only we could wind back the clock and change something; one small thing to change the course of events.

Oh, I missed him. I missed my boy so much. I missed all the happiness we hadn't had; all the summer days we didn't get to spend together; all the friends he never made; the photographs and videos we never had chance to take; the memories we didn't make. So much love and joy and life, all of it gone, wasted, and for what?

It would have been so easy not to have lost Daniel, so, so easy.

I knew it was a pointless exercise, I'd done it a million times before, but still I found myself tumbling down a rabbit hole of 'if only's'. If only we hadn't chosen that particular day to go into town; if only we hadn't mentioned our plans to

Anna; if only we'd told her we wanted to take Daniel with us; if only we'd realised that she needed to keep drinking in the same way most people need to keep drawing breath. No, that last one was wrong; if only I'd realised. Joe had his suspicions. I knew he did. I'd recognised it in those moments when we first found out Daniel was missing. I saw fear run across Joe's face like the shadow of a cloud. I'd analysed every moment of that day a million times and I knew that, in that instant, Joe had been thinking: *Oh dear God, don't let this be anything to do with Anna's drinking*, I knew it and when I challenged him about it, he admitted it. He admitted that he suspected Anna might be drinking all day, every day, that she couldn't go longer than an hour or two without a drink, but he'd convinced himself she wouldn't do it while she was looking after Daniel.

Why didn't he talk to me about it? Why didn't he mention his fears to me? If he had, would I have left Daniel with Anna for a single minute? No! No, I wouldn't have and Daniel wouldn't have gone missing and Joe and I would still be together and the three of us might well all be here on holiday, now, like a normal family; like normal, happy people.

Regret took hold of me and squeezed. I felt it in my heart, in my soul, in my bones.

The dock rocked beneath me, disturbed by the wake from a speedboat out in the bay. I sat down, leaned back on the palms of my hands, felt the movement of the water below. I looked over to the villa. It was lovely in the sunshine, the points of the cypress trees rising above the roof, the flowers tumbling over the wall, turquoise sea surrounding the headland, setting it off beautifully.

Our villa.

The villa we were about to sell. The villa that had been in the DeLuca family for more than two hundred years; the family whose lost babies were buried in its gardens.

What then? I wondered. What would become of us after the sale?

There'd be a little money for Joe and me to share. Not much, that was clear, but perhaps enough for me to put down a deposit on a small place of my own. I could move out of Fitz's spare room and into... what? Property in Bristol was expensive. I might be lucky and find somewhere tiny and cheap, probably not in the desirable area of Southville where Fitz lived, but somewhere. And then what? Without Fitz and the animals, how would I fill my life? And, in any case, did I really want to live in a small flat on my own, just because I could?

No.

Okay. So, I wouldn't use my share of the money to buy a property. What else could I do with it? I didn't want to travel. I couldn't ski, I wasn't interested in chasing the sun for the sake of it. I didn't want a car or a yacht, or fancy clothes or jewellery. There was nothing in the world that I wanted except what I had already lost; my son, my family, my former happiness – all the things that Anna had taken from me.

The bitter truth was that the money she'd bequeathed me via the villa, blood money, would not enhance my life. I didn't want it.

I supposed I could refuse to accept my share of the cash, insist that Joe took it all, or I could put it aside for Cece's children, not that they'd need it. The Sicilian villa might not be worth much but the London house Anna had left to Cece and her family would give them more than enough to see them through.

I could give the money to Fitz, only Fitz wouldn't take it.

I could give it to charity.

I looked across the sea at the villa. Somewhere in the gardens, amongst those riotous plants, the little black and white cat would be hunting; the sun would be warming the stones over the three tiny graves, the birds would be splashing in the birdbath, the light would be falling on the courtyard behind the kitchen. I thought of the afternoon light inside the villa, the dry smell of warm wood, the colours of the garden reflected in the mirrors that hung on the walls, the perfume of the flowers, always strongest at this time of day, drifting through the open windows and the reassuring, gentle sound of the sea. Something inside me shifted; a truth revealed itself to me. I felt more at home in the Villa della Madonna del Mare than I'd felt anywhere else in the past ten years. It was because I felt closer to Daniel there; because it was so easy to summon my son to me when I was inside the villa's walls, or in the garden close to the graves. I couldn't rationalise or explain this, but it was true.

My heart belonged to Daniel, and Daniel was with me in the villa. How could I leave the villa when it seemed to me that my darling boy was there? How could I abandon that sad, small place in the shade of the oleaster where lost DeLuca children gathered to wait for someone to come to find them? Matilde Romano had her memories of the place, but she wasn't family. Our ghosts weren't her ghosts, they weren't calling to her.

I had the strongest sensation, a visceral feeling, that the villa could only exist if it belonged to the DeLucas. If we were to abandon it, what would happen to the spirits who inhabited its boundaries? What would happen to Daniel? If we weren't in the villa, would he too be lost, forever?

* * *

I swam back to the beach, dug my phone out of my bag, wrapped the towel around my shoulders, perched on a rock sticking out of the sand and called Fitz. She filled me in on the news from Bristol and then I tried to tell her about the ideas that were somersaulting through my mind. I didn't talk about Daniel or the stillborn children because I didn't want her to worry that I was going crazy. I tried to sound like a reasonable human being. I wanted to hear her honest opinion.

'Fitz, do you think it would be a terrible idea if we kept the villa after all?' I asked.

'I thought you'd decided to get rid of it?'

'We had. We agreed. And I don't really know what it is we could do with it if we did keep it, but there must be something.'

'You could turn it into a wedding venue, like they do with those French chateaux.'

'I was thinking more of a retreat.'

'You've got Ragusa and other World Heritage sites on your doorstep. You could host history trips or culture tours.'

'Or walking trips.'

'Culinary trips!'

'Yes,' I said.

'Wine!'

'Yes!'

'But how much needs doing to it? Is it falling down around you?'

'It's not that bad. I don't think we'd ever be able to afford to make it immaculate, but that's kind of its charm. You'd have to come over, Fitz. You'd have to come and see it.'

We talked on, and every time a new idea was generated, the possibilities for the villa seemed greater, its potential more valid, and at no point did Fitz tell me I was being unrealistic, in fact she encouraged me. After our conversation, I felt invigorated. Everything was clearer in my mind.

On the way back from the beach, retracing my footsteps up the sandy path and planning how I would open a conversation about the villa's future with Joe, I caught sight of movement in the shrubs. A small goat was moving through the olive trees on the lower slopes of the hill. The old man from the cottage, Irma's husband Gabriele, was following it through the shadows, holding the end of its leash. He was hunched, moving slowly and carefully, none too steady on his legs. He was murmuring to the goat as they went, muttering a one-sided conversation in Italian. I could not catch a single word. I felt pity for the man, briefly, until I remembered what he had done.

But still, seeing him made me think. Life was short; you had to grab hold of it while you could.

26

It was late afternoon by the time I returned to the villa. I picked at crumbs of cheese inside the wax paper wrapper that we kept in the icebox of the old fridge – the insulation was enough to keep food fresh for a while – and ate the last olives from the jar.

'Hey,' Joe came up behind me and made me jump, as if I'd been caught doing something wrong. I swallowed the olives and made myself cough and had to pour myself some water.

'Did Liuni come?' I asked.

'Yeah. He brought a chipper. We can shred whatever we cut and use it for mulch on the flower beds.'

Why? I wondered. What was the point of doing anything if the gardens were going to be left to run wild again in a few weeks anyway? Or had Joe's mind been following the same lines of thought as mine? Perhaps, subliminally, he didn't want to sell the villa either.

I waited for him to say something else, to give me some clue, but he didn't. He opened the fridge door and looked inside.

'There's nothing to eat,' he said.

'No.' I screwed up the cheese paper and put it into the bag we were using as a bin.

'We could go to Eurospin,' he said, 'stock up and then eat at the pizzeria.'

'We could.'

'Don't you want to?'

'I don't particularly want to see Vito Barsi again.'

'We won't have to talk to him.'

I shrugged.

'He might be an idiot,' said Joe, 'but the pizzas at Vito's are amazing.'

'How do you know?'

He coloured slightly. 'Valentina made me one.'

I stiffened. 'Oh. Was that when you called in to see her?'

'Yeah.'

'That was nice of her.'

We stood in silence for a moment, in a kind of deadlock. 'Well, I'm going to Vito's,' Joe said at last.

'I suppose I'll come with you,' I said.

'Don't feel that you have to.'

'It would be nice to see Francesco.'

Joe gave me the kind of look that he used to give Daniel when he suspected Daniel of lying about something and I looked away.

* * *

That evening, I washed myself as best I could with a basin full of lukewarm water, soap and a flannel and put on the long, grey dress. I didn't have much of a tan compared to Joe, but my skin hadn't burned, and what colour I had, the dress showed off. I put my hair up into a messy bun and threaded a pair of earrings I'd found in Anna's dressing table drawer into my ears.

I stood in front of the dressing table in my bedroom and looked at my reflection in the mirror. Despite the freckles that covered my face, and my scruffy hair and unkempt eyebrows, I looked better than I had when I'd arrived in Sicily. Younger, healthier and less stressed. The place had been good for me. Perhaps getting away from the cocoon I'd built around myself in Bristol, my small, safe world, perhaps that had been good for me too.

As I went down, I met Joe coming up the stairs with his shaving razor and a can of foam in one hand. He had a towel around his waist, but otherwise was naked. It was the strangest feeling, but I wanted him to look at me. I wanted him to see that I was strong and that I was okay. I wanted him to look at me and really see me, because I had the feeling that every time he looked at me, what he saw was the woman I'd been ten years earlier, the bitter, furious woman who wouldn't listen to him and who had cursed him and humiliated him and left him. I believed what he saw was anger and resentment and judgement and cruelty, and who wants to look at that?

He glanced at me, but his eyes didn't settle, they skated over me as usual. 'I won't be long,' he said and walked past me into his bedroom and closed the door.

27

Vito's pizzeria was one shopfront wide, with an illuminated red sign over the entrance and a deckchair-striped canopy pulled out over the outside dining area. Most of the tables were occupied and there was a buzz of chatter and the clink of cutlery on china. The glass doors separating the outer and inner areas of the restaurant had been pulled back and inside was busy too, people were leaning on the bar or sitting at tables staring at the football match playing on a widescreen television. Inside, the restaurant was brightly lit, but its décor was tired: a wipe clean wallpaper with a fussy pattern of plates of food, dead fish and game and bottles of wine in straw baskets. The floor tiles were chipped and the signage on the walls was faded. The kitchen was behind the bar, separated from the restaurant by a counter that ran most of its length. An impressive, wide mouthed pizza oven took pride of place in the centre.

I spotted Francesco; he was wearing a short sleeved white shirt and black trousers and his hair had been gelled. He was moving amongst the tables collecting empty glasses and stacking them in a plastic carton. From the pavement, my eyes followed Francesco to the bar, and then they found Vito.

He was serving drinks, talking to the men perched on stools beside him. The men were animated, gesticulating, laughing in that slightly threatening way some men laugh when they are on the cusp of drunkenness.

While my gaze alternated between Vito and Francesco, Valentina came out of the restaurant, a tea towel tucked into her pocket, her arms balancing a number of large plates of pizza. She caught sight of Joe and acknowledged him with a warm smile and a nod of her head. She didn't see me. I moved a fraction closer to Joe.

Once she'd served the pizzas she was carrying, Valentina wove her way towards us through the wooden tables balanced on the cobbles, smiling, holding out her hands in greeting. She and Joe embraced and exchanged a flurry of words in Italian. I stood to one side, uninvolved, while my former husband chatted to his former girlfriend, until, just as I reached the point where I thought I couldn't bear it any longer, Valentina turned to me and her smile was so genuine I found myself warming in response, despite myself.

'It's nice to see you again, Eva,' she said.

'It's Edie,' said Joe apologetically.

'Oh, I'm so sorry, Edie!'

'It's fine.'

'You see, I like the name Eva so much, it's one of the names we had for the baby!' she laughed, fingers at her throat playing with the small, silver dolphin she wore on a slender chain. 'I like Edie too, of course! I'm talking too much now. Where would you like to sit? Would you like to sit outside? Would you like a view of the harbour?'

'Please,' said Joe.

'This table here?'

'That's lovely.'

'Give me a moment to clear it.'

'I can do that,' said Joe.

'No, you're guests! Sit down, sit! I insist.'

Joe and I sat opposite each other, with me facing the harbour. The moon was rising over the sea. I tried to keep out of Valentina's way as she piled up the dirty dishes and unclipped the paper tablecloth from the table. She dusted crumbs into the palm of her hand.

'Francesco will bring the menus,' she said. 'I hope you find something you like.' She disappeared and the boy appeared a few moments later with a candle in a glass jar, a carafe of water and two glasses. His expression was serious, although he smiled a shy greeting to us both.

'Hey,' Joe said. 'How are you?'

'I'm good, thank you,' said Francesco. The faintest ghost of a moustache ran along his upper lip and there were spots on his jawline. These signs of adolescence made me feel very tender towards the boy. He took a lighter from his back pocket and lit the candle. We thanked him, perhaps a little too heartily; he gave a nod of acknowledgement, disappeared and returned with bread in a basket, salt, a stoppered jug of olive oil and two laminated menus. Joe attempted to draw him into conversation and Francesco answered his questions politely, but his eyes kept flickering to the interior of the restaurant, to his stepfather.

At last, Joe said: 'Sorry, I'm keeping you from your work. You go and do what you have to do. We'll talk another time.'

Francesco said, 'Okay,' and he turned and disappeared.

Joe and I exchanged glances that acknowledged each other's concern for Francesco.

Valentina returned with two long-stemmed glasses and a bottle of wine. 'It's Siciliano,' she said, with a little flurry, 'it's on the house, for my dear friend, Joe, and his lovely wife, Edie.'

'Ex-wife,' Joe said.

'Lovely ex-wife,' Valentina corrected with a small roll of her eyes. 'Would you like me to pour the wine?'

'We can manage,' said Joe and I said: 'Yes, please,' at exactly the same moment.

Valentina deferred to me, opened the bottle with a corkscrew attached to a ribbon pinned to her apron and filled our glasses.

'Please,' she said to me, indicating my glass, 'taste.' She watched as I drank, her eyes scrutinising my face for signs of approval. 'What do you think? Do you like it?'

'It's delicious,' I said. 'Thank you so much.'

'You're welcome,' she said.

Now she was watching Joe as he tried his. He looked up to see her watching him and their eyes locked. Unconsciously, Valentina bit her lower lip and a flicker of sadness, or perhaps regret, crossed her face. I saw it and Joe saw it too.

'Which pizza would you recommend?' I asked Valentina brightly.

She turned back to me.

'Oh...' she smiled, 'any of them. They're all good. My personal favourite is the traditional scacciata. It's a speciality of the region: delicious local cheese, potato, broccoli, anchovies...'

'Edie won't eat anchovies,' Joe said.

'No?'

'Sorry, I'm vegetarian.'

'It's no problem,' Valentina said, 'I'll make you a vegetarian scacciata. How about you, Joe?'

'Do you remember Signora Ganzaria's scacciata?' Joe asked Valentina. 'She used to pack them for us to eat on the beach.'

Valentina smiled. 'They were the best I've ever tasted.'

'If you could make me one like that, I'd be the happiest man on the planet.'

'I'll do my best,' Valentina said, delighted to be presented with this challenge. She wiped her hands on the tea towel and disappeared back into the pizzeria. Joe watched her go. I saw his eyes following her. He was smiling. Me, I took a large drink of wine.

28

For the first hour of that evening, Joe and I didn't say much to one another, although we competed for Francesco's attention whenever he came to our table. Our pizzas were burning-hot, oily, salty and delicious. I was hungry and while I ate I forgot everything and simply enjoyed myself. I texted a photo to Fitz and as I texted I realised something inside me had changed in the days since I arrived at Catania airport. The weight of the sadness that I'd carried for ten years had eased, a little. My transformation was to do with discovering how close I felt to Daniel within the villa's walls: the time in the graveyard when I'd felt him run by me; the growing sense of him being amongst the DeLuca ancestors in that strange and lovely place. For ten years, my love for him had been subsumed into the overwhelming grief and anger, but now those emotions were receding, the love was emerging and it was helping me.

It had been good for me to come here. And yes, okay, it was Anna's will that brought me here, but that was all. She wasn't to know how I'd react when I arrived. Her part in this was negligible. I pushed her from my thoughts.

Time went by quickly. The night sky was beginning to dance

and the terrace outside the pizzeria was becoming noisier. I shouldn't have drunk so much. Soon it would be time to leave and Joe and I had hardly said a word to one another and I still couldn't think of a way to explain to him how the prospect of selling the villa had become almost painful to me.

While I dithered, Joe took out his phone and checked his texts and emails and while he was doing this, one of our fellow diners, an older man with a handlebar moustache, stood up and began to sing. Those who knew the words of the song joined him and those who did not clapped along. The terrace took on a convivial atmosphere, even more so when Valentina came round offering complimentary shots of limoncello. I took a glass. The limoncello was ice-cold and so sweet it made my teeth hurt. Joe pushed his glass towards me and I drank its contents too.

The moustache man had a rich voice, deep and powerful, and each time the ballad reached its chorus, the crowd joined in with increasing gusto, some swaying their arms, others banging out the rhythm with the flats of their hands on the tabletops. All the while, Valentina bobbed between the tables, bringing drinks, coffees, small bowls of ice cream, and Francesco cleared the empty glasses and took away the dirty dishes.

There was too much noise on the terrace for Joe and me to have any kind of conversation now. I stood up and made my way into the restaurant, heading for the Ladies'. I passed Vito leaning on the bar, his eyelids and jowls heavy with drink, his expression ugly. He did not move when Valentina tried to squeeze past him, carrying an armful of dirty dishes. As I waited, I watched her giving instructions to Francesco and he nodded and did whatever it was she had asked of him. It was almost midnight; Francesco must have school in the morning, his exhaustion was written on his face. Vito, meanwhile, was picking an argument with one of his drinking buddies. By the time I came out of the restroom, the argument had escalated.

I went back towards the door, giving Vito and his friends a

wide berth; still I saw the ugliness in Vito's face when Francesco went past him with a carton full of glasses. I saw Vito slap the boy on the back of the head, jolting him forward. Francesco ducked to avoid a second smack.

'Hey!' I cried. 'Stop that!'

I pushed through the tables to get closer.

'Vito Barsi!' I called. 'I saw what you just did! If you think you can...'

I felt a hand on my arm. Joe.

'Vito just hit Francesco!' I cried.

'I know!'

'We can't let him do that!'

'Vito's drunk and if you humiliate him in front of his friends, you'll make things worse for Francesco.'

From the corner of my eye, I saw Francesco hunched over, putting the empty glasses into a sink. Valentina was with him, standing beside her son, whispering to him, one hand on his shoulder.

'Leave them,' Joe said. 'Walk away. We'll think of a way to help him, I promise.'

I shook myself free of Joe's arm and headed back to the table, picked up my bag, then walked across the terrace towards the harbour, where we'd left the car.

'Edie...' Joe's voice behind me was calm.

I turned. He was holding out my shawl.

'You dropped this,' he said.

I snatched it from him and shoved it under my arm.

We drove in silence all the way back along the spine of the headland, past the Intimissimi billboard, the model's face graffitied with black spectacles and a curly moustache. We turned onto the coast road, but after half a mile or so Joe stopped the car.

'What are you doing?' I asked.

'There's a viewing point.'

I scowled at him, but I got out and followed him along a little path to a ledge with a railing jutting out over the cliff edge.

The moon was hanging over the sea, its silver light reflected tens of thousands of times on the spines of little lumpy waves. We stood together, looking.

'Why did you bring me here?' I asked. 'Why did we stop?'

'To give you a chance to calm down.'

'I didn't overreact.'

'I didn't say you had.'

'We need to help Francesco.'

'We will. Only that wasn't the time. You can't reason with someone when they're drunk.'

You should know, I thought. I didn't say it out loud.

We fell silent and watched the sea. Eventually I relaxed and the atmosphere between us felt peaceful. *If this isn't the right time to speak*, I thought, *I don't know when will be.*

I took a deep breath and began.

'Joe, I've been thinking...'

'What?'

'What if we don't sell the villa? What if we keep it?'

He didn't respond.

'We could convert it into a hotel,' I continued, 'or a retreat. If there's so little money to be made in selling it, then there doesn't seem much point, and at least it would remain in the family. What do you think?'

Silence.

'Joe?'

I couldn't make out his features, only the silhouette of his face. He stared out over the sea as if he hadn't heard me. An offshore breeze disturbed the hair above his forehead, otherwise he was motionless.

'I just thought...' I said, 'I thought a retreat... I thought it would mean...' I ran out of words.

'It wouldn't work,' Joe said, after a silence that became more uncomfortable each moment it lasted.

'How do you know it wouldn't work?'

'Because you and me can't be together.'

'Joe...'

'You despise me,' he said, 'remember? And if I'm honest, Edie, I don't like you very much either.'

29

We returned to the car and drove on in silence, Joe's words stinging all the way back to the villa. He'd never spoken to me so bluntly before; in the past, no matter how cruel I'd been to him, he'd never retaliated. I hadn't realised how much a few cold words could hurt. And it was painful to know that someone who once loved me now disliked me to such an extent he wouldn't even talk about the possibility of a mutual project. Along with the sorrow was frustration. We'd never talked through the implications of keeping the villa, never considered them because we'd both been so desperate to get away from one another. I wished, now, that we hadn't been so hasty.

Joe parked the Fiat in its usual spot and we got out. The air was still warm. The sea was gently patting the rock. The insects were singing and the bats were hunting above us, invisible ghosts blacking out streaks of the sky, stars twinkling.

Joe didn't say anything. I struggled to contain my emotions and act normally; I didn't want to push him further away by speaking thoughtlessly but it was difficult to keep quiet when there was so much I wanted to say. Mostly, I wanted to make him tell me that he hadn't meant what he'd said, but I was afraid, deep down, that he had. I lifted two bags of shopping from the back seat and carried them across to the gates. By the light of the lantern above it, I could see a small, dark lump on the gravel. I put the bags on the ground, went closer and looked down.

'Oh! Joe!'

'What is it?'

Joe came and crouched beside me, the two of us looking down at the body of the little black and white cat that lived in the villa's gardens.

'Is she dead?' I asked.

Joe reached out a hand and smoothed the cat's shoulder.

'Yes, she's dead.'

'Oh, dear God!' I clamped my hands to my mouth.

Joe looked around, as if he believed whoever had hurt the cat might still be lurking in the shadows of the villa's wall.

I shivered and my eyes searched the darkness too. That primordial fear, the sensation of being watched – hunted – was stronger than ever. My head turned from left to right. My ears were pricked. My senses were on high alert.

'What do you think happened?' I asked, my voice a whisper in case someone, or something, malevolent was nearby, observing us, waiting for an opportunity to strike.

'Perhaps she was hit by a car,' Joe said, but I could tell that he didn't believe it.

'Cars don't come down here.'

'Maybe she was hit on the coast road and made her way back.' He examined the cat by the light of his phone. 'She's got kittens.'

'What?'

'Look, she's been lactating. There must be kittens somewhere.'

'Where? Where are the kittens?'

'They'll be too small to have been with her. We'll find them. In the morning.'

'That might be too late!'

'Edie, we can't do anything about them now.'

The frustration that had been building all evening spilled over. 'First Francesco, now the kittens! It's always the same with you, Joe, it's "not now", it's "not the right time" it's "we wouldn't work"! You always take a step back and hope whatever problem it is will sort itself out and...'

'What do you want to do about the kittens then, Edie?' Joe's voice was still low, almost a hiss. 'They'll be hidden, who knows where. They might be in the gardens or they might be somewhere on the headland, they might be up at the Arnones' cottage. Where do we start to look in the dark? Huh?'

I glared at him over the body of the cat. I pushed my hair off my face. My skin felt cold and clammy. I heard a noise behind me, close to the villa wall, and I snapped my head round towards it, but nobody was there, or at least nobody I could see. I wanted to get away from this exposed space, into the villa, somewhere where we could lock a door behind us.

I looked back to the poor cat. 'It looks like she was trying to make her way back into the gardens,' I said. 'That means the kittens are probably somewhere close to the villa.'

'Unless someone put her here.'

'What?'

'I can't see any paw-prints in the dust.'

He targeted the phone's light at the area around the cat. He was right. There was no sign of the cat walking, or dragging herself, to the spot where we'd found her.

'Why would anyone leave the cat's body outside our gates?' I asked in a whisper. My skin was crawling, sensing those invisible eyes watching us, that hostile gaze.

'Maybe someone was doing us a kindness,' Joe replied in the same whisper. 'Perhaps they found the cat on the beach and assumed she came from here and brought her back.'

I hoped that was true but again I had the sense that Joe didn't believe what he said.

'Anyway, we can't leave her out here,' Joe said, 'we need to bury her.'

'Now?'

He nodded.

I unlocked the gates while he picked up the cat and wrapped her body carefully in a towel that had been in the back of the car.

Once we were safely back in the villa's gardens and the gate was locked behind us, I held the torch for Joe while he dug a grave for the cat. It was hard work; the soil layer in the spot he'd chosen was shallow and the blade kept clanging onto rock, but at last the hole was deep enough. Joe put the shrouded cat into the hole and covered it over.

At the last moment, before the soil fell on the bag, I panicked. 'Joe, are you sure she's dead?'

'Yes.'

'Only I've heard about people who buried animals and...'

'She's dead, Edie. She's stone cold.'

'Oh,' I said. 'Sorry.'

He looked at me, and in the torchlight I saw sympathy in his eyes.

I moved the torch so the beam didn't blind him and he finished the burial. We put stones on top of the grave to stop other animals attempting to dig the cat up and walked back to the villa, Joe leading, me following so closely behind that I kept treading on his heels. I was scared about whoever had brought the dead cat to the villa and I was worried about the kittens. I strained my ears, listening for mewling. I tried to stop my mind going down tiny holes, imagining them blind, helpless and terrified. I tried not to think about owls, or wildcats, or foxes that might be out hunting. I tried not to worry about the possibility that some malevolent observer, the killer of the cat, was still lingering beyond the villa's walls.

* * *

Inside the villa, I climbed the stairs, lit the candles in my bedroom, took off Anna's earrings and let down my hair. I stared at my reflection, ghostlike in the darkness of the wardrobe mirror, candlelight refracting in odd zigzags from the faults in the glass. I used to think myself the kind of person who wouldn't let life slip through my fingers. When I heard people complaining about the hand they'd been dealt, I vowed I wouldn't become like them. I would live expansively, experiment and be bold. Life hadn't turned out the way I'd expected. It had closed around me, becoming narrow and small; I lived in a rut – not a terrible rut, but a rut nonetheless. It was Anna who'd done this to me. She was responsible for my walls and here I was sitting in her family's villa staring at my reflection in her mirrors.

I gazed at myself. My chin was shaped like my grandmother's. The skin on my face was beginning to soften, like hers. My grandmother had no options in life. She'd been obliged to care for her family. There was never enough money and she ran out of time. My mother's life had been confined by the boundaries of ill health. I'd always had more freedom than either of them. And here I was, with a once-in-a-lifetime opportunity to step out of the rut. If my grandmother or mother had been here now, they'd have told me to pull my socks up. The poor cat, left dead outside our gate, wasn't a reason to run away, it was a reason to stay and fight.

Yes, I was afraid that someone was watching us, someone who didn't want us here, but I would be damned if I let them know I was afraid. And I could see why Joe had said what he'd said but things could change. We weren't exactly close but we'd been managing to work together in and around the villa. We'd proved we could still be a good team. We complemented one another in our skills and approach to life. And each of us was the only strong link the other had to Daniel. We had made Daniel between us. We couldn't walk away from that. We mustn't.

'Are you going to give up so easily?' I asked my reflection. 'Are you?'

30

I went back downstairs, padding barefoot. The chandelier twinkled in the hallway. I followed a slight draught into the kitchen. Joe was standing by the back door, gazing out into the darkness, a bottle of beer in his hand. He looked scruffy and tired.

'Joe,' I said, 'can we talk about the villa?'

He took a drink from the mouth of the beer bottle.

'I was wrong,' I said, 'to want us to rush into selling. I just wanted this whole thing over and done with. I hadn't given it any thought and you... well, you didn't really have a choice did you, because I couldn't sell unless you did. You don't really want to give the villa up, Joe, do you?'

He didn't answer.

'I mean, if there was an alternative...'

Joe sighed. 'There is no alternative.'

'There could be! If we work together!'

He turned slowly. 'If we work together? Seriously? You and me?'

'Why not? We were a good team before.'

'A good team? Are you crazy? We were a disaster.' His eyes

were bright, he was becoming angry. At least he was reacting now. It was a step forward.

'At the end, we were a disaster, but most of the time we were okay.'

'No, Edie. We weren't. We never were "okay". We pretended.'

'No! We weren't pretending when we were friends as children or when we started going out with one another. We weren't pretending when we were at university or travelling, or when we got married or when we had Daniel or when he was alive. We weren't pretending then! We loved one another. We made one another strong.' My voice was rising, the words coming from my heart.

'No,' Joe said, and his refusal to acknowledge what we both knew to be true made me angry.

'We were good for one another!' I cried.

'It wasn't real! We were going through the motions...'

I took a step towards him. 'Joe, how can you say that?'

He moved away from me, banged the bottle down on the table and turned his hands upwards. 'Because if we'd been even halfway strong, we'd have got through losing Daniel, but we didn't! Not even close! We fell apart like a... like a fucking deck of cards.'

'But we were in shock then, we were grieving. We should have had counselling or something but...' *you wouldn't consider it and I couldn't see the point.* 'I've talked to Fitz and she says we probably both had PTSD.'

He snorted.

'Don't!' I cried. 'Don't mock us! We'd been through the worst thing ever and nobody helped us and we didn't have the emotional tools to cope and—'

'Excuses! That's all those are! Platitudes! Lies you've told yourself to convince yourself. You were strong, Edie, but I wasn't. You were the one who went into the shaft after Daniel! You were the one who tried to save him! You were the one who kept your shit together even with your broken hip and your smashed-up leg! You were the one who didn't totally, completely, fall apart!' At this last comment he turned to hide his face from me and I was shocked as I realised how ashamed he had felt; how small I'd made him feel. Regret rose inside me; a lump of remorse like acid in my throat. I'd humiliated Joe as a way of assuaging my own pain. I'd destroyed him to shore up my own fragile sense of self. How cruel I'd been. How unkind.

'Joe... You didn't... You couldn't help it. It didn't mean you were weak.'

'That's not what you said at the time.'

'I didn't know what I was saying.'

'I think you did, Edie. I think that was when you were at your most honest.'

'Our son had died!' I cried again. 'I was trying to hurt you, to offload some of my hurt! It was awful and wrong and I'm sorry, but I couldn't help myself!'

Joe shook his head. Still he wasn't looking at me; couldn't bear to look at me. 'We could have helped one another though, couldn't we?' he asked in a quieter voice. 'We could have talked. We could have tried to comfort each other, but we didn't. I blamed myself and you agreed. You said it was my fault. You said you wished I'd died instead of Daniel. And you know what, Edie?' Now he turned to face me. 'You know what really eats me up when I'm lying awake at night thinking of what I could have done differently, what I should have done? It's this. You were right; about everything. It should have been me down that fucking shaft instead of him. I wish it had been me! If there was any way I could turn back time and put myself there and give Daniel back to you, then I'd do it! I'd do it now! In a heartbeat!'

We stared at one another across the kitchen. My heart was pounding; Joe's words – my words – the words I'd said to him, rang in my ears.

'I'm sorry,' I whispered, then I pushed past Joe and went

outside. I ran across the lawn, around the empty swimming pool, out to the decking and beyond to a dark part of the garden, and I fell onto my knees and cried until there were no more tears. I lay down on the grass, dampening now as the gentle night settled over Sicily, and the tears dried on my face. This was my fault. The words I'd said a decade earlier, my cruelty, all of it was coming back to hurt me.

I stared up at the stars twinkling in the velvet sky. The moonlight was silver slipping over the surface of the sea that rolled and turned and shifted, relaxed, crumpled, like the sheets of a weekend bed. The sky with its millions of stars was uncompromisingly beautiful. This place had been given to me and I wanted it now, I wanted it so badly, but I couldn't have it because of the person I used to be and now I was going to lose Daniel for ever.

Joe was right. We hadn't been a team, not when we needed to be. It wasn't his fault, not at all: it was mine. I was the one who murdered the last remnants of our love.

31

I woke late, exhausted and wrought from the emotional energy spent the night before. The sun was already high in the sky and the room was warm. I slid out of bed, put on my shorts and T-shirt and went downstairs. Joe was in the kitchen, his back to me, huddled over something on the table.

'Hi,' I said.

He turned. He was holding a towel in his arms. Wrapped in the towel was a tiny, white kitten, squirming, its eyes closed.

'You found the kittens!'

'Yep. Got up early. Couldn't sleep.'

I hadn't slept well either but it hadn't occurred to me to get up and look for the orphaned kittens. I studied Joe's face for a moment and saw the sadness and tiredness in his eyes and felt a pang of gratitude and something else: respect. I looked away before he had chance to see what I was thinking and took another step closer to him. I leaned over to look into the towel. 'It's so small!'

'Only a couple of weeks old.'

'Are there any others?'

'In there.' He nodded towards a cardboard box on the table.

I pulled back the flap and peeped inside. Two more kittens were curled together, fast asleep, snuggled into one of Joe's T-shirts. I put my finger into the box and drew back the fabric. One kitten was the colour of a ripened fig, the other mainly black with a tiny white spot on its nose.

'Where were they?'

'In the old stables. That's where my grandmother's cats used to live. I figured if they were their descendants, they'd probably still be there.'

I stroked the kittens in turn, very gently, with the back of my finger. They were warm and solid; tiny bones beneath the skin; a determined pulse.

'They're going to need feeding,' Joe said. His voice was softer than it had been last night.

'I'm so glad you found them,' I said, 'and they weren't on their own for too long.' I tried to convey my gratitude in my voice. 'How do we feed them?'

'We'll have to go into town for milk.'

'Okay.'

I looked at him tentatively over the top of the box.

'Joe,' I said, 'about last night...'

'Forget it,' said Joe.

'I just wanted to say that I'm sorry for—'

'Please, Edie,' said Joe, 'I don't want to talk about it any more.'

There were so many things I wanted to say to Joe, but the emotions uncovered last night were still raw and bloody. I didn't want us to end up shouting at each other again so I nodded and said nothing else. I'd wait until the right time came to raise the subject of the future of the villa again.

We headed off to Porta Sarina soon after. I sat in the back of the Fiat with the box on my lap. The kittens' eyes were closed and they were quite still. The sun came through the window, beat down on my shoulder. I put my hand over the box to keep its strong rays from the kittens. I promised them we'd look after them; I told them they'd be fine.

As soon as the car was high enough up the hill for my phone to receive a signal, it pinged several times with incoming messages. The first was from Matilde Romano:

What's the name of the agent? I need to get things moving. Please respond asap as a matter of urgency.

There was also a string of WhatsApp messages from Fitz. I could see from the preview that the first was a link to a biography of Guido Reni and the second was the URL of an auction house in Milan. I kept one arm around the box, but with the other I clicked on the link. It took me to an online catalogue for a forthcoming sale. There was a photograph of a picture that was captioned: Annunziata – Reni, Guido, C1620.

I expanded the picture with my fingertips. It was a beautiful painting. The face of the girl who had posed for the portrait of the angel in the picture was so vital, she could easily have been one of the young women who were currently opening up their parasols on the beach outside Porta Sarina. And the colours, the pale blues and pinks, the creamy complexion of the model's skin, the delicacy and intricacy of the needlework on her dress, oh, it was a lovely thing. To think that a work by this same artist had hung in the alcove in the hallway of our villa for two centuries! I clicked on the description of the Annunziata. Its guide price was half a million euros.

I wanted to tell Joe, but the coast road was busy and the steepness of the fall down the mountain was a constant source of worry to me. He needed to concentrate on his driving.

Instead, I read Reni's biography. He had been an artist of the high baroque style. He had mainly concentrated on religious subjects and had been prolific in his output. I found dozens of images of the Madonna that he had painted with the sea in the background, but none of them matched Joe's description of our *Madonna del Mare*.

A knot of excitement twisted inside me. Half a million euros! Enough money to restore the villa, put in a new swimming pool, do whatever we wanted! Ideas chased through my mind. I couldn't remember the last time I'd felt so enthusiastic about anything.

We drove on into Porta Sarina, my eyes on the kittens, but my mind in the villa, imagining it restored, with people in it; long lunches in the courtyard, children playing in the gardens, people sunning themselves around the pool; the graveyard made into a quiet, private place where we could go to remember Daniel and grow flowers for the dead babies; the kittens carrying on their cat heritage in the grounds. Once I found a way to apologise to Joe, to make him realise that I'd changed, then surely he'd be able to see the vision too.

The kittens were examined in the veterinary surgery and pronounced to be three or four weeks old and in reasonable condition. We bought worming powder, flea treatment, nursing formula, bottles and a supply of plastic nipples. The nurse showed us how to make up the formula because the kittens had already gone too long without a feed and were borderline dehydrated. We sat together, in a line, Joe, the nurse and I, each of us holding a kitten, encouraging it to take the milk. The one I held, the little black and white one, opened her tiny mouth and lapped at the yellow liquid, bubbles of milk on her chin. I held her close to my face, whispering encouragement. Her whiskers tickled my cheeks.

When I looked up, I saw that Joe was watching me, but when he saw that I had seen him, he looked away at once.

* * *

Back in the car, Joe turned towards the harbour road.

'I thought I could call in the pizzeria,' he said, 'seeing as we're here.'

'Okay,' I said. I wasn't in the mood to argue.

At the harbourside, two men in shorts and tattered T-shirts, brown as nuts, were stacking lobster pots on the harbour wall. Cats waited for titbits in the shadows of the roadside weeds. A dun-coloured dog sniffed at the feet of a bench. The boats moved gently in the water. Vito's battered old truck was nowhere to be seen.

Joe pulled up at the side of the road, a little way down from the pizzeria. A woman was sweeping the street outside one of the bars. Another was washing the windows with a long-handled squeegee. Sunlight glistened from the wet panes. The tables and chairs were laid out on the terrace outside the pizzeria, under the shade of the striped awning, and the door was open, although no lights were on inside and the place had an air of abandonment about it.

Joe switched off the engine.

'I won't be long,' he said.

He climbed out of the car and I watched him walk towards the pizzeria and step through the open door. It was too dark inside for me to see anything after that.

I put the box on the seat beside me and I checked that each of the kittens was still breathing.

My phone pinged. Matilde Romano had sent another text.

I don't think you're receiving my messages.

And another:

If you get this call me back.

And a third:

Edith? Is this the right number for you?

I deleted the messages. I'd have to do something about Matilde Romano, tell her something, but not yet. She would have to wait for an answer because I simply wasn't in a position to be definitive with her yet.

I looked towards the pizzeria. No sign of Joe.

I sighed, rearranged the shirt around the kittens, took some pictures of them to send to Fitz, then scrolled through some photographs of the dogs that she had sent me, smiling at their dear faces, their comical expressions.

Still no sign of Joe. Back to the phone. I read some more about Guido Reni, about how he'd been apprenticed to a Flemish painter when he was only ten years old. I imagined the small boy climbing up onto the seat of a carriage to be sent away, to live and work with a stranger in a different country. I imagined his mother kissing him goodbye. I wondered how she bore the pain.

More than half an hour passed before Joe returned to the car. I had made myself comfortable on the back seat and was half asleep. The sound of the door opening jolted me awake again.

Joe sat down and started the engine without looking at me. He pulled back out onto the road and was hooted by the driver of a dusty old van, who leaned out of the window, made an obscene gesture and yelled abuse at Joe. Joe ignored it. The van disappeared, dust rolling behind it. We followed at a distance.

'Did you see Francesco?' I asked Joe.

'He was out with Vito.'

He gripped the steering wheel tightly. His shoulders were hunched.

'Was Valentina okay?'

He grunted and then was silent for a minute. Eventually he said: 'Why does she stay with him?' Before I could say anything, he continued: 'How does someone like her end up with an asshole like him? What is there about him that would seem attractive to a woman like Valentina?'

'Well—'

'He's a bully, he's crass, he's thoughtless, he doesn't have a proper career, he makes her and Francesco work like slaves... It's not like he's even good-looking.'

I picked my words carefully and took care with the tone of my voice, to make sure it didn't sound jealous when I replied: 'It must have been hard for Valentina, coming back from America on her own with Francesco. Perhaps she met Vito on the rebound.'

'She didn't have to marry him. She didn't have to have his baby.'

'It's always easier to get into these kinds of situations than it is to get out of them,' I said.

Joe sighed wearily.

We joined the spine road and drove out of the town, marshland to either side. We'd reached the Intimissimi billboard junction before he spoke again.

'It's Francesco I'm worried about, Edie. You know that, don't you?'

'Yes,' I said. 'I know.'

I knew it was true. Joe was concerned about the young boy. But I knew he was concerned about Francesco's mother too.

32

Joe's mood lifted when we reached the villa. The morning was bright, but the heat of the previous day had been tempered by a fresh breeze that skittered small white clouds across the sky and ruffled the treetops. Birds were busy amongst the fruit cages; petals drifted from the flowers and settled amongst the gravel and the grass.

Joe carried the box of kittens into the villa. He put it on the kitchen floor, checked the kittens and then covered the box with a tablecloth.

'They'll be okay there for a bit,' he said. 'I want you to see something.'

'What?'

'Something I found.'

His words were spoken in a different tone to before. Whatever it was he wanted to show me, the fact that he wanted me to see felt like a peace offering.

'You might want to put your trainers on,' he said, and my heart lifted again. He was concerned for my comfort.

I did as he suggested and followed him across the garden. He led me almost to the gate, but then veered off into the mouth of a tunnel he'd hacked through the overgrowth close to the boundary wall. There was barely space for me to squeeze after him and the bare skin on my arms and legs was soon scratched and stung.

Joe ploughed on ahead, pushing through the climbers and brambles, disturbing lizards and birds, scattering leaves and twigs. 'Here!' he called at last.

He reached his hand back for me and I took hold of it – how strange it was to be touched by him; like something recalled in a dream. He helped me through the tangle and we emerged into a cobbled courtyard, with a tumbledown and overgrown building behind. The roof was pitched but had folded and collapsed in places and many tiles were missing. Inverted horseshoes were nailed to the stonework that was illuminated by shafts of dusty sunlight. A metal pump towered over a great stone water trough, a rusty old bucket was lying on its side, and the boundary wall ran behind.

'The old stables?' I asked.

'Yes. Old and forgotten. I don't suppose anyone's used them since my grandfather died.'

We stood, both of us slightly out of breath, looking at the building. A hay rake was propped in one corner, its tines rusting. The air was still, and I could feel the ghosts of old horses, imagine the clanging of metal shoes on the cobbles, the whinnying of the animals inside the stables, the smell of fresh hay and cold water in the trough. I imagined the ancestors of our kittens basking in the sunlight, or tiptoeing inside to hunt for mice.

'I knew they'd be here,' Joe said, reading my mind with the same prescience as before. 'There were always cats here. The Ganzarias encouraged them because they kept the vermin down.' He took a step forward. He put a hand on one of the two wide doors that stood slightly ajar in front of the building. 'My grandfather turned the stables into garages,' he said. 'And the groom's cottage,' he nodded to the roof of a slightly taller building, beyond the stables, 'is where the Ganzarias used to live.'

'This is what you wanted to show me?' I asked.

'There's more.'

Joe took hold of the door handle and pulled, using all his weight. The door creaked and complained as he dragged it over the cobbles. Swallows darted out of the gloom, so close that I felt the draught of their wings on my face. They swooped like arrows, lining themselves on the spine of the roof and the treadle of the weathervane, a three masted ship in full sail.

Inside the building, nests of fledglings fell silent.

Joe stepped inside and disappeared into the darkness. 'Come and see,' he called.

I followed him across the cobbles.

The interior was almost pitch-dark, thick with the smell of oil and hay and bird droppings. It took a moment for my eyes to adjust and then slowly something took shape in front of me: it was a car, one patch of its bonnet lit by a faint ray of sunlight coming through a crack in the roof. The tarpaulin that had covered it lay crumpled to one side. Apart from the tyres, all completely flat, it looked intact.

'My grandfather's car!' Joe said. He began to circle it. 'She was all wrapped up and protected from the elements. She looks almost as good as new.'

He came around, in and out of dim rays of light, his fingers trailing tenderly on the car's bodywork.

'Is it the same car you remember?' I asked. 'The one your grandfather used to collect you from the airport?'

'Yes.'

The car Daniel and Joe were going to drive around Sicily.

'What kind of car is it?' I asked.

Daniel knew. He knew exactly what it was. He knew a ream of facts about it. I felt him somewhere nearby; come in from the garden, hidden now by the darkness.

'It's an Alfa Romeo Disco Volante,' Joe said. 'An absolute classic.'

Daniel's small presence was right beside me. It was the most clearly I'd felt him in days, and I wanted him to stay. I couldn't bear him to leave me. If I didn't look, I could reach down and perhaps a small, warm hand would slip into mine. Time disjointed, moments shuffled like cards. Here was the car, the promised car, and there was Daniel, sitting on the counter in the kitchen of our London flat wearing his pyjamas, his wellington boots, his swimming goggles and his Ninja Mutant Hero Turtles cape, eating a piece of toast and jam and describing this very Alfa Romeo to me. 'It's a coupé, Mummy, with two seats and it can do nought to sixty in four seconds. And it's got a top speed of almost two hundred miles per hour.' He had jam on his chin – strawberry jam – as he demonstrated the velocity of the car with his hand. 'It's the best car ever!' he'd said. 'Nobody has never ever engineered a car even half as good.'

Daniel never saw this car, but he loved it. It should have been part of his future.

'Do you think it'll still work?' I asked Joe. The words came out sticky. I was too full of emotion.

'She'll need a bit of attention.' Joe bent to examine a tiny mark, then he straightened up and looked at me, through the gloom. 'I thought I'd ask Francesco if he'd like to help me get her back on the road. What do you think?'

Francesco? It should have been Daniel.

'That's a great idea,' I said.

'You're not sure?'

'Yes. No. I mean, I am sure. It's a really good idea. Do you think Vito will let him?'

'Vito doesn't have to know.'

'If he finds out Francesco's been lying to him…'

'We'll find a way.'

'It means we'd have to stay here,' I said quietly, 'at least until the car was fixed.'

'One of us would have to stay anyway, until the kittens were big enough to rehome.'

I nodded. We breathed together into the darkness.

Joe said: 'You could leave now, if you want, Edie. You could go home. I can take care of everything from here.'

'There's no rush,' I said. 'I don't have to be back in Bristol until the end of the school holidays.' I brushed a fly from my arm. I could hear Joe's breath, in and out. 'If you don't mind me staying, that is,' I said.

'No,' Joe replied. 'I don't mind.'

We were so still and quiet that a swallow dashed in above us and a chattering started from a nest tucked in the crook of one of the rafters above us. And in the next moment, we heard another sound: the sound of an engine coming down the track towards the villa. I knew who it would be. I'd been half expecting Matilde Romano to turn up and, in a way, I was glad that she'd come. I needed to get her off my back.

33

By the time we emerged from the tunnel of undergrowth, Signora Romano had walked into the villa gardens and was standing beside the derelict swimming pool, staring down into it.

'Who's that?' Joe whispered, and I remembered that he hadn't been there last time she came.

'Matilde Romano, your mother's one true childhood friend.' I reached up to pull a leaf from his hair. 'Grandma Mouse. Our potential buyer.'

'She looks too old to be Anna's friend.'

It was true that Signora Romano, in appearance, seemed old for a woman in her mid-sixties, which must be all she was, if she was the same age as Anna.

'She has a hard life,' I whispered. 'She looks after her house-bound father.'

'The puppet maker?'

'Yes.'

Matilde Romano must have caught the sound of our voices, because she looked up. She trotted towards us, little girlish footsteps, her handbag hooked over her wrist in a way that reminded me of the mincing women in 1960s TV sitcoms. 'The gates were open so I came in,' she said, 'but I was worried that nobody was home.'

'Well, here we are,' I said brightly. 'Joe, this is Signora Romano. Signora Romano, this is Joe DeLuca, Anna's son.'

The tiny woman beamed up at Joe. 'Of course it's you, Joe. I'd have known you anywhere. You still have the same look of your mother that you had when you were a little boy.' She tilted her head, robin-like, to one side. 'Look at you! You have her eyes! The same shape to your ears! I bet you're like her in personality too. Fun loving? Easily swayed? Always think you know best?' She said these things so teasingly and affectionately that I laughed. Joe smiled, but I could see he was embarrassed. Matilde Romano's hand twitched as if she longed to reach out and touch him. 'It's uncanny,' she said, her voice tender with emotion. 'It's almost as if Anna was standing here, looking at me from inside you.'

She turned to me then. 'I texted you, Edith, several times, about the valuation and the agent, but I haven't heard back from you.'

'I'm sorry, I—'

'Did you give me the wrong number?'

'No, it was the right number.'

The older woman pushed her head forward towards me and frowned. 'You didn't reply.'

'It's because the villa's not for sale... yet.'

'No? Why not?'

Joe and I exchanged glances.

'We've had things to sort out,' I said.

'But you told me you wanted to sell it quickly. "The sooner, the better," you said, and I'm ready and waiting; the cash is in the bank. The whole sale could be arranged this week if we pushed for it.'

'We'll let you know when we're ready,' Joe said.

Matilde's frown deepened. The previous friendliness vanished. 'What am I supposed to do in the meantime? I've told my father that we're coming here. He's been looking forward to it. He's old, you know, frail.'

'I'm sorry...' I began, but Joe put his hand on my arm.

'We'll let you know as soon as we've decided on a course of action.' he said this gently but with conviction, in a way that brooked no further argument.

Signora Romano's expression was one of quiet devastation. Her hands fluttered at her neckline. She had gone very pale.

'Are you all right, Signora?' Joe asked.

'I feel a little... I don't know...' She reverted to Italian and Joe took her arm, gesturing towards the villa. I took her other arm and together we guided her inside.

34

We took Signora Romano into the living room and settled her on the turquoise divan. I fetched some water, placed a cool cloth on her forehead and sat beside her.

She was so still and quiet that I feared she'd lost consciousness and was on the cusp of panicking when she groaned and asked if we had anything stronger than water for her to drink. I fetched her a small glass of wine, which she sipped in the same way a bird sips water from the edge of a pool, and, when the glass was empty, she asked for another and then at last she said she felt a little better.

She looked around the room.

'So many memories,' she sighed. 'The happiest days of my life were spent here.' Her eyes settled on the photograph of Anna's parents. 'It wasn't only Anna who I loved, but those two people too! Anna's mother, God bless her heart, looked after me. My mother died when I was still a child.'

'I'm sorry.'

'No, I don't need your sympathy! I was better off without my mother. She was a terrible woman.'

Joe was standing at the French windows. He caught my eye over Signora Romano's head.

'She humiliated my father,' the woman continued, 'in many ways.'

'Oh dear,' I murmured.

'Everyone knew what kind of woman she was. That's why Anna's mother liked me to stay here, safe from her depravity. That's how I came to learn English. Anna's governess taught the pair of us. It was our own secret language that nobody else understood!' She paused. Her eyes bright. 'This was more of a home to me than my real home. Anna's mother more of a mother to me than my own and Anna and I were closer than sisters. It's such a shame that such sadness came to the DeLuca family. Tragedy after tragedy; children lost, hearts broken. Local people have long believed that the villa is unlucky. Some even say it's cursed.'

Joe raised an eyebrow.

I'd been jolted by the 'children lost' comment, which I took to be an oblique reference to Daniel – although perhaps Signora Romano had meant the stillborn babies – and for a fraction of a second Daniel was there, on the other side of the living room beneath the mirror, staring at me, wide eyed. I blinked and he was gone.

'But you still want to buy the villa, Signora Romano?' Joe asked.

'I have no children to lose,' Signora Romano replied. 'There's only me and my father. We have nothing to fear.'

'What happened to your mother, Signora?' I asked.

'She fell in the marshes on her way back from an assignation. It was no more than she deserved.'

Something chimed in my memory. I felt as if I'd known this, although I reasoned that I couldn't have.

'I want to show you something?' Signora Romano said suddenly. 'Upstairs.' She must have felt fully recovered because she stood up and trotted across the living room in a spritely fashion. At the door to the hall, she turned and beckoned to us. 'Come on!'

We followed her up the stairs and into the room Joe was using – Anna's old room.

She went to the bed and leaned against it, pushed. She was slight and the frame was heavy. 'Help me, please,' she said to Joe.

He took hold of the headboard and pulled it away from the wall.

'There!' Signora Romano cried, triumphant. 'Look!'

Drawn on the wallpaper were two little female figures holding hands in the style of the old Love is... cartoons. They were enclosed inside a heart. Beneath were the words: Solo la morte ci separerà.

'Only death will part us,' Joe translated quietly.

'That's how close we were,' Signora Romano said with satisfaction. 'That's what we meant to one another. That's how much Anna loved me.'

Something else was written underneath, in a fainter, more familiar hand: Anna's. I leaned down to see and read: E la morte non avrà più dominio. And death will have no dominion – the same words inscribed on the gravestone in the garden.

I accompanied Signora Romano back to the Mercedes and watched her turn the old taxi round and drive away, trailing petrol fumes. As the car rattled up the hill, a movement to one side caught my eye. It was Irma Arnone, standing in the shade of the olive trees, blatantly staring at me.

'You made me jump,' I told her rudely, hoping she'd get the gist, if not the exact meaning of my words.

I gave her a hard stare. She stared back and then spat to one side.

'Disgusting,' I muttered.

I went back into the villa's grounds, pulling the gates shut behind me. I didn't look to see if Irma was still watching. I'd had enough of older women for one day, enough of them turning up and spying on me, taking up my time.

In the kitchen, I picked the kittens out of the box. I held two on my lap and one to my cheek. The kitten's heartbeat was like a finger tapping a rhythm on the palm of my hand. All three were so fragile; so helpless. It seemed such a responsibility to hold so small and vulnerable a life.

35

That evening, Joe left me in my usual spot in the courtyard at the table beneath the vine, candles twinkling in their little pots, while he went down to the cellar and returned with a couple of dusty bottles.

It was cooler that night, the sky clear and black and it glittered with a million stars. The moon was late rising. Occasionally, a plane disturbed us, whining high above like a mosquito, scratching a scar across the night sky.

I'd changed into jeans and a sweater and was wrapped in a blanket, curled up on a chair. I was imagining Daniel on my lap, his body relaxed against mine, one leg bent at the knee, the other dangling. His head, hot and sweaty, pressed against my ribcage, eyelids fluttering against the curves of his cheeks, his lips plump and soft, slightly open. My boy. My dream child. *Don't go*, I begged the ghost-child. *Don't leave me.* I held him closer.

I looked up as Joe returned to the table.

'My grandfather's wine,' he said.

He put one bottle on the table, tucked the other under his arm and picked at the wax that sealed the cork. He drew out the cork with a corkscrew. He sniffed the cork, then the mouth of the bottle, and poured a little wine into a glass. He held the glass close to the candle. The wine was a deep, ruby red colour and viscous, like blood.

'It looks okay,' he said.

He took a sip, then another, then passed the glass to me.

The wine was smooth, its flavour deep. It tasted of the past, of old sunshine and the hands that picked the grapes, the press that crushed them, the people who made the wine; their expertise.

'It's good,' I said, with a nod to the wine glass.

Joe filled a second glass for himself, then he sat down, huddled into his jacket, cradling the glass in his hands.

'I never knew about that picture scratched on the bedroom wall,' he said.

My shoulders tensed, only slightly, at this reminder of Anna's existence.

'I'm surprised you don't remember Matilde Romano,' I said. 'She's quite distinctive.'

'You know me,' Joe said, 'observation isn't my strong point.'

He swirled the wine around his glass. It coated the sides; such a deep red, it was almost black.

Joe and I were silent for a long while, then we both started to speak at once, then we both stopped, embarrassed.

'You go first,' I said.

'Okay,' said Joe. 'It's just... well. I've been thinking.'

'About the villa?' I asked. Hope fluttered in my heart.

'Yeah. The thing is, Edie, no bank would give us a mortgage, not in the state the villa's in. So if, theoretically, we did decide not to sell, how would we afford the renovations?' He stared into the wine glass and answered his own question. 'There's the car, I suppose, although that wouldn't nearly cover it.'

'Don't get rid of the car,' I said. 'It meant so much to Daniel.'

Joe flinched at the mention of our son's name.

'It's all we have,' he said.

'Let me show you something.'

I reached for my phone, lying on the table, and flicked through saved images until I found the screengrab from the auction house catalogue. I passed the phone to Joe. He stared at the Reni Annunziata and read the description and price. I saw his eyes widen.

'Bloody hell,' he murmured. 'Half a million euros!'

'There must be places we still haven't looked for the Madonna,' I said. 'It can't have vanished into thin air.'

'I'm beginning to think it must have been stolen,' Joe said.

'Let's look again, tomorrow. Perhaps we've overlooked something.'

'I don't think we have. I'm going to go to the police,' Joe said. 'I'll report the painting missing. At least, then, if it does turn up at some auction house somewhere, we've got a chance of getting it back.'

It was probably something to do with the old wine I'd drunk, but during the night I dreamed I was in the London flat again. This time, I was tucking Daniel into bed, covering over a little foot sticking out from the elasticated cuff of a pyjama leg, when I heard him crying somewhere else. I turned, and when I looked back again, he was gone from the bed. In my dream, I ran down the narrow stairs of that old house, the stairwell that always smelled of beeswax, and out of the front door, following Daniel's cries through the rain until at last I saw him standing at the edge of a shaft dug deep into the ground, the walls of the shaft strengthened with wire mesh and bolts. Daniel was looking down into the pit. I knew I must not panic. If Daniel heard panic in my voice, if he thought I was angry with him, if he lost concentration even for a second, then he would fall.

'Daniel, come here, sweetheart, come to Mummy,' I called, in my dream. I held out my arms. Daniel turned and looked at me, rain streaming down his face, his hair plastered to his skull. His expression was cautious; he wasn't sure if he was in trouble. He was so close. If I could only reach him, if I could touch him, take hold of the sleeve of his pyjamas. 'It's okay,' I said, 'Mummy's not cross; come here, Daniel.' I crouched, so my eyes were level with his, blinking away raindrops, 'Come to Mummy!' He came. I enclosed him in my arms. I felt the weight of him; I smelled the rain on his hair. He put his arms around my neck and his heart bumped against mine.

As I straightened, his legs wrapped around my waist and he pressed his head into my shoulder so I could feel the warm ferocity of his breath. My arms encircled him and I breathed in the smell of the skin of his neck and I thought: *Thank God, I've got you, it's okay, you're safe, you're not going to fall.*

But then I breathed again and my arms were empty and I was there at the building site, rain falling down, lashing down at an angle, puddles of red mud, and the shaft was ahead of me, the world tilting to show me, rain collecting at its base; rain puddling around the little body of—

'Edie, Edie! Wake up! Wake up!'

'Daniel!'

'No, it's me, Edie, it's Joe!'

'Joe?'

I sat up, panting, gasping for breath. I couldn't see Joe in the darkness of the room, only the negative shape of him; a shadow against the glow of starlight from the window; the moon now risen, a slender, tilted smile drawn onto the sky.

Joe was sitting on the bed beside me. I guessed he must have been shaking me to wake me, although he wasn't touching me now.

I pushed the hair back off my face.

'Sorry,' I whispered. 'I'm sorry I disturbed you.'

'It's okay,' Joe said.

'I dreamed... I... I dreamed of...'

'I get dreams like that too,' Joe said.

We sat together, side by side, staring at the moonlight on the floorboards. Then Joe reached across the inches that divided us and gently took hold of my hand, curling his fingers around mine.

36

The next morning, Joe and I were gentle with one another, trying to be considerate of the other's feelings.

Joe made coffee and passed a cup to me and I cut bread and unwrapped cheese and sliced tomatoes and laid them out on the table for breakfast. We sat on opposite sides of the table and drank our coffee and ate. We didn't talk, but we were comfortable.

When he had finished eating, Joe poured more coffee into each of our cups, then he sat down again in the same place, his hands on the tabletop, palms down. There was a tiny crescent-moon of dirt at the top of each of his fingernails; the skin of his arms was tanned a deep brown.

'There's nothing to be lost,' he said at last, 'in finding out how much it would cost to renovate the villa.'

'No,' I agreed, 'nothing to be lost at all.'

Signora Romano's face, her shocked expression when we told her we weren't ready to sell, jumped into my mind, the things she'd said about her father. Would it really be the end of her world if we didn't sell the villa to her? Surely not. She could always find somewhere else. It wasn't as if there was any shortage of homes for sale in Sicily.

Joe did a little drumroll with his fingertips.

There was a silence. We sipped our coffee.

I took a deep breath. Then I said: 'We wouldn't have to change much, just bring it back to how it used to be.' I moved my hand across the table until the tips of my fingers were almost, but not quite, touching his. 'We could make a list of what needs doing, all the separate work, and price it individually. Is that what you had in mind?'

Joe curled his fingers into his palms, taking them away from mine. 'That's what I was thinking,' he said, 'yes.'

'We could make a start now, this morning!'

'I was planning to drive into Ragusa this morning to report the painting missing.'

I withdrew my hand. 'Okay,' I said, 'yes, of course, you said. You go. I can make a start on the list while you're gone. That's a better use of our time.'

I smiled as if that was the outcome I'd hoped for all along.

As soon as Joe had departed for the police station, I found a notebook and wrote: 'Inventory of Works' at the top of a clean page. I underlined the heading and divided it into two columns, one marked: 'Description', and the other marked: 'Cost'. Fitz and I had watched enough property programmes on TV for me to know roughly what was required.

I made a list and beside each item, I wrote an approximate cost, then I added up the numbers. Realistically, we were heading towards six figures' worth of euros, and that was before we even thought about decorating or buying new furniture. For it to be remotely possible, we'd have to cut every corner and do as much work as we could ourselves.

I decided to make a start straight away. I scanned the list of works. Something that I could easily do now, without requiring any extra tools or materials, would be to make a start on demolishing the derelict swimming pool.

I changed into an old T-shirt, shorts and trainers, took the broom and a pail and climbed down the tiled steps in the shallow end in the smaller of the two interlocking circles that formed the pool. At the bottom, I tugged at the crumpled tarpaulin that covered the old drain. It was dreadfully heavy and had almost fossilised, folded and creased, stiff as rock. With persistence, I eventually managed to heave it up the steps, onto the lawn.

After that, I swept up the broken tiles, leaves, and other rubbish at the bottom of the pool and heaped the detritus on the tarpaulin. It was hot, dirty work, but it felt good to be doing something positive. The sun burned down on my back and shoulders. There was plenty of space for a new pool; a more natural pool. We could have a pebble beach leading into a shallow, paddling area for children and, beyond, a deeper pool for swimming. In the centre could be an island where we could grow water plants and encourage wildlife. Perhaps there was some way we could link the pool to the villa, so rain and flood water from the hills could be collected and recycled. Nothing need be wasted.

The more I planned, the more I liked the idea and the more I enjoyed the work. I was still in the pit of the old pool when Joe returned. He came to find me, a bottle of water in his hand.

'Wow,' he said, looking down.

I wiped my face. 'I'm making a start.'

'I can see.'

He tossed the bottle to me. I caught it and drank.

He crouched at the edge of the pool.

I shielded my eyes with my hand and squinted at him. 'What did the police say?'

'They're going to send someone over. They need a picture of the painting. They want to see where it used to hang, get some more details, that kind of thing.'

'They're not going to look for fingerprints are they, after all this time?' I asked.

He reached for the bottle and I passed it back to him. 'I doubt it. I think it's more to check we're not plotting an insurance scam. I found out something interesting though.'

'Oh, yes?'

'Vito Barsi has previous convictions for burglary.'

'Who told you?'

'Fredi's sister works at the commissariato. We went for coffee. Apparently he's been up before the court several times. He used to scout out the homes of wealthy people who called him in to do odd jobs and then return later to steal whatever he could get his hands on.'

Joe raised the water bottle to his lips and drank, a hint of satisfaction in his eyes.

I didn't argue with him, but I knew Vito Barsi hadn't stolen our painting. If he had, he wouldn't still be driving round in a clapped-out old truck; he wouldn't be unblocking drains for a living; and poor Francesco wouldn't be working all the hours God sent serving pizza to the hungry people of Porta Sarina. If Vito Barsi had come into a great deal of money, I was 100 per cent certain, he would be out spending it as if it was water.

37

I was cooking pasta when I heard the rapping at the kitchen window behind me. It was Francesco. My heart gave a leap of pleasure. I propped the spoon against the rim of the pan and opened the door wide.

'Francesco, how good to see you! Is Vito with you?'

'No, I cycled.' He indicated an old bike leant against the villa wall, with a plastic sign that said: 'Pizzeria Vito' attached to its parcel rack. He was wearing a backpack hooked over his shoulders. 'Mama told me Joe needs help with his car.'

'Yes,' I said, 'he needs all the help he can get.'

Francesco swapped his weight from foot to foot and tugged at an earlobe. 'I might be some use then. I know a lot about cars.'

'Then, Francesco, you're exactly who we need. You couldn't have come at a better time.' Behind me, the spoon rattled against the pan. 'Are you hungry?'

'A little.'

'Good. Why don't you go outside and find Joe, and after lunch, the two of you can get to work.'

* * *

After they'd eaten, Francesco and Joe disappeared off into the old stables.

Meanwhile, I had to abandon my work on the swimming pool for a more pressing task. At Joe's request, I passed the afternoon looking through old photograph albums in search of an image showing the *Madonna del Mare* in situ that we could give to the police. It was an interesting and pleasant task and soon I was engrossed in old photographs of the DeLuca family. I turned thick card pages to see century old pictures of family groups taken in the villa gardens; be-whiskered men and short, corseted women, posing with gaggles of children, all beautifully dressed in stockings and pinafores and pantaloons, and later on, smaller, but more relaxed groups, the women now in sunhats and looser fitting dresses, the men without jackets, braces pinning their shirts to their chests, the children barefoot, no longer standing to attention but posing with toys and animals. Almost all the pictures had been taken outside.

As the chronicles of the family moved forward, I found photographs of Anna's mother at various stages of pregnancy; it was painful to think of how much grief she must have endured each time she lost a child. But eventually there were pictures of a live baby and then a little girl, Anna. There she was, unmistakably Joe's mother, her hair as dark as her mother's, her skin as dark as her father's, some lucky combination of genes giving her the most attractive features of them both. In one of the pictures, Anna, aged five or six, was posing beside a swimming pool in the villa garden – not the same pool that was there now, but an older, smaller, rectangular version. The photograph was black and white, and she was grinning broadly, several of her milk teeth missing. Her hair was cut short and everything about her, from her skinny chest to her out-turned feet, the saggy swimsuit, her thin little legs and her arms held above her head as if she were about to dive, reminded me of Daniel. The resemblance was so strong, it made the hairs on my arms stand on end.

Neither Joe nor I as children had looked as much like Daniel as Anna did. They could have been twins, if it weren't for the fifty years that separated them. Had Anna realised, I wondered, how alike they were? When she looked at Daniel, did she see herself? Did she wonder where her life had gone off track? How had she felt when we lost him, when she lost him, when it was all her fault?

I kept going and found more pictures of Anna as she grew older, and then another character joined the cast at the villa; the young Matilde Romano. For several years, Anna and Matilde were the only children to regularly appear in the pictures, but later, probably around the time of Matilde's mother's death, a third girl started to appear. She was taller than Anna and Matilde and she was not conventionally beautiful, but there was something compelling about her; she wasn't looking directly at the camera in any of the images, but always slightly beyond, as if her thoughts had already moved onto something else; her chin was raised in a haughty, playful manner, one hand often on her hip. The face of the third girl made me smile. She looked as if she would be fun. She looked like a rebel.

I was certain they were the same three girls from the picture on the memorial wall, the picture where the face of the third girl had been scratched out.

I pulled a photograph from the album and turned it over. Written on the back were the names Anna, Matilde & Gina. Here was a picture of them in their swimsuits, by the pool; the old, rectangular pool, Anna posing like a film star in a pair of her mother's sunglasses, while the taller girl crouched, pretending to take a picture of her. Matilde was hanging back, looking at someone off camera.

Here was another image of the three girls, dressed up, standing behind the puppet theatre we'd found in the cellar. Each girl was holding the handles of a puppet. Anna had a female marionette, similar to the one Matilde had given me, the taller girl, Gina, had a knight – perhaps the same puppet we'd found on the floor of the cave beyond the cellar – and Matilde had some kind of animal, a wolf perhaps, or a bear. It was a charming picture. I removed that, and a couple of other pictures, to give to Matilde when we next saw her – I thought it would be a kind gesture and one she might appreciate. It might make up, in part, for us letting her down over the villa.

Another picture caught my eye. The teenage Anna was standing beside Gina and with them was a young man; a grinning, self-confident Sicilian, older than the girls, wearing an open-necked shirt and holding a cigarette between two fingers. He was wearing a hat that shadowed his eyes, but he was desperately good-looking and the pose, the physical confidence, showed that he knew it.

Who was that? I wondered.

Here was a whole chapter of Anna's life about which I knew nothing. What had happened in the months and years after this picture was taken to bring her away from Italy to England? What was it that had gone so wrong that she'd left her family and friends and this beautiful Sicilian man behind?

The last album I investigated included pictures of the new, bigger swimming pool with its overlapping circles, under construction and later, pictures of Cece and Joe, as children, playing in it. At last, I found what I'd been looking for: a close-up of the *Madonna del Mare*, that, according to the writing on the back (I translated with the dictionary), had been taken after its last professional clean, 'a process made necessary by an accumulation of tar deposited by decades of cigarette smoke and other dirt' on the surface of the image.

For the first time, I looked into the face of the villa's Madonna. It wasn't a great photograph, the colours were faded, and I couldn't make out any of the details, but I could see enough to make me realise that I would like to see the real picture very much indeed.

38

As the afternoon drew to its close, I went out into the heat, to the old stables, where I found Francesco and Joe working companionably together, their heads hidden inside the Alfa Romeo's open bonnet. Francesco had set up his phone on the dusty window-ledge and it was playing music.

I watched for a moment, enjoying seeing the two of them together, then I felt a little tug, Daniel, reminding me that he was present.

I called 'Ciao!' to let them know I was there and their two heads popped up; Francesco's dark hair silvered by cobwebs, Joe's silver hair stained dark in places by oil. Joe had given Francesco an old T-shirt to wear to protect his clothes. In the gloom of the stable, broken as it was by shafts of strong sunlight, I couldn't tell who was enjoying himself more.

* * *

After Francesco had left, cycling his bike back to Porta Sarina, Joe and I returned to the stables. While Joe tidied up, I walked round to the caretaker's cottage, squeezing between the saplings and creepers. It was an attractive, stone building with a concreted yard. A child's tricycle, the plastic sun-bleached and the metal rusted, lay on its side amongst the weeds pushing through the cracks.

At the boundary of the yard was a drystone wall. On the other side of that wall, the villa's perimeter wall ended and beyond was a drop into the open sea. The rocky shelf, at this point, was too high and wide for boats to come close to the headland, or for swimming to be safe. Leading up to the shelf was a grassy area

'This was where the Ganzarias kept chickens and goats,' Joe said, coming up behind me.

'We could do that,' I said.

'Chickens and goats?'

'Why not? And a donkey maybe, for the children to ride.'

Joe leaned down to pick up an old fence post that had rotted at its base. He stood it upright, balancing it beneath the flat of his hand. It trailed a tail of rusting wire.

'We could be self-sufficient,' he said. 'We could grow all our own food. Collect our own water. Recycle everything.'

'We could do holidays for kids.'

'Maybe. We could be somewhere people came to...'

'To what?' I asked.

'To heal,' Joe said. 'A place where people could come to heal.'

* * *

We went to the decking to watch the sun go down. We were still there as the stars began to show themselves, shyly at first, in ones and twos, and then in greater numbers.

For the past ten years, I hadn't been able to look at a night sky without thinking of Daniel, without feeling, with one heartbeat, love, and with the next, pain. That night, the love was purer and the pain was clearer because it was no longer obscured by the wall of anger and bitterness I'd hidden behind. That night, I realised, the barrier that surrounded my wounded heart was coming down and it was something to do with the villa; with this place.

We sat together, silent. Joe beside me but not touching me.

'I'm sorry,' I said at last. 'I'm sorry for the things I said to you, Joe. I'm sorry I was so cruel. Nothing that happened was your fault.'

I took a breath. I felt lighter for saying those words because although I hadn't acknowledged them before, they were true.

Joe rested his wrists on his knees. He gazed out to sea.

'I'm sorry too,' he said. 'I'm sorry I was so weak.'

'Loving someone isn't weakness.'

'Falling apart is.'

'No, Joe,' I said, 'no, it's not.'

I longed to rest my head on his shoulder. I longed to reach out for his hand, but I didn't dare. I was afraid he would reject me. This was the closest we'd been in ten years. I wished I could tell him that, in all that time, I hadn't wanted to be close to anyone else, but I couldn't speak. I was afraid of jeopardising the tentative peace that had come between us, fragile as the skin of a bubble.

The night air cooled and I began to shiver. Joe held out his hand and helped me to my feet. I wrapped my blanket around me like a nomad and we walked, side by side, back towards the villa. We were crossing the lawn when I felt something touch my shoulder and I jumped, but when I looked to see what it was, it was Joe's arm. He had put his arm around me. It was a kind of miracle.

39

As we walked, we talked about the future. We were pragmatic. We were too old for pipe dreams, too experienced to imagine that a ramshackle old building on a remote headland could ever play out as a romantic fantasy. We'd need help if we were to make something of our villa, but Joe had his Sicilian friends and they knew people, good people. We'd need a plan, but between us we could come up with something workable: Joe could design the gardens and I could work on the house. We'd need money. If we had the *Madonna del Mare* that wouldn't be a problem, but without her we'd need to work as quickly as we could and start generating income as soon as possible to fund the future work.

Most of all, we'd need faith in one another. This was always going to be our biggest hurdle. I'd let Joe down before. I'd walked away from him when he needed me most and it had taken me all this time to understand what I'd done to him. I still didn't know how – or if – I could convince him that I wouldn't let him down again.

There was some cold, leftover pasta, in the bowl on the kitchen table, but Joe said he was tired of pasta. Instead, he peeled potatoes while a big pot of salted water boiled on the stove. I made a salad and drank some wine. For the first time since our reunion, we moved about one another as we used to move in the tiny kitchen of our London flat. We moved like dancers, each knowing where the other was, predicting one another's gestures and requirements, passing knives and colanders between us. It was comfortable to be back in the company of someone who knew me so well. It was so straightforward and so nice. I wished we hadn't stayed apart so long; I wished I'd had the sense to reach out to Joe before; wished I'd tried to build bridges. Now it was so easy, I struggled to remember why it had seemed so difficult before.

There had been opportunities for Joe and I to meet in the past decade. Anna wrote letters that I tore into pieces and threw away unopened and unread. Many times, I had been invited, via Martha, to DeLuca family events, but I'd always found reasons not to go. The Christmas and birthday cards Anna sent to me were dropped straight into the recycling bin. Every chance I'd had to make things better, I'd rejected. And now it felt as if each of those rejections had been a way of hurting myself when, instead, I should have been looking for ways to heal.

* * *

Joe and I ate our meal and talked long into the night. When we were halfway through our third bottle of wine, I put my feet on Joe's lap and he massaged my left ankle. I watched him in the candlelight. His face was so dear to me, so familiar.

Joe must have felt my gaze on him because he looked over and his eyes found mine and we stopped speaking, we looked at one another. He reached for my hand and I gave it to him and our fingers twined. He drew me to him and we kissed. I was drunk, but not too drunk to recognise the rush of emotion when emotion had been so long suppressed; the longing for Joe, the pull towards him. The desire was as strong as it had been when we were young. The love was there, just as it had been the day that Daniel was born, when neither of us could quite believe that two hopeless cases like us could have produced a child as perfect as he. The affection was there too; the friendship. We were drawn together and I had no wish to resist.

After a while he took my hand and led me upstairs. We went up to my bedroom and Joe lay me down on the bed. It had been ten years, but our bodies hadn't forgotten what they knew about one another. Our arms, our legs, our heads, our tongues, our hands, they remembered what to do and where to go. So what that our bodies were older and less resilient than they had been; we were still the same people underneath. We were still us and we knew how to make one another happy.

It was as if we had never been apart.

Joe did not cry out, like he used to, when he came. He was quiet. He rested for a moment above me until I had to move, because he was heavier than he had been and his weight was pressing down on me.

'Sorry,' he said.

'No, I'm sorry,' I said as I squeezed out from underneath him. I wasn't as lithe as I used to be either. I wondered if he noticed the difference, the softness around the hips and breasts, the boniness of the shoulders, the loosening skin at my neck. Time had brought small changes to both of us, changes we wouldn't have noticed if we'd stayed together but which now were new territory. It was as if the comfort of being with a man I knew very well had been combined with the mystery of being with one I hardly knew at all.

Once we were settled, side by side but with our lower legs tangled companionably together and his arm around my shoulder, Joe smoothed the hair from my face and I felt a sudden shyness.

I tried to turn my ageing face from the moonlight, but he held it still.

'Let me look at you.'

I reached up my hand to cover my face; it was instinct – I had become used to hiding my face from anyone's gaze.

He said: 'No, let me see.' He looked at me for a moment, then he whispered, 'You're still as lovely as ever.'

'I was never lovely.'

'Oh, you were,' he replied, 'you always were.'

When he said those words, warmth spread through me. I remembered how I had loved this man when he was young. I remembered how good a man he was. I remembered how lucky I used to feel to lie in his arms at night. I remembered all the good things I'd spent so long trying not to remember.

I'd been so committed to anger and grief. How much time I'd wasted! What a fool I'd been!

'Are you okay?' Joe whispered, looking down on me with such tenderness.

'Yes.'

'Really?'

'Yes!'

'You're happy?'

'I'm happy. Are you?'

'If you're happy, then so am I.'

We settled again and lay together, quietly. The windows were open and a breeze drifted over us. I did not want to spoil the moment, and I didn't say anything to Joe, but I had the strongest sensation that we weren't alone in the villa. Its ghosts moved about us still, but they did not disturb us. That night, they let us be.

40

It was morning and Joe was gone from my bed. I went onto the landing, padded to the central arched window, pushed it open and stepped onto the balcony. A raptor soared in the sky above. The sky was white, the sea was choppy. It wasn't cold by Northern European standards, but it was the first time I'd felt cool in Sicily during the day.

I went back into the bedroom; the sheets on Joe's side of the bed were rumpled and piled together. Above me, on the other side of the ceiling, something scampered. I tried not to think about whatever it was, pulled on a cardigan and went downstairs.

I felt the breeze rushing through the ground floor before I reached the kitchen and found the back door open. I looked outside, but there was no sign of Joe – although he had cleared the mess we'd left on the table the night before.

I pulled the cardigan tight around my shoulders, and went into the living room, where we'd put the kittens. A note on the settee beside their box said: 'We've had our breakfast'. I returned to the kitchen and put a pan on the hob to heat water for coffee. I leaned back against the counter and looked around. I'd had a go at cleaning the tiles and the paintwork, but everything was old and worn; the accumulated grime of the centuries caught in the exposed plaster and the cracks in the wood. We needed more supplies, proper, hardcore cleaning stuff.

I moved closer to the hob, where it was warmer. I laid out the cups for coffee. I yawned. I felt like myself. For the first time in ten years, I felt as if my life was where it was supposed to be. I was with Joe and our combined love for Daniel was as strong as ever and Anna was gone and we had the villa and everything was going to be okay.

Two detectives came that morning to investigate the disappearance of the *Madonna del Mare*, one male, one female.

I hovered while Joe showed them the alcove in the hall where the *Madonna del Mare* had always hung and then gave them the photograph I'd found and answered the questions they asked. After that, we all sat in the living room and drank coffee. I fidgeted, unable to follow the conversation, but turning my eyes to whomever was speaking.

When they were gone, Joe told me the officers believed whoever had taken the painting must have had a key. My grandmother's keys, or the housekeeper's set, must have been copied over the years. Keys would have been handed out to relatives, tradesmen and so on. Trying to track down everyone who ever had one would be impossible, that line of enquiry simply wasn't feasible.

'But if Gabriele Arnone used to come in to do odd jobs, he might have had a key,' Joe said, 'and he might have passed the key on to Vito Barsi.'

'Or Gabriele might have come into the villa himself,' I said.

'Maybe.'

'We need to change the locks, Joe.'

'We'll make it a priority.'

'So, are the police going to question Vito?'

Joe said they weren't. Not yet. They had a dedicated squad for tracking down missing works of art and the *Madonna del Mare* would be added to the database of unaccounted for pieces. Auction houses and fine art salerooms would be notified to keep an eye out, but the main focus of the squad officers would be the dark web, where stolen paintings were sold to private collectors with more money than integrity. Once the painting was found – if it was found – then its provenance could be traced back to whoever it was who had taken it in the first place and he or she would be held accountable.

A great deal depended on the painting being recovered. Without it, I knew Joe and I would struggle to hold onto the villa, let alone restore it. I hoped the police would be successful, but even if they weren't, even if the *Madonna del Mare* never came home, it wouldn't stop Joe and me from doing our best. We would still be together.

41

While the police launched their search for the *Madonna del Mare*, Joe and I concentrated on the villa. One morning, when we were on our way back from the DIY hypermarket, Signora Romano called. I answered reluctantly and she asked what was happening about the villa and once again I felt waves of guilt about having raised her hopes for a sale. I suggested we meet to talk 'face-to-face' and she agreed that was exactly what we should do.

We offered to drive to her father's house, but instead she gave directions to a restaurant-bar close to the electricity station on the other side of the Porta Sarina marshes.

Joe knew it well, but it was a part of the far headland I hadn't been to before. To get there, we had to continue past the Intimissimi billboard and join the road that led down to the industrial area entirely hidden from the tourist part of Porta Sarina. The land was low, at sea level. A raised track led across the marshland to the electricity station. Stubby grasses and thistles grew out of the marshes and old mattresses and bags of litter had been fly-tipped; as if the area wasn't ugly enough already. We passed the putrefying body of a dead cat at the side of the road, black crows pulling at its flesh.

'You know the woman you said Gabriele Arnone murdered?' I asked Joe. 'You said she was found in the marshland. Was it here?'

'Somewhere round here.'

'Do you think it could have been Matilde Romano's mother?'

'Oh Jesus! Yes, of course! Must have been!'

'Do you think Matilde knows her mother was murdered?'

'Surely not. She was only a kid. They'd have told her some story.'

I recalled Signora Romano's bitterness when she spoke of her mother and the contempt with which she'd described her. I thought that maybe she did know but perhaps she thought her mother deserved her awful fate.

We drove on in silence, past the huge electricity station, and Joe pulled up in a car park separated from a wooden building by a boardwalk. A sign was erected at one end of the car park with pictures of the restaurant's dishes: Specialità Pesce.

'I can't believe there's a restaurant out here,' I said.

'I've heard the food's good. It serves the electricity workers and the guests staying with the nuns.'

'Nuns?'

'There's a little convent round the corner that takes in paying guests.'

We left the car at the side of the road and crossed the boardwalk. The restaurant was quirky, entirely made of wood, open to the elements save for mosquito nets. Most of the tables were occupied by workers in steel-toe-capped boots and hi-vis clothing, but Joe pointed out four nuns wearing coif, wimple and veil. We found a table, ordered Coca-Cola and gazed at the flatlands through the netting while we waited for Matilde Romano.

At last we spotted her coming through the restaurant's saloon doors. She looked around the restaurant where the manual workers were eating octopus and the four nuns were tucking into tiramisu. She didn't spot us until I stood and raised my hand.

'Oh, there you are!'

She trotted across to our table, taking little mousy steps, her handbag dangling from her wrist. She seemed nervous. When one of the workmen laughed loudly, she jumped and nudged the table, slopping my drink over the rim of the glass. I patted the spilled liquid with paper napkins while she apologised, and when all was calm, Joe asked: 'Can I buy you a drink? Something to eat?'

'I think I'd like a small brandy,' she replied.

While Joe went to the bar, I fished in my handbag, took out the envelope containing the photographs. 'I've a surprise for you, Signora Romano. Look what I found.' I passed the envelope to her. She opened it and shook out the photographs, the pictures of the three young friends: Anna, Matilde and Gina. She spread the pictures on the table. I watched her closely, anticipating delight.

As she recognised the subjects of the photographs, her hand went to her mouth, her fingers touched her lips and the colour drained from her face.

'They're such lovely pictures of you all,' I said gently.

Her mouth open and closed.

'I expect you haven't seen these for a long time. Do you remember when they were taken?'

'I... I...'

'This is a good one, this one here, you're closer to the camera. You're all wearing lipstick. It must have been some kind of celebration. And this one... with the puppet theatre, it's so sweet how you're standing together. Look, Anna's arm is over your shoulder, and Gina...'

She pushed the pictures away.

'I can't look at those,' she said, 'not with Anna only just gone and barely cold in her grave. I can't bear to see her face.'

'Oh!'

'I loved her so much! We were so close and you're putting pictures of her in front of me without so much as a warning! Don't you know how they make me feel? How they break my heart? I don't know how you can be so thoughtless! So unkind!'

'I'm sorry, Signora Romano, I didn't mean to upset you!' I gathered the pictures up and put them back in the envelope. 'I'm really, truly sorry. I thought you'd like to see the photographs. Never mind. Perhaps you can take them with you, look at them later, on your own.'

'I don't want them!'

'Are you sure? Not even one? The puppet theatre... Wouldn't you like to show that to your father?'

She gave an appalled gasp and pushed the pictures further away. I gathered them up.

Joe returned with her drink. He raised a questioning eyebrow and I made a face to signify that I didn't know why Signora Romano was so upset.

She took the brandy and sipped, making an effort to compose herself. I lay my hand gently over hers. It was so tiny, so thin, skin and bones and veins. It trembled beneath mine.

Joe and I exchanged glances.

I can't! I mouthed.

You have to, Joe replied silently.

I cleared my throat, dreading saying the words out loud.

'We do have some other news for you, Signora.'

'The villa?'

'Yes.'

'At last! Are you ready to sell? Do you have a price for me? I have my chequebook with me. I can give you a deposit today.'

'No,' I said. 'We don't have a price. Actually, we wanted you to be the first person to know that we've made up our minds not to sell. We're keeping the villa.'

She was pale already, now her skin drained to a deathlike pallor.

'We weren't sure before, but now we are,' I continued. 'I'm sorry, I know this will be a disappointment to you, but we wanted to let you know as soon as possible.'

'You're going to live there?' she asked, horror on her face.

'Yes.' Joe smiled. 'We're planning to turn the villa into a retreat.'

'But it's all in a state...'

'We're going to fix it.'

'That's crazy,' she said. 'There are only two of you... the work that needs doing... the expense!'

'There is a lot of work, but we're optimists,' said Joe.

'And we can do most of it ourselves,' I added.

'Edie's already made a start on the pool.'

'And, of course, you'll always be welcome at the villa,' I said, 'whenever you want to visit.'

Joe gave me a ferocious look.

'Always,' I said, desperate to appease her.

'You lied to me,' Signora Romano said.

'I didn't mean to lie, Signora. When we first spoke, I meant what I said and—'

She banged her fists on the table and leaned towards me, her eyes sparking with anger. 'You lied. You told me you were selling the villa and I put things in motion, things I can't stop!' Flecks of spit tapped the skin of my face.

'I'm sorry.'

'Sorry isn't good enough.' She waved her arms around dramatically. 'I've told father... I've started packing up the house, throwing things out.'

Joe said: 'Signora, surely you understand...'

She pushed back her chair and stood up. 'You lied. You misled me.'

'Signora Romano...' I said. 'We can't let you go like this.'

'Let me get you another brandy,' Joe suggested.

'No,' she said. 'No.'

I reached for her arm. 'Signora, please!'

'Get off me!' she cried, so loudly that the electricity workers turned to look at us. 'Get off! Leave me alone!'

She picked up her handbag and went, her heels tapping on the restaurant floor. She pushed through the saloon doors so violently they swung madly behind her. She'd hardly touched the brandy.

The envelope that contained the photographs still lay face down on the table.

42

'Well, that went well,' said Joe.

'I feel awful... what she said about her father... About packing up the house...'

'That's not your fault.'

'And the photographs really upset her, Joe.'

'You couldn't have predicted she'd react like that. Once she calms down, she'll see that it's not the end of the world.'

We ordered lunch and it was good, so some time passed before we left the restaurant. I felt as if a weight had been lifted from my shoulders now we'd made our plans clear to Signora Romano. Yes, her reaction had been even worse than expected but as Joe said, we needed to give her time. I'd let the dust settle then go to see her, make sure she was all right.

Joe and I came out of the restaurant laughing and talking, our arms linked, but our words died on our lips when we saw what had happened to the Fiat. Joe ran to it and I followed, dread like a knot inside me.

The back window was broken, little pieces of shattered glass lay inside and outside the car; a thick dent had been scoured into the metalwork along the passenger side, mud had been smeared on the boot; two letters scratched into the mud: VF.

'What does that mean?' I asked.

'It's short for "vaffanculo",' Joe said dourly. 'Italian for "fuck off".'

'Who would have done this?' I asked. 'Who?' I recalled Signora Romano storming out of the restaurant. 'You don't think she had anything to do with it?'

'No,' said Joe, 'it will have been kids.'

He said this in the same tone he'd used when trying to reassure me about the dead cat. He didn't believe it was kids any more than I did. I found myself looking around, looking to see if anyone was watching us. This didn't feel random. It felt as if we were being targeted and that meant somebody was following us; someone was aware of everything we were doing.

'What if it was the same person who killed the cat?' I asked. 'What if someone is trying to make us go away?'

Joe shook his head. 'We don't know that anybody killed the cat, Edie. And how could the two things possibly be connected? It's vandalism, no more than that. It's not the end of the world.'

It wasn't, but still, it was a horrible thing to happen.

We called the car hire company, who told us to take photographs of the damage and make a report to the police. We did. The following afternoon, a representative came to collect the damaged car and brought us a replacement, Fiat Two. He told us we should be more careful about where we left it. We would have to pay the excess. Another expense to add to our list.

* * *

Joe was in a bad mood for a couple of days after that. He spent some time bashing at the old concrete walls of the swimming pool with a sledgehammer. Then Liuni came and the two of them climbed into the attic, to make repairs to the feeder tank.

From the room below, where I was giving the kittens their milk, and taking pictures of them with my phone, I could hear the men's voices. I couldn't understand what they were saying because they were speaking Italian, but they were animated, united in anger about something.

When Liuni left, I suggested we went for a swim. Clouds had formed over the sea, obliterating the blue sky and the sun, but the weather was hotter than ever and humid. The air was full of tiny black flies. My skin felt slippery and dank and the joints in my bad leg were more painful than they'd been for weeks. We went to the decked area. Joe took off his boots and dived straight into the sea. He swam out towards the horizon, his arms chopping through the water, his head disappearing from time to time behind the bulge of a wave.

I changed into my swimsuit and then jumped into the water, hoping it would refresh me, but after the first delightful shock of cold, even the sea seemed viscous and gloopy. The darkening sky was reflected in the sullen water, the waves were black that day with none of the twinkle and spray that I'd come to love. I felt unaccountably nervous of whatever creatures moved beneath me – it was nothing more than anxiety about Joe's mood and a reaction to the changing texture of the sea, but I could not bear it and, after ten minutes or so, swam to the steps and pulled myself out onto the decking. I sat on the towel, holding my knees and, moments later, Joe's head appeared at the top of the steps. He leaned down and shook his head, spraying water like a dog, then came to sit beside me.

'We have to go back to the pizzeria tonight,' he said.

'Why?'

'Something Liuni told me.'

'Vito?'

'Yep. I'm going to have a word with him.'

'When I tried to have a word with him, you said it would make things worse for Valentina and Francesco.'

'Yes, but a) he was drunk at the time, and b) we didn't know we were staying then. If we'd caused trouble for Valentina, she'd have paid for it after we left. I want Vito to know that from now on if he touches Valentina or Francesco, he's going to have to answer to me. Every time. Every single time. I want him to know that he can't behave like he's been behaving; that it's not acceptable. That none of us likes it.'

'Joe...'

'I'm not going to cause any trouble. I'm only going to talk. I won't be combative, I'll be tactful.'

I stroked his damp hair. He reached for my hand, held it to his lips and kissed it.

'I might go and have a shower then,' I said, 'seeing as we're going out.'

'Okay.'

I pushed myself up to my feet, shook out my towel and tied it round my chest and turned to make my way back up the decking and suddenly felt a blunt, deep pain in my heel. 'Ow!' I cried, hopping, grabbing my foot. 'Oh God, what's that?'

'It's a hornet!' Joe took my foot, removed the insect and flicked it away. 'Oh Edie, that's going to hurt!'

He gathered me up and I put my arm around his neck. The sting was a needle of pain from my foot to my brain. I put my face against Joe's shoulder.

'It's okay,' said Joe. 'Lean on me.'

Together we shuffled back to the villa. Every time my heart beat, it pumped a new throb of pain.

In the kitchen, Joe helped me into a chair and lifted my ankle gently onto another, rested it on a cushion. He poured some vinegar onto a cloth and held it against the sting, his hand holding my foot tenderly, as if it was an injured bird.

'You've gone very pale,' he said.

My heartbeat had slowed, my breathing was shallow. I was

floating. The room was beginning to tilt, first one way, then the other.

'I feel like flour being sifted through a sieve,' I said.

'What?'

'Like flour being sifted…' I demonstrated the gentle shaking of a sieve.

'Edie?'

'I think I'm going to faint.'

'No, you're not.'

He pressed my head down and held me in that position until the dizziness eased. After that, he had me swallow an antihistamine tablet and a couple of co-codamol. He laid me like a princess on one of the grand settees in the living room, on the sunshine yellow, embroidered, shot-silk upholstery with a pillow beneath my head. I lay, draped, until the antihistamine kicked in and my breathing came back and the world stopped moving.

'Do you want to go upstairs?' Joe asked.

'No,' I said. 'I want to stay here.' I wanted to spend more time in the company of the elegant ghosts that inhabited this beautiful room. The sun was setting and the colours were softening and I felt very calm.

'I think we might have some rain tonight,' Joe said. 'I'd better get going.'

'Joe…'

'I have to go, Edie. I can't sit here thinking about what's going on over there. I promise I won't be long. An hour and a half tops. You'll be okay here.'

'Yes,' I said. 'I'll be fine.'

* * *

The painkillers made me sleepy. After Joe left, I closed my eyes and listened to the villa. I heard the wind soughing around the roof and I heard the calls of the house martins who lived in the eaves. Some conflagration of the weather and the woodwork made sounds that were very like whispers, but try as I might I couldn't pick out any words. Daniel came and curled up next to me and I put my arm around him and drifted off to sleep.

By the time I next opened my eyes, dusk had fallen and the room was in darkness. Daniel was gone. A good moon lit the garden silvery blue for a few moments, but then the clouds blew across the bright face of the moon and the light was muted.

Without putting weight on my sore foot, I limped to the kitchen and lit a couple of candles in case the lights went out. I hobbled around the ground floor, double-checking the windows were closed. I returned to the kitchen, wrapped myself in a blanket and picked up my book. I tried to read, but the rain had started to fall and the sound of the drops pattering against the windows made me jumpy. I poured a glass of wine and curled up in the old basket chair, listening to the rain. In all its years, the villa must have withstood far more severe weather than this and it hadn't fallen down yet. I sat in the chair and I worried about thunder claps making me jump and wondered if the lights would go off. I listened to sounds that seemed like whispers and others that resembled footsteps. I tried not to feel lonely; I tried not to feel afraid; I tried not to dwell on my isolation, but I was lonely and scared. I was desperate for Joe to return.

43

The rain was persistent. It drenched the two headlands on either side of the Porta Sarina bay, it pattered against the windows and the walls and the roof tiles of the Villa della Madonna del Mare. It came through the holes in the roof and dripped onto the floorboards and furniture. It seeped into the cavities between the floors and soaked into the old plaster walls. It was pervasive. It invaded my sleep; I heard the rain and it merged with a memory and it became a nightmare.

In the dream, Joe and I were standing in the foyer of a smart London department store. I was holding a bag in my hand. The bag contained a dress that I'd bought to wear at a prize giving ceremony for innovators in education; one of my colleagues had been shortlisted for an award. People were all around us, buttoning up their coats, fastening their hoods, opening umbrellas; we could see through the windows how the rain was bucketing down onto Oxford Street. The bus wheels were sending great showers of spray up over the legs of the people hurrying along the pavements.

Joe and I pulled up our hoods and went through the sliding doors, out of the dry, perfumed warmth of the store. The rain blew up at us, cold water mixed with car exhaust fumes; fans churning out fried meat smells from the backs of restaurants. Music.

I caught my finger in the catch when I opened the umbrella; pinched the skin. I sucked the blood as we walked, side by side, away from the main road. Wet pavements. People gazing blankly from the foggy upstairs windows of buses. We skipped the underground journey in the way that often happens in dreams and found ourselves in the neighbourhood where Anna lived. Snapshots: Joe reaching up to grab the overhanging branch of a lime tree and shaking it to spill the rain collected in its leaves. Me saying it wasn't funny. Joe laughing, pulling me to him and me telling him to get off, also laughing. A dog shaking itself. A woman running into the well of a block of flats, holding a folded newspaper above her head. A child stamping triumphantly in a puddle. Turning into Anna's road, the houses built of yellow and black London stock brick. Me shaking out the umbrella in the garden. Dusk falling too fast, making me giddy. Anna's living room and hall lights on and the front door open. A stain on the carpet where the rain had blown in. A large glass of wine left on the small table beneath the mirror just inside the hallway. Joe turning to me.

'Why is the front door open?'

'Why are the lights on?'

'Where's Anna?'

'Where's Daniel?'

* * *

I woke. I was in the kitchen of the Villa della Madonna del Mare, my neck was stiff and the sole of my foot was pulsing with pain.

The lights were out and the candles had burned low, but they still flickered. The rain had stopped.

Joe wasn't back. He would have woken me if he'd come inside.

Where was he? Had something terrible happened to him while I was sleeping?

I took the candle, picked up the phone and hobbled to the door. My flip-flops were tumbled with Joe's on the mat. I put them on and went outside, stepping into a puddle. I walked out towards the path and I saw the door at the bottom of the cellar steps was open and a faint light was glowing inside.

I limped down the steps and looked cautiously around the door. The light was coming from the wine cellar. I heard a chink of glass and a snatch of music: Nick Cave. Joe adored Nick Cave. I crept forward until I reached the vaulted archway and looked through. Joe was sitting on the floor with his back against the wall. He was listening to the song on his phone and that was the source of the pale blue light. He had a wine bottle in his hand and another lay empty on the floor beside him. Something alerted him to my presence. Slowly, he looked up at me and raised the bottle. The flesh around his left eye was so swollen that the eye was barely a slit. I had to work hard not to let the shock I felt show itself on my face. It wasn't only Joe's physical appearance: I was terrified he might have had an emotional relapse too. Why else would he hide away down here, on his own? I approached him slowly, gently.

'God, Joe,' I whispered. 'What happened? What are you doing down here?'

'Swelling.'

I limped towards him, struggling to keep a reassuring smile on my lips.

'Does it hurt?'

'Not much. How's the foot?'

'It's fine.'

I sat down beside him.

'We're a right pair,' said Joe. He was drunk but not incoherent. I relaxed a little.

The sound of the water slapping against the rocks in the cave was eerie and unfriendly and when the wind blew in a certain direction, the cave caught the sound as a bottle will collect breath, and magnified it into an eerie, low-pitched wail. I remembered the faceless knight puppet on the cave floor. I wished we hadn't left it there. I wished we'd got rid of it.

I stroked Joe's face very gently. 'You said you were only going to talk to Vito.'

'That was my intention. I did not intend to get hit.'

I felt a rush of rage at the thought of anyone hurting Joe.

'Was it Vito? Did he hit you?'

'Several times.'

'Did you hit him back?'

'I told him to stop being such a dick.'

'Good for you, Joe.'

'Then he hit me again.'

Bastard, I thought. The anger I was suppressing was changing into sadness. I swallowed back tears.

'He is such a dick,' I said.

Joe put his arm around me. I snuggled closer to him. We settled into one another.

'Can I tell you something, Edie?' Joe asked.

'Anything.'

'I wouldn't say this unless I was drunk.'

'Okay, say it.'

'I miss my mother,' he whispered.

'Is that why you came down here?'

'I didn't want to... I couldn't... It didn't seem right to grieve for her in front of you.'

Tears spilled over my eyes. They ran down my cheeks. I wiped them away with the back of my hand.

'I just needed a little time to think of her,' Joe said.

'Of course you did,' I said. 'You haven't really had chance. I understand.'

'Do you?'

'Yes,' I replied, and to my surprise, I found it was the truth.

* * *

In daylight, the next morning, I saw the extent of the damage done to Joe by Vito Barsi.

The left side of his face was swollen; the sclera of that eye bloodshot, the pupil yellow in colour. There were cuts on his lip and chin and bruises on his ribs and hips. He looked like a boxer after a prize fight.

The physical pain didn't bother Joe anywhere near as much as the worry that, despite his good intentions, he'd done nothing but cause trouble at the pizzeria. He worried about Valentina and Francesco. He was afraid he had made things worse, rather than better. I told him that he'd been right to call Vito out on his behaviour. I told him that people would talk about it now, and it would be harder for Vito to carry on. Surely one of the things about domestic abuse was that people pretended it wasn't happening. Once it was out in the open, like any dirty secret, it became less acceptable.

This was the truth, but on a personal level, I was afraid that Vito's pride would force him to take things further; that his dented ego would not feel whole again until he had defeated Joe. Humiliating a bully touches the deepest, sorest, root of their pain.

* * *

For the next few days, everything was calm. Work at the villa progressed well, and the amount of help we were receiving snowballed. Word of Joe's challenge to Vito had spread.

Strangers turned up at the villa, people with the specific skills we needed, and they treated Joe with consideration and respect. I saw him through their eyes, the outsider who'd had the guts to take on the town bully, and I was proud. I was proud to be with this man; I was proud to be associated with him.

I did what I could in the villa, and when I ran out of things to do, I climbed down into the swimming pool and bashed out a few more tiles. I made sketches of the natural pool and what I wanted it to look like. I stepped out the measurements over the lawn and drove in stakes to mark its footprint. It was my pet project and I was keen to see it through.

Joe called the police and asked if there was any news on the search for the *Madonna del Mare*. There wasn't, but it was early days, they said. These things always took time.

Liuni's sister came over and sorted out the electricity. Soon, the plumbing was fixed and at last we could run a hot bath. Cleaning became much easier. I began to work through the linen and soft furnishings, sorting everything that was usable, washing, airing and ironing. Francesco cycled over to the villa whenever he could to work on the car with Joe. He never talked about his stepfather.

One day, Francesco turned up with a tooth missing. He tried to hide it, covering his mouth with his hand when he smiled, but the bloody gap was there and there was bruising around his lips. Joe and I were in no doubt that Vito had caused the damage and our dislike of the man grew. We could hardly talk of him without the pitch of our voices rising and mutual anger souring our conversation. If ever we were in the Eurospin, or out and about in Porta Sarina, and we saw Vito walking towards us, we turned and walked the other way even though he called after Joe, and jeered; made chicken noises.

Other outstanding matters were attended to. I wrote to St Sarah's, telling them of my intention to resign my position at the end of the next academic year. I talked to Fitz and to Martha and to the handful of other people in my life who deserved to know my plans. The kittens' eyes opened and they grew stronger and became more active. We kept them in the villa. Joe said we should let them outside, so they could become 'streetwise' and learn to hunt, and I allowed them supervised access to the court-yard but was too afraid of losing them to let them run free.

Most of the time, there were people in the villa or its grounds; Joe and his friends, me, Francesco. Sometimes I was aware of the DeLuca ghosts; sometimes I sensed Daniel nearby, sometimes not. It was good to have people, voices, life in the villa again. Every day, it felt a little less abandoned, a little happier. The times when Joe and I were alone became more rare and precious. We worked together on the garden, we ate at the table outside, we swam, we took siestas, we made love, we planned, we worried about not having enough money.

Lack of cash was going to be our biggest issue and, time and again, we talked about how the *Madonna del Mare* would have solved all our problems if only we had it in our grasp. Without it, we had to improvise. We worked out what furniture we could sell; what would bring us the most profit. An antiques dealer from the city of Modica came and looked at the silverware, the clocks and the mirrors and took some items away for the following month's auction. We waited for news from the police.

We had the Alfa Romeo, of course, and it would provide a temporary lifeline, but of everything we had, I knew that was the one item Joe really didn't want to sell and I didn't want him to have to sell it either.

Irma Arnone didn't talk to us or approach us, but we were aware she was watching us, logging the comings and goings of the tradespeople and our friends; they saw her taking photographs of their vehicles as they passed by, making notes, they joked, of their registration plates. We didn't know why she was doing this but suspected she was keeping a record in case she wanted to lodge a complaint at some future date. We feared she might try to stop us opening the villa up to paying guests; that there might be some local bylaw or something that would prove a stumbling block. We told Francesco to be very careful when he came by the cottage. His bike didn't make a noise, but if Irma saw him, she was bound to take a photograph and she might well show it to Vito. This was a great worry to me.

We heard nothing more from Signora Romano. I considered driving over to the marshland and seeking her out to apologise directly to her father, but Joe persuaded me it was best to leave well alone.

For a while, everything was okay, and then things started happening to our friends' possessions while they were at the villa. Nothing terrible. Nothing that was obviously malicious, but small things that might well have been accidents. Nails in tyres; tools missing from the backs of vans; a car window broken by a rock, presumed thrown by children from the beach; a box of plants that were in the back of Fredi's truck dying for no reason, as if someone had poured poison over them – but maybe they'd been damaged in transit; a wallet taken from the glove compartment of an unlocked car.

We took more care of the vehicles left outside the villa, and the bad luck began to follow our friends home. Items that he hadn't ordered were repeatedly delivered to Fredi's elderly father's house; items that were costly and difficult to return. Someone reported Liuni to the police, they said he was responsible for the theft of a tourist's camera, taken from the post office in Ragusa. He wasn't, of course. He had a rock-solid alibi, but the police attention was embarrassing and inconvenient. Every time we saw one of our friends, someone who'd helped us, it seemed something minor but disturbing had taken place. All the incidents were seemingly unconnected, but each time I heard of some small disaster, my blood ran a little colder.

44

One afternoon, after an appointment at the bank in Ragusa, Joe and I found ourselves almost alone in a quiet, shuttered city. The sun was fierce and the shops were closed. The families had gone to the beach; the dogs were snoozing. Even the church bells were silent. It was the very height of summer and it was siesta time.

Joe said he wanted to show me something, and I said okay. We climbed to the top of the city, where the formal gardens, the Giardini Iblei, were laid out: green, shady and quiet. We entered through an avenue of huge old palm trees throwing deep shade across the hot, bright path. Starlings sang in the trees; cats stretched in patches of sunlight. The gardens were flanked by churches; one even stood inside its boundary – an arched door painted green and a saint standing up high beside its tower, one hand raised in benediction, baking in the glare.

As we walked past a monument to the fallen of the war, past pools and benches, dovecotes and columns and flower beds, I experienced the same sensation I had in the villa; feeling the ghosts of the past and the future converging in this space, walking with us as we strolled, pausing by the fountain and trailing their shadows over the surface of the water. At one point, we could smell the sweet apple scent of baking crostata from the panetteria down in the city below; at another, the smell was fried fish; at another, fresh lemons. These perfumes were becoming familiar to me. I was becoming used to Sicily.

'Cece and I used to come here for picnics with our grandparents,' Joe told me. 'We'd play chess with my grandfather and French cricket. Nonna told me it was Anna's favourite spot.'

'Anna didn't come with you?'

'She never left the villa after we arrived.'

'What? Never?'

'No. She wouldn't go beyond the villa's walls from the day we arrived in Sicily until the day we left.'

'Why not?'

'I don't know why. It was just how it was. Come over here.'

He led me to the parapet; stone balustrades at the end of the park guarding a steep drop over a deep, rocky ravine; trees dipping fronded branches over a slatted bench.

'Do you recognise it, Edie?'

'How could I? I've never been here before.'

'Go and stand by the balustrade,' Joe said. 'No, this way a bit, over there, by that lamp post. Stand with your hands on the stone and lean forward a little, now turn your head to the left, like you're looking back at me. Smile. That's it. That's perfect.'

He raised his phone high and then came over to show me the photograph he'd taken.

'Recognise it now?'

I did.

The photograph was a recreation of the painting of Anna I'd found in the wardrobe at the villa. I was posing in the same position as she had, in exactly the same spot, under the trees, beside the balustrade. The hairs on my arm stood on end.

It was an odd sensation, knowing that my mother-in-law had been standing exactly where I was now when she was less than half my age. Time had passed, years and years and years, but the stone would have felt as warm beneath the palms of her hands as it was beneath mine. The view would have been the same, or very similar; the breeze would have whispered through the leaves of the trees in the gardens in the same gentle, unobtrusive manner; she'd have heard the starlings' chatter and smelled the same smells. The years collapsed away. I lost track of where Anna ended and I began.

'Are you okay?' asked Joe.

'Yes. Yeah, I just...' I tailed off. I felt a pang of sadness for Anna and as I didn't enjoy feeling any kind of sympathy towards her, I shook it off.

We made our way back downhill and returned to the piazza at the front of the Duomo. The sun was lower in the sky now, the shops were reopening and the square was busy again.

Joe and I ate slices of pizza at a pavement café. We watched the pigeons and the tourists on the Montalbano trail. I was sipping espresso affogato from a teaspoon when a shadow fell across our table; I looked up to see Valentina Barsi standing nervously a few feet away from us, clutching her bag to her chest, balancing it against her pregnancy. Francesco was a few feet behind his mother, eating a hot dog that was oozing mustard and ketchup, trying to catch the overspill in a paper napkin he held in the palm of his free hand.

'Joe?' Valentina spoke anxiously.

Joe jumped to his feet so quickly that the chair fell over behind him. He and Valentina greeted one another the traditional way, a kiss on each cheek, and then he invited the two of them to join us.

Valentina sat down heavily in the chair beside mine with an 'oof'. Her bump was straining at the fabric of her dress.

Francesco stayed distant, finishing his snack.

Valentina turned to Joe. 'I'm sorry for what Vito did. If I could have stopped him, I would have, only he gets in such rages over nothing and—'

'Don't do that,' Joe said. 'Don't ever apologise for anything Vito says or does. You're not his keeper.'

'But your eye... it's still bruised.'

'It's nothing.'

Valentina looked down at her lap. She looked dreadful, as if she hadn't slept for a week.

'Where's Vito today?' I asked.

'He's looking after the pizzeria. I had to come to the ante-natal clinic for a check-up.' She put a hand on her belly. 'The baby's been a bit quiet lately. I was worried. I thought maybe the stress, you know, I thought it might have affected her – the baby, it's a girl. But she's okay. I'm okay. Even my blood pressure's low. The midwife said: "Whatever you're doing, keep on doing it, because the baby's doing great." Ha!' She pushed the hair out of her eyes. 'Francesco hates me talking about pregnancy stuff, he finds it excruciatingly embarrassing, don't you, Ciccio?' She smiled at her son, who rolled his eyes, put the rest of the hot dog into his mouth and then shook the crumbs from its wrapper.

Valentina watched him and smiled. She rubbed her temples with her fingertips.

'Are you really okay?' I asked her.

'Tired. There was a long wait at the clinic and then I had to find Ciccio, and by the time we got to the bus station, we'd missed our bus. We're going to be late back. Vito won't be happy.'

'We can give you a lift back,' said Joe.

'Oh no, I don't want to put you to any trouble.'

'We're heading back to Porta Sarina now anyway.'

'We are,' I confirmed.

Francesco balled up the hot dog wrapper and tossed it into a bin. 'Getting a lift will be better than telling him he's got to open the pizzeria on his own,' he said.

Valentina bit anxiously at the side of a fingernail.

'He'll go mental if we're late,' said Francesco.

'Yes,' said Valentina, 'you're right. Thank you. We'll accept the lift.'

45

We returned to Fiat Two. Francesco and I squashed together into the back so Valentina could have the passenger seat. She laughed as she attempted to make the seat belt cross her body.

'Oh mio dio!' she laughed. 'I'm like a whale!'

Francesco was embarrassed again and put his earbuds into his ears to listen to his music. He stared away, out of the window.

Valentina's gaiety was forced. She was using laughter and chattiness to deflect her anxiety and instead it put Joe and me on edge. We tried, and failed, to make light-hearted conversation during the first part of the drive, but after a short while we all gave up and looked through our windows, in different directions.

We had crossed the ravine and were approaching the tunnel when Valentina's phone rang.

'Vito,' she warned.

Joe muted the volume on the radio and we all went quiet.

Valentina spoke to her husband. 'Ciao, Vito! Yes!' she said in an artificially cheerful voice. 'Yes, I saw the midwife, everything's fine. The baby's as big as she should be, healthy. Yes, we'll be back in good time, don't worry. It would be great if you'd...'

We were sucked into the tunnel and her signal fell away.

Valentina looked at the face of the phone; its blank screen. 'Come on,' she said, to the phone. 'Come on!'

'You won't get a signal in the tunnel, Mama,' said Francesco. He had removed one of the earbuds.

'Vito'll think I've cut him off on purpose.'

'Call him back when we're out of the tunnel and tell him where we were.'

'I can't, I...'

The tiny arch of daylight at the other end of the tunnel was looming larger now.

I reached in front of me. 'Give me the phone, Valentina, I'll tell Vito what happened. He won't have a go at me.'

'No,' she said, 'no. It's best he thinks we're on the bus. He'll go mad if he knows we're in a car with you guys.'

'Why would he go mad?'

'He just would, wouldn't he, Ciccio?'

'Yeah,' Francesco mumbled.

In the seat in front of mine, Valentina was shrinking, becoming smaller. Beside her, I could sense Joe's anger, although he didn't say anything. 'It's easier for me, well, for both of us, if I don't do the things that make Vito mad,' Valentina finished in a little voice.

Francesco was staring out of the window, concentrating on the music from his phone, making a point of not listening to his mother so he did not have to hear her humiliate herself to us.

Valentina's phone rang again the second we were out of the tunnel; Vito must have been pressing redial over and over.

'Ciao!' Valentina said cheerily. From my position behind her, I could hear Vito's voice coming through the phone speaker as he bombarded her with questions. 'It was the tunnel,' she said, 'we've just come through the tunnel. No, no, no, of course not. No. No!' She covered her eyes with her free hand as if she was trying to protect them.

It was hard for her to get a word in edgeways through the torrent of questions Vito was firing at her.

We had joined the coast road and had driven past the Arnones' cottage before Valentina managed to say: 'Honey, my battery's about to go. The phone will cut off any second,' and then abruptly the angry voice at the other end disappeared. 'Quick,' Valentina said to Francesco, 'turn your phone off too.'

We were all silent after that until Joe took the turning for Porta Sarina beside the Intimissimi billboard. The poster was beginning to weather. It was torn in places, frayed at the bottom.

Valentina bit a knuckle, pretending to watch the countryside, but her eyes were wide and panicked.

'What if he comes to the station to meet the bus?' she asked.

'You didn't say you were on the bus,' I reminded her.

'No, but if we don't get off it, he'll know we weren't on it. He'll know that I lied.'

'You didn't lie. You never said you were on the bus.'

'But he thought I was. It's the same thing.'

'This is crazy,' I said. 'Valentina, it's crazy.'

Francesco sat hunched, his bitten-down fingernails worrying at a spot just in front of his ear. The skin around the spot flushed red.

As we neared Porta Sarina, we caught up with the bus that Valentina and Francesco should have been on. It was only a few yards ahead of us at the roundabout.

'What do you want me to do?' Joe asked Valentina. 'Shall I take you to the harbour or to the bus station?'

'We'd better go to the bus station,' Valentina said. 'If Vito's there, waiting, we'll say we were on a different bus. We'll say the schedule was different today. We'll think of something. If we go straight to the restaurant and he's waiting for us at the bus station, he'll be really mad.'

Joe tensed his arms against the steering wheel.

Francesco had picked off the skin from the top of the spot; there was a tiny flare of blood.

We followed the bus into the station.

'Is he there?' Joe asked.

Valentina was slumped in her seat, her head held very low. 'I'm not sure.'

I craned my head to look at the spot where the bus was pulling in. It was busy. 'Can you let us out here,' Valentina said, 'out of sight.'

'You can't carry on like this,' Joe said.

'I know. I know. But I can't face another fight, not now. Not with the baby and everything.'

Joe pulled over by the bus-wash, right next to an unmissable: Parcheggio vietato sign with a graphic of a car with a large red cross covering it for the benefit of those who did not speak Italian. The moment Joe pulled over, a man in dayglow-green overalls headed our way, waving his arms.

'Thank you,' said Valentina, 'thank you so much.' She heaved herself out of the car as quickly as she could, while Francesco climbed over Joe's seat.

'Take care,' I said, 'both of you.'

Valentina gave a half smile, and a nod, and then she, holding her pregnant belly, and her son, hurried away like hunted creatures.

46

Joe and I drove back to the villa in silence. As we came down the hill, my heart sank. Someone had been there in our absence. Seagulls were squabbling over the remains of a fast-food meal that had been scattered around the parking area and there was a discoloured patch of damp dust against the wall where a bottle had been smashed against it. Broken glass was all around.

I got out of the car and began to pick up the rubbish, shooing away the gulls. Joe got out too, slammed his door and muttered about it almost certainly being Vito who was responsible for this mess and that he bet it was Vito who'd vandalised Fiat One too.

'That can't have been Vito,' I said. 'How could he have known we were going to be at that out-of-the-way restaurant?'

'Maybe he followed us.'

'Joe, that's paranoid.'

'I know... Shit!'

I looked up, following his gaze. We had left the gates locked, as usual, but now they stood wide open. The padlock and chain were bundled in a pile on the floor.

My heart began to pound. We walked toward the gates. My

ears were ringing. This wasn't opportunists then. It wasn't accidental. Someone had come to break in.

Joe picked up the chain. The links had been cut.

'We should call the police,' I said, and in the next breath remembered the kittens; we'd left them in the villa, alone and unguarded. I put down the bags and pushed past Joe.

'Wait, Edie!' he called. 'Whoever it is might still be there...'

'I don't care!'

I ran towards the villa as quickly as I could, cursing the old injuries that slowed me down, dreading what I might find. It was a relief to see the windows at the front of the villa were intact, but in the next heartbeat, I saw that the front door was covered in red paint; an empty can lay on its side in the flower bed. The step and columns and the wall around the door were spattered too and the trunk of the magnolia and the thick old stem of the magnificent creeping rose that wound around the door; the plants looked as if they'd witnessed a gruesome murder. In the centre of all the red, was a black shadow. A crow had been fixed to the door by a nail hammered through its neck. Its head hung limp to one side; one cold, unseeing eye, a long, yellow beak sharp as a blade. Its wings dropped behind its talons; feathers and paint, the plastic white of the quills. The dead bird stank.

I put my hand over my mouth to stop myself retching.

Joe was behind me. He said: 'It's okay, Edie, it's okay.'

'No,' I replied. 'No, it's not okay! No way is that okay!'

This whole thing, the casual dumping of the litter, the broken bottle, the red paint and the dead bird; all of it was nasty, it felt as if whatever unpleasantness had been following us had been nudged up a notch. The vandalism of the car may have been random. The cat might have been killed accidentally, but this wasn't random and it wasn't accidental. This was horrible, gruesome; a deliberate attempt to frighten us.

My heart was in my mouth as we went round to the back of the villa to the kitchen, checking the windows and doors were secure – they seemed to be, although the dining room shutters were open and the lock on the French windows outside that room wouldn't close properly. They appeared to be shut, but it was possible someone could have gone in and out that way.

Joe unlocked the kitchen door and we went inside together, me behind him, the two of us creeping, turning on the lights as we went, talking loudly, just in case. When all the lights were on, I ran upstairs to check on the kittens – now they were so mobile, we'd taken to shutting them in Anna's old bedroom because it was one of the few internal doors we could lock. My fingers trembled as I turned the key and entered. The three kittens were in a line inside their box, all looking towards me with their ears pricked and their eyes wide and alert.

'Hello, babies!' I whispered, my heart pounding with relief. I went into the room and scooped them up, one by one, checking them over. They were all perfectly all right.

I brought them down, all three of them in my arms, the little tortoiseshell boy who was the boldest, climbing my hair. I slumped down in the basket chair.

'I've checked downstairs,' Joe said. 'There's no sign that anyone's been inside.'

'So, they cut the chain just so they could come in and nail the bloody crow to the front door?'

'Whoever did this is sick,' Joe said. 'If they've got something to say, why don't they just say it to our faces?'

He opened two beers and passed one to me. I took it and drank back several gulps. I lifted a kitten off my head, its claws dragging at my hair.

'What does it mean?' I asked. 'What does the dead crow mean, and the red paint? Is it something to do with the devil? With the occult?'

'It doesn't mean anything.'

'Then why do it?'

'It's how they get to you,' Joe said. 'It's how they operate.

They know their psychology. They know they hardly have to break the law; they do one small thing to frighten you and leave your imagination to do the rest of the work.'

'Who are "they"?'

'Whoever it is who wants to get rid of us.'

* * *

I took a bath. The bathroom was big as a ballroom and the lights in that room still didn't work, so I lit candles that flickered shadows over the walls and the huge old claw-foot bath. Steam clouded from the surface of the water. The dimness in the outer reaches of the bathroom meant I couldn't see the cracks in the tiles, or the mould stains on the plaster, the age-spotted mirrors, the basin with a corner missing, or the cobwebs in the high corners. I heard a pattering on the other side of the ceiling above me; a sound like a child singing. I thought of all the other people who had lain in this bath: Anna, Anna's mother. There were pictures in the albums downstairs of Joe and Cece, as children, in the bath together; their two faces grinning towards the camera. The bath, the room, was the same, only the people changed.

A draught touched my face. A tiny drift of plaster fell from the coving. A spider scuttled up the wall. The door was ajar and I could hear Joe moving around downstairs. From time to time, he called up to me, and I called down to him; each of us reassuring the other that we were okay.

When the water began to turn cold, I pulled out the plug and heaved my body out of the bath. I wrapped myself in a towel and padded back into my bedroom. I massaged oil into the skin of my legs to soften the vividness of my old scars. Through the window, I could see the moon beginning its nightly ascent, and its reflection in the water of the bay. I sat on the bed and rested back against the pillow – and jumped up again at once.

Something was beneath the sheet. Oh God!

I leapt off the bed, took hold of the end of the sheet between my thumb and forefinger and peeled it back slowly, my heart thudding.

Please don't let it be a dead animal, please don't let it be a dead animal, oh God, please, please, please.

It was a dead animal!

I screamed and dropped the sheet, backed into the corner of the room, crying, gasping for breath.

It wasn't an animal, it was the puppet Matilde had given us. It lay spread-eagled at the top of my bed, its head at a terrible angle, the painted eyes and lips gouged from its face. The marionette's limbs were arranged in a gruesome dance pose, hair torn from its head and stuffed, disgustingly, between its legs. In the middle of the doll's chest, between its two small, wooden breasts, was the blade of a knife, our knife, the kitchen knife, the one we used for cutting vegetables.

Joe burst into the room.

'Jesus!' he said when he saw the puppet. 'Jesus fucking Christ!'

'Get rid of it!' I cried. 'Get it out of here, Joe!'

Joe reached for it, but he didn't want to touch the disgusting thing any more than I did.

I pushed my damp towel towards him and he picked it up with that, swaddled it, took it out of the room and onto the landing. Two or three small, curly hairs still lay on the white sheet. I would never sleep on that sheet again.

Joe came back into the room. I was huddled in the corner.

'They came into the villa! They came up here! They could have hurt the kittens,' I whimpered.

'We'd locked the door to Anna's room...'

'But what if we hadn't? What if we'd left them downstairs? What if...'

Joe came to me. He put his arms around me and kissed the

top of my head. 'Shhh,' he said. 'Stop it. All that's happened is some sick fuck came into the house, found the puppet and put it in the bed. Nothing more than that. They want you to jump to the worst-case scenario. They want you to start asking yourself: "What if?" That's exactly what they want. If you start doing that, then they're winning.'

I nodded miserably. Joe held me tight.

'This will stop,' he said. 'We'll find out who's responsible and we'll make it stop. We will.' He took my hand. 'We can do this, Edie. We can get through this. We just have to hold our nerve.'

47

We slept in Anna's old room that night, Joe, me and the three kittens. We locked the door and bolted it from the inside. I wanted to push the wardrobe up against the door too, as an extra precaution, but Joe said that would be ridiculous – we weren't expecting anyone to come at us with a battering ram. Nonetheless, we brought the tools that could do serious damage to a door or a person, the axe, a large hammer and the chainsaw, up to the room and locked them in with us. We didn't really think anyone would break in, in the middle of the night – at least, we told ourselves we didn't – but if they did, we would be ready for them.

I couldn't sleep. Even with Joe beside me, snoring like a baby, I couldn't switch off the scenarios that chased through my mind. I imagined faceless people watching the villa from the gardens. I imagined them waiting until they believed we were asleep before they made their move. I jumped at the slightest sound: the creak of settling wood, the hoot of an owl, a kitten rolling out of its box. I lay on my back, in the bed, with my eyes wide open, adrenaline scratching in my veins. MYSTERY OF VILLA MURDERS!

British couple's throats slit as they slept. Was mafia behind gruesome DeLuca deaths?

Nothing happened. It was a peaceful night. The dark hours passed and day crept over the horizon and the night slid away.

I only relaxed enough to sleep when I heard the familiar sound of the Arnones' cockerel crowing up the hill. When I woke again, light was streaming through the slats in the shutters, making stripes over the floor and bed. The kittens were playing on the rug, tumbling over one another, pouncing on each other's tails, making cheerful skittering noises on the floorboards.

Joe lay on his back on top of the covers, one arm crooked above his head, his eyes closed and his lips parted. His T-shirt had ridden up so that a bulge of belly was exposed, a line of three red mosquito bites leading away from his navel. He had a hard-on, the tip of his penis poking cheerfully through the gap in his boxer shorts. He looked vulnerable, faintly ridiculous, completely adorable. How could anything bad happen to either of us when Joe was sleeping like that, innocent and uninhibited as a baby?

I didn't want to disturb him.

I slid my legs out of the bed, stood up and went to the window, easing the stiffness from my joints. The kittens gambolled to my feet, jumped on them, biting my toes. I unlatched the shutter, letting in a slice of morning light. It illuminated Anna's portrait, propped against the wall. It was a lovely picture. I wondered why nobody had ever bothered to frame it and why such a beautiful object had been left hidden inside the wardrobe. Perhaps Anna didn't like it. Perhaps she thought the portrait wasn't a good likeness (it was) or that it didn't flatter her (it did).

Or perhaps it was just that she couldn't bear to look at herself, to remind herself of how happy she once was.

* * *

Joe and I returned to the tool hypermarket to buy new locks for the gates and doors. On our return, we met Gabriele and Irma Arnone halfway up the track between the villa and their cottage. Irma had one arm around her husband and was persuading him up the hill. The old man was disorientated.

Joe slowed the car and leaned out of the window. He spoke to Irma and she answered his questions curtly. They had a brief conversation and then Joe drove on. He told me Gabriele had walked down to the villa on his own while Irma was inside the cottage bottling tomatoes. Apparently he was drawn to it like a magnet; she was forever having to run down the hill to fetch him back.

Joe and I exchanged glances.

'You don't think it's him, do you?' I asked, as we drew away from the old couple.

'It can't be, he's not well enough.'

Still, something Joe had said to me earlier, something about the things that had happened to us, small things that messed with our minds being the way 'they' operated, made me think the mafia might still, in some way, be behind the campaign being waged against us.

* * *

After the crow and the puppet, I thought it would take a long while for me to feel okay about being in the villa again, but the house had a way of making me calm, and the gardens and the sea beyond worked their therapeutic magic. Daniel was more present and, soon enough, Joe and I and fell back into our routine. I showed Joe the graveyard; he knew about the babies but had forgotten they were buried in the villa grounds, and he agreed we should restore the area, and the path to it, although we'd keep its surrounds untended for the benefit of the wildlife.

The woman police officer dropped by to say they'd been

tipped off about a Reni painting being touted for sale on the black market in America. Their US colleagues were going to investigate. There was a slim chance it might be our Madonna, but we were not to hold our breaths.

For days, we did not leave the villa, and each day I was a little less afraid. I felt safe when I was inside the boundaries of the garden wall because I was certain whoever it was who wished us harm was outside. As long as we stayed there, protecting the villa and protected by it, we would be okay.

Joe was happiest when Francesco was with him and they were together, working on the car. The Sicilian schools had broken up for the summer now, so Francesco was freer. Vito had some contract work in the city of Gela, more than an hour's drive from Porta Sarina, so for the time being we didn't have to worry about him either. Affection and respect were growing between Francesco and Joe and I was never quite sure if Francesco was an excuse for Joe to work on the car, or if the car was a reason for him to spend time with Francesco. The old tyres were off now and the body of the car was supported on bricks. Beneath the bonnet, Joe assured me, good progress was being made.

One afternoon, when I was upstairs cleaning, I came across Anna's old diary. I hadn't looked at it in a while and, this time, I realised it covered not just one year, but several: the years she never talked about – her last years in Sicily when she was aged between fifteen and eighteen. Apart from the diary, all that remained to speak of Anna's existence in those years were the few photographs I'd found and the portrait painted in the Giardini Iblei.

I took the diary downstairs, sat at the kitchen table and flicked through it. Some of the entries were no more than a few words: many referred to Anna's boarding school in Rome. She enjoyed listing the 'disgusting' meals the pupils were forced to eat, clearly regarding them as a form of abuse. Some entries were in Italian, the lyrics of songs Anna had painstakingly transcribed from the radio and then written into the diary – she had told me she used to do this when she was a girl. I remembered her saying: 'We'd spend hours beside the radio waiting for our favourite songs.'

We, she had said. We. Anna and who else? Matilde Romano?

Soon enough, I found some lyrics written by a different hand. The other writing was smaller, neater and more playful. The dots over the 'i's were little hearts, full stops had become smiley faces, rabbits and cats had been doodled amongst the lyrics. The doodles illustrating the transcription of 'Sympathy for the Devil' were little horned men with tails, holding pitch-forks. They'd been drawn in a similar way to the two characters on Anna's bedroom wall, which meant, I assumed, that this was the work of the young Matilde Romano, although I had no sense of Matilde in the drawings at all.

48

The new tyres for the Alfa Romeo arrived early one morning, chained to the back of a pick-up truck. Behind the truck, cycling as fast as he could, was Francesco. He dropped the bike just inside the gates and waved to me as he ran over towards the stables. The drive had been cleared now. There was no more need for scrambling through the overgrowth.

By the time I reached the stables, the Alfa Romeo had been jacked up and the wheel arches were being examined. Joe introduced me to Signor Mastrolembo, who ran a tyre and exhaust fitting business, and his mechanic, Antonio. The atmosphere in the stables was crackling with anticipation and it was noisy with laughter, the men shouting instructions to one another. I watched as Francesco came up with the solution to some technical problem.

'Bravo!' Signor Mastrolembo cried. 'Bravo, Francesco!' He patted Francesco's back and the boy glowed with pride, grinning broadly, forgetting to be self-conscious about his missing tooth. I could not have been more proud; I only wished Daniel could have been there too; it was a situation he'd have loved.

While the men were occupied with the Alfa Romeo, I took

Fiat Two to Eurospin, did the shopping and, on an impulse, decided to buy some flowers for Signora Romano. I'd make a gesture of apology and after that I wouldn't think of her again.

There was a flower shop close to the farmacia. I left the car where it was and walked through the town until I arrived in the piazza. The posters on the memorial wall had been removed or pasted over with a new batch, different images but the same mixture of the very old and the very young, with a smattering of people killed in road accidents and by untimely illness in between. My Italian had improved sufficiently for me to make out some of the messages, but it was the faces of the dead that drew me in. It would be naïve to say that their eyes carried a foreshadowing of what was to come, but as I looked at them, I was certain I detected a kind of knowingness in their expressions, that even as the shutter clicked on the camera, those people were aware their image would end up on the memorial wall.

But we're all going to die. We all know, I reminded myself, and then I stopped, because I found myself looking into young Anna's eyes. There she was, sitting bareback on a horse; her hair cut in a short bob, her smile wide. She was wearing jodhpurs and a sleeveless shirt tied at the waist, riding boots. The horse was a handsome piebald with a long mane. The reins were loosely looped through the fingers of one of Anna's hands. In the other was a cigarette. Anna did not look as if she was thinking about death. She looked like a young woman who was loving life; loving every moment of it. Her face was charismatic, happy, strong.

Standing slightly behind the horse was the same young man I'd seen in the photograph at the villa: the good-looking young Sicilian. He was looking down, the brim of a hat shadowing most of his face, so that only his smile and jaw were obvious, and Matilde was there too, half in, half out of the picture.

I was compelled to stare at Anna's face for a while, several minutes, before I felt a gentle touch of a hand on my elbow and I turned to see a nun in full habit, with a gentle expression. She asked, in Italian, if I was all right and I realised she assumed I was grieving. I assured her that I was fine. She murmured some kind of religious assurance, which was kind, and we went our separate ways.

* * *

The woman inside the flower shop was about my age, with short black hair and a long fringe held off her face with a clip. We communicated successfully with the help of the translation app on her tablet. She introduced herself as Benedetta, the proprietor, and when she discovered who I was, she told me her mother and grandmother used to deliver flowers to the Villa della Madonna del Mare for parties and special occasions.

'When the villa is restored, I'll bring flowers for you!' she said. I said that would be wonderful.

On her recommendation, I chose a tasteful arrangement of sweet peas, interspersed with rosebuds, ribbons and foliage to give to Matilde Romano. Benedetta put the arrangement into a cardboard box and wrapped the box in cellophane.

I returned to the car and drove back to the marshes, past the turning for the electricity plant with the weeds that grew thick at the base of its razor-wire fences, past the restaurant shack where Fiat One had been vandalised and on until I reached a thin, desolate house with a steeply pitched roof and crumbling paint-work standing on its own. The battered old taxi was parked outside.

I slowed the car. It may have been nothing more than a reluctance to see Signora Romano again, but something about that thin, old house filled me with dread.

I turned Fiat Two so it was facing back towards the coast

road, ready for a quick getaway, before I bumped it onto the dusty verge outside the house and climbed out.

The air was very still; it had a dank, marshy smell to it and was thick with the buzz of flies and mosquitoes. The land here was flat, only the metal towers, the pylons, transformers and girders that supported the cables of the electricity station shimmered in the heat of the horizon. Sweat slicked the surface of my skin. I reached into Fiat Two and lifted out the flower box.

The door of the house had been painted the colour of dried blood, although the paint was peeling, revealing older, black paint beneath. Rubbish bags were piled to one side, empty meat cans stacked haphazardly in a plastic crate with plastic milk cartons. I lifted the knocker and rapped on the door, half hoping that nobody would come and that I could leave the flowers, with a note. But I could hear the sound of a television turned up loud inside and, after a moment or two, bolts slid back and there was a fumbling at the latch and the door opened.

It was Signora Romano, only she wasn't neat and tidy as I'd always seen her, now she was wearing a nylon housecoat that must have stifled her in the heat of that day. Her legs were bare, the skin mottled and hairy, and her feet were in slippers. Her hair was scraggy, like a bird's nest, and her face, without make-up, wrinkled and coarse. One side was creased and flattened; she must have fallen asleep in front of the TV. Behind her, in the gloom, I could make out a wheelchair and the vague shape of somebody, with their back to me, sitting in it.

Signora Romano was confused for a moment, and then she recognised me and immediately stepped out of the door and pulled it to so that I should have no further glimpse into the house.

'Edith,' she said, flustered, scrabbling to make sense of my appearance on her doorstep.

'I'm sorry if I disturbed you, Signora, but I brought you this,'

I showed her the box. 'It's a small gift to apologise for any trouble you went to over the villa.'

Signora Romano frowned. 'What is it?'

'Flowers,' I said. 'I thought you might like them.'

She took the box without grace, without a smile or a 'thank you' or any indication of being pleased by the gift. I had a feeling she would discard the arrangement as soon as I was gone; toss it out with the rest of the stinking rubbish. I felt a pang of pity for the flowers.

'I hope you and your father haven't been too inconvenienced on account of Joe and me,' I said, 'and if there's anything you need... anything I can do to help...' I was anxious for reassurance that there was no bad blood between us.

'We've waited for the villa this long. We can wait a little longer,' she replied curtly.

'There's no point waiting, Signora, the villa's not for sale,' I said. 'We meant what we said. We're not going to sell it.'

'But you will,' she said, 'because if you don't, you'll lose everything.'

It was a mean thing to say, and uncalled for when I'd been trying to make amends.

I kept my voice calm. 'Joe and I know what we're doing. We know it won't be easy, but we're going to make it work.'

She snorted. 'You'll regret staying. You'll see. That villa will bring you nothing but bad luck.'

She shook her head and then she turned and went back into the house, pulling the door sharply shut behind her.

49

I drove back to the villa feeling cross and miserable. It had been foolish to hope that Signora Romano would accept the gift graciously, but I hadn't expected her to be so unkind. I turned her words over in my mind, wondering what she'd meant exactly, and eventually convinced myself that they had only been words; that they meant nothing, that she was a lonely woman with too much time on her hands, a woman who had come close to realising her dream and now was bitter because it had been taken from her.

I found Joe outside the villa tinkering with the Alfa Romeo. He told me he and Francesco had been taking turns to drive it up the track.

'You let Francesco drive?'

'I'm teaching him. It goes like a dream. Would you like to go for a spin?'

'Yes,' I said. 'I'd like that a lot.'

We drove a route we hadn't taken before, sitting low in the car, held secure in its big sports seats. The wind was in my hair, the sun on my skin. The car clung to the road, the slipstream grabbed at all the secrets and worries that had been playing on my mind and snatched them from me. We went fast enough to outrun them – almost. I'd never ridden in a car like it. I'd never understood that driving could be a joyous thing to do.

It was late afternoon by the time we reached the seaside town of Punta Secca, and the hottest day of the summer so far. The surface of the roads was beginning to melt and a heat shimmer blurred the greys and buffs of the buildings. Red and purple flowers cascaded over flaking walls; and the verges were littered with little white dog turds, cigarette ends and discarded sweet wrappers. The town was quiet; the oppressive heat was keeping people away. Joe and I were almost alone as we walked along the seafront, the sea too bright for our eyes in the sun's glare, towards the famous lighthouse and Montalbano's house.

We ate at a small café overlooking the sea. I ordered pasta with tomato sauce, and Joe asked for the house speciality. The waiter returned with a plate of fried sardines, their eyes popped and the bones of their fins shining slender as hairs through an oily batter. He put the plate in the centre of the table with a flourish, along with chunks of bread and a jar of mayonnaise.

'They came out of the harbour this afternoon,' he said. 'You won't get anything fresher anywhere.'

Those fish would have been shoaling in the shallows a few hours earlier, flashing through patches of sunlight in the water, darting amongst the weed. Now, they were little zombified corpses. They repulsed me. I drank some water. Joe ate enthusiastically.

I pulled my legs out of the sun and, under the table, a sparrow, startled by the movement, fluttered into the air and then settled again.

'Is something wrong?' Joe asked, nodding at my plate.

'I'm just not very hungry.'

'If you're not going to eat it, can I have it?'

'Help yourself.'

He took the plate from me, and forked the pasta into his

mouth.

'What's up?' he asked.

'Nothing.'

'Edie?'

'I went to see Signora Romano,' I said, 'to apologise. She said we should give up now or lose everything.'

Joe looked at me but continued eating.

I moved grains of salt around the tabletop with the tip of my forefinger.

'She's nuts,' Joe said after a while.

'I know. But things have been going wrong.'

'Random things.'

'The crow wasn't random.'

'I thought we weren't going to let that get to us.'

He broke a piece of bread and wiped the edge of my plate.

'Edie, Signora Romano's trying to spook you. She's upset about us not selling the place to her. She wanted to live in the villa and swan around pretending she was a DeLuca and now she can't and she's cross with us.'

'She says it's just a question of time before we leave.'

'She's mad, Edie; mad as a box of frogs. Forget her.'

* * *

We went onto the beach. A thin but steady stream of fans turned up to take photographs of one another standing in front of the balcony at the back of Montalbano's house.

We spread our towels on a rocky patch of ground. I pulled my dress over my head, folded it into my bag and sat on the towel. The shadows should have been lengthening, but the sky was peculiar that evening. Everything was a heat haze. Everything was close and sticky, choking.

Joe took off his shirt and squatted on his heels behind me. He lifted the hair from my neck and kissed the top of my spine.

'You've got a tattoo,' he said, when he found the little bird-in-flight just beneath my hairline.

'Yes.'

'Is it for Daniel?'

'Yes.'

'I might get one the same.'

'That'd be nice,' I said. I felt terribly sad all of a sudden. It was being here without Daniel. I was missing him. I had a sudden craving to be back in the villa, where I felt closest to him.

Joe said he wanted to swim.

'You shouldn't,' I said, 'not after all you've eaten.'

'That's an old wives' tale.'

'Don't expect me to rescue you if you pretend to drown.'

Joe laughed. He ran into the sea, diving forward as soon as the water was deep enough and disappearing, emerging seconds later, deep in the bay.

I stayed on the beach and watched the light catching the water displaced by his arms. I'd only been half joking about the drowning; I was actually afraid that he might run into trouble, or get cramp and disappear under the surface of the sea, and that if I didn't watch him, I might not notice he was gone and I might lose him again, but this time forever.

The sun slid down from a sky so hot it was white-grey, and the heat haze so intense it was difficult to differentiate between the sea and the sky. It was as if the sky had melted as the sea steamed in the heat and now they were melded into each other, obliterating the horizon.

I could still smell the marshland in the crook of my arms. Death and putrefaction was stuck to the tiny, pale hairs. I rubbed sand onto my arm to scrape away the smell.

* * *

Joe and I were quiet on the journey home, both of us thinking our own thoughts. The wind buffeted me and my hair kept going in my eyes. I held it back and gazed at the countryside, its greys and ochres sliding in the heat. We drove over bridges that crossed dried up rivers, passed old people fanning their weary faces and shepherds moving small herds of recalcitrant, long-legged sheep through Sicily's rocky landscape, the pale stone colours dotted by the brilliant pinks, blues and yellows of wild flowers. I had fallen in love with the country, but it wasn't my country nor my landscape; I didn't belong here really. I didn't understand Sicily, it was all contradictions, too much was understood but unspoken. Perhaps you had to be born here to know it properly.

My phone pinged. It was an email from an address I didn't recognise, random letters, numbers and symbols. The subject line read: Bitch. I baulked at the word. I should have deleted the email straight away but I opened it and in the body was a copy of one of the more lurid newspaper reports of Daniel's death. There was a picture of the building site, and the tent that was erected over the shaft where he had died. The headline read: BODY FOUND IN SEARCH FOR MISSING DANNY. We never called him 'Danny'. Never. Only the media called him that. The subheading was: WHO WAS REALLY TO BLAME FOR LITTLE DANNY'S DEATH?

I'd read that article before, ten years earlier. I didn't need to read it again because the phrasing haunted me still. It was a spiteful 'think piece' written by a female journalist who believed I was responsible for what had happened to Daniel because I hadn't paid enough attention to Anna's behaviour. She said I should have known it was dangerous to leave him with her, that any truly loving mother would have seen the risk. That article had pushed me closer to the edge than any of the other horrific things that happened in the wake of Daniel's death. I hadn't thought about it in years; until now.

I deleted the email, but no sooner had I done so than another popped into my inbox, then another. Each time, the subject line was 'Bad Mother' or something similar. I closed the app and dropped the phone into the footwell.

'What is it?' Joe asked.

'They've got my email address,' I said quietly.

'Who has?'

'*They*. Whoever's doing this stuff to us. They know about Daniel.'

'What have they said?'

'They're sending copies of the articles; the ones that blamed me.'

'Fuck them,' said Joe.

I nodded and kept my chin held high, but I didn't feel strong. I felt as violated and shamed as I had done ten years earlier. I'd forgotten those feelings; it was shocking how easily they could be recalled.

'Delete the email account,' Joe said. 'Don't even look at it again. Set up another.'

We turned onto the coast road and drove along, the bay to our right, a cloudy, thunderous night weighing down heavy over the sea. I had a stone of anxiety in my stomach. How had 'they' found my email address? How did they know how to get to me, how to hurt me? How did they know so much about me?

Our headland came into view. Something was moving around the roof of the house. I couldn't make it out. What was it?

Joe leaned forward, craning over the steering wheel, and in doing so misjudged the hairpin bend around the Arnone cottage so the Alfa Romeo bumped up onto the side of the road and then bounced off again. I grabbed hold of the door.

'Sorry,' Joe said, 'sorry, sorry, sorry,' as I rocked in my seat and the car lurched on its big new tyres.

We were both still staring at the villa, trying to work out what was causing the movement. We realised at the exact same moment.

'Oh Jesus!' Joe cried. 'It's smoke.'

50

Joe was out of the car before it stopped at the bottom of the track. I pulled on the handbrake and followed. He battled with the key and the new lock at the gates. I looked over him, upwards. A thin line of smoke was drifting from the villa's red roof tiles into the glowering sky.

Joe let the lock fall and pulled the gate open. I followed after him, the gravel skittering beneath our feet. I could smell the dry, peppery smell of wood burning with a thick, ugly under-smell.

Joe reached the villa door ahead of me. I was anxious about the kittens – we hadn't taken our usual trouble to shut them upstairs before we left. I was right behind Joe as he opened the door.

Before him, smoke was hanging viscous and dreamy in the hallway; the stairs drawing it up to the first floor. The kittens, one, two, three, darted out of the doorway and disappeared into the shrubs. Joe disappeared the other way, into the smoke.

'No! No! Joe!'

My instinct was to go after him, but we needed help. My phone was in the car. I turned and ran back towards the gates. Figures were emerging from the rocks at the top of the path to the beach, holidaymakers who'd seen the smoke and come scrambling up to see what was going on.

They questioned me in Italian. I answered, frantic, in English and they made mimes of the telephone and I understood that the fire brigade had already been alerted.

I pointed back towards the villa. 'Joe, mio marito, he's inside! Help, please help! Aiuto!'

Two men ran past me towards the villa, followed by a young woman. Other people surrounded me, patting my arm, muttering reassurances.

We were back at the villa. I pulled towards the open door, smoke billowing out; someone tried to hold me back, but I peeled their hands from my arms and plunged into the hallway. 'Joe!' I thought I saw him, a dense, dark figure in a tangle of swirling shadows.

I pulled the neck of my shirt over my mouth and nose and made my way to the living room; flames were licking across the floor, flickering on the edges of the rug; smoke danced around the chandelier and investigated the nooks and crannies of the ceiling coving. I went forward, stamping on the rug, furious with the fire. I grabbed Anna's diary from the table, and the photographs I'd left with it, and staggered forwards to the French windows. I lifted the catch, and the window swung back so suddenly that I fell out onto the terrace beyond. The smoke rushed after me, tumbling gleefully into the sky.

I crawled onto the lawn and lay there, my body heaving to draw oxygen. After a moment or two, I had the strength to drag myself forwards, and as I raised myself onto my elbows, I saw a couple ahead of me, standing beside the hole where the old swimming pool used to be. They were looking towards the burning villa and their faces were illuminated by the fire. I saw them clear as daylight, but they did not see me, down in the grass. It was Gabriele and Irma Arnone. His arm was threaded through hers and confusion was written on his old face. She wasn't looking at her husband. She was holding something up to her face; a camera. She was taking pictures of the fire.

* * *

Joe found me a short while later. He was sooty, smuts on his skin and ash caught in his hair. I shouted at him for going into the villa: he said he'd been in and out, closing doors, trying to contain the flames. He was shocked, but there was exhilaration in his voice, in his words. Joe liked action. He liked being able to do something to solve a problem. He told me to keep back, and he, meanwhile, joined the chain of volunteers, most still in their beach clothes, filling buckets from the pump and passing them into the villa. I watched them working in silhouette, this line of determined people in their swimsuits and kimonos working like ants. I would never forget that scene; the strangers who came to help us, nor how hard they laboured to save the villa.

The fire brigade arrived in a giant contraption that came through the gates and churned up the flower beds, digging into the gravel of the drive. The officers made everyone move back and they set up their hoses and pumps and we stood and watched as they sprayed water into and onto the building, dousing the burning furniture and dampening the walls and floors and ceilings until the fire was exhausted and the flames had nowhere left to go. The fire still danced in my eyes and I kept imagining I saw new flames breaking out. I kept sensing them behind me.

The fire officers went through the villa to be sure no tiny remnants of the fire were still smouldering quietly, sneakily, under the floorboards or in the cupboards. Steam drifted from the windows and dissipated into the night air.

I couldn't see, but I imagined people gathered on the harbourside at Porta Sarina, watching the fire, and now its after-math, from the other side of the bay. I imagined them talking about the haunted villa, blaming us, perhaps, for bringing trouble to the headland.

Some of the strangers had stayed to watch the fire being extinguished. They were saying things like: 'It could have been so much worse' – and they were right, it could have been. The damage appeared to be more superficial than structural, but the beautiful furniture in the living room was ruined; the glass in the doors of the bookcases had cracked and smoke and water had spoiled the books; the rugs, the wallpaper, the curtains, everything that made that room what it was, had been destroyed. The chandelier in the hallway had fallen to the floor. The firefighters had stomped all over it. If the *Madonna del Mare* had been hanging in its alcove, it would surely have been ruined too.

When they were satisfied the villa was safe, the fire officers left and the strangers drifted away. The kittens came creeping back, sniffing the air. The night became very quiet. The villa no longer seemed viable to me. It looked like something dead. Wisps of residual steam were its spirit, departing.

'They think it was an electrical fault,' said Joe, answering a question I hadn't asked, 'a loose wire that made a spark that caught on a piece of dry timber inside the wall.'

I didn't bother to argue. We both knew this wasn't an accident.

In my mind, Signora Romano's words echoed. 'You'll lose everything,' she'd said. 'Everything.' It looked as if her premonition was already starting to come true.

51

We couldn't sleep in the villa that night, not with the smell of smoke clinging to every wall and the downstairs waterlogged. Neither Joe nor I had the energy or inclination to drive back to the hotel in Porta Sarina. Instead, we collected some bedding and took it over to the stables. Joe made a nest for us on the mezzanine, in the old hayloft. I got into the sleeping bag and pulled it as tight as I could around my neck. We'd left all the villa's doors and windows open. The kittens could come and go as they pleased.

The birds were fluttering and the mice were scampering and I was worried about everything. I couldn't sleep for the churning of my mind. Holding onto the villa wasn't worth it, I thought. Nothing was worth this; this risking of people's lives, for what? A dream? A fantasy? I should have listened to Signora Romano. I should have heeded her warning. I should have realised when the emails pinged into my phone earlier that whoever it was who was conducting this campaign against us meant business. They weren't going to give up. Were we really going to persist until something terrible happened? Until someone died?

I lay quietly until I heard Joe snoring, then I climbed out of the sleeping bag, wrapped it around my shoulders, climbed down the ladder and wandered back into the gardens. I meant to find somewhere quiet to sit and listen to the sea and think.

The moon had moved across the sky and the clouds were breaking apart. Moonlight dimmed the stars, but shone on the villa, outlining it in silver, picking out its features. I walked towards it and then stopped, caught my breath.

Someone else was in the garden. A man was standing at the side of the old swimming pool, an old man, his shoulders slumped, pyjama bottoms held up by a string tied around the waist, clogs on his feet. From the shape of the head, the protruding ears, I knew it was Gabriele Arnone. His little goat stood beside him, attached to her leash.

For a moment, I stood paralysed. I didn't know what to do. If I ran to wake Joe, the old man might wander off. He might go into the villa or he might trip and fall into the empty pool, or the sea. I certainly couldn't leave him while I went all the way up the hill to fetch Irma. He was frail and vulnerable, but still I was afraid of him. He had killed people; at least three people, maybe more. He had probably killed Matilde Romano's mother. He had probably murdered her and left her face down on that dreadful marshland close to the Romanos' thin, family home.

I stood, hardly daring to breathe and, thirty feet from me, the old man stood, and I thought: *This is ridiculous, are we going to stand here in the dark until dawn?*

I called out to him. 'Scusi, Signor!'

He didn't hear me.

I began to walk towards him, talking all the time so that he shouldn't be surprised by my approach. As I drew closer, I saw that his chest and shoulders were bare. I could see bushy white hair on his naked skin, the bullish shape of his neck now slack with wrinkles. His lips were moving as if he was praying. The goat looked up at my approach, her little jaw rotating.

'Signor Arnone,' I said quietly, when I was almost, but not

quite, close enough to touch the old man. 'I need to take you home. A casa. To Irma. Irma will be worried about you.'

He looked up then. 'Irma?' he asked.

'Si, Irma.' Now I was close enough to see the confusion in his eyes.

He pointed down into the pool and mumbled something. I couldn't understand a single word.

I smiled with as much confidence as I could muster and nodded back towards the villa's gates. 'Andiamo,' I said, 'let's go.'

'No, no!' he said, and pointed down again.

'There's nothing there,' I said. 'It's just a clapped-out old pool. Come on, let's get back up the hill to Irma.'

* * *

We walked slowly around the side of the villa, Gabriele leading the goat and following me. He was meek as a lamb. Occasionally, he broke wind unashamedly and I had to clasp my hand to my mouth to stop myself laughing at the surrealism of the situation in which I found myself; the goat, me and the farting Mafioso. Moonlight rimmed the tracks gouged into the ground by the fire engine.

'Careful,' I said to Gabriele and he heeded my words, stepped carefully over the disturbed ground.

The moon was bright enough for us to see where we were treading, but I kept my phone clasped in my hand and was relieved when we were close enough to the road for it to light up with a signal. If I needed help now, I could call for it.

We climbed the track up to the Arnones' cottage and I saw Gabriele and the goat through the gate into its garden. I was tempted to leave them there, but my school-teacher's sense of responsibility obliged me to make sure they were safe. Gabriele sat down in his usual spot on the stool as if it were mid-morning, not the middle of the night.

I went to the cottage door, which was ajar, and knocked. A lamp was still burning inside.

'Signora Arnone!' I called. 'Hello!'

She appeared wearing a long nightdress that buttoned at the throat, her hair tucked beneath a nightcap. When she saw me, first shock and then fear flooded her face.

I held up my hands to calm her. 'It's okay,' I said. 'Gabriele is fine, he's outside. He was at the villa…' I pointed behind me, 'but I brought him back. He's here. A casa. Outside.'

I showed her and she relaxed and touched my arm in gratitude.

'Grazie!' she said. 'Mille grazie!'

We went out and she tied up the goat and then led Gabriele back into the cottage, one arm around his waist. His lips still moved silently. She indicated that I should wait while she took him into the bedroom and I heard her scolding him one moment and muttering endearments the next. I imagined her sitting him on the bed, taking off his shoes.

I looked about me. The interior of the cottage was cosy in the lamplight. It wasn't fancy, but nowhere near as run down as I'd imagined from the state of the exterior. On the wall was a photograph of Gabriele and Irma on their wedding day: Gabriele standing proud, puff-chested, squeezed into a suit that fitted badly, his hair oiled back. Irma was tiny beside him, wearing a dark dress that came to just below the knee. There were flowers in her hair, but her shoes were old and shabby. Shortly afterwards, it seemed, babies came along; here was Irma, still very young, holding a bundle of bonneted lace in her arms and Gabriele slightly to one side, a cigarette held to his lips, his eyes narrowed against the smoke, swaggering, proud, not so much of the infant, but of his own potency and masculinity. He had once been a good-looking young man.

'Oh God!' I whispered as I realised that I recognised him. I stepped closer, studied the photographs again to be sure. There was no doubt. The Gabriele pictured here, on his wedding day, was the same youth from Anna's photographs, the young man I'd assumed was her boyfriend. Here he was a little older, a little more confident, certainly, by this time a killer, definitely the same man.

I stepped away from the photographs as Irma emerged from the bedroom, the palms of her hands flat together in a praying gesture. Behind her, I could see Gabriele in bed, lying flat on his back, his head on the pillow. My heart was pounding. If things had been different then Anna might have ended up married to Gabriele Arnone! Only she wouldn't have, she couldn't have, her family would never have countenanced such a union.

While all this was rushing through my mind, Irma went to the dresser, opened a drawer and took something out. She pressed a little plastic key ring into my palm. Attached to the chain was a plastic charm in a shape that I took at first to be a chilli fruit. Then I realised; it was a horn. Irma was giving me a gift to protect me from bad luck.

She folded my fingers over the charm and nodded, to show that I should keep it. It was an old gift, cheap, second-hand, but still, coming from someone who, not so long ago had pointed a gun at me, it meant a great deal and I was grateful.

52

Joe was up at dawn. I, exhausted by my adventures the previous night, didn't stir from my bed in the hayloft until he woke me with coffee. It was bitter and dark and smoky. Everything was going to smell and taste of smoke for the next few days.

I turned the plastic key ring between my fingers.

Joe sat beside me, rubbing his eyes. He was coughing a good deal.

I patted his back. 'Are you okay?'

'Tired,' he answered, 'but we need to get on. We've got a lot of clearing up to do.'

I stared into my coffee cup.

'Where are we even going to start?' I asked.

'We'll take one room at a time.'

'It'll take forever,' I said, 'and everything's filthy. We don't have any paint. We don't have any money, we'll need special stuff for cleaning the curtains and the upholstery and...'

'Hey,' Joe said, 'we've got water. We've got soap. We'll manage.'

His voice was upbeat but I heard a weariness behind the

words. He was struggling to muster enthusiasm for all the work that lay ahead too.

We finished our coffee and headed back towards the villa, me trailing behind. I had the strongest feeling he knew what I was thinking and was trying to get ahead of me so he wouldn't hear me when I said: 'Joe, I don't want to do this any more.'

He stopped then. I saw his shoulders slump. He turned slowly and looked at me through bloodshot eyes.

'We can't stop now,' said Joe. 'We've done so much already. The gardens are almost finished and you've worked so hard inside the villa. If we stop it'll all have been for nothing.'

'It hasn't been wasted time,' I said. 'We can still sell the villa; maybe we can ask a bit more for it now the gardens have been cleared. I don't particularly want Signora Romano to have it, but if she wants it so badly...' I tailed off. 'It's two steps forward and one step back, Joe. All the hours I've spent cleaning and washing and now I'll have to start again and everything's in a worse state than it was before. And it's not just that... every time we leave the villa, we don't know what we're going to find when we come back. I'm worried about the kittens, I'm worried about everything. It's too much. I'm tired. It's not how I want to live.' I paused again. 'I can't bear the thought of anything happening to the kittens, Joe, and something will happen if we stay.' Another pause. A gulp of breath. 'I don't want anything awful to happen to you either.'

Joe could have argued. He could have pointed out that I was the one who'd persuaded him to give it a go, to keep the villa. He could have reminded me of all my grand ideas but he didn't do any of those things.

'I'm sorry,' I said.

'I understand,' Joe said. He sighed. We both stared at the ground. 'Well, that's it then,' he said. 'It's over.'

* * *

Ten minutes later, a motorbike drew up outside the villa. It was followed by a convoy of cars and vans, a truck stacked with scaffolding poles. The vehicles arranged themselves in the parking area, around the Alfa Romeo and Fiat Two and people got out.

Joe opened the gates. There was Fredi and a woman I didn't recognise, a couple of teenagers in apprentices' overalls, Liuni, and his sister, the electrician, a cashier from Eurospin and other people, people who knew Joe, who had known him – his childhood friends, friends of the family. Here was an older man in paint-spattered jeans and an old shirt; only when he came to kiss my cheeks did I recognise Avvocato Recupero, the lawyer.

Dozens of people were here, at our villa, all of them smiling and explaining in slow, meticulous Italian who they were, how they knew Joe and how they were going to help us. Word of the fire had got out and the Sicilian community had been called to action. They had come to help us fix the villa.

They were doing this for Joe. They said it was for us, but it was Joe they loved. I was so proud of him. I only wished Daniel was with us, to be part of this, to see how respected his father was, how people liked him and cared for him.

I wished our son had had the chance to see his father in this light.

It was a good day. With so many hands to help, with volunteers to run into town if there was anything any of the skilled tradespeople needed, masses of work was done in a short space of time. The scaffolding was erected. Liuni's sister and her colleagues attended to the old wiring, pulling out yards and yards of ancient cabling and feeding in new. I joined the cleaning team, and with several of us at work taking down the curtains and lifting furniture out into the gardens to be examined and cleaned, the chore became fun. Another team replaced the broken window-glass, others stripped off the ruined wall-paper and chipped away at scorched plaster and burned lathes.

There was laughter and constant joking. I couldn't follow most of it, but I went along with it and people made sure I was included. Within a few hours, I had forgotten the feelings of the night before and the insecurity that had brought us so close to giving up. I forgot the fear I'd felt when I saw Gabriele Arnone standing in the night garden staring into the pool. I forgot how alone I'd felt, facing our faceless, nameless enemy. With our friends behind us, Joe and I were unstoppable.

In the early afternoon, we congregated on the lawn and spread ourselves out and shared the food that people had brought: cold pizza, bread, cheese, olives and a huge bowl of tomato and basil salsa that we could spoon onto bread toasted over a fire fashioned inside an old metal pan. Bottles of beer were opened, wine was poured; the kittens were petted and admired. Everyone was relaxed, everyone was laughing, talking about their memories of the villa and of Joe, and his family. There was an intense discussion about the *Madonna del Mare* painting and what might have happened to it. The painting was famous in Porta Sarina; everybody knew of it.

I looked across to Joe. He was sitting on the lawn, leaning back on his hands. He caught my eye and smiled. His smile was one of reassurance. We weren't going to give up on the villa: why would we when we had so much support, so many friends around us? We weren't going to give in to cowardly threats and acts of malice. We were going to stand our ground until whoever was waging this campaign against us stopped and let us be.

It was good to see Joe so content and buoyed. It was wonderful to have these good people with us. I should have been happy, but above us, storm clouds were gathering, great, heavy, violent clouds obscuring the peaceful blue sky.

53

Four days passed before Joe and I were on our own again. The villa hadn't looked as good as it did then since the day we arrived in Sicily; the interior no longer smelled of smoke but of fresh paint, soap powder and wood polish. The windowpanes were clean, the floors shone, cobwebs, dust and ash had been cleared from the coving and pelmets, even the shutters had been painted. It had been an exhausting and exhilarating few days and so much had been achieved. The clean-up and repair project wasn't finished by a long stretch, but our friends promised to return to complete jobs and to bring us replacements for items that had been irreparably damaged. They promised to stand by us. They told us we weren't alone.

In the afternoon of the fifth day since the fire, Joe went for a swim and I went up to Anna's bedroom with the diary I'd saved from the flames. I propped her portrait on the bed beside me so she could sit with me while I pried into her past. I wanted to find out the truth about her relationship with the young Gabriele Arnone.

Now I knew that he was the young man in the photographs, a whole new range of scenarios was opening up; possible reasons why Anna might have decided to leave Sicily, reasons why she might have married Patrick Cadogan. Maybe she hadn't been rejected or betrayed by her young lover, as I'd imagined. Maybe she'd found out that he was a killer and had fled from him, in fear of her life. That would explain why she never left the villa when she came to visit in her adult years – to avoid any possibility of running into Gabriele Arnone; because she was so afraid of him or because he still had some kind of hold over her. It must have been horrendous for her, him living just up the hill where he could spy on her.

Or maybe it wasn't Anna's choice to leave Gabriele. Maybe her parents had realised what was going on between the two of them, and they'd forced them apart. Maybe they'd sent Anna to live in England to get her well away from Gabriele. Both versions made sense to me.

I retrieved Anna's old vodka bottle from the wardrobe, unscrewed the lid and took a drink. It tasted fine and I enjoyed the burn in my throat.

'Here we go, Anna,' I said quietly.

I opened the diary and skimmed through entries that grumbled about boarding school food and little intrigues between Anna and her classmates until I came to this:

> It's happening. We're going to do it. G sent me a book, with the places marked. It's all planned. We're going to go somewhere where we'll never be found, where we can be together, where we can be free.

Oh God! Anna was planning to run away with Gabriele. The book she mentioned 'with the places marked', was that the Australian guidebook that I'd found in the bottom of the wardrobe when I first searched this room? It must be! So the young lovers had made plans to elope but something stopped them. Neither of them made it to Australia. Gabriele never left the headland and Anna only went as far as England.

I read on:

I'm making lists in my head, changing my mind about what to take, knowing that anything I leave, I might never see again. It's only now I'm forced to think about it that I realise how little I care for anything except my love.

I can't sleep for excitement. I lay awake and stare at the ceiling and think of the adventures to come, the happiness we will share. I feel my life is about to start. These last eighteen years have been a rehearsal. My school friends keep asking me what's going on, but I don't tell them. Miss Gallo wonders if I'm ill. I tell her, no! I have never felt healthier in my life.

She was in love. She was describing the elation of first love. I felt happy for her. I also felt terribly sad because she couldn't have picked a less suitable sweetheart than Gabriele Arnone.

A few pages further on, I read:

Papa is coming to pick me up from school. He looks fine to me, but he says he hasn't been well and he's going to use the opportunity of being in Rome to visit his doctor, but the doctor's very busy and we might be stuck in Papa's apartment for weeks. WEEKS! This is terrible news. I can't have my return to Sicily delayed. Not this year! Please God, not this year! Please, please, please let there be a doctor's appointment available for my papa soon.

So maybe Anna's parents were aware that something was afoot. Perhaps they were concerned about a possible scandal. Maybe the doctor's appointment was a ruse to keep Anna in Rome, well away from Gabriele Arnone.

Two weeks later, the entry read:

We're still in Rome. It's driving me out of my mind knowing that G is waiting & not knowing what's going on. I sent a postcard, but it won't arrive until next week. What if G thinks I've changed my mind?

I asked Papa if I could travel to Sicily alone, but he said: 'No'. His attitude has changed lately. It's scaring me. I came into my room the other day and this diary had been moved from its hiding place. It might just have been the maid, but I suspect he's been snooping. Papa doesn't speak English, but there are plenty of people who would translate for him. I must be more careful.

I flicked forward a few more pages, over a number of entries in which she expressed her frustration and rising panic time and time again:

Matilde telephoned this morning. She's been staying at the villa, sucking up to Mama. She talked for hours about the new swimming pool. It was so boring. I don't care! Why would I care about a stupid pool? I asked her to go to the convent and she promised she would, but I don't trust her. That girl can be so spiteful sometimes.

The convent? Why would Anna want Matilde to go to there? To pray? To ask for divine intervention?

A few days later, in Rome, Anna's situation was deteriorating:

Papa's not affectionate, like he used to be. We don't go out for dinner like we used to. I asked outright if he'd take me to the Trattoria Vecchia, our old haunt. He said no. He watches me all the time. He's definitely been through my things and he's suspicious of everything. He challenged me with my bank account book and asked what's happened to the savings. When I wouldn't tell him, he shouted at me, called me a little traitor. I get the sense he'd like to peel me like an onion; take away layer after layer of me until he's seen right into the middle, seen everything there is to see and there's nothing left that's private to me.

The next day:

Mama telephoned from Sicily. She didn't want to speak to me, but she talked to Papa for hours. When he came off the phone, Papa went into his study and didn't come out until evening. I tried to leave the apartment, but the door was locked, and when I asked Papa for the key, he flew into a rage. He says he knows everything, but how can he know? G wouldn't have said anything to anyone.

Two days later:

I telephoned Matilde while Papa was sleeping. She said she 'hadn't had a chance' to go to the convent yet. I pleaded with her. I won her round with promises of things we'd do together when I'm back. I made her swear on her father's life.

G might be able to change the tickets. It might not be too late. I feel bad for Matilde, but what else can I do?

Three days after that:

Nothing from Sicily. I called M, but her father answered and told me to get off the line.

Later the same day:

Papa tried to make me tell him everything and when I wouldn't, he grabbed me by the arms & shook me & locked me in my room. I hate him.

And that evening:

I will not cry. I will not. I'm not ashamed. Love is nothing to be ashamed of. Papa confronted me again. He took off his belt and beat

*me. He said he'd rather I was dead than perverted. I have to let G
know. It's not safe in Porta Sarina.*

Later:

*Papa said I would bring shame on the DeLuca family name, that he'd
be a laughing stock in the business world if this got out. And after
that he became morose and wondered what he and Mama had done
to make me what I am. He stood by the drinks cabinet filling up his
glass with brandy and blamed himself for the 'disgusting creature'
that I have become. When he left the room, I took his glass and drank
what was left. It made me calm. I finished the bottle. Papa was
drunk. He'll think it was him.*

The following week:

*We're not going to Sicily this summer. Instead, Papa and I are flying
to London and he's going to take me to a psychiatrist to 'cure' me. I'll
pretend to go along with it, it's the only way I'll ever get back to G.
It's our only chance.*

That was the last entry.

I lay the diary open, face down, on the bed and sat there for a
long time considering what I'd just read. It was shocking that
Anna had been pretty much held prisoner by her father to keep
her away from the lover with whom she was planning to elope.
It was sickening to think of Anna's own father treating her so
badly, beating her, and in some ways even worse to read of her
mother's coldness in refusing to speak to her. But I could understand why they were behaving like this. Anna's parents were
panicking. They'd uncovered her plan and were desperate to
stop her leaving with Gabriele Arnone. I had a niggling sympathy. I'd seen the pictures. I knew that Gabriele had been an
attractive young man, confident and charismatic. He probably

had a strong sexual appeal to which Anna responded. How terrifying for her wealthy, respectable parents to think of her absconding with a young thug, a Mafioso; marrying him, bearing his children. She was their only surviving child. She'd been burdened with the weight of their expectations. They were deeply religious and once Anna was married, as far as they were concerned, that would be her lot, for life. Anything she inherited would go to Gabriele too. No wonder they were trying to keep her away from him. No wonder they were doing everything they could to keep the young lovers apart. Their efforts to protect Anna might have been clumsy, cruel even, and even if their motivation was partly to avoid scandal, they had also been acting out of love. It was an awful situation for them all.

I went outside in search of Joe and I found him in the sea, floating on his back.

'Come in,' he called. 'It's beautiful.'

I pulled my dress over my head, dropped it on the decking, climbed down the steps into the sea and swam towards Joe and at the same time he swam towards me. We met and we kissed as we trod water; below the surface, our bodies broke and reformed in the refracted light. Joe's skin was so much warmer than the sea, his mouth so gentle on mine.

We parted, swam quietly alongside one another.

The last entry in the diary was bothering me. Anna had written that her father was taking her to see a psychiatrist in London. Perhaps the DeLuca parents believed Anna could be persuaded out of her infatuation with Gabriele Arnone or perhaps they were hoping she could be prescribed drugs that would make her easier for them to control. I'd read of horrendous 'treatments' inflicted on young women diagnosed as being 'promiscuous' in the wake of the sexual liberation movement during the 1960s. Or maybe they thought a psychiatrist would be able to persuade Anna to understand how unsuitable a match Gabriele would be.

Patrick Cadogan had been working as a psychiatrist in London at that time. Had Anna originally been Patrick's patient? I knew they'd met when Anna was young and at a low point in her life, no more than that.

Joe was floating on his back with his eyes closed. I swam up to him.

'Joe? Do you know how Anna met your father?'

'She never used to talk about it.'

'Didn't Patrick ever say anything?'

'No.'

'Do you know if...' I tailed off.

'If what?'

'If Patrick ever treated Anna for anything, as a patient I mean?'

Joe snorted. 'He didn't treat her. He was the one who gave her most of her problems.'

That was true.

I lay on my back and let the sea hold me up. The sky above me was lovely. I thought of that eighteen year old girl being dragged to England against her will to have her hopes and dreams dashed.

Poor Anna, I thought. *Poor her.*

54

Valentina and Francesco came to the villa. Vito was safely out of the way, working the night shift in Gela, and Francesco wanted to show Valentina the Alfa Romeo.

Valentina was heavy with her pregnancy and it was exhausting her. Dark circles were like bruises around her eyes. When she stood, she leaned backwards to adjust her centre of balance. She breathed through her mouth and she constantly looked for things she could rest against: trees, benches, walls. She winced as the baby moved inside her. She looked as if she needed to lie down in a quiet place and sleep for a week.

Francesco was keen to take his mother for a drive in the Alfa Romeo, but Valentina was too tired to contemplate any such outing.

'You go,' she said to Francesco, 'you and Joe. I'll stay here with Edie while you're gone.'

I was longing to get back to Anna's diary and the photograph albums, but I couldn't abandon Valentina, so the two of us found a shady spot in the garden where we could sit well away from the graveyard. I didn't want any DeLuca bad luck rubbing off on Valentina or her baby.

Valentina hooked her bag over the branch of a tree beside us.

'Don't let me forget it,' she said. 'My phone and my birthing plan are in there.'

'I won't.'

We talked of inconsequential things at first and then, somehow – probably because she was so much on my mind – the conversation moved back to Anna. Valentina was an easy person to talk to and I found myself baring my soul about the way I'd treated Anna after Daniel's death. I told Valentina how I'd blamed her for everything; how I'd hated her.

Valentina was sympathetic. 'Wasn't she supposed to be looking after Daniel when he went missing?'

'Yes.'

'Then it's no wonder you were so angry with her.' She looked at me carefully. 'What happened? Can you talk about it?'

I wasn't sure if I could, but once I started, it wasn't so difficult.

'There's not much to tell. Daniel was almost six. He was playing in the back garden of Anna's house in London. She went inside to fetch herself a drink and he slipped out of the gate.'

'Oh.'

'We didn't know he could open the gate by himself. There was a complicated latch and... well, he must have watched us and figured it out. He knew he wasn't supposed to go out of the garden, but there was a building site just round the corner and he couldn't resist the diggers.'

'Francesco was the same,' said Valentina. 'Lorries, cranes, they were like a drug to him.'

'It was raining,' I said. 'Joe and I had gone into town. When we got back to Anna's house, it was empty. She'd already called the police.'

I'd never talked about this before, about the awful, mundane details of the day Daniel died, although I'd often ranted about Anna's alcoholism or her carelessness. It was odd to speak of the events in a normal tone of voice, to report them objectively rather than through a mirror of hatred.

'You must have been so frightened,' said Valentina.

'We went round the streets,' I told her, 'Joe and me. We were circling; going along all the alleyways between the houses. Everyone we saw, we asked them: "Have you seen a little boy? This high, dark hair, wearing a tracksuit, a blue anorak." Everyone joined in the search, all the neighbours. We could hear people calling Daniel's name for miles. We kept meeting people who were looking for him and they didn't know we were his parents, they asked us to help, described our own son to us. Everyone was so kind. Everyone was trying so hard and I was thinking: "It'll be all right. It'll be okay. How can anything happen to him when all of London is looking? When everyone wants to be the one who finds him?"'

Valentina was watching me intently. Her hands were on her belly, protecting the baby.

I turned the key ring that Irma had given me between my fingers and continued: 'We reached the building site, and it seemed secure, there were signs everywhere saying: Danger, Keep Out! and signs saying there were dog patrols and we thought it would be impossible for anyone to get in, but we walked the perimeter anyway, to make sure, and there was a hole at the foot of one of the hoardings, only a small hole, but big enough for Daniel to crawl through. As soon as I saw it, I knew.'

I remembered every detail, how my hair had been plastered to my head and mascara was in my eyes, making my vision blurry. Joe and I had tugged at the hoarding, kicking it until the hole was big enough for us to wriggle under like commandos, and we found ourselves in a wasteland; acres of mud and piles of rubble, giant machines standing still, stacks of pipes, huge wooden bobbins wound with stressing cables. My hands and knees and front were plastered in mud. Joe began walking around the inner circumference of the hoarding calling Daniel's name. Something had drawn me forwards.

'They had dug a hole,' I told Valentina, 'a shaft for the lift to go down to the basement of the building they hadn't even started to build. I didn't know the hole was there, but I could feel Daniel, as if he was calling me and I...'

I'd gone forward, mud clagging my shoes and the legs of my jeans, my feet so heavy. I kept slipping, but I continued moving forward and I reached the edge of the shaft and I looked over. I could see Daniel at the bottom, twenty feet below me. I could see him lying there like a doll; he looked as if he was running, only he was lying flat on the mud and a puddle had formed on the bottom, he was half in, half out of the puddle. I called his name, but he didn't answer me. I tried to climb down, but I slipped.

'I fell too,' I said quietly. 'I broke many bones but I don't remember feeling any pain; not from the bones, I mean. I couldn't think of anything beyond Daniel.'

'Was he dead?' Valentina asked in a whisper.

'Yes.' I let out my breath. 'And I blamed Anna.'

'Of course you did,' she said softly. 'Of course you did. Any mother would have done the same. You mustn't blame yourself for blaming her.' Valentina's hand was gentle on mine.

Blaming Anna kept me going; it was the blood in my veins, it was the metronome that measured my heartbeat; since Daniel's death it had become the single, biggest part of me, it was my raison d'être. 'But I shouldn't have blamed her,' I said quietly.

'What do you mean?'

'Once,' I told her, 'I had a headache and I went to the shops for some aspirin. I was home boiling the kettle before I realised I'd left Daniel asleep in his pushchair outside the chemist's.'

'We've all done things like that.'

'And once, in London, he climbed onto a tube train ahead of me and the train pulled away before I could get the buggy on. A woman realised what had happened and waited with him on the platform at the next station. If she hadn't noticed, God knows where he'd have ended up.'

'You were lucky,' Valentina said.

'Very lucky.' I sighed. 'All Anna did was take her eye off Daniel for a few minutes while he was playing in the garden of her home where she believed he was safe.'

'She was unlucky,' Valentina said quietly.

And, like that, the wall around my heart came down. Because it was true. It had taken me ten years to acknowledge that Anna was not to blame for Daniel's death. Anna wasn't perfect, but she loved Daniel. She loved him with every ounce of her being, every beat of her heart. Even when I hated her, deep down I never doubted that. She had left him playing in the garden for a few minutes while she went inside to fix herself a drink. She hadn't killed Daniel. She'd been hideously, appallingly unlucky.

55

I went to fetch some water and when I returned, Valentina was dozing, her legs stretched out in front of her, her body propped against the chair, her belly like a hill stretching the fabric of her dress tight. I didn't like to leave her there alone, so I fetched a blanket and lay down on the grass beside her, a book open in front of me but not paying it much attention. If a fly or mosquito landed on Valentina's bare ankles, I shooed it away.

My thoughts were all about Anna and what might have happened to her after she was sent to the psychiatrist in London. What had they done to her? I wondered. What had happened to change her from a feisty, courageous teenager to the cowed, anxious, damaged woman I had always known?

* * *

When I heard the roar of the Alfa Romeo's engine that signalled Joe and Francesco's return, I pushed myself to my feet and met them at the gate. We were standing by the car, Francesco raving about how wonderful it was, his eyes bright and cheeks flushed, when another vehicle came down the hill. In amongst the approaching cloud of dust and exhaust fumes was Vito's truck.

Francesco glanced anxiously from me to Joe and back again.

Joe straightened his shoulders and did his best not to look worried.

'It's okay, Francesco,' he said. 'Everything's going to be okay.'

'I'll talk to Vito,' I said to Joe. 'You take Francesco to find Valentina.'

'I'm not leaving you with Vito,' said Joe.

'He won't do anything to me.'

The truck bumped onto the parking area.

'Joe!' I hissed, signalling that he should take Francesco away, but before either of them could move, Valentina stepped out from behind us. She walked calmly towards the truck and met Vito when he was already almost upon us, holding his arms out to her, his face a mask of concern.

'There you are!' he cried. 'I didn't know where you were, baby! I've been looking everywhere.'

Valentina stood stiff as he embraced her, pulling her close so that her back bent awkwardly. He kissed her on the mouth as she remained rigid.

I looked to Joe, desperately uncomfortable. He was looking the other way.

Vito was staring into Valentina's eyes, holding her face between the palms of his hands so she had no choice but to look at him.

'We finished early and I went back to the pizzeria to surprise you, baby,' he said, squeezing her face. 'You weren't there. I've been looking everywhere. You never said you were going out. I thought something had happened to you!'

'What would have happened to me?' Valentina asked.

'You know how I worry about you when you're not at home! You shouldn't have come all this way without me. You're supposed to be resting, baby.' He shook his head and pulled the kind of face a parent pulls when a toddler does something stupid. 'I phoned my aunt. I said: "Auntie Irma, I'm so worried, I don't know where Valentina is!" and she told me she'd seen you being dropped off at the villa. She told me you'd been here for hours. Why didn't you let me know where you were, baby? You know I always like to know.'

Valentina didn't answer. Over her shoulder, Vito sent a look of pure malice towards Joe.

'Get in the truck, baby,' Vito said to Valentina. 'Come on, kid,' he beckoned Francesco, 'you too!'

'I want to stay here,' Francesco said sullenly.

'No,' Valentina said sharply.

'It's time you were off, buddy,' Joe said to Francesco. 'Go with your mama. We'll see you soon.'

Francesco scowled, but he approached the truck and climbed into the back. Vito gave him a push as he went in.

'Francesco...' I called.

Valentina turned to me and shook her head.

I stepped back.

'There,' said Vito, helping Valentina up into the truck. 'The family's back together again. Everyone where they should be.' He slammed the door shut so hard that the truck rocked. Valentina's face was in profile, staring straight ahead.

Vito started the engine and a plume of smoke gusted from the truck's exhaust like a great black fart.

'Bastard,' Joe murmured.

I took hold of his hand.

56

Heavy clouds loitered ill-temperedly in a gunmetal grey sky, glowering over the sea, turning it a threatening colour. The birds fell silent. Heat was trapped between the land and the clouds. Joe tramped off to be by himself somewhere, to dwell on his hatred for Vito. I had a headache. My vision was disturbed by a silvery shadow, like mercury on a mirror. For a moment, I imagined it was one of the ghost children, Daniel perhaps, but soon realised it was only the onset of a migraine.

I went upstairs, took a couple of tablets with a glass of water and lay down on Anna's bed. I picked up the diary and flicked through it, searching for entries I hadn't yet read. I found a sweet little sketch of Anna sitting on the same bed I was on now, with her back against the bed frame. Matilde's work, I guessed; it had been executed with the same lightness of touch as the figures drawn on the wall behind the bed.

I touched the drawing gently with the tip of my finger and the villa played its time trick on me; the bed, the pencil mark, the diary, all these things were always here, only the people came and went.

I searched the diary again. I was missing something. I knew

that I was. There was something I needed to know to make sense
of it all; some clue I didn't yet have.

I reread an account of a day the three friends – Anna,
Matilde and Gina – had spent on the beach. They'd taken a
picnic prepared by Signora Ganzaria – the food described in
detail – and played beach ball. After that, they'd gone for a
swim. I'd skimmed the entry before, finding it insignificant. Now
I read on.

Anna had written:

The sea was so cold that my hands were blue when I came out. G
blew on them to warm them and wrapped her towel around us both
like a blanket.

'G'. Not Gabriele, Gina.
Here was another one:

Gina and I went to Ragusa on the bus. We climbed to the Giardini
Iblei & G made some sketches of me. She's going to paint a portrait of
me for my birthday!

Gina! It was Gina who had painted Anna's portrait! I smiled
at the picture, propped against the wall.

I flicked through more pages:

Matilde came over today. Mama invited her to stay the night. She's
sleeping in my bed now and I am by the window writing my diary
by moonlight. I'd rather be here, on the chair. I don't like sleeping
beside Matilde. She's such a fidget. I miss Gina. I wish she was here.

Two days later, a local builder brought his labourer down to
the villa to look at the swimming pool and discuss plans for
demolishing the old one, built in the 1920s, and replacing it with
a modern pool, which Anna described in her diary:

Two interlocking circles, one deep, one shallow, with a sloping shelf linking the two, & tiled steps into the water at the shallow end. There'll be filters & a pump house, systems for keeping the water clean. It's going to be 'state of the art' according to Papa. The best pool in Sicily, he says.

One of the labourer's boys, Anna reported, was a good-looking young man called Gabriele Arnone:

He has taken a shine to G & G has been playing along.

Slowly, slowly, the penny dropped. My mind shifted as I reordered Anna's story, mentally crossed out what I'd believed up to that point and wrote a different version. Because if 'G' was Gina and not Gabriele, then everything I'd read before had been misinterpreted, everything I thought I knew had been wrong.

I read on:

In two weeks, I'll be going back to Rome. G's going to be on her own in Porta Sarina with that asshole Gabriele sniffing around her like a dog. I keep telling her she needs to be careful, but she just laughs and says she knows what she's doing. I don't like this boy. He looks like a prince but has the reputation of a thug.

The following week there was a shock entry:

M knows. She saw G and me together 'accidentally'. She made out she was so upset that we could have 'betrayed' her like this. 'Oh, how could you do this behind my back? Aren't I your best friend? Don't I care about you the most? Haven't we been friends the longest?' etc. I'm sure she's been spying. She says we can trust her, but sometimes I catch a look in her eye and it tells me quite the opposite.

I closed the diary and sat back against the wall.

Oh, I thought, *that explains everything.*

Anna loved Gina and Gina loved Anna. Of course, their love had to be secret! They lived in a small town in Sicily, where homosexuality was regarded as such a deviance that the mafia executed a gay couple to make an example of them and as a warning to others. And Matilde knew about Gina and Anna. Matilde who loved Anna, who loved Anna's parents, who believed herself to be like a sister to Anna. I could see how, to Matilde, Anna and Gina's relationship would have seemed a betrayal of her loyalty and friendship.

Matilde would have told Anna's parents what she knew, I was certain of it. She'd have seen it as her duty but that wouldn't have been her only motivation. She must also have been painfully jealous. Telling Anna's parents about their daughter's love affair was the most effective way of making sure Gina and Anna were separated. And once the DeLuca parents knew, once they realised the danger Anna was in, it was no wonder they kept her away from Porta Sarina. No wonder they sent her to a psychiatrist to try to 'cure' her. Now everything made sense.

Behind me now, behind the bed frame on the wall, was the drawing of the two female figures. Matilde Romano had drawn our attention to them; she said they represented herself and Anna, but Matilde wasn't the artist, Gina was. Gina had painted the beautiful portrait of Anna; Gina, I was certain, had drawn the sketch in the diary, Gina had made the drawing on the wall.

Matilde had lied about the image. She'd lied because even when Anna was dead, her jealousy knew no limits. She would not acknowledge that Anna had ever loved Gina, not even now. She was crazy.

I slid off the bed and went to find Joe.

Outside, the storm clouds were growing heavier. Flickers of thunder rumbled above. The peninsula seemed to be holding its breath. The sea had flattened, its surface barely moving. The light was weird, bright and artificial; the villa, the trees, the headland, all of them looked unreal.

I walked across the garden and saw something hooked over the branch of a tree: a fringed leather bag – Valentina's. 'Don't let me forget this,' she'd said and I'd promised I wouldn't, but when Vito turned up, Valentina's bag had been the last thing on my mind.

57

I found Joe in the stables. I told him about the bag and that we had to return it to Valentina as quickly as possible.

'We'll go now,' he said.

We crossed the gardens together. The storm clouds were expanding, lightning deep inside them, flickering; it seemed as if they were preparing to explode. We heard the distant rumbling of thunder. Joe grabbed the car keys and together we ran to the parking area.

When we reached Fiat Two, it was on a slant. Two of its tyres were flat.

'Two?' Joe said, incredulous. He leaned down. 'They've been slashed. Jesus! What the fuck's going on?' He stood up and walked round the sports car parked beside it. 'The Alfa's fine. We'll have to go in that.'

'What if the storm breaks while we're out?'

'Then, my darling, we'll get wet.'

* * *

The moon was bright behind the clouds as we drove around the

Arnones' cottage and headed out along the coast road. Lightning flashed over the sea, licking its surface. The Alfa Romeo's engine roared. Joe took the bends very fast. I clutched Valentina's bag on my lap.

There was no wind that night, but still I was buffeted by hot air. The road felt bumpy beneath us.

Joe jolted the steering wheel from side to side.

'What is it?' I asked.

'Something doesn't feel quite right.'

I didn't pay much attention. My mind was full of those young girls; Gina, Anna, Matilde. They danced through my mind.

I held onto the top of the car door as we rounded another corner and the car lurched.

'Sorry,' said Joe, 'I took that one a bit fast.'

I gripped the door tightly. My hair was blowing across my face. I gulped at the air.

* * *

Without moonlight shining down on it, the town of Porta Sarina was dark, its narrow roads malevolent. I couldn't see into its shadows, didn't know what might be lurking around the corners that the Alfa Romeo's headlights didn't reach. It was a relief when the vista opened up and we saw the harbour lights, lightning jittering above the sea.

Joe parked outside Vito's. He turned off the engine but left the keys in the ignition. A group of men were sitting beneath the awning at the harbour-front tables, drinking. There was no sign of Vito or his truck.

'Wait here,' Joe said. 'I'll take the bag.'

I sat in the car and watched as he went inside, disappearing into the light. I could hear the men's voices, the sound of a television; the distant rumble of thunder. Sitting in the open-topped car made me feel vulnerable so I climbed out. I walked along the harbourside a short distance, looked back. I could see Joe inside the pizzeria's kitchen. His face was lit by the glow from the oven. Valentina was there too. It looked as if he was remonstrating with her.

'Come on,' I murmured. 'Hurry up.'

A breeze blew in from the sea. The waves were dancing erratically, white horses whipped up by the wind. I crossed the road, came closer to the pizzeria entrance, stepping slowly, cautiously. I couldn't hear what Joe was saying but now Valentina was holding the hem of her apron to her face, wiping her eyes.

'Come on,' I whispered. 'Come on!'

I stood, waiting restlessly, moving from foot to foot. The storm clouds bloomed larger. In the distance, thunder boomed. I kept putting my hand in my pocket but the phone wasn't there: I'd left it at the villa. I couldn't check the time but Joe had been inside the pizzeria for ages; at least ten minutes. The bulbs in the streetlights flickered. Someone turned up the volume on the TV.

'Come on!' I said again, but it was too late. I heard the sound of a truck approaching and I knew it must be Vito. Shit!

I went into the pizzeria, through the bar, and stood beside the counter that separated it from the kitchen. On the other side, Joe was comforting Valentina, his arms around her. She was sobbing.

'Joe,' I hissed, ' we need to get out of here!'

'I can't leave her like this!'

'Vito's coming! I heard his truck!'

'Valentina,' Joe said, straightening, holding her shoulders so that she had to look at his face, 'come with us. We'll take care of you.'

She shook her head. 'I'm not going anywhere without Francesco.'

'Vito will be here any minute,' I said. 'You have to come now.'

'You go,' Valentina said. 'Get out of here. I'll wait for Francesco.'

'Where is he?' I asked.

'I don't know. He got in between me and Vito earlier and Vito hit him. He went off on his bike. He... God! He took a bottle of grappa.'

'We'll find him,' said Joe. His face was flushed with the heat. His T-shirt was dark with sweat. 'Come with us.'

'I can't go without him,' said Valentina.

'Please, Valentina!'

'I can't.'

I stared pleadingly at Joe. The heat from the oven was overbearing. My skin prickled. 'If we don't go now...'

But it was too late. We heard a crash and turned to see Vito pushing aside chairs as he strode through the restaurant towards us. I made an attempt to stop him but he barged past me. His breath was foul with alcohol and tobacco.

Valentina stood at the entrance to the kitchen, half sobbing, half pleading with her husband to calm down. Vito pushed her aside with no regard for her pregnancy. All his focus was on Joe.

'You can't stay away, can you!' he snarled at Joe. 'You just can't leave my wife alone.'

'She shouldn't be working in the kitchen in this heat,' Joe said calmly. He took a step back, away from Vito but closer to the oven behind him. It belched out searing air, the wood inside burned white. The casing must be blisteringly hot. *Don't lean on it, darling*, I thought. *Don't burn yourself.*

'Don't you tell me what my fucking wife should be doing.' Vito moved closer to Joe, the muscles on his arms tensing. Joe took another step back.

'Joe, careful!' I called.

'She's my wife,' Vito snarled, jabbing his finger into Joe's chest. 'She does what I tell her to do, that's how it is!'

'Don't you touch him, Vito,' Valentina said. Her voice was steely.

'You stay out of this, baby.'

Joe's back was almost touching the oven now. I took my eyes off him for a second, looking around for something I could use as a weapon but Valentina was quicker than me. She picked up the pizza paddle and lifted it.

'How many times do I have to tell you to leave her alone?' Vito asked Joe, his fist clenched, his arm raised. 'How many times do I have to punch you before you get the fucking message...' and then he was silenced as Valentina swept the paddle round, slamming the metal tray into the side of Vito's head. He fell sideways, down onto the floor.

'I told you not to touch him!' Valentina screamed, the paddle clattering on top of her husband.

Vito groaned, doubled over in pain, his hands clasped to his cheek. Blood was bubbling between his fingers.

'I told you!' screamed Valentina.

Joe was trapped between Vito and the oven. He caught my eye 'Get her out!' he called to me. 'Quick!'

'Not without you!'

'Get her out!' Joe cried again.

'Come on!' I told Valentina. I took her arm. Vito was still hunched, staggering, grabbing at Joe's legs with a bloodied hand. Joe kicked him away.

'I can't go without Francesco!' Valentina cried.

'You can phone him from the car. We'll pick him up!' I tugged her arm and at last she moved. We hurried through the empty restaurant, bumping into the furniture as we went.

I glanced behind me. Joe was trying to keep Vito in the kitchen but Vito was flailing. Joe wouldn't be able to hold him back for long. Valentina and I reached the door and were halfway across the road when Vito came crashing towards us, blood streaming down his face. Joe stumbled behind. His shirt was torn and there was blood on his cheek too.

'Hey!' Vito called drunkenly. 'Valentina! What you doing, baby? What d'you think you're doing?'

'Leave me alone!' she called.

'Baby! Angel! Come on! Come to Vito!'

'She doesn't want you!' I yelled at him.

Vito roared in anger, grabbed a wine bottle from the table on the terrace and threw it. Valentina screamed and we both ducked, our hands over our heads. The bottle hit the side of the Alfa Romeo with an awful thunk and bounced back onto the road. It shattered and wine frothed over the tarmac like blood. The men from the table at the terrace pushed back their chairs and huddled round Vito, trying to restrain him.

While all this was going on, something moved in the periphery of my vision; something small and quiet emerged from the darkness; Francesco. He cycled up to the Alfa Romeo, put one foot on the ground and looked around him, taking in the scene. He dropped the bike, jumped over the driver's door and slid into the seat. He leaned across to open the passenger door and called to his mother. Valentina crawled into the seat beside him. He started the engine. The engine roared, smoke plumed from the exhaust and Francesco drove the Alfa Romeo away. It all happened in five seconds, maybe ten and then the car was gone; and all that was left was a grey trail of exhaust smoke, hanging above the roadway.

On the terrace outside the restaurant, everything went quiet. Vito stopped raging, the men fell silent, I went to Joe and we stood together, listening to the sound of the Alfa Romeo's engine fade. Up above, thunder rumbled, like applause.

'Scusi! Scusi!'

It was one of the men from the terrace. He put something in Joe's hand: a set of keys.

He pointed to an old car parked a few yards away and made the motion of driving with his hands.

Joe began to ask a question but the man snorted with impatience and waved us towards his car. Behind us, Vito was becoming noisy again, arguing with the other men.

'Come on,' said Joe.

We jogged over to the old man's car and climbed in. It was dusty and battered and smelled of fish. The seats were torn and the steering wheel held together with duct tape, but it rattled into life at the first attempt and Joe steered it through the town as fast as he could, with me bracing myself against the dashboard. Only one headlight worked, giving us a narrow view of the road ahead. When we reached the open road, Joe ramped the car through its gears, and it rattled and bumped, gaining speed. We rose up the headland spine and, ahead, I glimpsed a pair of headlights zigzagging smoothly along the coast road ahead of us.

'Is that Francesco?' I asked.

'Looks like it,' said Joe.

He put his foot down and we reached the billboard junction perhaps two minutes after the Alfa Romeo and joined the coast road. I held tight to the seat; Joe was gripping the steering wheel, his face close to the windscreen, concentrating on the road.

We turned tightly round a bend and suddenly Joe slammed on the brakes and we stopped with a great jolt that threw me forward with such violence I hit my face on the dashboard before I bounced back.

'What?' I cried, my hands clasped over my nose. 'Why did you stop like that?'

Joe was already out of the car, moving towards something that I could not see. I followed him, blood dripping between my fingers, and then I saw what Joe had seen. The Alfa Romeo was crashed into the side of the mountain.

58

The sports car was skewed across the road, its nose pressed against a sapling that was broken in the middle, falling crooked across its bonnet. The lights on the passenger side were broken, glass fragmented on the road, but the driver's-side lights were still on, illuminating the scene like a chiaroscuro painting.

Francesco was standing to one side, his hands on his knees, panting; he'd been sick, strings of saliva trailed from his mouth. Valentina was kneeling awkwardly on the road, cradling a gaunt figure in her arms. It was an old man, and he was wearing pyjama bottoms, a piece of rope tied around the waist, rubber clogs: Gabriele Arnone.

Gently, Joe prised my fingers from my face. He took off his T-shirt, scrunched it up and gave it to me to hold to my nose. Then he took out his phone and as he called for help he went to Francesco, put his free arm around him, held the boy's head to his chest.

I headed towards Valentina and Gabriele. I stepped on something pulpy and recoiled in disgust, but when I looked down, I saw that tomatoes had been spilled on the road, that was all.

Valentina was holding Gabriele upright as best she could.

I crouched beside her.

'He was in the road!' she said. 'He was right there in the middle of the road!'

'Capretta,' murmured Gabriele.

'It's Vito's uncle,' Valentina whispered, her eyes glistening. 'Francesco tried to steer around him, he did his best.'

'I know he did,' I said. 'Are you okay, Valentina? Did you hurt yourself?'

'I'm okay.'

Gabriele's wet old eyes swivelled from one of us to the other. A crust of spit had dried in the corner of his lips. His skin was waxy and yellow, he looked dreadful.

'Help will be here soon, Signor Arnone,' I whispered. I took hold of one of his big hands. It was cold. His breathing was laboured.

Valentina repeated the reassurance in Italian. The old man didn't seem to understand either way, but he was calm.

'Francesco couldn't help but hit him,' Valentina whispered again. 'It wasn't his fault!' She beckoned me closer. Her eyes were frantic. She whispered over Gabriele's big head, 'He's been drinking grappa. He took the bottle after Vito beat him.'

'I know,' I said, 'it's okay, try not to worry.'

Joe came over to us. Francesco was behind him, his hands hanging limp by his side.

'The ambulance is coming,' Joe said, 'and the police.' He held my eye meaningfully. 'We don't all need to be here when they come.'

I gave a small nod of understanding.

He bent low and carefully took the weight of the old man from Valentina. 'I'll look after Signor Arnone. You go back to the villa with Edie,' he told her. 'Take Francesco. He needs you.'

'Tell the police it wasn't Francesco's fault,' Valentina said. 'Tell them he did his best! Tell them—'

'Don't worry,' said Joe. 'I'll take care of everything.'

* * *

Francesco, Valentina and I squashed into the fishy car. We set off, heading jerkily along the road back towards our headland, when the first thunder cracked the sky like a sledgehammer. We all jumped and Valentina began to mutter something that sounded like a prayer. She was sitting in the front, beside me, her arms around her belly, her eyes closed. Francesco, behind, had one hand on his mother's shoulder. From time to time, he sniffed and wiped his face with the back of his hand.

I kept the car in second gear and we puttered along barely faster than walking pace as the first fat spots of rain began to fall. I couldn't work out how to turn on the windscreen wipers. Raindrops exploded on the windscreen. We were approaching the Arnone cottage. I was leaning so far forward that my sore nose was almost pressed against the windscreen.

'Careful!' Valentina cried.

I hit the brake hard and stalled the car. Rain was spotting onto the road, turning it black.

Walking towards us, hurrying through the downpour was a figure; an elderly woman – Irma Arnone. One hand was held to her eyes. The headlight was blinding her.

I climbed out of the car and met Irma on the road. Raindrops fell around us and on my head and my shoulders, stinging my sore nose.

Irma Arnone squinted to see who I was. She screwed her face up against the rain and the light. She kept repeating Gabriele's name.

I pointed up the road. 'He's hurt. There's been an accident.'

She didn't understand what I was trying to tell her. I thought: *I'm going to have to take her to Gabriele.* I couldn't leave her on the road, alone, not like this.

Thunder crashed above us; we ducked out of instinct and

then, thank God, we heard the sound of a siren approaching from the Ragusa direction.

We stood together, in the pool of the single, wonky head-light, rain lashing onto us and around us, until the blue lights of an ambulance came around the corner and then I stepped into the road and waved and the ambulance stopped.

Irma spoke to the paramedic who helped her into the cab and together they drove off up the road.

I returned to the car. Valentina and Francesco were cowering inside.

My clothes were stuck to my skin. Rain was dripping from the ends of my hair, my eyelashes. Another flash of lightning lit up the headland.

I climbed back into the car, started the engine and we set off again, slowly.

A police car flashed past us, heading towards the accident, and that was a relief. If the police car was there, even if Vito tried to reach us, he wouldn't get past it. We would be safe in the villa tonight.

59

Back at the villa, Valentina, Francesco and I hurried inside. Claps of thunder echoed across the bay. Lightning skipped across the horizon, razors of light slashing the sky.

We sat in the kitchen, the gas flames burning on the stove. The kittens came out of their hiding places to find us. I made peppermint tea, gave cups to Francesco and Valentina. Francesco looked at me and Valentina from hooded eyes, wondering if we were angry with him.

Valentina reached across to take his hand.

I told him he was a hero, that he'd done nothing wrong.

'What about the old man?' he asked.

'You couldn't help him being there in the road,' said Valentina. 'It wasn't your fault.'

Francesco began to cry. We tried to comfort him, but he was inconsolable and all Valentina could do was hold him while I paced and waited until the crying passed.

After that, we sat in silence, listening to the rain. The kittens played about us. When Valentina said she had to lie down, I took her upstairs into Anna's old room, moved my things and made up a clean bed. Valentina climbed onto the bed, a candle flickering in a jar beside her. I covered her over. She asked Francesco to stay with her and he lay beside her on the bed. They lay there quietly, in each other's arms. It was good to see them together, mother and son. I remembered how I used to climb into Daniel's bed when he couldn't sleep and how we used to lay like that too. Poor Francesco's face was swollen with crying; his heart was breaking.

Valentina whispered endearments and reassurances. 'It'll be okay, honey. Everything's going to be okay.' I could see the baby moving inside her.

Hours passed and the storm had abated before I heard the front door open and Joe's footsteps in the hall. He came to find me in the kitchen. I saw his eyes run over the injuries on my face. He stood beside me, his hand holding mine. His breathing was slow.

Outside, somewhere beyond the window, the first notes of birdsong rang out.

'Is there any news on Gabriele?' I asked.

'It's not looking good.'

'What did you tell the police?'

Joe was silent.

I lined up the pieces of his silence. 'You told them you were driving the Alfa Romeo, didn't you?'

'Yes.'

The darkness pressed in around us. A gust of wind blew raindrops against the window, and then it became quiet outside.

Silence. Our breathing. A mosquito in a high corner of the room whined.

'If Gabriele dies, people will believe you caused his death,' I whispered, 'they'll hold you responsible.'

'I'd had nothing to drink,' Joe said. 'I was insured. I've passed my driving test.' All the things that Francesco didn't, wasn't, hadn't.

I heard a movement upstairs, a floorboard creaking, but it was nothing. It was my mind playing tricks.

The white kitten appeared. He tiptoed along the edge of the wall and disappeared into the shadows. I glimpsed Daniel's face at the window; pale and ghostly, anxious, watching.

'Everything's going to be all right,' Joe said quietly. 'Everything's going to be fine now. It's sorted.'

And I could tell from his voice that, finally, he was at peace with himself. He couldn't save our son, but he believed he could save Valentina's.

I looked back to the window. Daniel was gone.

I rested my head on Joe's shoulder. He rested his head against mine.

More birds were singing now and a melancholy light was creeping across the sky, a reluctant dawn breaking.

Joe and I were so close I couldn't tell where I ended and where he began.

60

The dawn came in, fresh and cool. I moved about the kitchen cutting bread and cheese, washing fruit, boiling water to make tea. I'd barely slept, but I didn't feel tired. We were at a cross-roads, and I didn't know if the next road would take us to the end of our journey, or to a different kind of beginning. All I knew was that I must be strong and look after the people I cared for. I must stand by them. They needed to know where my loyalty lay.

Francesco came downstairs and stood in the hallway in a T-shirt and underpants. His legs were teenage skinny, dark with hair, his knees bony knots, his feet long and thin. His hair was untidy, sticking up around his face, moppet-like. I'd have liked to take him in my arms and comfort him, but I was afraid that would be too much intimacy, so I crossed my arms around my own body and held back. Francesco was going to need me. I couldn't afford to alienate him now.

'Hi.' I smiled.

Francesco was doing his best to hide the fact that he couldn't bear to look directly at me. My swollen lip and nose and the dark bruises beneath each eye reminded him of all he'd endured the previous night.

'Where's Joe?' he asked.

'Asleep in the living room. Would you like a drink? Something to eat?'

'I'd like to watch TV.'

'We don't have one.'

'Oh.' He sighed. 'My phone doesn't work here.'

'There's no signal.'

'How can I find out if the old man from last night is okay?'

I pulled my cardigan tight round my shoulders. 'You come and make tea for Valentina,' I said. 'I know where to find a signal. I'll go and check.'

I pulled an old sweater of Joe's over my top and went out. The rain had washed the fire smuts from the garden. It had brought out flowers, flowers everywhere; the garden was a kaleidoscope of colour rinsed in the freshness of the after-rain smell.

I walked uphill until my phone latched onto a network and then I checked the local news website. The headline read: INCIDENTE STRADALE: UNO MORTO.

Uno morto. One dead.

'Oh no,' I whispered. 'Oh no!'

How could I deliver that news? How could I look into Francesco's eyes and tell him Gabriele was dead?

The unfairness of the situation bit down on me. Francesco had been trying to take his mother from danger. He had never instigated any trouble or violence. He hadn't known, when he drank that grappa, that in a few hours he'd have to drive his mother from her brutal, drunken husband. Now, no matter what story was told to the police, no matter how many times Francesco was reassured that he couldn't have done anything differently, his whole life would be shadowed by the fact that he'd killed a man and that it might have been because he'd had a drink.

As I stood there, worrying and grieving for Francesco's future, Joe came striding up the hill. I looked at him, his silver head, his tanned skin, the blue jumper, the shorts, and I felt a little calmer. I watched him approach and I no longer saw a scruffy, middle-aged man, a half stranger; I saw Joe; Joe who I loved, who I'd never stopped loving; Joe, my soulmate, my husband, my best friend.

He slowed as he came closer and looked at my face.

'Did he make it?'

I gave the smallest shake of my head.

'Oh, dear God,' he whispered. 'Jesus, Edie, what do we do now?'

'We have to tell the truth and let Francesco and Valentina decide what to do.'

'I don't want to put that responsibility on Francesco's shoulders.'

'You have to, Joe. It'll be better if the truth comes out now. Better for Francesco, I mean. I know you want to protect him, but you can't hide this from him.'

'He'll go to prison.'

'He's too young for prison. And plenty of people saw what happened at Vito's. The witnesses will explain why he had to take the car.'

'The grappa...'

'It wouldn't have changed anything.'

'Nobody will believe that.'

I shook my head sadly. 'We can't change what people believe, Joe. We can only tell the truth. It's all we can do.'

* * *

We walked down the hill together, dawdling, putting off the awful moment when we had to break the news of Gabriele Arnone's death to Francesco. We went through the villa's gates and into the gardens. The birds were singing their hearts out. All the plants and trees, even those that had previously wilted in the heat, stood upright. The sky was blue, the light was bright, the colours vivid. We took the long way around the garden, around the edge of the flower beds, past the great oleaster that sheltered the little graveyard, past the old pool house, across the lawn. The area around the pool was muddy and puddled, the pile of concrete and tiles that had been dug out had collapsed in the downpour and the walls of the pool had subsided. I leaned over the hole, expecting it to be half full of water, but it wasn't. Only a couple of inches of muddy water lay at its base, and a largish brown object half submerged in the mud at the bottom.

'What's that?' I asked Joe.

'I don't know.'

He looked around, found an old bean cane, went to the pool and slid down the bank so he was standing in the puddle at the bottom. He poked the object with the end of the cane, turning it over. The other side of it stared back up at us. Joe looked up at me.

'Jesus,' he whispered.

At his feet was a human skull.

61

'Is it real?' I asked.

'I think so. There's something else here...'

'What?'

'Some big bone. Part of a pelvis, I think.'

'Oh God!'

Other bones were in the mud. A knobble of a spine, part of a leg; the delicate curl of a rib and another, broken ribs.

'It's a whole skeleton,' Joe said. He suddenly jumped and shook his foot. A piece of cloth was attached to it, ancient, filthy. Joe stepped back and cried out as he trod on another bone. He scrabbled for the side of the pool.

I stepped away, slipped and sat down in the mud. I reached down to help Joe and heaved him up. He stood beside me, covered in mud and panting heavily.

'Jesus,' he said, 'Jesus Christ!'

We clung to one another, appalled. Joe was trembling.

'How did it get there?' I asked.

'I don't know.'

'D'you think it's another of those things like the cat and the crow?'

'It looks old, like it's been there for ages.'

'You mean it was there all the time? Under the pool?'

We stared into the mud. The bones were settling again now, the skull tilted to one side. A brown bubble emerged from one of the eye sockets and broke on the surface. We both shuddered.

'Maybe the pool was built over an old graveyard,' I whispered.

'It wasn't.'

'How can you be sure?'

'Because the DeLucas were superstitious about such things. They just wouldn't do that.'

'Where did it come from then?'

'I don't know!'

I felt the chill of those old bones in the puddle at the bottom of the pool. I felt the dread in my own bones. I recalled how Gabriele Arnone was drawn to this old pool, how I'd found him standing, staring into it.

'You'd better go and call the police, Edie,' said Joe. 'Tell them what we've found. I'll stay here and talk to Francesco and Valentina.'

It was still early, not yet seven o'clock. Less than twelve hours had passed since we set off for Porta Sarina to return Valentina's handbag; it felt like a lifetime.

* * *

I walked up the hill for the second time that morning. The sun was growing stronger now; the earth was drying. I could smell the fallen rain as it evaporated back to the sky. My mind clattered with all that had happened. That body must have lain in its secret grave beneath the swimming pool for years. All that time, those bones were in the dark, underground, the flesh rotting in the cold, while just above them children played; that poor lonely body below and all the happy, warm bodies above, kicking and diving, floating on lilos, doing handstands on the base of the pool – so much living above such a lonely resting place.

When I had a signal, I called the commissariato in Ragusa and explained what we'd found. The officer didn't speak good English but managed to convey that police were already nearby and that they would be with us soon.

I started walking back towards the villa, but something was niggling at me.

On the night of the fire, I'd thought it was the flames that drew Gabriele Arnone to the villa, but it wasn't the fire, it was the pool; he was obsessed with the pool. And hadn't Anna mentioned in her diary that a local contractor had been employed to build the new pool, and hadn't she said that Gabriele was one of those called upon to help with the construction work?

The pool was being built that same summer that Anna and Gina had been planning to run away to Australia together.

An awful possibility was dawning on me. I knew what had happened to Anna but I had no idea what had become of Gina. I hoped with all my heart that she was alive and well and living a good life, but it was entirely possible that some harm had been done to her while poor Anna was being held captive by her father in Rome.

'Think!' I told myself. 'Who would know about Gina's fate?'

Matilde Romano would know. She'd been in the thick of the events here in Sicily while Anna was in Rome. She'd been in touch with Anna and was supposed to have been acting as a go-between for Anna and Gina. But Matilde didn't like me, it sounded as if she'd hated Gina and despite all her protestations, she'd been a terrible friend to Anna.

There must be someone else who could help. I wracked my brains until I remembered. There'd been a clue in Anna's diary.

She'd mentioned several times that she'd asked Matilde to go to the convent. If that was where Gina had been lodging, then there was a chance that someone there might still remember.

62

Instead of going on towards the villa, I diverted down the tiny path that led to the beach. The sand was clean, covered with tiny holes where the rain had punctured it. I took off my trainers and hooked my fingers into their heels. The beach was empty apart from a single dog walker and two figures, a long way ahead of me, walking along the narrowest arc of the beach across the sand. I raised my hand to my eyes to shield them from the sun. The figures were moving away from me. One was a woman and she had a small child with her; a boy. They seemed familiar.

I hurried after them but by the time I reached the far end of the beach, I'd lost sight of them; it was as if they'd disappeared.

To my right, the road led into Porta Sarina. To my left, it went back out towards the billboard junction. Directly ahead of me, on the other side of the road, was the track leading through the marshland to the electricity station, the café and the Romanos' house.

It was also the road that led to the convent.

I dusted the sand from the soles of my feet, put my trainers back on and set off along the marsh road. The flatlands were strewn with rubbish thrown from the windows of passing cars:

food detritus, plastic bottles, disposable nappies. Crows shimmered in the heat – sharp, black mirages – as they tore apart the carrion. The turrets and cables and pylons of the electricity station towered over the marsh; giant silver gatekeepers. There was a stronger, underlying stink too, one that caught on the back of my throat. I kept going, the soles of my shoes sticking to the melting surface of the road, until the electricity station loomed close and there was a small sign pointing down a track. It said: Convento S. Ciara.

I followed the track into a clump of trees obscured from the road by the electricity works. Amongst them was a small, neat building. A fountain trickled into a stone basin at the front and a statue of the Virgin Mary stood beside the door.

I walked along a paved path, lined with clumps of lavender and other herbs doing their best to obfuscate the stink of the surrounding land. The trees gave cool shade and there was birdsong, not wild birds singing, but poor creatures trapped in cages suspended from the roof of a covered walkway where two old nuns were folding laundry. I could hear the rumble of washing machines coming from a small outbuilding beyond, smell the artificial perfume of detergent.

As I drew close, the nuns turned and I recognised the elder: it was the nun I'd met at the memorial wall.

I bowed to each of them, and the older nun explained to the younger that I was English and, fortunately, the younger spoke English fluently. I told her I was seeking information about someone who had stayed at the convent fifty years ago.

The nuns considered this for a moment, then the younger one beckoned me to follow her. 'Sister Alfonsa,' she told me with a smile. 'She remembers everything!'

Sister Alfonsa was a very old lady with only a handful of teeth left in her mouth. She also had trouble hearing so ours was a difficult conversation conducted with help from the young nun, who translated for us, speaking to Sister Alfonsa with the help of an old-fashioned ear trumpet. I asked Sister Alfonsa if she remembered a young woman called Gina who had stayed here once, a tall girl who liked to paint. The old woman's face lit up. Did I mean Gina Accardi? Of course she remembered Gina, she'd never forget her; such a kind and vivacious girl.

'We used to have breakfast together,' the old nun said. 'Gina ate early, before our other guests, because she had to catch the early bus to work in Ragusa. She had a good appetite.' She smiled and nodded, clasped her hands together, sucked in her lips. I was delighted that the nun remembered; it had been worth coming all this way.

'Where did Gina work?' I asked.

'At the bakery in the piazza at Ragusa. They were famous for their cannoli pastries. They were always busy, especially in the summer.'

'Do you remember when you last saw her?'

'One morning.'

'An ordinary morning?'

'A Friday. It was the day before Ferragosto.'

'That's a big religious festival in August,' the young nun explained to me.

'Was anything different that day?'

The old woman shook her head. 'We ate our usual breakfast and then Gina cleared away and laid the table for the other guests. She left for work at the usual time but she never came back. That was the last we saw of her.'

'And she hadn't said anything about... not coming back?'

'Not a word. That morning, we talked for a long time. She was troubled. She'd received a postcard from her best friend. The friend had been delayed in Rome and Gina was upset about it.'

I was glad that Anna's postcard had reached Gina. At least she'd have known that Anna hadn't forgotten her or changed her mind about their plans.

'So do you think Gina might have gone to Rome to try to help this friend?' I asked, turning the key ring that Irma had given me between my fingers. Sister Alfonsa frowned. 'No, not Rome. She didn't go to Rome.'

The younger nun asked: 'But she did go somewhere?'

'She left to catch the bus for work at the usual time and I didn't give her any more thought until later that morning.'

'What happened then?'

'Someone came to collect Gina's belongings. She said she was a friend of Gina's and that Gina wouldn't be coming back. I asked why not and she said because Gina had gone to Australia. I said it was strange, people don't just up and go to Australia like they'd up and go to the shops, and the visitor said Gina had been secretly planning the trip for weeks. I didn't believe it.'

Now my heart was racing. I could hardly bring myself to ask the next question in case the answer confirmed my worst suspicions.

'Why didn't you believe it?'

'Because Gina was a thoughtful girl. She wouldn't have left without saying goodbye. She wouldn't have left the day before Ferragosto, leaving her colleagues at the bakery in the lurch on its busiest day of the year. And if she'd gone to Australia, why would she have left everything behind? Her bag, her clothes, the letters from her friend?'

'Do you still have the letters?'

'She took them.'

'The other friend? The one who came here?'

'Yes.'

'Did you report Gina as missing?' I asked.

'We spoke to the police. But it turned out that Gina had bought a ticket for Australia and she'd mentioned her plans to a girl she worked with in the bakery. That was enough proof for the police that she'd gone of her own free will. We waited and waited, but we never heard anything from her. Not so much as a

postcard. But what could we do, apart from pray and ask the
dear Lord in his mercy to bring our girl back to us safe.' At this
juncture, both nuns murmured some kind of prayer and crossed
themselves. I waited until they'd finished.

'This person who came for Gina's belongings,' I asked, 'do
you know who she was?'

'Oh yes. She's a neighbour of ours.'

'Neighbour?'

'Si, si,' said Sister Alfonsa, nodding her head vigorously. 'She
lives in the thin house on the marshes. La figlia del tassista.' The
taxi driver's daughter.

63

I thanked the nuns and set off again, out of the scented sweetness of the convent gardens and into the stink of the marshland. I went as fast as I could, jogging along the track past the electricity station, the zing of the charge in the air hurting my teeth. The sun was high now, the heat oppressive. I should have put on sunscreen; the skin on my face and shoulders was burning, I could feel the damage being done to the cells.

I was worried that Joe would be worried about me: I'd been away for a while now, but I figured he'd still be tied up with the police, making sure Francesco was all right. I was so close to the Romano's house that it seemed crazy not to go there. I had no plan of what I would say to Matilde Romano when I saw her, but I wanted to look her in the eye and ask her what had happened to Gina Accardi, and if she lied to me, I would know, and if she told the truth, then I'd know too. One way or another, I'd know if Gina had gone to Australia, or if those lonely bones lying in the mud at the back of the villa were hers.

In the distance, through the distortion of the heat shimmer, I could see the narrow house perched on the marshland by itself, the house where Matilde Romano and her father lived. A long, low car was parked outside with an old yellow sign on its roof. The taxi. Good. That meant Matilde was home.

It would be quicker to shortcut across the marsh. I stepped off the track and regretted it at once as my feet sank and green-grey slime clotted around my ankles. The air was thick with mosquitoes competing for my burning skin, my blood. I staggered on through the marsh, drawing great gasps of breath, heat thick as soup. The half liquid land on either side of me was evaporating, the air above its surface seething. Steam rose from the greasy ponds where the mosquito larvae grew, the smell, the very air was moist and foul. In the distance, the thin house shimmied grotesquely like a mirage in a nightmare.

As I came closer, I saw that rubbish had been dumped behind the house as well as in front of it. Black plastic bags and boxes were heaped high. It smelled like death.

I slowed as I approached, crept along the boundary at the side, mud drying on the skin of my ankles, the sun beating down on the back of my head. I went to the front door and knocked hard, with my knuckles. There was no answer, but when I tried the handle, the door opened. Probably Matilde never bothered to lock it, because nobody ever came out this way, and even if they did, who would want to rob a house as run-down as this one, surrounded by trash?

'Signora Romano?' I called. 'Are you there?'

Nothing moved inside the house. I stepped out of the burning heat of the marshland into a dark hallway only slightly cooler. There were stairs in front of me and a door to the left that I pushed; it swung open into a shuttered room. Flies followed me and circled the room haphazardly, describing its spaces and crevices with their wild looping.

When my eyes adjusted to the gloom, I saw a living space furnished in the Sicilian style: a sofa, a dresser, a large television set, shelves containing plates and bowls, a vase of faded silk lilies. It would have been an unremarkable room if it weren't for the pictures. The walls were covered with framed photographs; pictures of Anna from when she was a small child to a middle-aged woman. These were photographs I hadn't seen before, dozens of them, in all sizes; Matilde Romano was in some of the pictures, standing beside Anna.

On the dresser, was a framed picture of Anna, Matilde and a third girl, each wearing party gowns. It would have been a lovely picture, if it weren't for the fact that the face of the third girl – Gina – had been scratched out.

I went back into the hallway. A second door, downstairs, opened into a small, dark kitchen and a third into a bathroom that had been converted for an invalid; bars by the lavatory and the kind of shower that can accommodate a wheelchair. There was no sign of Matilde or her father.

I went to the bottom of the stairs, steep and narrow, the space further constricted by an old-fashioned stairlift.

'Hello!' I called. 'Signora Romano, are you there?'

I heard nothing.

I don't know what it was that compelled me to climb the stairs even though the prospect filled me with dread. It must have been some desire to know everything, to satisfy my curiosity, a desire that was stronger than my fear. Up I went, slowly, as quietly as I could, my hand shooing the flies from my face. Bites were itching and swelling on my exposed skin.

Two doors opened from the landing; both were ajar. I pushed the first and went into a bedroom, sparsely furnished with a bed and wardrobe. It was gloomy because the shutters were closed but as my eyes adjusted they were drawn to the marionettes hanging from hooks on the walls. There were dozens of them, grotesque, hand carved puppets, each facing towards the centre of the room, to the bed. Each, individually, was as macabre as the one that Matilde had given to me. Together they made a sinister little army. God knows how she slept with all those mean little painted eyes staring at her. I backed out of the room quickly, pulling the door shut behind me, wishing I'd never gone in.

A neatly made hospital bed was in the centre of the second room with a drip stand at the head end and various cabinets and tables around. On the table next to the bed were framed photographs. I could see at once that whoever had been at work on the picture downstairs had also interfered with the pictures here. They were family photographs: Mama, Papa the taxi driver – a rat-faced, bearded man and little Matilde Romano, a flossy-haired toddler dressed in ribbons and lace. They would have been sweet pictures except for the fact that Mama's face had been gouged out of them all. The Romanos were a family who certainly knew how to bear a grudge.

A fly bumped against the window glass. The room was airless, as if all the oxygen had been breathed from it. I went out onto the landing and at that exact moment the light that had been falling through the front door was extinguished. I heard a key turn, a lock slide shut, a grunt and then the squeak of badly oiled wheels.

Signora Romano had come home.

I leaned forward, very slowly, until I could see over the top of the banister. I saw the handle of a wheelchair and the top of a wheel; a figure slumped in the chair; the rim of a black fedora, a thin shoulder in a too-big black jacket, a strand of grey hair. Matilde's father, if that was him in the wheelchair, wearing too many clothes for such a hot day. His head lolled forward. His hands were folded on his lap.

I stood absolutely still, trying to breathe slowly and quietly, praying nobody would come upstairs. Signora Romano's footsteps went along the hallway into the kitchen. I heard the fridge door opening and closing, the pouring of something into a receptacle, and then she returned to the hallway. She spoke to her father, who didn't respond. She said something curt but affectionate, the Italian equivalent of 'silly old fool' I guessed, and went into the living room. I saw enough of her over the banister to observe she was carrying a tray. She turned on the television. I heard the machine-gun rapid banter of a game show host, canned laughter.

I couldn't see into the room but imagined Matilde was sitting down in front of the TV, enjoying the snack she'd prepared for herself. If I was going to get out of her house without her seeing me, this was my best opportunity. I crept down the stairs, one at a time, testing each board to ensure it didn't creak beneath my weight, my heart pounding like a drum. The front door key was in the lock and bolts above and below had been slid home. A fly bothered my face, its buzz loud as a chainsaw.

At the foot of the stairs, I held my breath. The wheelchair was facing away from me, and no sound came from Matilde's father. I thought he must be sleeping. I stepped down into the hallway; took the two steps across the tiles that brought me to the front door. I reached up my hand to the top bolt and tested it. It was stiff, it wouldn't move. I tried the lower one. That slid back easily.

A roar of laughter came from television and Matilde laughed too. I held the door handle to keep it steady while I turned the key. The lock retracted with a clunk that nearly stopped my heart. I held my breath, waiting for the old man in the wheel-chair to jerk upright or ask what was going on, but he didn't move. I only had to slide back the top bolt now and open the door. If Matilde heard, I'd still be out before she could reach me. I counted backwards from three, then grabbed the bolt with both hands and pushed as hard as I could. It slid back and I gave a gasp of relief and reached for the door handle. I tried to turn it but it didn't give. The door wouldn't open. I'd missed some mechanism. I rattled the handle. It still wouldn't open.

Shit, shit, shit, what now?

In the living room, the television went silent. I imagined Matilde sitting still, listening out for me as I listened for her.

There was no time to dither. I had to get out quickly, before she reacted. I turned and squeezed between the wheelchair and the stairs, aiming for the kitchen, but as I did so Matilde came out of the living room. She was holding a metal fire poker that she pointed at me from other side of the wheelchair. She was shocked to see me: I saw the horror in her eyes.

'What are you doing here?' she asked. 'What are you doing in my house?'

I could have made up some excuse, but I was too wired for that.

'I came to ask you about Gina Accardi,' I answered truthfully.

The woman winced. It was as if a shadow had fallen over her face. She hated Gina so much she could not even bear to hear her name.

I tried to keep my voice steady. 'I want to know the truth about Gina,' I said. 'I've been to the convent. The nuns told me you came to collect her belongings the day she disappeared. You told them she'd gone to Australia. Did she go to Australia, Signora?'

Matilde said nothing.

I continued. 'Anna loved Gina, didn't she? She loved Gina more than she loved you. They were going to go away together. That was their plan.'

'No.'

I glanced to the kitchen door. It was perhaps four paces away.

'It was. They were going to go away together and leave you behind: you and Gabriele Arnone. He liked Gina, didn't he? And you loved Anna. That must have been very hurtful to you, Signora, when you found out they were going to desert you.'

The woman's lip trembled. Pain was etched onto her face. I almost felt sorry for her.

'No wonder you told Anna's parents what was going on,' I

continued. 'You made sure they kept Anna away from Porta Sarina that summer. But Gina was still here, wasn't she, living in the convent a few hundred yards from here, like a thorn in your side. You needed her to be gone before Anna came back. What did you and Gabriele do to make *her* go away?'

I was still hoping I was wrong, hoping Matilde would tell me not to be silly and offer up some proof of Gina's existence in Australia, but she was silent.

I felt a great sorrow in my heart.

'We know why you wanted us to sell the villa to you, Signora. We know why Gabriele was so obsessed with the old pool. The truth has found a way to reveal itself. It always does.'

Still she said nothing and I knew then that the bones were Gina's.

'Who killed Gina?' I asked. 'Was it Gabriele? Or was it you? Did you do it together, or did you make the plans and he carried out the act?'

Silence.

'She must have been killed on the marshland, like your mother,' I said. 'She must have been killed early one morning, somewhere between the convent and the bus stop on the Ragusa road, and then someone took her body back to the DeLucas' villa and buried it beneath the swimming pool. I expect Gabriele had a vehicle of some kind. I don't suppose it was much of a problem. He got rid of the body and you cleared out Gina's room at the convent; you disposed of the evidence.'

Matilde was distracted by a fly that spiralled and then landed on the back of her father's hands. How thin the hands were, literally skin and bone. The nails were long and yellow. The skin had sunk between the bones.

'Is your father all right?' I asked, moving slowly around the chair. I was no more than three steps from the kitchen now. 'He's so still.'

'Flies don't bother him,' she replied. She was watching me, holding my eye.

Three steps to the kitchen; four at the most. I was about to move but Matilde pre-empted my escape. She lunged at me with the poker, stumbling against the wheelchair, which tipped. Her father slumped forward. I saw that he was falling and instinctively crouched to catch him.

And two things happened.

Firstly, as the body of the old man crumpled and fell into my arms, the fedora slipped and I saw the rictus grin on the face beneath and the sunken eyes and the skin, mummified and yellow, and the grey hair sparse on the almost-bald head, and secondly, the front door burst open and Irma Arnone arrived, brandishing her gun.

64

I caught the corpse of the Porta Sarina taxi driver as it fell and then, realising what it was, scrabbled away from it, screaming, so I didn't see the scuffle between Irma and Matilde, all I heard were their shouts as I crawled away towards the kitchen and then I heard gunshot and pain drilled into my back.

I panicked. I kept going, half crawling through the kitchen and out of the back door, and I climbed over sacks of rubbish in the backyard, swollen plastic bags splitting beneath my hands and their insides spilling out. I climbed and scrabbled over that vile collection of detritus until I reached the marshland and then I staggered across the marsh. I was so full of fear that the pain was dulled, but I knew Irma's gun had fired and the shot had found me and that with every breath I was becoming weaker.

It was a huge effort to cross the marshland and I knew I was going the wrong way, heading away from civilisation; away from the road and the electricity station and the billboard and the town, but fear forced me on. The pain in my back became a heavy ache and my head began to spin and nausea rose up inside me. The world tilted, this way, then that. Hot turned to cold. I shivered. I was freezing. The adrenaline surge was replaced by a dreadful weakness. I'd never been so tired. There was darkness at the periphery of my vision.

I could lay down, I thought, lay in the marsh. The ground was soft and pulpy. The insects that swarmed round me, drawn to the smell of blood, would feast, but the marsh would keep me warm and I could sleep for a while.

I could rest.

I relaxed my knees. I let my body fall, and as the marsh came up to meet me, I heard a voice.

Not yet, Edie. You can rest soon, but not yet. Come this way. Come with us!

My sight was blurred, as if I was drunk, but I could just make out the figures in front of me; the woman and the child I'd seen earlier on the beach. They were standing just out of reach. I narrowed my eyes to try to focus.

'Daniel?' I whispered.

'This way,' the child said.

'Daniel!'

He turned and pointed and then the woman took hold of his hand and the pair began to walk away. The pain, the nausea, the panic receded. I forgot the fear. They were moving slowly, giving me time to follow. I felt an immense calm. I focused on the child, my darling boy, as he walked across the marsh as if it were a grass meadow on a summer's day, and I didn't notice the flies or the blood or the heat.

All I had in my heart was love.

* * *

They found me on the boardwalk that led across the marshland to a hide beside a pool where migrating birds came to feed. I was unconscious but in the shade of the hide, the only spot in that vast flatland where the sun couldn't reach me. They took me to the hospital in Ragusa and I was bathed and rehydrated, the shot removed, my wounds treated alongside the sunburn and the insect bites.

Joe sat beside my bed reading a book about traditional methods for the restoration of old buildings while he waited for me to wake. And when I did wake, he told me that Irma Arnone had called the police and told them that I was out on the marshland somewhere, wounded. They hadn't held out much hope of finding me alive, but they drove to the boardwalk, to start their search from there, and there I was. It was a miracle, they said.

'It wasn't a miracle,' I said. 'Daniel showed me where to go.'

'Daniel?'

'Yes. And Anna. She was with him.'

I didn't say any more because I could see that what I'd already said was too much for Joe. But I knew what had happened and I knew they were together, Daniel and Anna. I knew she was looking after him. I knew he was safe.

* * *

Later, Joe told me that Matilde was behind all the awful things that had happened at the villa. She'd poisoned the cat, she'd cut the chain that secured the gate and nailed the dead crow to our door, she'd set fire to the villa and she had tampered with the steering on the Alfa Romeo. She'd known exactly what to do because she'd been taught, by her father, all about cars and how they worked.

'She was trying to kill us,' Joe told me, holding my hand, turning it over in his. 'She set it so that the mechanism would fail when the wheel was turned sharply; on a bend or trying to avoid something – or someone – in the road.'

'We could have driven over the cliff.'

'We could have.'

I let the implications of this sink in for a moment, then I

asked: 'So the steering failed as Francesco tried to avoid hitting Gabriele?'

'Yes.'

'So the accident wasn't his fault?'

'No. And Irma knew. She has proof.'

'How did she know?'

'She knows everything. She watches the villa. She takes photographs. She saw Matilde slashing the Fiat's tyres. She saw her get into the Alfa Romeo and do something to the steering column. When the police told her what had happened to Gabriele, she knew it was Matilde's fault.'

'So she went straight over to Matilde's house with her gun.'

'Like Clint bloody Eastwood,' said Joe.

'Like the cavalry.'

* * *

On the third day that I was in hospital, Valentina came to visit. She came to the side of the bed and lay a small bundle beside me. The face of a newborn baby gazed out from its swaddling.

'Oh, Valentina, she's beautiful.'

'Her name is Mia,' said Valentina. 'I wanted you to be the first to meet her. Well, almost the first. Francesco's seen her.'

'How is Francesco?'

'He's doing okay. He knows the accident wasn't his fault.' She sighed and shook her head. 'It's still a terrible thing to have to live with, but he'll be all right. I'll make sure of it.' She looked down at the baby, gazing back up at her. 'We'll make sure of it, won't we, Mia?'

* * *

A week after that, Joe took me back to recuperate at the villa. The police had finished their examination of the swimming pool and Joe had already begun to fill in the hole. We didn't want to be reminded of what had happened there. We thought it better to cover the place over and we'd think of a way to remember Gina and to commemorate her life later.

I didn't feel afraid in the villa. There was nothing to be afraid of any more. Matilde Romano, who only suffered flesh wounds when Irma's gun went off, had been removed to a secure psychiatric hospital. There had been enough evidence in the house to be certain that she had been behind Gina's murder. Gina's clothes and belongings were still up in the attic along with Anna's letters. The police also found correspondence between Matilde and Gabriele: letters in which Matilde expressed her hatred for Gina, and which encouraged Gabriele to think of her as a tease, a girl who had led him up the garden path, even though she never had any intention of being with him: the girl who preferred other girls to him: who had afforded him the ultimate humiliation. Matilde had sketched the route Gina walked each morning from the convent to the bus stop and added instructions to Gabriele on the best place to ambush her.

The Romano house was going to be demolished and the land around it would be assimilated into the wildlife sanctuary. Later, Matilde's father's inquest would reveal he'd died of natural causes several years earlier. Matilde had continued to care for the corpse, keeping it clean, taking it for walks and so on, as if it were one of her collection of puppets.

Valentina had left Vito and she, the baby and Francesco, were staying with her grandparents in Punto Secca. Irma had moved in with Vito and was helping him to run the pizzeria. She sent a letter to Francesco assuring him that she did not hold him responsible for Gabriele's death and that he shouldn't blame himself. She wrote that he was a good boy for looking after his mother and that she was going to try to knock some sense into Vito and that she wished Vito was more like Francesco.

Joe had taken responsibility for the Arnone animals, so now

the little goat, Capretta, and the chickens were resident in the villa grounds along with the kittens. We lacked dogs, but Joe assured me it was only a matter of time until a stray in need of a home came along.

Joe's friends, my friends now, came to the villa. They brought us food and drink and did little jobs around the place while they were there. Children came; old people. Everyone had their own skills. I loved to hear the laughter, the footsteps on the stairs, music. It was wonderful to know the villa was being brought back to life.

Now the source of the malevolence we'd experienced in the villa had been removed, it was a happier, more relaxed place. I was conscious of the DeLuca ghosts but I never resented them; they seemed to me like friends. I never spoke again of what happened to me on the marshland or how I was saved but I liked to hope that Anna's spirit was around somewhere, taking care of the lost children, making sure that Daniel was never alone.

One last thing. I did some research into Patrick Cadogan's background and discovered he had been Head Psychiatrist at the Grey House Clinic in Holland Heath in London at the same time as Anna was with her father in Rome. For some years, the clinic specialised in the care of young patients with 'emotional and personality disorders'. I found a prospectus from that era reproduced online and was disgusted that people who called themselves medical professionals could inflict such crude and cruel 'treatments' on young men and women who 'suffered from hysterical outbursts, depression, eating disorders and/or homosexual tendencies'. The clinic assured the wealthy parents of such young people that, with the correct therapies, all of these 'afflictions' could be corrected. The clinic had closed some years earlier and now a new business had taken over the premises. It carried out cosmetic surgery procedures.

I couldn't be 100 per cent certain that Anna had met Patrick at the clinic, that he was the psychiatrist employed to look after her, or that he abused his position to take advantage of her, but it seemed likely. So did the possibility that she, in her vulnerable state, having been told, no doubt, that Gina had left for Australia without her, was coerced into marrying Patrick. I wondered if Patrick treated Anna so badly because he could not forgive her for never loving him the way she had loved Gina. Did she inadvertently make him feel so insignificant that the only way he could make himself feel big again was to humiliate her?

Whatever had happened, it must have been a terrible time for Anna. It filled me with sorrow to think that Anna had spent her whole life believing that Gina had gone away to Australia without her. God knows what lies she was told by her parents, by Matilde. There was nothing to suggest that Anna's parents knew what had become of Gina, but they must have been relieved she had disappeared from their lives.

As I moved around the villa, I couldn't help picturing Anna moving in the same way, decades earlier. I wondered if she was conscious of the villa's ghosts, if, perhaps, she felt some connection with Gina here, if she found some comfort. I hoped with all my heart that she did.

65

ONE YEAR LATER

Here's Joe. Here he comes, my man, tousle-haired and sleepy
eyed, in his shorts and sweater with a cat in one hand (we kept
all three). He's tanned now and his hair is longer and he's
reverted to his normal, scruffy ways. He comes and sits beside
me, his knees falling open. He kisses the cat and puts her down.
She winds around my legs. He's brought the parcel with him. He
yawns; we smile at one another.

'Well,' he says, 'we got it back.'

'Yep,' I say. 'We did.'

He peels off the sticky tape, tearing the newspaper and
unwraps the parcel. Inside is a beautifully restored ornate,
gilded plaster picture frame. Inside the frame is a small, bright
oil painting, its jewel colours glowing as they must have
glowed the day it was painted. It's Guido Reni's *Madonna del
Mare*.

Joe holds the picture on his lap, admires it at arm's length –
he's not wearing his reading glasses, so he has to squint a little to
see the detail.

Sunlight catches the corner of the frame, illuminates its reds
and bronzes. I lean over to study the lovely face of the Madonna,

her skin peachy, her expression confident, vibrant and modern. We are lucky to have the painting here. So lucky.

'That was some good karma that brought the picture back to us,' Joe says.

'Ah, Joe,' I say, 'we were due some good karma.'

* * *

At Easter, when we opened the restaurant in the converted stable block, we opened up the villa, the gardens and the cellars so that people could come and explore. We wanted to let our neighbours in Porta Sarina know what we were doing, give them the chance to ask questions and address any concerns they might have. Amongst the visitors two young women, university students. They approached Joe and asked if there would be vacancies for seasonal staff during their summer vacation. Joe took their names. One was called Ema Ganzaria. Joe said that was a coincidence: the couple who used to work for his grandparents as caretakers to the villa were also called Ganzaria.

'Yes, I know,' the young woman replied. 'Alberto and Ignazia. My great-aunt and uncle.'

There followed an emotional discussion about the old couple, that led to Joe opening a bottle of his grandfather's finest wine from the cellar and Valentina cooking some spaghetti with aubergine, chilli and courgette and all of us sitting down and sharing the food and drink with Ema and her friend, while Ema filled us in on what had become of the Ganzarias. Alberto had, sadly, died of old age five years previously, but Ignazia, now eighty-seven years old, was still alive. She was in good health, although frail and confined to the apartment where she lived with her niece and her husband in the fishing village of Aci Trezza on the other side of Catania.

Ema promised she'd remember Joe to her great-aunt and sometime later we received an invitation for us to go and visit

Signora Ganzaria and we'd made our way to the village. The Ganzarias lived on the second floor of a modern block over-looking the sea.

The niece met us at the door and led us up the stairs to the apartment. We'd bought gifts: flowers from the villa gardens, a bottle of wine from the cellar, and photographs of Alberto and Ignazia outside their cottage that we'd had copied and framed. The niece was delighted with the gifts and said she'd show us into her aunt's room. We could chat while she made coffee.

'She's rather deaf,' the niece explained, 'and she tires easily, but she still has all her marbles.'

We went into a narrow, pleasant room with sliding doors opening onto a small balcony that overlooked the bay. The first thing that struck me was that the balcony was full of potted plants; their blooms emitting colours and scents that together formed a miniature version of the gardens of the Villa della Madonna del Mare. We could hear the sea and the voices of the fishermen on their boats in the harbour and the sunlight came through the windows, lighting up the room.

Signora Ganzaria was sitting in an armchair. She was small, her face wrinkled and soft as a grape left too long on the vine, her hair white and thin, hidden by a black scarf and all her clothes were black too. She was hunched, but when she saw Joe, her eyes widened and then became glossy with tears and she straightened out a little.

'Joe! Joe! Look at you!' she cried and she pulled herself up on her stick to embrace him. He had to bend almost double to kiss her, she was the size of a child. When they'd finished their embrace, she took my hand and indicated that I should sit on the chair beside her, which I did. I showed her a picture of her and her husband taken more than three decades earlier. The couple were standing outside their cottage, and with them was a little boy with dark hair and a solemn expression. He was holding the housekeeper's hand.

Signora Ganzaria laughed. 'You were a handsome little chap even then, my Joe!'

'You were biased, Signora Ganzaria. You always were on my side.'

She reached out and touched his wrist. 'Why wouldn't I be?' she asked. 'You were such a good boy. You were like your mother. You didn't have a bad bone in your body.'

* * *

We stayed for an hour, until Signora Ganzaria's eyes became heavy and her head started to nod. Then we stood up to leave and the niece, who had been hovering around us for the duration of the visit, said: 'Wait, my aunt has something for you.' She touched the old lady's arm. 'Shall I give it to them now, auntie?'

'Yes, yes, it's under the bed,' Signora Ganzaria said.

With some difficulty, the niece got down on her hands and knees and pulled a battered old suitcase from under the bed. She blew dust from its surface and Joe helped her lift it on to the bed.

'Open it,' said Signora Ganzaria. 'Go on, Joe, look inside. It's something of yours. Something I've been waiting a long time to give back to you.'

He flicked open the catches and pushed up the lid. Inside was a bundle of rags. He unwrapped the rags. Carefully, he lifted out the object they contained.

He turned to show me what he held in his hand.

It was a 400 year old Renaissance masterpiece; Guido Reni's *Madonna del Mare*.

* * *

Signora Ganzaria had been thorough with her attempts to keep the villa safe: a bag of salt spilled at every doorway; olive oil smeared on the frames; as many sheep and goats' horns spread about the place as she could manage, but she wasn't sure it was enough to keep the evil out. Too many people knew the villa was unoccupied and the painting was still there, she said. Irma Arnone knew about it. Vito Barsi knew about it. And Matilde Romano was always snooping round the headland, using any excuse to come into the villa grounds, even at night. Signora Ganzaria had never liked that woman, never.

She and her husband had talked about it a great deal and between them they'd decided to go back to the villa and remove the painting for safekeeping. She'd been keeping it safe, under her bed, ever since.

And now the Madonna is back from the restorer, and it looks as vibrant as it must have looked the day it was painted. We're going to send it to auction. It will provide us with the money we need to pay our debts and to set ourselves up. I hope it goes to a good home, somewhere where it will be displayed, where everyone who wants to see it will have the opportunity to do so. We don't need it any more.

Now, Gina's portrait of Anna hangs in the alcove in the hallway of the villa, which we've renamed Villa Anna. Valentina, Francesco, and baby Mia, live in the restored cottage where the Ganzarias used to live, and the stable block restaurant belongs to them too. We are family; we eat together most days, we share our joys and our problems. It's wonderful to have them so close.

Joe lays the painting down carefully on the table. He pulls his chair closer to mine and sits beside me to drink his coffee. His left arm bridging the small space between us.

We will never regain what we have lost, but we have accepted that the losing was not the end we thought it was.

There are hours and days and years ahead of us still, and we're going to fill them and make the most of them. Daniel will be with us, every single moment he'll be here, running beside us. I feel him now, close by, beloved. We love him as we've always loved him and always will. He is not lost. He never was.

Joe and I are looking forward, in every sense, to everything that life brings to us. We know that happiness is ours; all we have to do is choose to take it.

ACKNOWLEDGMENTS

Thank you to everyone who's been involved in bringing this book into the world. I'm more grateful than I can say to Marianne, to Alison and also to Vicki and Pat, all of whom have been so patient and supportive. I'm thrilled to have joined Boldwood Books and to be working with such a talented, enthusiastic and friendly team, especially Sarah, who's done so much to shape the book. Many thanks also to Jade and Rose for their insight and Becky who designed the beautiful cover, but also sincere and heartfelt thanks to everyone in the wider team.

Thank you also to everyone who supports me and my books in real life and social media, family, friends, booksellers, bloggers, libraries and readers you are the best and I really do appreciate you.

MORE FROM LOUISE DOUGLAS

We hope you enjoyed reading *The House By The Sea*. If you did, please leave a review.

If you'd like to gift a copy, this book is also available as a ebook, digital audio download and audiobook CD.

Sign up to Louise Douglas' mailing list for news, competitions and updates on future books.

http://bit.ly/LouiseDouglasNewsletter

ABOUT THE AUTHOR

Louise Douglas is the bestselling and brilliantly reviewed author of 6 novels including *The Love of my Life* and *Missing You* - a RNA award winner. *The Secrets Between Us* was a Richard and Judy Book Club pick. She lives in the West Country.

Follow Louise on social media:

facebook.com/Louise-Douglas-Author-340228039335215

twitter.com/louisedouglas3

bookbub.com/authors/louise-douglas

ABOUT BOLDWOOD BOOKS

Boldwood Books is a fiction publishing company seeking out the best stories from around the world.

Find out more at www.boldwoodbooks.com

Sign up to the Book and Tonic newsletter for news, offers and competitions from Boldwood Books!

http://www.bit.ly/bookandtonic

We'd love to hear from you, follow us on social media:

facebook.com/BookandTonic

twitter.com/BoldwoodBooks

instagram.com/BookandTonic

Made in the USA
Monee, IL
13 June 2020